SHADOW of the LAST MEN

SHADOW of the LAST MEN

The NEXT MAN Saga – Book 1

J.M. SALYARDS

© 2013 by J. M. Salyards
All rights reserved.

No part of this publication may be reproduced, stored in a retrieval system or transmitted in any form or by any means, electronic or mechanical, including photocopying, recording, or otherwise, without written permission from the publisher. For information visit www.xchylerpublishing.com

This is a work of fiction. Names, descriptions, entities, and incidents included in this story are products of the authors' imaginations. Any resemblance to actual persons, events, and entities is entirely coincidental.

Xchyler Publishing,
an imprint of Hamilton Springs Press, LLC
Penny Freeman, Editor-in-chief
www.xchylerpublishing.com
1st Edition: September, 2013

Cover and Interior Design by D. Robert Pease, walkingstickbooks.com
Edited by Penny Freeman and McKenna Gardner

Published in the United States of America
Xchyler Publishing

ONE

The Outlands,
Insurrection of the Next, Day One

As they tracked along in their column of three, the teenage boy habitually slipped to the rear, placing the man and woman ahead of him.

"Why do you keep walking back there? Is the pace too much?" the woman, Alouine, asked.

"No, I'm fine."

"You *can* walk with me, Quintain."

"Thank you for your concern," the boy replied, "but I really only care that we are going together. If I follow, I can watch over the two of you."

They did not need protection, but Quintain let them know he took an interest in their welfare. It was an obviously flimsy reason, but true all the same. The older pair fascinated the teenage mystic. He took every opportunity to study them, even if only to stare at the backs of their heads as they strode on through the wasted belts of tundra and wintery pine forests of the Outlands.

The man was tall and imposing, even menacing. His broad, warrior's shoulders and powerful, rangy frame made him loom over the others. Severe, grim eyes shone like crystals from a pale, almost ashen and weathered face. He wore a close-cropped beard and tied back his wild, dark hair into a wolf tail by a series of leather thongs to keep it from his eyes. It gave him a twisted and dangerously skewed look.

SHADOW OF THE LAST MEN

Dressed in black over his entire form, numerous hand-sewn belts and pouches, bulging with ammunition and gear, crossed his torso and legs. He had two rifles slung over his back, an ancient, scoped bolt-action next to a modern, military-style automatic, a pistol holstered on his right thigh, and a long fighting dagger at the diagonal on his hip, for drawing with either hand.

His coat and pants were so caked with dust and dirt that they helped him blend into his surroundings. Metal gave a dull glint from his gauntleted hands. His clear blue gaze reached out a thousand meters with the intensity of a madman.

The warrior's female counterpart was likewise mesomorphic and tall, though thirty centimeters shorter and half the mass of the man ahead of her. She cut a dashing figure, a marvel of form and function. Her grimy, dark clothing was analogous to the man's. A simple but thick, grey overcoat, poncho-style, draped over her shoulders, took the brunt of the cold. Underneath, a darker, throat-to-toes synthetic bodysuit contoured the shapes of her thighs and led to black, ankle-high boots. It all fit her like a tough, thick hide of armor and warmth.

Unlike the man, she was not obviously armed, but she moved with a primal, feline grace that was as dangerous as it was pleasing to the eye. Her sable hair was held back by a scarf wrap, exposing her own penetrating, black gaze.

They were aphotic, human-shaped holes in the withered grey landscape, untouched by the freezing winds and constant pallor of decay surrounding them. Each one was near twice the teenager's age, and he hoped that his own adulthood would bring such magnificent presence.

Quintain could see their thoughts. Not the substance of them, but their effect on the sapient field, or aura, which permeated their bodies. Both of their minds engaged in constant simulation, not flabby surface instincts like those which consumed most Outlanders.

The people of the Outlands thought about food and warmth, safety and shelter, and little else. In contrast, both the man and woman took the reins of their respective fates in hand. They seemed to shape events to suit them by pure power of will. They appeared forces of nature—an earthquake and a hurricane. Individually, they upset the collective order of existence wherever they went.

Together, the possibilities were endless.

Quintain found it remarkable. He was not only intrigued, but ecstatic. He saw the future happening before his very eyes. These two humans, and the product of the alchemy between them, wrote the fate of the world. He tried hard to temper his excitement.

For a mystic like him, the pair embodied the flame of life, and he, the only moth around. In his mind, he gave the cosmos an eye through which the true ruler of destiny could observe itself and the two heroes, man and woman; its creations.

The teenager recalled his mother's words as he admired the older warriors ahead of him.

"In times of great crisis and peril, heroes may rise to bring balance to the world," she had told him. "Sometimes it is a lone and anonymous hero, a single man or woman, dedicated to overthrowing a corrupt organization. Other times, more driven heroes are needed, and sometimes there is a demand for the most powerful of us to rise.

"For the past ten generations or more, it has been the Outlanders, by ones and twos, which have answered the highest of calls. It has been us, alone, who have fought back the creeping darkness and restored the balance.

"But we are weak creatures, we humans, and our power has been withered for too long. The tide of cruelty, greed, and ignorance has advanced too far. It has dug its heels into the earth, and if a hero tries to confront evil alone he will drown within it. His blood will vanish from the face of the earth forever.

"But there is hope. New heroes arise. They will innovate and create new weapons, new means of fighting their ancient foes. And you, my son, will present them with the ancient knowledge that has vanished from the mind of history.

"Before the spirits bent to the wills and intents of mortals, there was a symbiosis; the time is once again upon us for the ancient ways to return. Soon, you will be standing at a crossroads with a terrible decision to make. One path, the brightest and easiest path, will lead to the absolute destruction of the heroic urge, and the fall of mankind. If this path is followed, the race of men will vanish from the realm of the living within a single century. All hope will be lost and the world will become a lifeless void floating through the endless heavens.

"The second path is filled with pain and fraught with danger. The heroes must walk upon a road paved with the blood of all those around them, even allies and lovers. Enemies will come screaming in from every side in a never-ending flood, trying to shove the heroes headlong into the cold embrace of death.

"Many times will these heroes bleed and many times will the blood of enemies and allies alike stain their hands. There will be harsh decisions ahead of them—decisions that may strip them of their humanity and leave them lying naked in a pit of despair.

"They must do this to have only a sliver of a chance to succeed. The odds are long, but only through unimaginable suffering will they triumph.

"These two paths are connected at a hundred points. If a hero takes even a single step down the path to nothingness, there is no hope, and everything he touches and loves will turn to ash. The choice is love or fear."

He remembered that the youthful, kind woman, his mother, had looked up at Quintain so fast, he had jumped in surprise. Something was wrong with his mother's eyes, as though he could see the memories and souls of thousands of people within them. Those souls were not trapped or in pain. They were Quintain's ancestors, trying to reach out to him, to help him. They formed an unbroken chain which stretched backward in time for a million years—back to the very beginnings of humanity on earth.

His mother was channeling them, allowing those spirits into her mind, to use her mouth to speak and her eyes to see. "The path to the future is through the heart. Many people the heroes trust and respect will unknowingly try to guide them down the path to the Void, but they must do what is in their hearts."

Quintain could see images projected into his mind: some were people, some were places he had not been, but all of them were so out of focus he could barely make them out. His mother, the etheric traveler, the astral psychonaut, shaped the spirits of the past into a mirror to glance at the future.

"In the shadow of a black fortress, in the Valley of Death," she said in a soft, faraway voice, "a hero stands strong before the intense rage and hate of his enemy. He is alone. His family is either dead or fighting for their lives below him. Agony and pain await his people. Unless he commits to the path of the heart, they will all be slaughtered."

Quintain remembered swallowing in terror.

"The hero must throw himself down the throat of the beast, fight his way past the fangs of the monster and the ones he cares for. Broken will be his body, but whole will be his heart. Defeat the dragon he may, but he'll never see the sun rise the next day."

"With thoughts of friends and loves in his heart, he throws himself onward. For several moments, he stands with his back to a precipice and fights on, his enemies fall and freedom is only a step away."

As a boy, Quintain had been horrified by his mother's words. "Is there nothing else to see?"

Her voice fell to a whisper, barely breathed. "Countless, enormous columns of flame."

The woman fell silent. As she freed herself from her trance, he begged her, "This hero—it's not me, is it?"

She smiled, but her eyes, human and hers once more, were sad. "I cannot say. I do not know. Only one thing is certain, my son. Your fate is braided with your bloodline. Together they will guide you until the end of your days."

Quintain smiled fondly at any memory of his dead mother as he walked behind the warriors and marveled at how he had never suspected her of being such an accurate prophet.

Lost in his memories, Quintain pitched forward, arms windmilling as his toe kicked something hard and unyielding. The ground swept up to meet him as he fell flat on his face, driving the air from his lungs with a grunt and scratching his chin open.

"Ouch."

Harrow and Alouine stopped to look back at him. The male warrior simply gazed without judging, while the woman hastened to his prone form.

"I just warned you to watch your step. You've got your head so high in the clouds you can't even see the ground."

He grinned sheepishly, even though his jaw hurt from the impact, as Alouine helped him to his feet and brushed the dirt and gravel off his chest.

Quintain dared to hope that he had found the hero: the stoic, silent, powerful Outlander hero his mother had prophesized about. Next to him, upbraiding him for his carelessness was the one who held the hero's heart. She had to be. A great and powerful relief flooded the youth with joy. The choices his mother had spoken of were not his to make, and the pieces of the puzzle were finally falling into place.

He wanted to hope and wish and pray so fervently that the force of his desire screamed through the astral world, but that natural inclination was counterproductive. He knew that the easiest way to destroy his hopes was to smother them.

He held the fragile prayer lightly in his heart.

It was simple for Quintain. He liked it when things were simple. If that tall, dark warrior was the man his mother spoke of, he needed only to keep the hero from dying in fury or fire, and all would be right in the world. Devils and dragons would be slain, and all would return to the paradise the earth was meant to be.

Alouine asked if he was all right, and he nodded in response. Without a word, Harrow turned once more and renewed his stride.

Simple did not always mean easy.

TWO

FOUR YEARS BEFORE THE INSURRECTION OF THE NEXT
THE OUTLANDS, EIGHTY KILOMETERS
NORTHWEST OF THE ENCLAVE

The demon watched the family for nearly a week. A man in his early twenties, and a woman, slightly younger, and their small girl of perhaps eight summers. It was rare to see a complete nuclear unit in the Outlands. They intrigued the demon.

The young girl's parents possessed no skill as warriors. They both cared for her deeply; the demon could tell. But they avoided danger as best they could. Her caretakers were simply not equipped to face hostility.

The girl's father earned his living with skillful gambling. The demon never gambled with anything, but he recognized that there was a great gulf between luck and skill. Luck, the product of random selection, refused to be influenced in any way. When the father gambled, he did so with skill and only in games which involved reading other people. He knew when to bet and when not to, and he did not cheat—at least, not that the demon could see. The man quit when he was ahead and left a village or camp with more than he entered.

The girl's mother handled barter and knew the best ways to get food into everyone's bellies. It was not often nutritious or tasty food, but the girl—little Nina—rarely felt the kind of hunger that hurt. The demon imagined that most of the time her hunger was just an itch, and only when times turned really tough did it become painful. The three of them frequently traveled because her mother and father knew they would be safer that way. The demon knew the truth of it. In some ways, the ancient Roaming Empire had it right.

They moved on, and the demon did, too. Their paths through destiny had run parallel for long enough; he had observed them without being noticed and now contented himself to let them be. Come the morning, the demon would be gone. The small family prepared as best they could for the long and arduous trek ahead of them, stockpiling food and material for barter. The demon did likewise.

To the unprepared, a sojourn in the biting cold of the Outlands was suicide. It was especially true there in the piedmont, the foothills of the great, uninhabitable mountains to the west, where the ripping winds channeled down the slopes and, in some places, could freeze a man to death in an hour. Clusters of hilly, scraggly evergreen forests marbled the land, separated by wide swaths of grey tundra, and dotted by widely spread Outlander niches where the most shelter and resources could be had.

The man, woman, and girl set out before dawn, travelling to the south, and the demon followed shortly after.

Nina was a quiet child and knew how to be sneaky, the demon observed. She always stepped carefully and made very little noise. In the right hiding place, perfect stillness could make her invisible. She even knew how to conceal the fog that her breath caused. Many people would hurt her if they could, and her stillness helped her parents protect her. She demonstrated a genuine desire to help them, to repay them, by being a good little girl.

On that morning, with the rising sun still smothered in thick clouds and a fresh coating of snow on the ground, she could not lend aid. Like her father had said, sometimes skill couldn't overcome sheer bad luck. In a game, you just play the hand you were dealt, take the loss, and try again.

It wasn't a game when they ran into the hunters. Little Nina was rightly terrified because they would kill and eat anything, even people—especially people like her and her parents. They were big, dark shapes, simian and savage, and they ambushed people to rob and murder them.

Nina and her parents instantly knew the danger; they had run and hidden from it so many times.

That day, they could not run, and there was nowhere to hide. Her mother and father's luck had run out. If luck was a lady, as the Outlanders sometimes said, she was a cruel and heartless one who always betrayed those who relied on her.

Watching from a distance, the demon saw the savages leap out from behind bushes, trees, and an ancient hedgerow. They broke the father's skull open with a club and left him leaking his blood and brains into the dirt.

The evening prior, the girl's mother had promised her mate that if they were ever in trouble, she would fight back, that she would make the hunters kill her, rather than submit to the awful things they would do. She kept her promise.

After she bit down on her captor's bearded cheek, they beat her with clubs, and another one of the hunters stuck a knife in her chest. He twisted it cruelly. Nina watched her fall down. Her mother weakly told her to run, and she tried, but the big men were faster. Their boots kicked the frozen dirt into the air, and they caught her easily.

The demon watched, weighing his options. It was precisely the injustice he sought to eliminate, but to attack the symptoms, and not the root cause, was an exercise in futility. Still, the spectacle enraged him. Such was human brutality at its worst, destroying something good for spite and temporary gain.

Nina kicked and struggled but wasn't as strong or fierce as her mother. She couldn't make the men kill her so that she could be with her parents again. She was alone with the hunters, held in a painful grip while they chuffed and hawed and congratulated one another. The demon watched her small, dirty face as she resigned herself to her fate. Even in her tiny mind, he knew she accepted it as the beginning of the end, that life would be pain and suffering for however long the remainder lasted.

The men who attacked the girl's parents and then held her against her will were animals, feral and savage. But the demon—he was something else entirely.

The demon let his presence be known. The entire world's ferocity was barely held in check within the dark blight walking up the ancient road.

The girl's father had told her a story about the demon before they set out that morning. He had listened as her father warned her that they would be traveling through lands that the monster was known to haunt. He said that the demon, called 'the Harrowing Rain', killed Outlanders by scores, but it also fought the Last Men wherever it found them. It roamed like a storm cloud, dumping bad luck on whomever it fell.

Her dad told her that if she ever saw the demon, she should not look in its eyes. She should run away as fast as she could and it would let her live. Nina had said that the demon sounded more like an angel.

The monster was there, and the small child could not run. Soon her sweat and tears and bruises would become blood, and she and her mother and father would be the same again. The thought seemed to calm her and gave her some comfort.

She ceased her struggling and waited for the demon to deliver her from the grip of hunters and send her back to her parents who loved her. She wanted to be just like them; not scared, just broken and dead and finished. This play of emotions on the child's face saddened the demon immensely. She had given up.

The demon was, in fact, a man. The Harrowing Rain, endless wanderer of the ancient byways, was living, human flesh, a human mind. He did not know who had coined his moniker, but he did not disagree with it, so he took it as his own. Those few Outlanders who knew him personally called him Harrow for short. It was fitting enough for his purposes.

The man considered it a challenge.

He knew that taking life by blade or bullet was not difficult. Only the tiniest of threads held the soul to the person. The physical systems of the human body operated within a thin band of efficiency. Disrupt them, move them away from that band by even the slightest margin, and incapacitation or death will result.

He simply knew how to kill efficiently. The world saw his power over life and death and thought it demonic. He was only a man with tools and skills and knowledge. How quickly the mundane used superstition to explain phenomena they did not understand.

He had tuned his hard and muscular body for this. He had built it, tested it, and refined it, to inflict pain and trauma. He calibrated his augmented brain for battle and strife. He had inured his heart to suffering, hardened in the fires of loss and grief.

He held all the tools necessary to fulfill his destiny as a bringer of the earth's great revenge.

The road he walked was blocked. It was so often blocked. He had been content to follow the nomadic family for another day, perhaps, had they continued to the northeast.

Had they been anywhere else, they might have lived to see the sun rise again the following morning. But what had been whole had been broken, and the lives of two Outlanders had ended.

Six more would be little issue, he decided. Five were grubby murderers, beating a man and woman to death with clubs of wood and iron. The tiny child's limp form was crushed against the sixth. Tears carved channels through the grime on her face. She had dirt and blood in her blond hair.

He saw their satisfaction, the promise in their eyes of full bellies and a new slave. When the child grew, they would use her to slake their lusts. In the meantime, she would be a pet. A plaything fed from scraps.

Such an event repeated itself endlessly, there in the Outlands. Harrow told himself that he cared nothing for a girl or her dead caregivers or the gaggle of thugs preying upon them. He told himself that the freedom to travel without limit was his only concern, but he knew deep down that it was a lie.

The man and the woman had lives of peace that were ended by violence. Harrow resolved to avenge them.

Harrow was on top of the hunters before they saw him. They only noticed him when he stopped ten paces away. The nervous energy of the hunt returned to them, making the figures hunch and their knees bend, readying them for action once more. They refused to share their catch and circled the one holding the girl like wild dogs defending a kill. One of them, brandishing a dull, grey pipe, slick with blood, pointed the weapon at Harrow.

"Get the fuck out of here," he wheezed in a guttural snarl.

The men were large, all of them, well-fed on rich protein. All wore dirty patchworks of stiff canvas and leather, beards thick with remnants of old meals, hair matted where it hung from hoods or caps. Metal and eyes glinted in the feeble light of dawn. The fools did not recognize him. They were ready to fight, to chase him off or add him to their bounty. The little girl, though—she knew who he was.

Harrow ignored the hunter's words. "You are blocking the road. Stand aside or die." His voice was clear and even, though raspy from disuse. It had already played out. It happened one hundred times a day in this cruel wasteland. It was the law: eat, be eaten, or run away. Running was wise. It was the same as choosing life.

Harrow did not need the wisdom of the deer or the hare. He was simply better. They were hyenas; cowards and scavengers. As the only lion around, they were beneath him, unworthy of his time or attention, but the unwilling recipients of both nonetheless.

The fools laughed like jackals, a hoarse barking. One warning for them was the most he would offer. He had allowed himself to hope that they would stay and fight to preserve their kill, and he was not disappointed. Overconfident in the weight of their numbers, they broke up out of their knot of limbs and staves, mocking and taunting and slowly moving to encircle him. He would not let them.

His long fighting knife, KA-BAR, flashed from its sheath and into his right fist even as he sprang, in a downward, stabbing grip.

No man stood against lightning. He struck as a thunderbolt from the dark canopy of night splits the sky.

Fibers of stern canvas could not resist Harrow's blow. Subcutaneous fat and muscle parted, bones splintered. The warhead found its mark at a downward angle just under the clavicle, eight inches of hardened steel penetrating without remorse. He rammed the weapon to its hilt, seeking, finding, and severing the heart's major artery, and then withdrew it, twisting, in one quicksilver motion. A sanguine stream trailed the blade in confused, unexpected freedom.

The attack pushed the target backward. Jerked forward by the blade's extraction, the man fell, first to his knees and then onto his belly, and began his journey to the void at the speed of thought.

The little girl froze, aghast by the ferocious alacrity of the attack. It stunned the other men. Harrow never waited. There was no wasted motion, ever. On to the next, the killing was a cycle, a blur of movement. He reversed his grip and stabbed another man in the belly before the first had begun to fall. His dagger-tipped arm lashed like a bullwhip. Each crack drew blood in sheets. The thick, dark fluid coated all with its slickness.

Blade extended, he punched past the gawking face of another. Razor steel unzipped windpipe, carotid and jugular alike. The fresh smell of rare meat—that coppery, heavy scent—clashed with the air again. It settled on top of the growing pools of the previously perforated victims.

Surprise and wide-eyed fear filled Harrow's vision. All the sadism and bravado had dissolved in an instant as three men fell bleeding. Their eyes bulged as a blow from a metal club was deflected by Harrow's forearm with the unexpected ring of iron on steel. Harrow found one of those bulging eyes with the point of his dagger and destroyed it. A cacophony of panic drove the universe insane.

Hunt those cowards who live without deserving it. Horror and agony given come around again. Harrow was content to be their harbinger. The hamstring, the kidney, the armpit became his targets. He found them again and again. The remaining men struck back feebly, trying to fend him off, but it was too late. They belonged to him now: the price of failing to heed his warning.

That one which held the girl dropped her roughly and reached for his knife, a short, rusted and dull thing. Harrow snapped his weight-bearing leg with a powerful, sideways kick. As his victim fell, Harrow stepped in and smashed his face with a forearm that iron could not crack. The jackal dropped, dripping blood and mucus, teeth and tears.

Harrow left them a pile of groaning flesh, leaking their life into the dirt, dying at varying paces. He stabbed the last man in the thigh of his unbroken leg, aiming for the largest blood vessel to speed him along to oblivion. He wiped his blade clean on the torn shirt of a man becoming a corpse.

Sheathing the weapon, he straightened to walk on his way. A tiny voice behind him gave him the slightest pause. He was impressed that the child had the presence of mind to say anything after being party to such a violent spectacle.

She examined the pile of twitching, stinking, blood-soaked corpses, her parents among them. "Can I go with you?" It was a simple question, with no pleading.

He did not turn around to answer the child. "Do as you please."

Hours passed. They covered mile after mile, their footfalls sounding endlessly in a rhythm of heavy boots, punctuated by a faster pattering. Harrow found his pace slowing without intention.

The girl trailing him was admirably keeping up, but her stamina was not the tiniest fraction of his. They traveled an ancient, rotting artery of the old Empire of the Roamers. A long forgotten civilization of nomads had built these ancient highways for their chariots of steel and plastic and rubber. Now it was all broken down and overgrown with gray weeds, crumbled nearly to nothingness and, in some places, easy to lose sight of.

Corpses of those discarded 'automobiles' littered the path, but their metal bodies were so disintegrated and putrefied by the passing of time, they amounted to little more than rust-colored stains on cracked and decayed pavement. Every material which had gone into their construction in that long-passed age was already scavenged by generations of outliers, eager for any metal or glass.

The ancient nomads had once zoomed from place to place along these roads, ever moving in their chariots which drank from wells tapped into the earth, and used its black blood for fuel. Harrow had seen Outlanders try to patch together the remains of these chariots, but without the refined liquid they used for blood, the monstrous imitations were largely useless and lifeless. Outlanders were now cursed to travel forever on the soles of their own feet and nothing more.

"Those men," the girl said, her panting and tiny voice cutting into the silence, "they killed my mom and dad."

"Yes."

"They were going to eat them."

"Yes."

A long moment passed, before the small voice resumed.

"Why are we here?"

Harrow blinked, and nearly lost a step. He had struggled with that question his entire life.

"I asked Mom and Dad, but they said they didn't know."

The man took a measured moment to craft his response. "People have been asking that for a very long time. Some made up myths and fairy tales to explain it all."

"Do you know any?"

"No."

The girl cast her gaze downward.

"They're a waste of time," Harrow continued. "I know the truth."

"What is it?"

"We each decide why we're here for ourselves."

They trekked on over the endless wastes. Harrow kept a steady pace that was agonizingly slow for him, but one that he could sustain indefinitely. Still, the girl fell behind. Her scrawny legs could not carry her. Her parents might have stopped several times by then to rest. Eventually, she fell. Harrow had outdistanced her by ten meters.

He stopped and turned. The tiny figure lay on her side. He could tell that her underdeveloped muscles had seized completely. The pace and distance had defeated her. "You have a choice, young one," he said softly, just enough to carry his voice over the wind.

The girl groaned a weak and pathetic sound.

"You must stand up, or die where you are."

Harrow spoke with no cruelty or malice. He refused to face anything but the reality before him. He never went backward. He could stop or rest, but never retreat.

"I don't want to die," the little girl whined, breathlessly. "Please."

"Stand up."

She placed her tiny hands on the ground and strained against it. Shuddering, the small human managed to get one knee under her, then the other. She swallowed, fighting her pain. Tears ran down her filthy face.

"Stand up," Harrow gently repeated.

She shook like a newborn calf but managed to get onto her feet. Arms out to balance herself, she wobbled in the breeze, as a sapling shorn of leaves.

"Walk to me."

He watched her take a step, then another. Those tiny legs struggled under even her feathery weight. Several times, she was forced to catch herself as she nearly fell again, posting her arm and pushing the ground away with her miniscule palm. The ground was her enemy. Gravity was trying to kill her, just as those men had done to her parents. The girl bit down on the insides of her cheeks.

Finally, inch by agonizing inch, she arrived before the man who had saved her life hours before. He knelt down to put himself at her eye level. His arm shot out and caught hers as she nearly toppled once more. He seemed a giant to her, and his giant mitt wrapped around her entire upper arm with room to spare in its grip. He righted her again, roughly. Her streaming eyes fluttered from exhaustion and pain, but he caught her chin between thumb and forefinger and the girl managed to focus.

"This is the sacred power of 'no'. To live, you must learn to say no to death." His crystal blue eyes locked onto her hazel ones.

"Living on this earth is the same as refusal to die."

"No . . . to death." The girl's eyes rolled back into her head and she lost consciousness, spilling forward into Harrow's ready arms.

He arranged the sleeping girl on his back, her warm head tucked into the nape of his neck and arms hung over his shoulders. Orienting himself, he carried the girl the remainder of the way along the roads of the Roaming Empire.

— — —

Harrow thought back to the last time he had seen his father.

The adolescent Harrow and the man, his father, stood facing one another. They had been through so much together, but the father was leaving his son for the last time. The memory, a pain which had dulled over the years, was still bittersweet.

Blood flowed freely from the man's many wounds. His paling face, already passing into shadow, was bereft of expression, but his eyes, clear and blue, radiated a blissful serenity. Cold zephyrs tore at them both, ripped at their sturdy clothing to reach into their flesh, to no effect. Neither man nor boy would allow a reaction to such a trivial thing as the constant, pervasive cold.

The boy's journey had taken him through twelve winters but had not yet truly begun. The path ahead would be immensely difficult, as the man well knew. But he had inured the boy against sorrow and suffering, hardened him against pain, fear and hunger. He taught his son to fight, to protect himself, to shoot and to hunt and to live. He taught him not to merely survive in the harsh conditions of earth, but to thrive.

Even then, an earnest young man, Harrow must have looked severe and statuesque. A complete human soul locked away inside that fortress of a small body, which had scarcely begun its trek through life, not even puberty. In a world which had forced the man to raise the boy in such a way, events rarely found a person who was ready for them. He had prepared his son for everything as best he could.

The man had mastered life, and taught its skills to the boy. All the things his own great father had handed to him, right or wrong, humane or inhuman, the man had passed to the boy. Together, they were a teacher and a lone student more than a father and his only child. No time for affection. Any bond of love or companionship was forsaken for the relationship of master and apprentice.

There were only hard lessons, each and every day. Hunting and trapping, all forms of combat, language and computation, geography, and history—the most important lesson of all. Every moment of twelve years, the man had spent pouring a life's experience into the vessel of the younger soul.

In another world or another time, the boy would have every reason to hate the man. There was never a childhood for him. No time for play and too little for self-expression. His father loomed over him as the most powerful man in the world, and insisted that it was his son's destiny to eclipse him. The man knew that the boy would grow into those oversized talents and skills and knowledge. Experience would be his only teacher now. Fate would finish the work the man had begun.

He had nothing left. He gazed into the void. The void looked into him and saw itself.

"You're going to die, now?" the boy asked.

"I have to, son. Fate prepared this for me and me for it."

The young man nodded. He knew that his father would find only death where he would soon be walking. No emotion showed on his face. He was hard and smooth and flawless as crystal.

The man released a pain-laden breath. "Things will be difficult for you. I will not lie about that. But I trust in you. Your wounds will make you stronger because you must refuse to die from them. Understand? I want you to remember that even though fate guides you, it is your will that becomes reality."

"You could live. Refuse to die. You said yourself that winning is never quitting. Don't quit now." Though calm and composed, his voice carried an element of pleading.

"I've run my race and you have to take over. This is the end." The boy showed nothing. "Tell me you'll remember."

"I won't forget."

"No, you won't." The man leaned tiredly and laid his hand on the boy's shoulder. "Fate speaks with a voice of encounters and opportunities. Listen to it, be thankful for it, but always act with your own will."

He gripped the boy's shoulder, felt the leather of the rifle sling under his fingers. "Humanity is over, son. You have to blaze a new trail. Be the next kind of man, better than the one before." He unfastened the long, fighting knife that was another of his prized possessions and pressed the sheathed weapon into the boy's hand.

"The Next Man," the boy repeated, accepting the blade.

"That's right. Love your fate and be like lightning. We did not start this war, but you can finish it. You have everything you'll need."

The man smiled at the boy, his first smile in so very long. He had forgotten. That smile might have been his very first. The boy reflected it back at him for a beat before tucking it away and hiding it.

"Don't worry, Father. I do have everything I need. Thank you." The young man's devastating seriousness and severity rolled off in waves, and prodded the old man to straighten. "I'll think of you often."

Harrow's gritted teeth and grimaced face curled into a sneer at the memory as he adjusted the sleeping girl on his back.

"Just do what is necessary," had replied his father, his voice even. "Fight the Last Men. Pile their corpses high. Avenge me. Avenge our people."

That man had endured a lifetime of surviving the bleak, dead earth. His existence was a pinprick of light in the unending shroud of darkness.

Despair was his oldest enemy, his constant, unwavering foe. The future was beautiful. His life was beautiful. He was the storm cloud; the herald of his son's coming. The boy was the lightning bolt which the man had hurled to punish his foes and re-energize the shattered earth. The only thoughts he would have for the rest of his life were focused with clear exactness on the boy, the man's gift to the world.

Harrow recalled trying his best in order to fulfill the man's highest hope. He recalled lowering his head in respect and saying softly and precisely, "Goodbye." Another glance, searing the bleeding, tired, proud man into his memory, and then he had turned and walked away, alone.

Harrow strode on, carrying the girl, fighting the chill and his memories. The wind picked up and he felt the child unconsciously tighten her grip on him, trying to burrow into his warm back. *The strong are strongest alone*, he reminded himself. But if that were true, why did the girl feel so light? Why did the warmth of her tiny body energize him, make him feel more alive than he had in years? It impelled him, interfaced with his magnetic field, charged his willpower and stoked his soul-fire and pushed him onward. It swept away his fatigue and made him forget the pain of his wounds. He carried her on, to a place where he knew she would be safe, and, to any possible extent, happy. He wondered vaguely why he was helping her. No one had ever helped him.

Harrow remembered those early days, when he was not much older than the girl he now carried on his back.

It had taken some time to learn to be alone, after the boy, not yet known by the appellation of 'Harrow', had left his father for dead. He did not know what to do, so he walked.

He walked for days, aimless and adrift and hungry. The cold

wastes of the Outlands were not yet his happy hunting grounds, and he passed from one clutch of Outlanders to the next like a ghost.

There were occasional offers of kindness, but the young Harrow turned these down. He knew those charities would fade. Those few Outlanders who still maintained family units might, with pity, gift him with a scrap of food here and there, but as he grew to manhood, this would cease. Healthy suspicion would replace sympathy. On his own, he became an accomplished hunter, trapper and scavenger.

In four years, he also learned how to kill people. His father had warned him of this; had warned him not to hesitate, to listen to the dictates of necessity. Everything he possessed—his weapons, equipment, clothing, supplies, his flesh, blood, and even hair—were commodities that others would seek to take from him, if they could. They tried, again and again. His rifle and pistol were tempting prizes since an Outlander would only bother to carry them if he possessed the ammunition to feed them, and the big fighting knife was worth a fortune itself.

"Want to lighten your load?" a big man asked him, a kindly smile plastered on his face. The little shanty town was just one more stop on young Harrow's journey, and the hulking, dark figure had called to him from a doorway as he walked down the center avenue of the row of squat, derelict buildings. "I have things for trade, kid. You know, barter?"

Harrow stopped and turned his head to look at the man. "What things?"

"Come in. I'll show you."

The dwelling had only one internal light source—a tiny fire crackling in an iron stove in the corner. Its dim rays did nothing to dispel the cloying shadows, but Harrow instantly made out the forms of two other large men to his left as he walked through the door. As soon as he was inside, they pounced, and the first man slammed the door shut behind him.

The teen had no choice but to let the much larger and stronger men bear him to the ground, but he showed them no fear as they held him down. The young Harrow vaguely hoped they had not knocked the scope of his rifle out of zero with their jarring tackle.

"Look at all this stuff. A kid doesn't need all of this. We'll have to teach you to share," one of the men whispered in his ear as he kneeled on his arm, pinning it to the floor. The man on the other side did the same. Harrow saw a hunger in the third man's eyes that went beyond simple greed and knew that he was the type of savage filth who would force himself on a captive without a thought. With one hand pressing down on Harrow's shoulder, he massaged the crux of his thighs through his trousers with the other.

"So, what have you got for us, you little idiot?" the original man taunted. The others laughed.

"Pain," Harrow replied darkly. He exploded to the right and the overly phallic aggressor's hand slipped off of his shoulder. Using the newfound leverage, the boy arched his back, tipping the pervert off balance and freeing one arm. He snagged the throat of the other man who grappled him.

Harrow hooked the man's larynx between his thumb and forefinger and squeezed until he felt the fibrous tissue of the windpipe give way. It sent the assailant reeling backward, his eyes bulging as he choked and pawed at his ruined airway.

With both arms free, he grabbed the pervert's ear and ripped it clean off of his head, then thumbed him in the eye with the same finger which had just crushed the other's throat. Rolling sideways and onto the man, Harrow dropped his knee hard onto his testicles and drew KA-BAR in anger for the first time.

The scream of agony and fury over his wrecked eye and disarticulated ear escaped as a groaning gurgle as Harrow planted all of his weight on the disgusting man's genitals and, pushing off, rose to his feet.

Shock and fury crossed the face of the initial man, the deceiver. He bid a retreat toward the door as one friend, or perhaps brother, kicked and rolled on the floor, his face reddening as he clawed at his neck for breath. The other man blubbered pitifully and cringed into a ball.

Their intended victim may have gotten the jump on the others, but he was still just a kid. The big, bearded man's eyes flashed to the knife and searched for a way to turn the tables.

Harrow watched as indecision swirled across the man's expression, but did not give him more time to act. By the time the man had made his decision to fight, Harrow was already stabbing him. He drove the point of the dagger into the big man's liver, stomach, heart, and both lungs in rapid succession, backing him up to the door and hemming him in as he performed his butcher's work.

Something savage roared in the pit of his stomach: a powerful thirst for blood.

"Pain . . . and death," he amended, letting the heavily bleeding man sink to the floor. Satisfied that man was dead, or would be in a matter of seconds, he turned on his other attackers.

The man with the crushed throat was likely to die already, so Harrow helped him along with a single, punching stab in the side, slipping the blade between the man's ribs, puncturing a lung and probably nicking his heart. However, the other man did not find the relief of death.

Mouth set in a grim line, Harrow began kicking and grinding and stomping the man in the groin, castrating him with his boot, as the disgusting fool weakly tried to fend him off, and only stopping when his legs burned from the exertion. A sick, alien feeling snarled in Harrow's mind, insisting that this man did not deserve the precision of his blade.

After the would-be rapist passed from consciousness, Harrow took a moment to collect his breath and steady himself. The adrenaline roaring through his veins shook his entire body. The thick scent of blood hung in the air and he had to fight to keep the contents of his guts inside him and to contain the sudden urge to defecate. Long moments later, the nausea passed and the red haze cleared from his vision.

He ransacked the house and made off with a good haul of food and other items. He carefully packed up and stowed away on his person, dried meat, tobacco, liquor, sturdy clothing, and several useful household items, stuffing his rucksack and satchel. The healthy suspicion the men had taught him was also valuable, and he tucked that away in his mind, never to relinquish it.

Harrow sighed as he adjusted the sleeping girl on his back once more. It was not her fault that her father did not teach her what his father had taught him. The Outlanders lived under the rule of the jungle, and only the fittest survived, but this girl could be taught; she was still young enough. She was brave and had a strong will, and she could become strong enough to live on her own. Harrow knew a place where she would be sheltered until that day came.

Walking on for five more hours, he stopped only to trickle water between Nina's lips and to feed her a crushed and bruised apple.

When they arrived at their destination, he set her on her feet and shook her gently awake. The strange place frightened her all over again, as did the woman standing over her with skin as dark as night.

Harrow gazed down at the girl, hunching so that he could look into her eyes. "This woman will look after you until you can do it yourself. Obey her in all things."

Nina swallowed hard and looked as though she might cry; nonetheless, she nodded, her hair falling into her face.

The tough-looking woman, sleeveless even in the intense cold, gently wrapped one hard, wiry arm around Nina's shoulders and guided her toward a nearby hut.

"You're all skin and bones, girl," the stranger said, offering the girl a friendly smile. "Let's get some food in you."

"I will return soon." Harrow gave the woman a curt nod and bid them both farewell.

THREE

"This may be new to you, but have confidence. Let your nervousness subside. Relax, close your eyes, and let your bodily sensations gradually fall away."

He did as his mother bid him, taking deep, rhythmic breaths.

"Now recite the scriptures and come home."

He murmured the vibratory sounds he had been taught. A spiritual membrane stretched as his consciousness tested itself against the tension. His body—the amniotic sac holding his spirit form—finally broke, and his soul burst free in a rush of warm ecstasy.

As he beheld his surroundings, a stabbing of fear struck at him, but he was comforted by the silver umbilical tying him to his sleeping body and the familiar shape of his mother's luminous astral projection next to him. Under her proud, patient gaze, he extended his wings and flew.

"Congratulations and welcome, Quintain. You have passed through the gateway of the spirit—the first step in becoming a wielder of Magick. From here, we may proceed to where the spirits dwell and speak with them. This is the home of your soul."

Quintain learned quickly that astral projection was no escape from the perils of life on the derelict earth. The spirit world and the earthly formed a two-way street—each affecting the other in a perpetual spiral. Demons of flesh inhabited one realm and formless nightmares stalked the other. He could see both and observe their interplay grinding down an already beaten world.

His newfound ability proved the culmination of seven years of training and study. It opened his vision to the earth beyond mere seeing. He read the ebb and flow of consciousness, and what he glimpsed there often terrified him—what humans like him had made of the world. Their images reflected in the blood they spilled as they slew one another.

He searched for acts of love and goodness and found them few, far between, and always stained in scarlet and born in tragedy. Innocence blighted by hate. Decency raped by greed. For each good deed, a thousand killings first.

Though the answers disgusted him, Quintain never regretted asking the questions. He thought back to the time when his mind first began to stretch beyond what his narrow, single-spectrum vision could show him—when his ignorance was blissful and he had yet to know the flame of indignation.

He grew up underground. The surface was not safe. He did not know how many years passed since his birth before he even saw the sky, which was nothing special to him. For all its expansiveness, it was simply a carpet of grey clouds. A ceiling of atmosphere, not unlike the stone ceiling of the lair he called home.

Stacks upon stacks of books filled the underground cavern. Some of them his mother had required that he read; others he read because he was interested. All of them harkened back to a better time, a time when men had built a great community on the earth. There had been an age of wealth and prosperity with abundant food and entertainments. He remembered asking his mother how they were reduced to living in what amounted to a hole in the ground.

"There was no single, great, murderous cause for the sorry state of things, my son; but it was all manmade. It boils down to overflowing ego."

"What's that?" the boy asked.

"Ego is a part of the mind. It is our sense of self-worth. It is not healthy to lack it completely, but too much of it is even *more* dangerous. It is a necessary force to protect the psyche of man from trauma, but it can also grow out of control and absorb or smother all else.

"The ego spawns all deceit," she said. "The out-of-control ego lies to everything, even the self it is supposed to protect. Strong egos prey on weak ones. They give rise to the kinds of people who take power and land and slaves for themselves. Those people become kings and priests, lords and ladies, politicians and bureaucrats, moneychangers and monopolists. The quest for increase is foremost in their thoughts. They will do anything— lie, cheat and steal—for more. If more for them means less for all others, so be it."

"So, egos make them greedy?" the boy mused.

"Yes. They conspire and collude with others, all seeking to fill their hollow lives with gold and jewels and slaves. Their anthem is, 'Me against my brother. My brother and I against our cousin. My cousins and I against our clan. My clan and I against our tribe. My tribe and I against the nation. My nation and I against the world.' Loyalty and honor are foreign to them. They view those things as weaknesses, and care for nothing outside themselves."

"It sounds like a sickness. Like a fever."

The woman nodded, seeming pleased. "Indeed it is. It is a disease of the mind."

"How many people are sick with it?"

"I do not know, but it has always been a small number. Those of us who are healthy and free from that curse—we outnumber them greatly, despite all their attempts to wipe us out. They think that their disease is actually a special blessing. They are jealous and smart, and they know that we would recognize their sickness if we saw it, so they hid themselves. For a long time they met in secret, formed webs of connections so that our ancestors would not discover their plots.

"In their impaired minds, these people believe that death is the end, and that nothing exists and no more treasure can be had afterward. They have children to pass on their knowledge, their accumulated wealth and treasure. These children inherit the illness from their parents, who teach them that it is a great power, that people like us and our kin are the same as animals—sheep, worthless save for our 'wool' and 'meat', our labor and our bodies. Ego has become a god to them. They worship their disease."

"That's terrible. You and me—we're not animals. Why would we do their work for them?"

"It is a bit complicated. They set themselves up as rulers and hoarded all wealth and food. Suffice it to say, they used a great fraud to force our ancestors to work for their lives. They have forced our people to kill our neighbors when it suited their plans. They forced the 'sheep' to tear out each other's hearts and murder their children.

"Eventually, our kind built for them a great civilization, and their every material desire was satisfied from birth. By then, the sickness had consumed their hearts. They became addicted to the feeling of power and wanted yet more. With no conception of need, no strife, no struggle for food, no striving for means, their minds became warped. Desire and gratification became everything to them."

"Even after they had everything, they still wanted more?"

"Pleasures repeated become pleasures expected, my son. That is human nature. Constant overstimulation numbs us. New heights of pleasure must be found. Depravity and corruption inevitably follow. They played ever more extravagant games with their influence."

"Why didn't anyone try to stop them?"

The woman put a finger to her lips and considered. "For centuries—for millennia—they have behaved as though they were unconnected, to keep that illusion alive. They fed each change they wrought to our ancestors drop by drop, so that suspicion would never fall on them. It was an illusion so vast and ever-present that it escaped their sight. Those who could manage to see through it and cried out were branded insane by those who could not.

"They kept the minds and bodies of our kin weak, and their life spans short, while pretending to do the opposite. They have used their knowledge of science and technology in subtle ways, so that we could not see what was happening to us. Their families have never mixed with ours. Their sickness seeks to remain undiluted. We were divided from the beginning and have only grown further and further apart."

The child listened, horrorstruck.

"We outsiders were poisoned with despair, and when our ancestors reached out to the false fronts of safety and security for help, they were fed even more poison."

"They sound so cruel. I hate them," the boy growled.

His mother shook her head. "Hate is their ally, son. By using our hatred against us, they directed our ancestors to destroy what remaining wealth of the earth was not in the sick men's hands, like a plague of unfeeling insects. They spent their remaining time fighting and killing, blinded by hatred, and the diseased ones emerged as rulers of everything."

Silently, the boy fumed.

"I know it is a hard story to hear, son. You asked, and as ever I will tell you nothing but the truth."

Silence reigned as the boy paused to consider. He looked to his mother, his face grave and severe. "Is there anything we can do?"

His mother glanced away. "They have taken everything from us. Their vast illusion has served its purpose and there is no longer any use for it. They live in palatial cities of steel and glass, topped with mighty domes to keep us out. They have robbed the greater human family of everything, starved and impoverished our people, raped and murdered, sown disease and ignorance. The entire world outside their magnificent Enclaves has been reduced to wasteland.

"They have seeded the earth with soft metals to ruin our God-given intelligence. They put chemicals in our food and water to accelerate our aging and have rendered the very air toxic to breathe. That is why we do not stay outside for long.

"Some few of us, the Outlanders, remain. But, to them, we are as ineradicable as rats, and they blanket us with poisons wherever we turn. The reach of their poison even touches babies in the womb, killing or deforming children before they can be born. Even those of us who have our health, like you and I, are rendered weak and docile before the elite. Our race has been utterly subjugated."

The boy frowned and his eyes welled. Still, his mother pressed on.

"The evil ones now call themselves the Order of the Last Men. They believe that they are the eternal meaning of the earth, the highest humanity has to offer. They imagine their victory is complete, that the point of no return has been crossed for generations beyond recall.

"In truth, my son, they are not wrong. They stand far above our race, whose fields of experience cannot compare with their mastery of the secrets of the absolute. When a light comes to shine among the outsiders, they extinguish it—at first by ridicule or exile; now by simple annihilation.

"They think that we Outlanders are helpless against them, that we have no weapons and no will to fight. They crush us like insects if we rise up against their Order. The Last Men have raised monuments and monoliths to their victory. Their version of Outlander reality now owns us."

Tears slid down the boy's cheeks and he clenched his eyes shut. He wished that he had never asked for this. It was better to not know.

The woman's voice softened and she gathered her son into her lap. "Don't despair, my son," she murmured. "All is not lost. For one hundred years now, the Last Men have guarded their victory with indolence and the worthless vigilance of slaves. And if Outlanders, as a race, discover that the Order of the Last Men can be vanquished, they will have no place to run. It is not their power, but the illusion of it, which keeps the Outlander crushed under their heel."

The boy took a shuddering breath.

"That we may even speak of this is already a sign," his mother said. "That this knowledge even exists among us is already spawning a spirit of justice that will release the fury of God on the Last Men—a fury that will cast them into a pit from which there will be no escape." She gave him a gentle squeeze. "Mankind will finally live where he was born to live: bathing in green and blue, under a great and golden sun."

Quintain knew that his mother always spoke the truth. At that moment, her quest for the world's absolution became his.

FOUR

One Month before the Insurrection of the Next
Temple of Understanding, Third City Enclave

Gerald Morningstar was a patient man. His rise to the Highest Chair of the Third City Enclave was anything but meteoric. It had taken him thirty years to reach his position after he had decided to continue on the path. Looking back on his life, he realized that he had never really wanted that power. What should have been pride and satisfaction, well-earned, turned out to be little but weariness and *ennui*. He had reached the highest fruit and it had turned sour on his tongue.

The High Circle's grand marble chamber was empty, save for Gerald. The other Circle members visited infrequently; only rare, pressing business could gather all thirteen men together at the same time. He sat in the Chairman's seat, a high, straight-backed chair of hard, polished stone. It was uncomfortable, but unlike most of his compatriots, Gerald understood the significance of intentional suffering, the value in sitting in the chair because it hurt to do so. It was his favorite place to sit and think.

His progression through the initiations of the Order had been steady. Due to his intense, studious nature and unending curiosity, he never faltered. He had ever wanted to be a scholar, a keeper of knowledge. It was a humble ambition. He was a humble man. It came to him naturally and without effort.

Too much of the Order was bound up in meaningless cruelty

and followed traditions that made little sense to him. That his peers had elected him to enforce the Order's protocols and manage its control, made even less. Perhaps that carefully cultivated persona of benign, fatherly patience, and his ability to remain utterly objective, had landed him the ultimate mediator's role.

Still, the view from the top amazed him, and the secrets open to him dazzled. Holding the High Chair was an honor.

The Order of the Last Men was a global entity which struck Gerald as far too arbitrary. The population of its members was highly regulated, and regimented by a strict, hereditary hierarchy, while the numbers of those outside the Order- the Outlanders- were limited by famine, disease and widespread interpersonal violence.

The Order owned the world's only military force: the soulless, near-robotic men of the Death's Head battalions, but they were merely vat-grown slaves used to keep Outlanders under heel. Privately owned firearms and ammunition by outsiders were strictly forbidden and punishable by death. The Death's Head often busied themselves executing the unenforceable doctrine.

The Outlanders had nothing to bind together their separate tribes, and their pathetic, individual lives were brief and brutal affairs of base survival. Only the religion of the Order was legally celebrated, a mystery cult of ancient origins—dubious origins, Gerald thought. It made no allowance for individual freedom or liberty, sovereignty or rights.

National and racial pride had been stamped out among the outsiders and reserved solely for members of the Order. The Last Men had destroyed the concept of marriage among Outlanders— the essential building block of their civilization. The custom was still practiced among the Last Men but only rarely and as a form of sociopolitical contract.

Only membership in the Order could save a woman from being

degraded to mere flesh. Outsider women became slave stock, an object for the pleasure of Last Men and nothing more. Even female members of the Order were property in all but name. They enjoyed the same rights and luxuries as the men but were rarely, if ever, given any real power, even over their own lives.

The Last Men instituted a thoroughly chauvinistic society. To that end, the Order had seeded the world outside their lush Enclaves with pornography and drugs many generations ago, lacing food and water supplies with mind-altering chemicals, to crush any esteem in which the Outlanders may hold themselves.

Gerald, as High Chairman, had shut most of those activities down, arguing that the damage had already been done and that the resources devoted to such practices were better used elsewhere. None of the other Last Men, including his fellow High Circle members, had argued against the tax breaks and lax duty requirements which resulted from Gerald's slashing of the programs.

The people outside the Enclaves were, to all appearances, thoroughly defeated. Their behavior was reduced to the level of beasts with no will of their own, easily regimented, controlled, or enslaved. All the wealth of the world resided in the hands of the Last Men, as did all control of industrial production and agriculture.

Gerald felt it excessive. Something about the paradigm did not sit well with him, even though he had been chosen by the Last Men to maintain it. He held two main duties to the Order: to maintain its control over the world, and to continue his predecessors' Great Work.

The Last Men had been trying for centuries to scientifically create an apotheosis machine, a soul or consciousness preserving hub—a device which would allow them to incarnate and reincarnate at will. Gerald was fascinated by the prospect and devoted nearly all his energies to it.

He sat in his hard, uncomfortable chair for hours at a time, poring over holographic diagrams and schematics projected by glyph-readers in the massive circular table before him. To break the hold of the body on the soul, without destroying the soul or damaging the memories, was a massive and ambitious undertaking. Maintaining the Order's domination over the outside world was banal and unnecessary by comparison.

Gerald's data link chimed in his head. He mentally activated the link and connected the call to the internal cellular transmitter/receiver device that all Order members had patched into the language centers of their brains. "Yes?"

"It is Carver Delano, my lord," came the transmitted reply. "I await an audience with you."

Gerald blinked and rubbed at his tired eyes. The hours had melted away without his realizing. "Where are you, my young friend?" he asked.

"The Highest Circle's threshold."

Gerald inwardly chuckled. The Order's insistence on propriety bordered on insanity sometimes, particularly between members of differing rank. The dependence on careful etiquette and slavish deference was silly to him. The system of hereditary compartmentalization was so engrained in the fabric of Order society that it would take the Chairman three lifetimes to overturn it.

He sighed. "Well, come in, then." He stroked the controls on the table in sequence. The massive doors to the High Circle chamber slowly but smoothly slid open. The doors themselves were two meters of solid steel with a polished marble façade, capable of standing against all attempts to breach.

Gerald found it ridiculous and pompous beyond measure, a throwback to a more paranoid time when the room he occupied had been the center of the most dangerous and ambitious conspiracy in human history. He supposed that the chamber still owned that distinction. Still, the doors were preposterous.

He spied Carver Delano, his vassal, and the man's Lictor bodyguard outside. When the doors opened, the man approached but left his hulking warrior slave in the entry hall. The Highest Chairman did not bother to hide the holograms before him, though they were considered the most sensitive secrets of the Order. He keyed the controls to shut the door again.

"Apologies for the interruption, my lord," Carver said with practiced reverence.

"Not necessary," Gerald replied. "What can I do for you?"

He knew from experience that the much younger man before him was his precise opposite in nearly all things—cruel and ambitious and utterly ruthless. Carver seemed the kind of man to lord his position as the High Chair's vassal over his own subordinates. Gerald tried to keep the ceiling low for men who were not deep thinkers or spiritually enlightened. Still, Carver proved useful to have around, if only to delegate duties to.

"I have just returned from the techno-research facility at grid C34," his coadjutor reported. "Here is the data you requested." He proffered a thick, faux-leather portfolio containing information too sensitive even to be delivered by data link.

Gerald gestured to the table and Carver approached. He walked into the open semicircle to place himself directly across from the chairman, and then set the packet down. Gerald had no doubts that his aide had already read the contents despite the fact that they were for the High Chairman's eyes only. He slid the crisp folder closer and flipped it open, perusing its contents.

While he did so, Carver was desperately trying to keep covert his attempts to memorize the holographic diagrams and sigils displayed between himself and the Chairman. Gerald inwardly smirked.

The file itself was short and concerned an experiment Gerald had ordered on Intrinsic Field research. It was but one of many avenues the Chairman was willing to explore to complete the Great Work. He nodded slowly, and when he glanced back up at his vassal, Carver's eyes snapped back into focus on Gerald's face.

"Very good." Gerald closed the folder. "Thank you, Carver."

"Your pardon, my lord, but that is not all."

Gerald nodded and let the man continue.

"Security forces detected unauthorized use of the facilities in grid C33. Being that I was on the scene, I sent a Death's Head security team to investigate. It turns out that an Outlander had managed to break in."

Gerald pursed his lips, intrigued. "An Outlander?" he asked softly.

"Yes, my lord. There was evidence that it used the facility and the surgery suite to fabricate some kind of machine for itself. The scum covered its tracks well and erased all the data on whatever it was building down there."

"And so may I assume that it is dead?" the Chairman asked mildly.

"No," Carver replied. His gaze fell to the floor. "The vermin escaped."

The chairman mentally checked the facts via data link. A report to the Death's Head High Command had already been registered. Three soldiers had been killed and another nine wounded. Four of those still alive would never recover nominal function without extensive surgery and cybernetics. They were written off, as it would be easier and cheaper to have them euthanized. Cloned Death's Head men were already being decanted from their growth vats and programmed. Carver left these facts out of his verbal report.

Gerald folded his hands and laid them on the table. "You did well in detecting this threat, young Lord Delano. I think you know what you must do. If unanswered, this could set a dangerous precedent."

Carver nodded. "Yes, my lord. My duty is clear. I shall find and eliminate the Outlander thief."

Gerald mentally activated his data link to lock in Carver's obligation. It would remain on file in the memory banks of the Enclave's Hall of Records until discharged. The Chairman nodded, satisfied. This simple matter of finding and killing an Outlander would give the young vassal something to vent his energies on.

For the briefest of flashes, Carver did not conceal his hatred of Gerald. Gerald caught it, but he did not react. He knew the man's temperament. Carver despised being considered an errand boy and hated the thought of being underestimated. As the youngest of a large generation of his family, Delano carried a huge chip on his shoulder.

Gerald found it irrelevant. All Order members had to work their way to higher echelons of power. There were no short cuts.

"That is all, Lord Delano," Gerald said as he keyed the massive chamber doors open again. Carver bowed, lower than was strictly necessary, then turned on his heel and strode out. Gerald watched as the younger man marched off, his brutish Lictor quickly falling in step behind him.

The High Chairman did not dismiss the danger that Carver Delano represented. He would have to deal with the man sooner, rather than later. The vassal was demonstrating too much interest in the Great Work, a secret that was far beyond his station. Although Gerald did not personally put much stock in the Order's overwhelming dependence on secrecy, the situation was not to his liking.

Carver Delano was too cunning and hungry for power in the High Chairman's estimation. Loyalty and a reasonable amount of deference were important to Gerald, and Carver could not be counted on for either.

He decided to let the young Delano expend some of his pent-up emotions in chasing down the Outlander intruder. After he fulfilled that duty, Gerald would make certain to transfer Carver to another Enclave. He started the arrangements via data link.

Gerald also arranged to have dinner with his daughter a few hours from then, and was already looking forward to it. He cracked the hand-delivered folder once more and returned to his work, blissfully unaware of the forces marshaling against him, and of the poisoned pages he turned with his bare fingertips.

— — —

Alouine Morningstar trembled in her seat. She was not cold or fearful however much those things beat on the shell of her emotions. Instead, a barely contained disgust manifested in the slight tremors that caused her body to shake.

The Third City's Grand Mausoleum was a sacred place, built and decorated in the style of the pharaohs of old. Here, the Order's dead were prepared for their journey to the afterlife, to merge with all the memories of their ancestors and to bathe gloriously in the illuminating light of their god, the Fire-Bringer.

Alouine came to bury her father. The place was polished black marble and gold, with huge vaulted ceilings and enormous expanses which were designed to evoke feelings of awe and solemnity. She felt neither of these things.

She already reviewed the autopsy report on her personal data link. The cause of death was listed as simple heart failure. Alouine knew better. It was nonsense. She had taken personal care of her father's health for the past ten years, monitoring his nano-machine injections and guiding him, step by step, through the DNA regeneration phases.

Like any Order member, her beloved father took full advantage of humanity's most advanced youth-restoring and age-defying technologies. His heart was in perfect health. He was over a century old and appeared half that. The autopsy did not tell the whole story. The organ would not have failed without reason—without being acted on by an undetected outside force.

Someone betrayed and murdered Gerald Morningstar. The Order had access to a hundred poisons, any of which could overcome even the most hardened of defenses and stop a human heart cold. An hour later these toxins broke down into simple proteins, leaving no trace behind. There was no proof, of course. Gerald had taught his daughter when she was only a tiny girl that there was a world of difference between knowing and proving. She had investigated the crime herself and found nothing.

Carver Delano, one of Gerald's hatchet-men and most ambitious vassal, had murdered his lord. Everyone knew it. No one could prove it. He alone had motive and opportunity, but not a shred of evidence could indict him. There, at a man's funeral, the daughter of the deceased and, she was certain, his murderer, stared at one another across the sarcophagus.

His face was schooled into an expression of humility and respect, which he held as still as a statue. He did not show a hint of guilt. When his flinty eyes met hers, they utterly lacked contrition.

"My condolences, my lady," he muttered softly. It was a practiced tone, meant to weave sympathy into his inflection. The woman was unimpressed. Her gaze bored into his forehead.

She could only utter a quiet "thank you" in response, pushed through her clenched teeth. The queue of sycophants moved on, taking Carver away. Mercifully, the hate which drove her to murder the man, to square the accounting, faded as he moved away from her presence.

A Chairman of the Highest Circle was dead, and the entire Enclave paused briefly to mourn. For the past three days, Alouine was bombarded with false sympathy, well-wishes, and assurances that her father dwelled in the light of the divine, a reward for his decades of service.

After the ceremony with all of its pomp and ritual, Alouine would have nothing more from the Last Men of the Order. She was expected to process her grief and move on. Sympathy was antithetical to the Order, and with her father laid to rest, she would receive no more of it. They considered care for the dead a vestigial remnant of a bygone age. To Alouine, it was more a symbol of the Order's overweening pride and vanity. They did for others what they could expect to be done for them in return and nothing else.

Only ten days remained until the High Holy Day of the Order, the Feast of the Cremation, when Last Men worldwide gathered to symbolically consume their compassion upon a pyre. It marked a new year for the Order, and Gerald Morningstar's funeral seemed trite and hypocritical in light of it.

As Chairman of the Highest Circle, Gerald would normally preside over the Cremation for the Enclave. Now his death had created a vacuum, and there would be more throat-cutting to come, to determine who would step into his rightful place in time to lead the ceremony.

Alouine was alone on the raised dais, for the first time wishing that her father had given her a sibling or that she had other blood-relatives. Her few remaining friends were lost to her in the sea of funerary robes and hooded faces.

Pallbearers in robes of bright white, the color of death, lowered her father's sarcophagus into an honored position in the floor of the Mausoleum's most sacred space, reserved only for heroes of the Order. Only a High Circle Chairman could be buried here. It should have been a great and burning honor, inflaming Alouine's pride. Instead it was hollow and patronizing. She wanted nothing but to have her father back.

The Order's priests had to use an anti-gravity carriage with powerful robotic arms to lay the immense granite slab, laser-engraved with all of Gerald's achievements and honors, over his coffin, sealing his body into the building forever. With great precision, the high priest, wearing his silvered Death's Head mask, delivered his reading from the book of the Dead and added Gerald's name to the rolls of the Order's fallen, and his deeds into the annals of its history.

Many came to eulogize the departed chairman. Alouine fought a sneer. She would not speak in praise of her dead father while looking into the eyes of his murderer. When called to deliver some words on the dead man's behalf, she took a steadying breath.

She had been taught from the youngest age, her earliest remembrance, to maintain body-mind disparity. No matter the emotions swirling within, her features and manner were trained to remain nonplussed and tranquil. It pained her deeply that her dear father was remembered not as a kind and intelligent man who cared greatly for her, but rather as an efficient cog in the Order's hierarchy and a valued manager of its machine of control. Praises were sung of his accomplishments, not his virtues. No one mentioned his desire for reform. She took the podium, her feet on autopilot.

Her voice was clear and even as she said to the crowd of sycophants and two-faced mourners: "Gerald Morningstar is dead. He is laid down forever. We worship the rising, not the setting sun." With a nod and a final glance to the tomb, the noble woman dismounted the podium and, with everyone watching, began to march out of the mausoleum on her way to the sky-tram platform and her home. It was a statement as well as a way to hide her tears.

She passed Thaira, her dearest friend who shared her home, on her way out of the tomb. The other woman reached out from her seat, slipping her warm hand through the mourning robes to catch Alouine's and give it a comforting squeeze.

The princess of the Last Men smiled at the other woman through her tears and squeezed her hand back, transmitting her sorrow and rage and desire to be alone. Thaira, ever gracious and understanding, released Alouine's hand.

— — —

During the long ride back to Morningstar Manor from the Temple of Understanding, Alouine allowed herself to reminisce under her black funerary veil.

Gerald had told her once, when she was only a little girl, that after years of searching, he had finally found his match in the genetic database. Unlike many of his compatriots in the upper echelons of power, he had personally approached the woman, Alouine's mother.

Rather than simply selecting an ovum from the catalog and having the Bureau of Reproductive Concerns "brew" him up a child, he had offered the woman an incredible sum of cash, honors, and favors to carry his child to term the so-called "old-fashioned" way.

The other members of his circle found it quaint but well within his rights. Everything was for sale, and Gerald was merely buying what he wanted. He wanted a child conceived within the womb of a human being, rather than created in the sterile glass of a test tube.

Alouine recalled asking after the mystery woman whom she had never, and would never meet, but her father had been evasive. He merely mentioned that she had family among the Aldobrandinis of the First City, and that when she had grown into a woman that information would be enough to go on to find her mother, if she wished.

Being a father was something Gerald prepared for like anything else, with diligence and keen attention to detail. He wanted a battery of in vitro modification but left the question of the fetus' sex for natural processes to decide. He had made up his mind to cherish his child whether it was a son or daughter.

However, he spent a fortune in genetic retooling that his

offspring would not go without: genome optimization for muscle and bone density, neural growth stimulation, and the splicing into her genetic code instructions for the growth of additional specialized organs, but unlike many Last Men and Women, he did not customize his child's features or coloring in the womb. The destiny of his genes was not a plaything.

Alouine was born a girl. Gerald had prepared for this. Power had always passed through the Order's generations from father to son, and all male Order members were expected to eventually provide male offspring, but Gerald had rarely given any concern to what he was expected to do. Expectations gave rise to disappointments. Expect nothing, he used to tell her, and you will never be disappointed.

He knew that his daughter would have to make her own way within the insular world of the Last, to perhaps eventually find a man of her station and breeding to whom she could bequeath her incredible genetic code and create a new generation of Last Men.

Truly equal male and female partnerships were uncommon but could be a potent means for a Last Woman to secure power. But that was just as well. Gerald could have as many sons as he needed to satisfy his duty to the Order. His firstborn child was his gift to himself.

She recalled her training, which among scions of the Last Men was a lifestyle one could not refuse. Dedication and a desire for constant improvement had been drilled into her head since birth. Her father had insisted on a primer course for the young girl which began at the age of five and would continue until she was in her forties, when she would be initiated into the ever higher strata of the Order's secret knowledge. Before she could learn to summon forth and command the forces of the universe, to enslave discarnate beings and disembodied intelligences to her will, she had to learn self-mastery, to pursue personal perfection.

There was no set curriculum. Her dear father selected Alouine's areas of study and after receiving feedback from the young girl, had tailored them more to her interests. He was supportive and kind but demanded much, and Alouine had always wanted to make her father proud. She absorbed the teachings he had arranged for her with all of the cognitive cleverness he expected, but her true passion was for the energy of the martial arts.

Gerald never threw a punch in his life, for practice or in anger. The idea of physically fighting someone was not one he valued as a man in his position. His inferiors simply did what he told them to do and that was that. There was never any need for him to learn how to defend himself when he possessed an entire team of genetically and cybernetically enhanced Lictor bodyguards and another thousand loyal and dedicated servants besides, who would give their lives in an instant to preserve him. Not to mention the ever countless dupes and puppets that could be heedlessly thrown into the path of any threats, and the mind-controlled spies and assassins which were provided as simply an aspect of the Order's power structure.

The martial arts were not a priority for the instruction of Order members. It was something they simply did not need. The elite of the earth pulled the strings of power; they did not engage in brawls.

Yet, Alouine enjoyed energetic, kinetic pursuits, like the martial arts, which required strength and dexterity. She possessed a natural affinity for fighting, which pleased her father. More than that, Gerald could see the positives in allowing his daughter to practice both armed and unarmed combat techniques. They strengthened her already deep wells of psychic energy and gave her a natural framework by which to develop her inherent power. They also provided a natural trump card.

The Order's gender relations never truly put male and female on the same plane. Men ran the Order, and very rarely were women allowed to ascend to the upper reaches of power. Nearly never did women take that kind of power for themselves; Alouine could be an exceptional case.

Her father had remarked that ruthless ambition and the ability to discard empathy and compassion came less naturally to the female of the human species. But he had wanted to give Alouine every opportunity, and saw no need for his child to play sidekick to a man merely because she had been born a woman. By mastering these forms of martial prowess, Alouine would be respected. All Order members, men and women, would have to give her the right-of-way, or she would break them.

On occasion, he watched her as she trained, when he was not called away by business or other duties. By the age of twelve, she had mastered numerous styles and was well beyond instruction by the powerful, encyclopedic computer programs she learned from. The girl was a dedicated and passionate student of all knowledge and demonstrated competence in the areas of mathematics and sciences, but her gifts in the realms of physicality and psycho-spiritual awareness overshadowed those purely mental pursuits.

He swelled with pride when he witnessed her complete mastery of inner energy. Call it Orgone or Chi or Ki or Prana or Essence or whatever else, his daughter was a prodigy at using her psychic power. Chakras blazing with invisible energy, she could regularly perform impossible feats: cracking solid stone with her fingertips and flitting about off of walls as if gravity had no purchase. Her father had been unsure from whence these talents sprang; perhaps they were traits latent in the girl's mother, or in his own genetic code.

As the towering structures of the Third City Enclave rushed past the sky-tram window, Alouine remembered her thirteenth birthday, clarity rushing back to her.

She was nearing womanhood. When her waking chime had sounded before dawn, she had quickly dressed and ran through the lavish corridors of the manor, her family's own corner of the Enclave, to find her father. She dashed around and between servants and leapt over the robotic servitor which cleaned and polished the marble floors each morning, enjoying the contest, the little game she played with herself upon waking—to rise and dress herself quickly, and report to her father for instruction in as little time as possible.

She remembered clearly the smile on her father's face as she chimed at his door. That morning, she had cut a full two seconds off of her best time yet. His eyes, slate grey, crinkled at the corners. "Good morning, dear," he had said to her, "and happy birthday."

"Hello, Father. Thank you," she had beamed back at him. She loved the smell of her father's office. Some comforting and achingly familiar smell permeated the room, which gave rise to a feeling of inclusiveness. She never feared leaving the warmth of her bed and blankets because it was only a short trip to Gerald's rooms, his presence.

He was not alone that day. In truth, he rarely was, but Alouine did not count the endless menagerie of servants. The host of butlers, stewards and clerks were will-less, soulless, and subhuman; without worth, aside from fulfilling their duties. However, that day, his father was entertaining a guest.

They sat on either side of the breakfast table where man and daughter usually took their morning meal. Alouine's father was not yet old, but his salt and pepper hair and slow, easy movement betrayed his years. However, the man sitting across from him was near ancient by comparison. It appeared that he could call two centuries of life his own. Scant wisps of white hair clung to the older gentleman's wrinkled scalp. Alouine detected the smell of leather and sweet pipe tobacco. The man's jacket was tweed, of all things, a blatant anachronism. Sizing him up, she decided that he was a vassal, a lower ranking member, without the full rights that a lord of the Order like her father possessed.

"Come here, Alouine," Gerald said, gesturing to her usual seat. "Have some breakfast. I'd like you to meet Mr. Landgrave. I have invited him here to continue to instruct you." His choice of wording was for the older man's benefit. An invitation that could not be refused was not much of an invitation at all, she mused. Even so, the wizened man appeared pleased by Gerald's polite introduction.

She nodded and approached, and the old gentleman stood creakily, pushing down on his cane. He took her hand and waved his nose over it in approximation of a kiss to her knuckles. "Lady Morningstar," he grumbled in greeting, his thick Old World accent rounding off his words. "I have heard much about you." She smiled, nodded and sat, and the man took his chair again.

Her father picked up the conversation. "Valdemar was the Master of Security for the whole Second City," he explained. "He knows a thing or two about the arts you like to study, so I brought him and his own daughter over to stay with us for a time."

Valdemar Landgrave cleared his throat softly and sipped tea from the china cup before him. "Your father has told me how impressive your skills already are," he said. "If you like, I'll teach you some things you won't find in those old manuals. Things an AI can't teach."

Alouine had nodded furiously. The thought of access to someone with real experience sent a jolt of excitement down her spine. "That would be fantastic. When do we begin?"

"You have an eager student," Gerald had remarked, without concealing his pride. Alouine allowed herself a sad smile at the memory.

The old vassal had smirked. "We'll see how long that lasts. I don't do anything by halves, as my own daughter well knows."

"How old is your daughter?" Alouine asked. By this time, she was well accustomed to holding her own in conversations with adults, and felt nothing about posing frank questions to a vassal or grilling a servant for information.

"Thaira is twelve," Valdemar replied. She recalled feeling surprised and nervous that the old man had the pluck to stare straight at her. It was not a breach of protocol, since he was not a slave, but it certainly lacked obeisance. He may have been a vassal in the Order, but the man was a master of his craft and held the stern visage of a world-class teacher—a man who demanded respect and would not be gainsaid by anyone.

"She's my youngest. With my oldest son taking over as Master of Security for the Second Enclave, she and I had an opportunity to cross the pond and see what life is like on the other side. When your father told me about your talents, I wanted to see for myself. Thaira is looking forward to meeting you. We're a family of warriors, after all. And competition, for a warrior, is the key to growth."

After breakfast, Alouine and Valdemar left her father, who had excused himself to attend to business. They walked to the wide gardens in silence, and there Thaira was already engaging in warm-up exercises, incorporating ancient techniques to limber up her young and flexible muscles.

Thaira Landgrave was a more plain-looking girl than Alouine, shorter and stockier. It would remain that way as the two of them grew up together. Her eyes were a lovely bright green, unlike the coal-dark gems set in Alouine's face.

Through this man, who had become a great teacher of hers, Alouine had also met her best friend. They drilled together in the mornings, a special time for their family. As a Morningstar, she was taught to worship the rising sun.

"One punch is never enough," the stern, old man had grumbled. Alouine and Thaira were sparring, wearing their workout clothing.

One stiff punch from Alouine had knocked the other girl to the hard floor, and she had paused, waiting for her friend to rise again. That earned her a solid swipe across the back of her thigh from Valdemar's cane. The man stepped between them. "We throw our punches in bunches," he said. "Attack until the enemy is still and lifeless."

--- --- ---

Departing the sky-tram and entering her father's home, Alouine remained lost in thought. She supposed it was her home now, but she suspected that she would never truly see it that way.

She banished her servants from her presence via data link and crossed the expansive halls to her late father's study. His presence had faded from the room, and the ghost of his familiar scent was already dissipating.

By the time she was fourteen, Gerald and Valdemar had run out of means by which to continue to instruct her. In the space of a single year, the vast materials contained within Valdemar's ancient databases had all been digested thoroughly. She routinely broke her robotic training devices into their constituent parts. Alouine could kill without a thought and honed numerous techniques for doing so.

She had no partners with which to train, having outgrown all other practitioners on the entire earth, including Thaira, who was herself a deadly warrior. Outlander slaves were sometimes used as training tools but they died, often accidentally, with ease. Indeed, the Order members who did practice any martial arts at all refused in any way to engage in the pursuit with Alouine, in fear of their own lives. Those members who studied things like the Order's ancient breathing and stretching techniques for the health and esoteric benefits they offered could only provide stale crumbs of knowledge anyway.

Her training with Valdemar and Thaira had reached its apex.

She could no longer learn from either of them but continued the routine at the insistence of both her instructor and her father.

"When you throw your front kick, your left guard dips," the teenage Alouine had informed her slightly younger friend.

Thaira was sweating and fatigued from their workout, unlike her friend. Her father had taken to observing, for the most part, during their sessions, while Alouine effortlessly completed her routine and simultaneously offered critique and advice. The slightly younger girl broke her guard completely and stood straight, frustration overcoming her patience and focus.

She huffed out a loud sigh. "You know," she blurted, "I thought we were supposed to be training together. Why does it feel like I have two teachers now, instead of a classmate?"

Alouine was taken aback. "I didn't mean to offend," she began to say, but Valdemar pushed past her, cutting her off.

"Thaira dear, I know this is hard for you. We all reach our peaks at different times, and Alouine is only trying to help you reach yours."

The girl had blown out another frustrated breath, which fluttered her bangs. "I know," she murmured. Locking eyes with the slightly older girl, she quietly said, "You're just . . . so perfect. Everything comes so easily to you."

Alouine stepped forward around Valdemar's flank and looked at Thaira plainly. "Don't make this a competition, Thai. I just want you to be strong. I don't want to be alone."

The younger girl looked at the floor for a moment, humbled. "You're not alone, Ally." She wrapped Alouine in a warm hug. The older girl was shocked by the gesture, but Thaira refused to let go and, eventually, they settled in and the embrace became mutual.

The old, wizened master allowed the hug for a moment. He was proud of both of them. When he interrupted, he did so gently. "The two of you should find other things to do together. Maybe we all need a vacation, and I'll consider changing up our training routine. You both need new challenges and I'll have to study hard in order to find them."

Thaira's excitement could not be contained. "We get some time off?"

Her father chuckled. "Well, I'd expect you would want to keep your skills sharp. But you are both coming of age now, and life is not all about lessons. You should see what the Enclave has to offer."

His daughter had squealed and grinned, scrunching her face and pulling on her friend's sleeve, but Alouine remained composed. "My father only allows me to leave our wing when he is with me. He's very busy," she reminded her teacher.

"Yes," Valdemar replied. "But you are nearly a young woman now. I will speak with him about allowing you more freedom to move about."

By then, the aged man cared for both of the girls equally—as though Alouine were his own, and he knew exactly how to inspire confidence in the young pair. "I doubt there are many dangers within this fine place, and together, you could overcome them anyway."

Easily excited, Thaira launched into a wild list of all the things she wanted to see and do, as her father ended their training for the day and retired to make an appointment to see Gerald Morningstar as soon as it was convenient for the higher-ranked man. Where Gerald's daughter was concerned, he always made time for the tutor and listened carefully to his advice.

Thaira led Alouine off to her room, gushing on about the tours they would take together of the galleries and museums, the trips to the markets and slave auctions. Her excitement was so palpable that Alouine could not help but feel encouraged as well.

"I guess we'll have to wait until we hear from Papa if we'll be allowed to leave the manor. It's about time, isn't it?" Thaira asked. An entire year had been far too long to be cooped up, even in a palace-sized house. "You've seen the Third City, right? What's it like?"

Alouine put a finger to her lips as she considered. "Well, my father doesn't really go anywhere except for the High Circle chamber. It's in the pyramid Temple. I've been, once or twice. We usually take a tram on the skyways. It can be pretty, I suppose, but it depends on the weather."

The younger girl gushed, "Maybe we'll get to meet some boys!"

Alouine smiled and shook her head as the two of them stripped their training clothes and washed, then dressed again in their normal attire. Form-fitting and made from luxurious blends of all-synthetic fibers, the servants insisted the outfits were the height of couture, but the older girl was skeptical.

In a small way, she hoped that her father denied the request. Alouine never lacked in things to do and chalked Thaira's excitement up to restlessness, something that inferior blood could often lead to in a lesser being. She did not hold it against the girl. It simply was what it was.

It took nearly an hour for Valdemar to return from his video conference with Gerald. Alouine suspected that her father was busy during that time of the day, and had bid her aging instructor to wait. The two girls chatted over refreshments until they both received instructions through their data links to report to their instructor immediately.

Valdemar inspected the two girls in the room set aside for his office, and addressed Alouine directly. "I suggested to your esteemed father that it might be time you two stretched your legs a bit, and he agreed. But I want you both to be very careful. Follow all the protocols and don't speak out of turn." He handed Alouine an envelope. "Lord Morningstar has trusted you with this." He locked his eyes onto hers. "I trust you with Thaira. Be responsible. Both of you keep each other out of trouble." He led them out of his office. "We'll expect you back for dinner, of course. Off you go."

The pair ran down the corridor in the direction of the tram loading area, with Thaira giggling and squealing. "This is so great! Where do we go first?"

Alouine shrugged. "I suppose I'll leave that to you."

Still at a trot which sent servants scrambling from their path, Thaira glanced sidelong at Alouine again. "Okay. I'm sure I'll think of something. What did your father give you?"

The older girl opened the envelope and took out a shiny but flimsy-looking card of transparent orange plastic. Golden circuits crossed it here and there, and it possessed a gem-like lens offset to one side. She marveled at it. "Well, we have some money," she offered as explanation. "Let me put it in my Mark account."

The pair slowed to a walk, and Alouine held the card to her right wrist, where the implanted, genetically-keyed microchip signifying her membership in the Order of the Last lay under her skin. The card beeped and the tiny lens which protruded from her skin blinked red a few times. Alouine closed her eyes and mentally accessed the account, and then immediately stopped in her tracks.

"What's wrong?" Thaira asked.

"Maybe he made a mistake," Alouine murmured, more to herself than to her friend.

"There wasn't any money on the card? That's a bummer." The younger girl got carried away, as she sometimes did. "That's all right. I have a little—enough for a snack, at least. Let's get some cake or something."

Alouine took her eager friend by the arm and gently pulled her to the side of the corridor. "He gave me all of it," she whispered. Over three hundred and forty billion credits were stored in the girl's Mark account. Certainly there were more wealthy families among the Last Men, but only a scant few. The entirety of the Morningstar fortune was hers to command.

"Wow," Thaira said. "He must really trust you."

The young Lady Morningstar nodded gravely. "I won't make him regret it."

Thaira laughed heartily. "You're so serious all the time, Ally. Don't worry so much! I know your dad is ultra-rich. Isn't he the High Circle Chairman? It's not like we could put a dent in his money in one afternoon. He knows that."

Alouine sighed. "When you're right, Thai, you're right." She smiled at her younger friend. "Let's go."

With the Third City open to them at last, the girls purchased tram tickets for the skyway and set off for the center of the vast and expansive enclosure. Riding the skyway was a new experience for Thaira. Like Alouine, she had spent every moment of her life confined within Morningstar Manor since her arrival from the Second City to the Third. Their every need and desire was instantly met in the palatial building, but both girls luxuriated in the feeling of open spaces.

The exciting and new sights and sounds stimulated both of them, as they walked among the statues and obelisks in the main forum. Huge and black, peaked by a golden capstone, the pyramidal structure at the end of the forum cast a colossal triangular shadow from its great height over the entire area. This was the Third City's crowning landmark: the Temple of Understanding. Rising two kilometers into the sky, its black capstone backlit by the Enclave dome's artificial, holographic sun. The sight of it made Alouine's heart catch in her throat.

"Doesn't your father work there?" Thaira asked as they walked from one of the great museums to another.

Alouine nodded. "The chairmanship carries with it office space in the capstone area." Again, the younger girl's excitability proved too much for the older girl to restrain.

"Let's go check it out."

Within Alouine's presence, human life existed by her leave. She feared nothing and no one, and that was the reward for all of her blood, sweat, and tears. Still, there was a distinct impression that she was entering an area that was as yet beyond her, where all others were initiated into profound and powerful mysteries. The pyramid was a place where wills were tested against other wills, where the weak were weeded out and those who were powerful and skilled at manipulating lesser minds thrived.

FIVE
The Outlands

A landmark of consciousness is the ability to intentionally expand it, Harrow thought. He took that step for himself. On the whole, he sought low-tech solutions to battle his high-tech enemy. He fought harder, which enabled him to win more easily. But, in the end he was forced to make concessions to the power of technology.

His enemies were predators, using cowardly violence which hides in the shadows. They always had done so. He was convinced that brave and honorable violence would defeat his foes. The problem was awareness and perception. He had to be able to see into the darkness of secrecy and occultation his great enemy used to cloaked itself.

His sight would have to penetrate the layers of the astral planes, the so-called spirit worlds from whence the Order of the Last drew their power.

Harrow understood little of what went on in the Order's strange magical practices, despite having eavesdropped on their rituals. The temples, blood sacrifice, sexual excesses, and haunting chants made little sense to him, but he knew one thing for certain: if there were no powers to be gained, the Order would not perform them. If nothing else, these so-called Last Men of the Order hated to waste their time.

Summoning spirits, discarnate intelligences, or disembodied

consciousnesses was the root of all the Order's magic, and Harrow refused to fall victim as so many Outlanders, past and present, had done.

Already a master mathematician, thanks to the stringent and severe drilling of his late, draconian father, he had purpose-built and installed SIMON himself, with quantum technology from the Order's massive Enclave. An entire ring of the facility was dedicated to research and development of ever more incredible technologies to serve the Last Men, and Harrow turned this center of knowledge and progress, used for centuries to advance the Order and neglect the Outlanders, to his own ends.

With only the schema his father had left him, his repeated and daring incursions had at last paid off. He had finished the design, snuck into the Enclave's techno-research facility, and programmed the automated robotic cyber-fabrication and surgical suite to build and install the device for him. The entire process had taken an hour, and by the time the Order knew what was happening, it was finished.

Using SIMON, he destroyed all the data afterwards by frying the local servers. The trial run of the quantum device had been his battle to escape the facility.

The Quantum Engine's hardware, by itself, was useless without the SIMON to utilize it. Using its simulation matrix, Harrow found he was able to overcome the eternally present moment and glimpse the future. With only his prestigious sensory input as the limiting factor, the Torus field-driven crystal device continually simulated the causal effects that nearly all of Harrows physical actions could produce, shaping all things within his body's magnetic field to match his needs. It was a future projector, and with it, Harrow was more able to actively shape his life to his precise specifications.

Using the engine brought with it an understanding that the brain is not the source of consciousness, but a receiver of it. It put

Harrow in touch with the conception that the universe was alive and intelligent and the product of a cosmic, creative principle. He was a human being, one of the most sophisticated manifestations of this constant and all-encompassing universal life-energy.

His human destiny came within his own grasp, and thanks to the machine built and installed by his own hand, Harrow could fire the great flame of his righteous indignation, to focus it, and to unleash it upon the enemies of his race, those plunderers of the future: the Last Men.

He conceived of this energy as his soul-fire.

With that spiritual fire as fuel, the machine could warp the laws of probability and affect quantum changes within the sphere of his body's electromagnetic field.

Piggybacked to the simulation matrix and quantum engine was a smaller device which projected a monomolecular fiber into the pineal gland of Harrow's brain. Inserting the fiber had been a dangerous task, but the Order's mastery of computer, laser and robotics technology had made it possible.

The device was a tiny factory devoted to the synthesis of certain chemical compounds which occurred naturally within the brain but responded well to conscious control. In particular, Harrow found that by regulating his body's supply of dimethyltriptamine, endorphins, and epinephrine, he became an even more capable combatant and frightful warrior.

Used to regulate his body's natural reactions to life and death situations, Harrow tuned the device to keep him from entering into what his father referred to as "condition black". At a heart rate exceeding one hundred seventy-five beats per minute, the body loses its fine motor skills. Harrow's constant battling of the Order and its pawns helped to inure him to this condition, but having a backup, a safety net, was, to his mind, preferable to the alternative: death.

At the trying moment, he refused to freeze, and in situations where he might otherwise have devolved into the primitive, 'fight or flight' of condition black, he instead kept his wits, loosened his muscles, and triumphed with precision and intensity. This was, as his father had told him, the definition of a successful warrior: an average man with laser-like force.

That which drained from Harrow, stemmed from an inexhaustible supply. Not mere blood, precious but ultimately secondary, but willpower, in such immense reserve as to never cease flowing. He was a master alchemist of the spirit, summoning a great and fiery something from the nothing of the abyssal void of the Outlands. To try to match his expenditure would grind even the most warm-hearted to dust in no time, but Harrow could spend of himself recklessly; the well of his soul was bottomless, and he drew its water without end.

He spent the product of his overflowing spirit to stave off the cold. It burned in the furnace of his heart and kept him bright and warm. Loneliness could not touch him. Despair, tracking behind him always, had no chance of gaining a foothold in his tempered mind. The man's tolerance for solitude was galvanized in the nuclear forge of his brilliant, quantum-augmented soul.

No one knew exactly how old he was, and if he did know, he never mentioned it. Most were sure that judging by his build and beard that he had left his teenage years behind, but his bright eyes and fresh face marked him as one who had not yet lived through thirty winters. None could say where he came from or where he went in his endless travels. They only knew the warmth he brought. Angel some called him. Savior, others whispered.

The people saw it wherever he went. They crowded around him, seeking to shelter themselves from the all-pervading chill within his aura of heat and strength. They smiled at him, offered him refreshment and spoke to him ceaselessly, most without consciously knowing why. He never said a word to them. He was not poor enough in spirit to offer alms in such a manner. But he listened and accepted their gifts and nodded his thanks, and coming from him, it was enough.

He brought them gifts, taken from the clutches of their oppressors. Fresh food and clean water, medicines, ammunition, and other treasures he liberated from the hordes of dragons, were left in his wake.

Like a river, he flowed through the world. No obstacle could contain him, and though he could provide for those nearby, he was also very dangerous. Few dared to stand in his way or arrest his travels. Those that did became corpses. The river could flood, leap its banks and consume all those who made their homes on its shores. It destroyed those who sought to dam it or divert its course. Demon, some called him. Monster, others whispered.

He carried a scoped, bolt-action rifle, an automatic pistol and a long fighting knife, and did not hesitate to use any of these. Exposure to the perpetual winter of the Outlands could kill a grown man in a day, but the icy grip of Harrow's disapproval was so much more deadly. He could be colder than cold when the time to kill arrived; a frost so chilling that it burned. He scorched everyone he met with intensity or frost, or both. The difference was a nuance very few could understand.

Once there were cities, but that was long ago. Now there were derelicts of metal and concrete, cracked and decayed. A world of rusting bodies gutted and scraped to dry bones by human worms. The youth often thought that perhaps he was a worm as well, that the only difference was that he could glow with the light of soul-fire. The other worms would gather around and call his light glory. He knew he was only a man, but his longing was an arrow he launched to the heavens. Perhaps he could be more than a man.

Home was a foreign, alien concept, but the young man did have a location where he would stop for rest and relative safety. In the exclusively barter-driven economy of the world, a man as rich as he often was could not stay in one place for too long without the locals becoming dependent on him, and that simply would not do. Others could rely on him, but he could never rely on them. He certainly did not desire to be viewed as a savior, so he did not encourage them by loitering.

There was a tiny village in what usable farmland existed forty kilometers north of the massive Order enclave—what the Order called the Third City and the Outlanders simply referred to as 'the dome'. The village took its name from an ancient sign rooted in the soil nearby, with the words "Mason-Dixon" still legible but slowly fading. Harrow would watch this village for a full day before entering, to ensure that none of the Order's enslaved military troops had occupied it and were waiting in ambush.

Just after dawn, he strode down the lane between cornfields to the piled ring of rusted automobile hulks that formed the village palisade and adjusted the large sack he carried over his shoulder. Village life started early, and already lookouts had spotted him. The place was secure, as Outlander villages went. The men were cautious and typically alert to threats, and the palisade was patrolled night and day.

In his youth, he had learned the hard way that simply approaching the gate was safer and more preferable to forcing his way in. Regardless of his personal feelings about them, the Outlanders were his people, and unlike the castle-like enclave or the sporadic outposts of the Order with their high-tech security and fat larders, their villages were safe from the man's predations, especially this one.

"Harrow!" a familiar voice hollered the warrior's name. He saw the young girl of perhaps twelve years squeeze her still-tiny frame through the gate without waiting for it to fully open. She pushed past the farmers and scavengers heading out for the morning's work. "You're back!"

Harrow nodded. The girl ran to him as fast as her scrawny legs would take her. Her ratty blond hair flew behind her and her patch-filled, oversized clothing billowed. She wrapped her spindly arms around his hips and buried her face in his side.

"Hello, Nina." He greeted her, resting his palm for a moment on the top of her head. Had he wanted to, he could not avoid the girl. Like a rare butterfly, she needed no excuse. "I've come to see Joanna."

"Sure, I'll take you," the girl grinned. Harrow was sure that the little orphan had a notion of infatuation with him. It was her prerogative, of course. His visits had been somewhat infrequent in the four years since he had taken her to Mason-Dixon, to leave her in the care of Joanna, the artificer, engineer and blacksmith of the village. Nina quickly became a favorite mascot in the tiny, remote colony. Though she was still quite thin and had not yet begun to blossom into true womanhood, Harrow had no doubt she was well cared for.

As he followed the exuberant blond child, men and boys leaving to tend the fields and flocks waved and offered salutes to Harrow as he passed them. The village was a circle of shanty homes, crudely constructed from whatever materials could be found and built on the strange concrete foundations that occasionally dotted the landscape. There were three working wells which drew clean water, more than enough for the people here. A dozen families called this area home; sixty souls, no more.

Joanna's work area was little more than a lean-to adjacent to her tiny cabin, all of it cobbled together from timber, bricks, stone and sheet metal, and insulated with dried mud and cattle dung. Her kiln and forge were already hot, and Harrow could hear the ebony woman pounding away at some metal item on her anvil. She never slept past dawn, and her hammer served the village double as a call to reveille, each and every morning without fail.

Wiry and hard-muscled, sleeveless and sweating despite the cold, she beat what appeared to Harrow to be the blade of a plow into shape from the springs of some relic truck as he approached.

"Look, Miss Joanna, Harrow's back!" Nina's chirpy voice cried over the ringing sound of the hammer. The hammer paused for a beat, then resumed. The older woman did not usually respond immediately to anything, and Harrow was content to wait and admire her focus and dedication. He gently set the sack containing her payment on the ground next to her workbench, scattered with the tools of her various trades.

Nina's incessant yammering provided a melody, set to the industrious beat of Joanna's hammer. Half-listening to the child fill him in on her adventures, Harrow stood watching the blacksmith. The woman was a jack of all trades and master of several. She could heat, shape, cut, and weld metal, blow glass, reload ammunition, treat injuries, and was an amateur chemist and electrician.

Harrow had once asked her where she had learned her skills, and she merely responded that insects had the luxury of specialization; humans did not.

Nearly an hour passed, and Nina had gone to draw water, heating it for Harrow and leaving it cold for Joanna. When the plow blade was finished, the tough older woman flopped onto a stool and took a long drink before finally fixing her gaze on Harrow.

"What do you want?" she asked in her gruffly affectionate tone. The hint of her white smile told Harrow all he needed to know; she was glad to see him.

"My blade needs sharpening, my armor repairing, and I have brass," he replied evenly, his features schooled into a blank mask. After months of use in countless duels and killings, Harrow's weapon, called "KA-BAR" because of the engraving on the black blade, had grown dull. Human bone, he found, would eventually blunt even the sternest steel.

His armor was custom-made for him by Joanna, a pair of thickly padded sleeves with steel bracers for his forearms, worn under his coat and, likewise, steel shin-guards to protect his lower legs, under his trousers. The armor had saved his life numerous times.

In a world where firearms were plentiful but ammunition rare, fighting had become intensely personal. Blades and clubs were improvised from pipes, dowels, and shards of metal or glass. Rarely did a person possess a weapon like KA-BAR, made for the intent of killing. "The time has almost come," he added softly.

"I know what you're up to, but it'll still cost you."

Harrow paid a lucrative retainer fee several times again what Joanna's services were worth. With a client like him, Joanna was becoming a rich woman; normally the most dangerous type of woman to be. In her case, the client was worth even more because everyone in the village knew that if they crossed her, Harrow would kill them.

He valued her that much; she was integral to his plans. No one else worked steel as well, or cast lead for bullets, or hand-loaded such quality ammunition. Harrow carefully emptied the sack.

Eight eggs, wrapped in cloth to cushion them, came first. Joanna arched a brow in silent question. Harrow merely smirked in response—of course they were fertilized. Nina followed this exchange and her jaw dropped. This would be a chance to have more chickens, which was a welcome luxury.

Joanna, however, continued to stare at Harrow expectantly. He drew out a folded, finely woven grey blanket, relatively clean, that the eggs had rested on, two bottles of kerosene and a box of matches stolen from an Order outpost, and his prize: a stocked first-aid kit of the zippered-orange-canvas variety. He also dug a small bottle of hand sanitizer and two foil-wrapped chocolate bars out of his coat pocket. The alcohol-based lotion he placed into the pile of treasure, adding to his offer. One of the bars he handed immediately to Nina. "Save this for a rainy day," he said, knowing full well that she would not. The other bar he held.

"Stay for breakfast, throw in the chocolate, and you've got a deal."

— — —

Quintain still made his home in the shadow of the Enclave. Its massive dome blotted out what little sunlight escaped the thick curtain of clouds, casting impenetrable darkness over his home in all seasons. His neighbors were cruel and barbarous, but exceedingly far-sighted. A mere sixteen kilometers east of their great dome, he was as invisible as a field mouse to them, tucked safely into his burrow at the corner of their house.

His mother had been a shaman, a medicine woman, a healer. She was also widely considered to be a deadly witch, who, if crossed, would place powerful curses on her assailants. Quintain knew these descriptors were only partially accurate. The Outlanders loved and feared his mother in equal measure. The tightly bound community which had once surrounded her lair had been a thriving one, thanks to her vast accumulation of knowledge.

He knew that they lived in the rubble of an ancient library, one which she tried to augment further at every opportunity. He had been taught to read from the innumerable stacks of books by his third winter, and even now he did so for about six hours every day, soaking everything up like an ever-absorbent sponge.

It was not enough to read; his mother had tested him for comprehension regularly. Now, he could digest and reason through the thickest tomes in very short periods by entering into the reading trance. Mother had taught him about brain waves and how to settle into the theta range, which facilitated high-speed language processing and computational ability.

She was a problem solver, and well-paid for her efforts. She knew where to find clean water, how to grow nourishing food which could be kept over long periods without spoiling, how to dress wounds, treat illnesses, and keep the body pure and healthy.

Likewise, she knew how to tend to the mind, to set the emotions of her fellow human beings on a balanced path, and to see to their spiritual needs. She gave them hope.

Outlanders desperately needed hope. The community in which the mother-and-son pair had lived was a shanty town of mostly underground dwellings which had grown up at the outskirts of the Third City Enclave. The towering, domed structure stretched for miles to the southwest, reflecting the weak sunlight by day and blotting out half the stars of the sky by night.

It was a constant reminder that Heaven was closed off to them, that the Outlanders were a cursed race, destined to struggle to survive. Quintain's mother had intended to change that.

She attempted to forge techniques for unfolding her fellow Outlanders' higher natures. Elevating them out of the muck of starvation and tribal warfare was one thing, but those things were merely symptomatic of deeper root causes. The world of the Outlands had no spiritual sense. Occasionally, some charlatan or would-be demagogue would attempt to deceive others into doing his will, but this was a contribution to the problem, not a solution.

No. Quintain's mother sought to use her accumulated knowledge of the human mind to exert a potent influence on the entire personality of her fellow Outlanders, to produce integrity, a new, equilibrated perspective toward life, and a unification of the various strata of consciousness collectively known as mankind.

She had tricks, which she taught to her son. Tricks for hiding herself from the conscious perception of others; tricks for dispelling hostility, aggression, and suspicion. Tapping into the higher, astral realms, she knew precisely how to alter the viewpoints of others and guide them into more receptive states of consciousness.

"Every human being has access to higher realms of thought and feeling," she had said to him. "They must first overcome their physical and spiritual degradation."

Implementing her desire for humanity's rebirth, his mother was beginning to make a difference. She brought together Outlanders from many separate communities and from incredibly diverse backgrounds. She healed them, taught them, provided counsel and guidance, helped them form a congress of a kind, to share in what bounty could be wrung from the wastes, and to develop a spirit of cooperation.

Voluntary associations began to spring up into a fledgling network. It was the beginning of a structure, the very first flowering of a new civilization. Out of chaos and anarchy, the brave woman was building a society.

The Order of the Last Men learned of this. Quintain had never found out exactly how, but he now suspected that they had bribed various Outlanders, men who were becoming leaders of new communities, to turn traitor to the entire enterprise.

They killed his mother in cold blood when Quintain was eleven years old. Struck down by a sniper's bullet fired from more than a kilometer away, it had carved a huge and ragged wound in her torso that no amount of medicine or sacred energy-healing could repair.

She did not die in terror or agony, but was happy to give her life in pursuit of her goal. If the Last Men had gone out of their way to kill her, it had meant that she was on to something.

The young Quintain managed to keep her alive and relatively comfortable for another two days.

"Do not give in to despair, my son," she had spoken weakly. The woman, a mother for many years, was still beautiful, with the soft firmness of youth, but paling and beaded with cold sweat. Death was upon her, it lay next to her like a lover in the bed where she would find her end. The mounds of bandages and cloth pressed to her abdomen had soaked through with her blood. "Despair is a surrendering to your basest instincts. Remember that hope is a gift you give to yourself. That is the meaning of inner strength."

Quintain's tears fell without regard. "I don't know if I can do it, Mom," the boy said. "I haven't learned enough yet. No one is going to listen to me."

His mother smiled. "You are not just my son, but your father's, as well."

The boy swallowed dryly. "You never mentioned him before."

"I did not know him well," she answered weakly. "When I found him, he was wounded badly, as I am now." Lightly coughing, she squeezed her son's hand. "Perhaps worse," she amended. "I tried to nurse him back to health, but he passed on. Not before he gave me the greatest gift he could have bestowed: you."

The young Quintain had pressed his forehead to his mother's knuckles, wetting her fingers with his tears.

"The Last Men have killed us both for our power," she said. "Your father gave his life to defend the people, just as I gladly offer mine to heal them. Do one of these, my son, or both. Defend or heal the people of the Outlands. They are your kin. Their blood is your blood."

"All right; I'll try," the boy mumbled.

"You have a half-brother," she whispered. "Your father wanted to search for him, but he never regained his strength. Your father was a great warrior. God willing, his other son has become one as well. Find him, if you can."

Her voice was fading, her strength nearing its end. With much effort, she reached up with her free hand and plucked the glittering jewel from her forehead, the crystal which helped to focus her spiritual power. The light within the gem guttered and died as it was removed.

All her remaining vitality engaged, she took the boy's chin and lifted it. Shakily, she placed the gem on his forehead, in the position of the Third Eye. It locked itself into place, sinking into his flesh and painlessly embedding in his skull. It gleamed softly; its light faint and weak compared to what it had shown when fueled by his mother's power. Even dying as she was, the boy felt eclipsed by her spiritual might.

She smiled her last, and as her final breath left her, she shaped it into words. "I love you."

"I love you too, Mother."

— — —

Quintain shook himself out of his reverie with a full-body twitch. He was not sure how long he had walked, aimless, through the wastes, lost in his memories, but at least he recognized where he was. His lair was another three kilometers to the west, so he re-oriented himself and trudged on.

His mother's dream was shattered. No one lived within two days walk of his lair anymore.

In the interceding years since the woman had died, Quintain mastered the techniques of meditation. Before she had been murdered, he had only managed to enter into a somnolent state. Now, his perception had widened. He could experience deep, spiritual insights and an unveiling of arcane knowledge, and could snap into and out of the trance near instantly.

The entire spirit world was open to all five of his senses. He could enter the lower and even the higher astral planes at will. It felt like his first real victory; the practice of conscious meditation had widened the band of frequencies that the young man could receive.

Growing experience of the psycho-spiritual world around him

had given him practice in dealing with spirits—the disembodied intelligences which occupied other dimensions of thought and being. The Last Men of the Enclave used these spirits as familiars, bound in occult pacts to do their bidding. In the physical world, the Enclave was a domed city. In the etheric plane it was a pit, swirling with demonic entities that battened on the spite and hatred and malignancy of the Last Men, their masters.

For his part, Quintain threw in his lot with the Archangels, the great astral spirits that loved, protected and guided mankind. He made these powerful beings his allies and teachers.

Wheels were turning; the young magus could feel it. He knew that events were cyclical, spiral-like, that time was marked by periods and that anything happening in the physical world was simply a shadow, a projection, of events in the spiritual world. Time affected the material world, and because it did, every event on physical earth was preceded by an event in the spirit realm.

His mother had explained it to him, but the boy still was not confident in his understanding. She had likened it to ripples in water. The more spiritual force that events exerted on the astral planes, the faster they traveled and were felt on the earth.

He took a deep breath as he gazed off toward the fortress-city of his enemy, staring at an astral scene of carnage and upheaval. *It looks like the devil is trying to break loose from hell. How long until that manifests and brings more destruction on the people*, he wondered.

In the wake of his mother's death, Quintain had tried to use his occult knowledge to form a bulwark against these hostile forces and keep them contained, at least. The task had proved incomprehensibly difficult. For all their bluster, Quintain thought, spirits are subordinate to the will of humans. *We are everything they wish that they could be.*

Unfortunately, my people do not have the strongest of wills.

Most other Outlanders gave these entities power over them by being lazy, by losing focus, by not being conscious and present in their own lives. It opened the door into their subconscious minds and allowed those dark forces to invade their psyches, cutting them off from their higher natures and ruling them without their ever becoming aware of it.

However, the Last Men of the Enclave actively worshipped and employed dark spirits. They imagined their wills were strong, and they were in command of great power over their fellow men.

The boy scoffed.

"There is no difference between being spiritually awake and spiritually free, Quintain," his mother told him. "Practically, they are one and the same. Only when we are blinded and cut off from the unity of creation do we descend into madness and perversity."

His skinny legs carried him home. He was, once again, empty-handed. The thought made him sick with disappointment. Again, he had gone gallivanting across the endless Outlands and had found no great hero, no kin, nothing resembling his mother's prophecy; only rumors of some demonic entity and a warning to be wary of it from frightened, superstitious Outlanders. They told him the demon murdered the servants of the Last Men and the Outlanders alike, butchering either without a care.

That did not sound very heroic to Quintain. He was fully prepared to cease his months of fruitless searching and try a new approach. Judging by the eruptions of demonic energy coming from the pyramid temple of the city, he was running out of time.

It occurred to the boy that he may have been squeezing his hopes too hard, strangling them. *The cosmos was perverse in that way*, he thought. *Hold on to something too tightly and you are bound to crush it, or to watch it slip away.*

He checked his satchel and found that, as predicted, his stores of food for the long trek had worn down to crumbs. Though some of the chambers of his lair were dedicated to producing food, he knew that the fungus and what few vegetables he could grow with artificial light were still weeks from being ready to harvest.

No matter, he thought. He knew where plentiful food was always available for the taking. *Besides, I always think more clearly with a full stomach.*

He turned again, putting the colossal dome of the Enclave directly in front of him, and made ready to play the mouse again.

SIX
Morningstar Manor, Third City Enclave

The Landgraves and the Morningstars were essentially one family, and had been for fifteen years. Alouine considered Thaira to be as a sister and the aging Valdemar was akin to a favorite uncle. The wizened man, her cherished tutor, could not replace her dead father, but he came very near to filling the void left in the wake of Gerald's murder.

The three ate lunch together every day in one of the common rooms of Morningstar manor, and that day was no different, save only the topic of conversation.

Valdemar cleared his throat to gain the attention of his daughter and his student prodigy. "I'm retiring for good," he announced.

"What does that mean?" Thaira asked with anxiety laced through her words. She obviously did not want to leave the Third City. Alouine perked up as well.

"The two of you are grown women now, and you'll need to begin finding your own places in this world," the old man mumbled. "With my liege gone, I am free from all obligations at long last."

He sounded tired, which was not unusual. While his health maintained a stable level, the man was losing what vitality remained to him in his last years. "It is time to withdraw, and live the rest of my days in peace and quiet. This city is getting to me. There is nothing to look at, and the weather is foul."

"I like it here," Thaira said weakly. She left the importance of her relationship with Alouine implied but unsaid.

"Yes, my dear, I'm aware of that. Stay, if it pleases you. The day is coming soon when I'll want to join my friend Gerald. Besides, a man should die with pride when he is no longer able to live with dignity. Until then, I want to feel the sun on my face and sand between my toes."

"Father," Thaira addressed him sternly, "there's been too much loss around here already. Surely, you can stay another year."

Alouine focused on her plate and said nothing. She hated being spoken around, and the euphemisms of 'loss' and 'gone' her friends used to lessen the bitterness of her father's death annoyed her. She would miss Valdemar terribly if he left, but, she felt she had no hold over him. She respected him too much to command him to stay.

The old man sighed. "The wheel of time keeps on turning for gods and mortals alike. The decision has been made, Thaira. I will go, right after the Cremation. You'll have all the revelry and debauch to take your mind off of a feeble old man. We'll spend the next few days together and wrap up our loose ends. Then I'll be off."

Alouine chose to speak. "We're going to miss you." The slightly younger woman sighed heavily with resignation, blowing air through her auburn bangs and dropping her gaze.

"Yes," Valdemar said. "Well, I imagine you'll soon move on to bigger and better and younger things. Now I have a favor to ask of you, Thaira."

The Lady Landgrave nodded distractedly.

"This afternoon I'm going to spend a bit of time with Alouine here. I have one more thing to teach her. Will you join me for dinner tonight? And I thought we might spend the day together tomorrow."

She smiled. "Of course, Father."

The two women exchanged a meaningful glance. Alouine understood Valdemar's intent completely. The older woman had just lost her father a week previous, and it was as good a time as any for her mentor to retreat somewhat from his own daughter's life. She reached under the table for Thaira's hand and gave it a reassuring squeeze, which was meekly returned. She could see awe in her younger friend's eyes, awe of her strength and how she managed to stay so composed despite the raging sorrow which roiled like a swirling undertow below the calm surface.

Valdemar finished eating, stood and gestured to Alouine to follow him. "I'll see you this evening, dear," he said to Thaira, gripping her shoulder softly and stooping to plant a kiss on her cheek.

"Okay," she replied, putting on a brave front. "Have fun, you two."

Master and apprentice went to the gardens, their traditional training grounds. Valdemar leaned heavily on his cane. "My daughter looks up to you," he said with no preamble.

"She has been a great and loyal friend to me," Alouine replied. "I only want to return her kindness."

He stopped and faced her. The man had always managed to see through her masks, to strip her down to bare bones and see the real Alouine Morningstar. "Stop it."

She nearly missed a step, taken aback. "Excuse me?"

"Thaira relies on you too much. It is truly a wonderful friendship that the two of you share, but she must learn to stand on her own two feet if she is to survive in our Order. You have learned this lesson well. I know how much your dear father meant to you, sweetheart. But you have not needed my help to get through this, or Thaira's. You have no need to borrow the strength of others. This is what I desire for my own daughter. I am nowhere near cruel enough to ask you to end your friendship with her, but surely you must see that she needs to step out from your shadow and find her own ways to thrive."

Alouine nodded, but was not ready to concede. "Thaira is popular and well-liked by everyone she meets. She's adaptable and strong and has her own interests."

"Yes, this is true. But she lacks independence—the one thing a person cannot have the liberty to follow her fate without."

"Are you asking me to distance myself from my best friend? A mere week since I lost my father?"

Valdemar sighed. "I am not asking you for anything. I am simply sharing a concern of mine. Besides, you can never tell where destiny is taking you. I never suspected that I would spend so much of my rapidly shrinking time in this stinking backwater of an Enclave."

Alouine cracked a smirk.

"The two of you have shared much," he continued. "Nothing lasts forever."

The high-born woman pursed her lips. "Do you know something you're not telling me?"

"It is just a feeling. When you get to be my age, you become somewhat practiced at reading between the lines."

"And?"

"You should be prepared to let Thaira go." The old man stepped into the training circle. Alouine lingered outside of the boundary, absorbing his words.

Valdemar allowed himself to look at her as she ruminated. His features softened from pride.

She grew up in that circle. Alouine had become awe-inspiring in presence and stunningly beautiful in face and body, as numerous Last Men attested. Her tall, natural grace and fluid dexterity were marvels of the human form. Her dark hair and brilliant eyes, thin, straight nose, high cheekbones and full lips were those of a goddess manifest, but they could not belie her complete competence and utter deadliness. She was a warrior, proud of her achievements—as was her teacher.

She was his favorite student of all time, barring no one. Still, she was not his daughter. She felt this keenly. The old man felt many things for her as she neared her thirtieth year, but a father's love was not one of them.

"Come into the circle," he said. "You can kill messily and brutally, but you have one more lesson to learn. I will teach you the Death Touch Enlightenment. Hone this technique, for I may call upon you to use it on me, in time.

"Without a weapon, the act of physically destroying a human body with another human body is difficult and often a painful exercise. As you know, where life and death are at stake, your opponents will hit back, and though you may outmatch them, nothing is as dangerous as a human being desperate to survive.

"The Death Touch focuses our inner energy, changing it from Subtle to Manifest. We breathe in the intention of Kali'prana," he intoned, demonstrating the exact technique. "And draw up the Shakti of Durga from the earth."

He placed his feet so, and coiled his ancient body specifically in sequence to draw both physical and spiritual power from the ground.

"This power twists through us, and we expel it through our blow into the body of the enemy. It may be the harshest blow which skewers a man like a lance, or a slight tap of the fingers. So long as the energy is formed properly and released fully, and the blow thrown at a crucial node, the enemy will die."

Alouine took her stance and followed her master's instruction. She could feel the deadly power of the technique, which filled her with a chilling, life-blighting hatred as she moved slowly through the steps. Absorbing the subtle energy of the universe and twisting it to the purpose of causing destruction of human life gave her a shiver of awesome, godly power, but also a frigid, nauseous feeling. She blanched.

"Be sure to release all that you gather," Valdemar admonished. "It is not wise to keep any of this energy trapped in your body for long. Thrust it out, into the air. Just be mindful of where you throw it."

Alouine did so, and the cold, sickly feeling left with the energy. She breathed a sigh of relief.

"With your great power, you may find that you may use it from a distance when you perfect the technique," the old teacher explained. "You may be able to stop a heart with a glance. The greatest masters of long past ages used it to kill from even beyond the horizon. With your abilities, you might find it easy to use from a world away. Project it through space or matter, it makes no difference; nor will it lose any potency."

Locking the technique into her muscle memory, Alouine bowed her respect. "Thank you," she murmured.

Valdemar shook his head. "Don't thank me for this. I am casting my burden on you. That is all. When I finally give up the ghost, you will be the only living master of the Kali'prana."

Alouine said nothing, glancing at the ground.

"It is a great power. Perhaps it is better off lost. I hope you forgive me for pushing that choice off on you."

"What choice?"

"Whether or not you will take this technique to the grave with you," the aged man mumbled softly. "Consider this your fair warning: using the Kali'prana is not without its costs." He looked the woman in the eyes. "I am not nearly as old as I appear. Your father and I are the same age, give or take a few years."

Alouine blinked.

"What did you expect? One does not channel the very essence

of entropy and become a conduit for killing intent without paying a steep price. The use of the technique will age you, break down your body and mind. Heavy, repeated use leaves you with a bitter chill which never goes away, no matter how many blankets you cover yourself with. It can lead to loss of all twelve of the senses. The first to go are the senses of smell and taste. I lost these many years ago.

"At the end of his life, my father, Thaira's grandfather, slipped into a coma. I remember it well. He had used the technique so many times that there was nothing left but an empty shell. He had no sense of balance or movement in his last years, was utterly numb from head to toe with no tactility anywhere on his body. He could not sense warmth, had no powers of speech." Valdemar took a shaky breath. "In the end, he could not even think. He had lost his sense of self."

His student swallowed hard, her lips tightened to a line.

"You are mature enough for this," Valdemar said. "Do not doubt yourself. I am not warning you to never use it, only to use it sparingly. It is a double-edged sword, my young lady. Unsheathe it only when absolutely necessary, but do not hesitate if it comes to that."

The pair fell into silence as they polished Alouine's technique to brilliance, Valdemar demonstrating until he was exhausted and Alouine copying the movements until they became natural and part of her body's arsenal.

Quickly, the time came that Valdemar could not go on, his scant vitality used up. Bowing again to each other, he excused himself, leaving his student prodigy to practice on her own. She was not allowed much time before her data link chimed.

Biting down on her disdain, Alouine answered the invitation she was sent, and agreed to respond in person.

— — —

Making a fist of her small, diamond-hard hand, she knocked lightly on the door. The empty sound bounced back at her. Clinging to the internal hope and prayer that the man was not inside, the woman fidgeted from one foot to the other, counting out seconds until she could make her escape and skip that horrid meeting altogether. She took a breath, found her center, and steadied herself. He was her number one suspect in her father's murder, she reminded herself, and she still needed proof that he had done the deed before she could exact her revenge.

"Come in," came that rich, imperious purr she dreaded. Two simple words could dash all her hopes of the moment. She dreaded what even just a few more could do.

The door handle gleaming, she reached and nearly cursed when it had the gall to open easily, like warm clay under her clenched fingers. With no other option, the woman entered into the man's furnished and warm office.

He stood near the dumbwaiter on the far side of the room, retrieving what appeared to be a bottle of rare whiskey. He looked at her, and her gut tightened of its own accord.

"My Alouine," he said in greeting, a pleasant smile dressing his lips.

"Allow me to be clear, Carver. I am not yours, nor have I ever been." Alouine was again forced to mentally castigate herself as the words flew from her mouth. Despite the disgust she felt toward the man, it was imperative she remain courteous in his presence.

Damn him all the same, she thought. He had no accomplishments of his own but had merely ridden her father's coattails into his current power. He had also benefitted greatly from Gerald's demise; this new office was proof enough of that.

However, Carver seemed utterly nonplussed by her cavalier attitude. "I think you're wrong, my dear. Your great father promised you to me, before he met his unfortunate end." The man possessed a reptilian cruelty hidden under his amiable veneer. It sickened Alouine.

"How many times have we gone over this? My father was not the type of man to make verbal agreements with no witnesses or documentation. But that is far from the real issue," she replied evenly.

"Which is?"

She wanted to punch him in the face, to ruin his flesh and bones, but that was the usual effect of Carver's audacity on her. If she was anything, Alouine Morningstar was a woman who hated to be condescended to, and Carver's constant playing at stupid did nothing but infuriate her.

She held a firm stance in the doorway with the door still wide open. "My father was not the arbiter of my future, even if he did make some kind of agreement with you. Which we both know he did not," she added pointedly. "It is and always will be mine to do with as I wish. I belong to no one but myself."

"Very well." Carver poured bourbon into two glasses, which came as no surprise. Alouine did not drink, but she knew he entertained himself with his belligerence. She felt keenly aware that her genetic line was the strongest among every single female of the Enclave. Her father had been Chairman of the Highest Circle. She understood Delano's compulsion to have her. If he were to satisfy his ambitions, he would need to make her power his. Attempting to ply her with alcohol was no surprise. "I will refrain from saying that, if you close the door."

She did so, clicking the door gently closed, sure that Carver believed it to be a sign of submission. To Alouine, it was a sign that she was completely unafraid of him.

He strode across the room and proffered the drink. She stared at it, and then at him, until he set it down on a nearby table.

"Will you remove your coat?"

"I am not planning to stay long."

His eyes bored holes through the coat, into her flesh, making her skin crawl. The man's proclivities were well known to her. Aristocrat or filthy slave, it made no difference to him. Female was female to Carver Delano. She suppressed a shudder.

He is only trying to frighten you, she reminded herself. *As if I would be scared of the likes of him*. "This visit is merely a courtesy, in respect to my father. He once told me that he found you a very useful vassal."

"Pity about your plans. I doubt you'll be leaving anytime soon. We have so much catching up to do." He sipped from his glass as he moved away from her, around his desk, beckoning her to come forward and registering no surprise when she silently declined to do so.

"No such business exists between us."

Carver's pretense dropped heavily to the floor. "On the contrary," he snarled, taking several long strides to again close the distance between them. Alouine was prepared from prior experience for his wildly shifting demeanors. She was certain she could kill him easily. It was a credit to his instinct for self-preservation that he stopped short of touching her, but he did press his face very close to hers.

Carver's voice lowered to a hissing whisper. "I think you have failed to grasp the subtleties of the situation. Your thrice-damned father is rotting in a hole, and you have absolutely no protection. Were it not for me, you would be awash with suitors—men of far, far lower Circles than mine.

"I am the best option you have. Like it or not, your gene sequence is the purest in the Order," he growled, putting his mouth an inch from her ear, breathing hot alcohol breath into her face. "But that is all you are. You had better learn to play ball, girl."

He straightened but remained very close. "Surely being with me and bearing my heirs, the future rulers of earth, would be preferable to being made into spare parts for the preservation of the Order."

Alouine very slowly turned to look Carver in the eye. "You would not dare."

"Oh, I am very daring, and capable, as you well know. My word, like the word of the Creator, is all that is required. Your ova will be harvested and your sequence added to the catalogue. I will get what I want, one way or another. The only choice is whether you are living or dead when you supply me with what I need."

Her bravado slipping, Alouine knew she had to leave quickly, before she did something rash, something to endanger her standing in the Order. "Do you think I'd cave in to threats from the likes of you? Just how foolish do you think I am?"

A reptilian smile drifted over Carver's lips. "Well, you are here, are you not?"

She felt that his threat was sincere. He would do anything for power, anything to make his descendants the masters of the Order. Securing her genes for his offspring was the crucial first step.

Even under the weight of his ambitions, she knew the prospect of exploring her hale, hardened body tempted him, and Carver was always willing to explore an opportunity that tempted him. He relented, but only just. "Perhaps you require some time to weigh your options," he remarked, veneer of amicability in place once more as he slid past her, to the door. "All I ask is that you remember that choosing me is choosing life. Anything else would be . . ."—his eyes narrowed—"foolish, indeed."

He opened the door, gesturing to the hall. "Please return at this time tomorrow with your answer."

Alouine found that she was unable to speak. Her wits failed her. Fortunately, her instincts spun her, and she found her feet taking her away from the vile creature, the bane of her existence, Carver Delano.

"Thank you for your visit," he added pleasantly, before she could retreat from audible range.

SHADOW OF THE LAST MEN

— — —

As she angrily marched away from Carver's office on her way home, Alouine remembered why she had never lost her nervousness about visiting the Temple of Understanding, the pyramid on the 'Hill', as it was called. She and Thaira had gotten into a long-standing habit of going there once a month, just to revel in the feeling of standing beside and inside a building so incredibly massive.

Alouine understood that this powerfully evoked feeling was intentional. The Last Men who had built the structure intended it to literally last forever, to be a constant reminder of their power and prowess, and their Order's control over the earth.

The pair had, from their teenage years on, toured every centimeter of the structure that they were permitted to enter. They traced over every ancient rune, each mirror-smooth, marble panel, and soaking in every laser-carved statue or relief. Alouine particularly enjoyed the giant, chromed statues of crouching men, some of them fifteen meters tall and each one an Atlas who served as a pillar to hold up ceilings and arches.

The two girls became women as the years slipped by. Both continued sharpening their skills, though Thaira had begun to focus on more immediate pursuits. In private, the younger girl was affable, friendly and open as ever, but publicly she began to develop a commanding persona for dealing with the Order's security forces.

When she focused on her studies, Thaira, like her father, had an incredible talent for analysis and problem-solving. Heredity was a thing no Last Man or Woman could easily overcome, and the girl was already being groomed to succeed her father as a Master of Enclave Security thanks to Gerald's influence. Indeed, it was repayment for Valdemar's service to advance Thaira's career.

Meanwhile, Alouine prepared for life within the upper limits of the Order's leadership structure. The Order needed a bolt of lightning to shake it up, and Alouine would soon provide it.

Unlike her more imminent friend, Thaira had developed an early interest in the opposite sex that was often returned by Last men of similar age. Those same young men tended to find Alouine cold and closed off from their attentions.

She recalled Carver's Establishment celebration, fourteen years past. It took place only a short time after Thaira and she had made their social debuts.

"Relax, Ally. This is going to be fine. We'll just sit in for a while and see what happens."

Alouine only gave her friend a fraction of her attention. She tugged at her pewter-grey dress to smooth out the wrinkles.

"Stop fussing. You look great. That dress really suits you."

With a huff, she followed along as Thaira led them to one of the parlor rooms. "You know I never enjoy these things."

Thaira stopped outside the door, checking her hair, cosmetics, and bust, in a convenient, gold framed mirror mounted on the corridor wall. "That's because you won't relax and let yourself enjoy anything."

Alouine's mouth formed a tight line and the younger woman relented. "You're beautiful," she murmured. "Eventually, we're bound to find a man with enough courage to bask in all this." She gestured up and down Alouine's lithe and fit form. "Besides, maybe if you dressed in friendlier colors people wouldn't be so arm's-length with you."

"That's actually a good argument for discarding fashion and cosmetics altogether."

"Oh, hush. There's no harm in looking good."

The pair entered and Alouine could not help but feel self-conscious. Her attire truly was fashionable enough, she supposed, but it was specifically chosen to help her blend in. She selected it as much for its properties of camouflage as its aesthetics. Thaira's bright-red dress, with its revealing cut, could do nothing other than stand out.

The massive hall was packed with partygoers, servants, slaves and food. Here, the younger men and women of the Last could mingle, gamble, connive, and conspire. No younger member of the Order needed a particular excuse to enjoy the debauch and extravagance the Enclave offered, but tonight was a special occasion.

The Establishment was an important social event coinciding with the thirty-third birthday, a time for a young member to be considered established and to begin to contribute in meaningful ways to the rule of the Last Men. It was also a time for the unveiling of the man's Lictor, his warrior-slave. Every Circle within the Enclave sent their offspring to an Establishment party. Alouine took a deep breath, as if a diver preparing to submerge.

Thaira immediately began to whirl through the crowd. Alouine watched her out of the corner of her eye, laughing politely or smiling demurely as appropriate, teasing her suitors and touching everyone. She knew from experience how tactile Thaira was. With only a hint of pressure from her fingertips, the younger woman could move others to her will.

Alouine, on the other hand, was acknowledged as the single-most, physically deadly member of the entire worldwide Order. She was sure that the same men whom Thaira entertained were the ones who, in private, likened Alouine to those cold-blooded insects of legend, which felt nothing and devoured their mates once their utility had run its course. They were afraid of her, Alouine reminded herself. Others leaned into Thaira's touch, but shied away from hers.

All around the hall, Last Men and Women dined and drank, engaged in gossip, and observed as entire teams of slaves in various states of bondage performed crude sex acts for an audience. The

Order members crowded around with commands and suggestions, prodding the slaves into position with painful slaps or cruel twists, and heckling when their demands were not met.

Uninterested, Alouine played roulette at one of the beautiful, gold-plated wheels for a lark. Gambling held little attraction, but it was a convenient way to pass the time while keeping an eye on her friend. Thaira had learned her lesson concerning intoxicants the last time they had gone to one of these parties together. Remembering the scene made Alouine blanch, and she had not let Thaira off the hook for forcing her to rescue her friend from certain predation at the hands of greedy and self-serving suitors. The incident had solidified both of their reputations: Thaira as a freewheeler and Alouine as an ice queen.

"You favor black, it seems," a purring male voice from beside her spoke. Alouine resisted the urge to snap an annoyed retort and merely glanced to the side. The host of the evening's gathering and object of the celebration, Carver Delano, offered her a glass of champagne.

Alouine took it, but did not drink. "I know the game," she said softly, "and I don't require instruction."

"I would not presume otherwise, Lady Morningstar. It was merely an observation." The man, her elder by some seventeen years, placed a bet of his own. "Might I inquire as to how you are enjoying yourself?"

"Time passes."

Carver nodded. Not physically in the best of shape, Carver had an already receding hairline that he apparently did not care to treat. Nevertheless, he managed to look somewhat dapper in his richly tailored suit. He was not an imposing man by any means, but there was something in his eyes.

Thaira had often complimented Alouine on her eyes. She compared them to gems, or dark diamonds. Carver's eyes were more like beads of amber color. While not unattractive, they did give him an almost reptilian countenance and betrayed a predatory intelligence. She felt the blood empty from her gut and flow into her arms and legs. Something about him set her on edge.

He was so artificial and synthetic. She was glad that she originated within a living woman's womb; tube-grown Last Men, like Carver, were too plastic for her taste. That she was in a small minority of the Order in that regard only heightened her disdain for the social milieu.

"I assured your illustrious father that you would be safely entertained for the evening. As in all things, I do not plan to disappoint him."

Alouine set her teeth. That was the crux of her anxiety: that others would look at her and see only her father's power and influence.

"If I might make a humble suggestion," the man said, though Alouine barely heard him, "we might retire from the table for a time, to return later, perhaps. I could make some introductions. With your unique skill-set, perhaps you could assist me in a small matter."

Arching a brow, she again glanced from the table to the face of the imperious man. "What matter?"

"Well, tonight is the debut of my Lictor," Carver replied. "I must admit that I am quite proud of him and the work it took to mold him. Perhaps you could offer critique. Your personal prowess approaches legendary status, and I am sure it has gifted you with a trained eye for these matters."

She nodded, feeling hollow, but eager to get the entire farce over with. "Very well."

"This way."

As Alouine turned to follow him, she left her full chalice behind on the edge of the table, forgotten. He led her to a large, adjoining room, where several more young, Last gentlemen were already deep into a discussion and well-fueled by alcohol. Conveniently located around the richly dressed males were their barely clothed, pleasure slaves. Each one wore a mockery of an outfit, to accentuate their bodies in the most pleasing manner.

Alouine struggled to hide her disdain. Even so, despite their intoxication, the men deferred to her, inclining their heads in greeting with a passable semblance of civility.

Carver signaled to one of his servants that he was ready to begin, and the remainder of the party's guests slowly shuffled into the grand chamber.

"Gentlemen, ladies, Last Men and Women, you have my thanks," Carver began. "As you well know, today is my thirty-third birthday. Therefore, it is my pleasure to present my Lictor to you." He gestured to the back corner of the room. "Armiluss, won't you join us?"

From a small service door used by staff, the hulking Lictor appeared. He stood well over two meters tall. The audience broke into polite applause.

Alouine found the practice of creating Lictors to be rather barbaric, but she understood why the Last Men did so. The elite men of the Earth were fearful beings, forced to compensate for the toll which their pleasure-seeking took on their bodies. Unable to safeguard their own well-being, they created the grotesque creatures as bodyguards. In truth, they were murder machines, ready to kill at their masters' whims and used as proxies to settle irreconcilable conflicts in brutal, single combat. She was not impressed.

Armiluss did not say anything. He simply walked out before the crowd and let them look at him, as instructed. The party guests circled around him. His master reached up and placed a hand on his massive shoulder, and they posed for digital remembrance icons together.

One of Carver's retinue, a Circle member named Heid Acheson, made his way close to offer his congratulations. "A fine specimen, my lord. Truly, you must have gotten ahold of a good batch."

Carver shook his head. That cruel grin pasted itself on his features. "On the contrary, this one was the runt of the litter. I must say, it took quite an effort to build him up."

"Oh, I see! He must be possessed of incredible toughness," the man prattled on, inspecting Armiluss as though he was window dressing. Carver nodded slightly, and turned, spreading his arms wide so that he could keep his hand firmly gripping his Lictor while encompassing Alouine with his other arm. He did not touch her but succeeding in corralling her closer. She inwardly winced; he reeked of cigars and too much aftershave.

"Heid, I believe you know the Lady Alouine Morningstar," the Order Lord said. "She is my special guest for the evening."

Heid bowed, lower than was necessary. "Indeed I have heard of the lady. The rumors fail to do your beauty justice."

Straight-faced despite the flattery, Alouine simply inclined her head. "The pleasure is mine," she lied. The idea of being Carver's special guest was unpleasant, but it was too late to gainsay him.

The man seemed pleased, though, whether it was an act, Alouine could not tell. She only wanted to leave. Carver kept his hand hovering mere centimeters from her bare back, which suddenly felt pitifully cold and exposed in her gown.

"It's said that even trained marksmen with firearms stand little chance against your prowess, Lady Morningstar," Heid was saying. "All the Circles I belong to agree that nothing short of an airstrike or well-aimed artillery barrage are sufficient to stop you." He smiled without kindness. "Here is a lady who will never have need of a Lictor."

Alouine's lips formed a tighter line as the man confirmed that he considered her no differently than anyone else did.

Heid and Carver prattled on about the Lictor for several more minutes as Alouine half-listened. He had selected Armiluss fifteen years ago from the brood pits. Alouine noted that she and the twisted behemoth were close in age; Thaira had only recently turned fifteen.

She listened more intently as Carver related the story of how the now-overgrown Armiluss was then the runt of his litter, which had included nine or so brothers and sisters; Carver could not recall the exact number. The fertility drugs and growth hormones applied to the Lictor's mother had disfigured her beyond belief. The Order's Eugenic Development Wing had impregnated her with ten embryos that were genetically programmed to grow as quickly as possible. The woman had become a monster, little more than an oversized womb. The men had a laugh over this.

Carver had selected the runt, he said, partially because if they survived, they were often the toughest and most cunning of the litter. Size and strength could always be added later, as Armiluss was walking proof. He wanted his servant to have a ruthless initiative and resourcefulness that could only be developed through an early struggle to survive. By the age of four, Armiluss had killed two of his brothers and one sister as he fought with them for food. It was a good start in what would become a life devoted to violence.

As the man grew, Carver had introduced himself. He would show up to the Rearing Center to shower the young Armiluss in gifts of food and sexual partners, then take him to specialized areas in order to subject him to growth hormone and genetic cleansing treatments, cybernetic implants, and a full course on how to be the most useful human tool to achieving Carver's ends.

"So, Alouine, what do you think of Armiluss? Please, be honest," Carver admonished.

"He could be considered frightening," she hedged.

"But not to you. You could destroy him easily."

"Perhaps. I do not plan to find out."

"No, of course not. The idea is reprehensible. However, you must know that a Lictor is an ongoing project. Armiluss here is . . . a work in progress. There are many more improvements to be made. I had rather hoped you would assist me—as a consultant, of course."

"He looks cumbersome. Ensure that he is not slow." She passed along one of the gems that Valdemar had given her: "Slow is dead." Taking a half step to her left, she removed herself from Carver's encircling arm. "If you'll excuse me, the hour grows late, and I must find my friend."

Carver nodded and bowed slightly. "Thank you for the advice, my lady. I will endeavor to follow it. Do you require an escort?"

She decided to be cheeky and gave the man a smirking smile to shine him on. "I never will," she practically purred. With a polite, recognizing nod to Heid, she made her escape. The charade had gone on long enough, and the evening was over regardless of Thaira's thoughts on the matter.

Alouine always remembered that incident. She had hated Carver Delano even then. Now, he was her father's murderer, and she intended to have sweet, longed-for justice the moment she could prove his guilt. The desire for a pummeling vengeance swirled in her mind.

— — —

Alouine took a deep breath through her lips and exhaled through her nose to push out her anxiety. Lost in her reverie, the walk and the sky-tram ride from the Temple had passed by unnoticed.

She retreated into her private quarters. After closing the door, she stood with her eyes softly closed, focused on every part of her body, relaxing the tension in each until she felt complete ease and total openness.

Drifting on a sea of bliss, she visualized the choppy waters of her own mindscape becoming as tranquil and still as a mirror at her gentle insistence. Heading to her meditation mat, she carefully folded her body into the lotus position until her sense of it fell away.

She lit her chakras in turn, using the ancient gnosis of her people, her divine birthright. One by one, she released any blockage in each vortex, from the base of her spine to the crown of her head, feeling the power entwine its way, like a serpent, up the central column of her body temple. Patient and careful, she lit her inner eye and allowed her body to become living light, tuning into the underlying, undulating vibration of the cosmos.

The light of the Arcanum Magnus entered her. It showed her all of creation and her part in it. She saw the perspective of the Ultimate Observer through her All-Seeing eye.

There is a schism in humankind, she felt. A voiceless emotion conveyed this fact to her from the Observer.

"That's obvious," she thought. No person with penetrating knowledge of herself and the world was unaware of this fact. *I wish to be enlightened as to the true nature of myself, my people, and the earth*, she projected.

For the first time in her life, the Order to which she belonged appeared to her not as an organization of warmth, inclusiveness, support, and pleasure. The loss of her father and her experience with Carver Delano had already begun to crumble that façade. *The Last Man is untrue*, she felt the Observer state. Waves of fear washed over her, but still she pressed on.

"Untrue? How?"

This Man must become the Next Man. He is misnamed.

She saw the Three World Enclaves of wealth and luxury. She saw the Third of these great cities, in which the woman had spent her entire life. It dominated the landscape, walled away from the gray earth and the anarchic turmoil outside. Those inside were the rulers of mankind, the Last Men, the keepers of 'civilization', using gene therapy and cybernetics as weapons in their constant struggle with inbreeding and corruption.

"What?" Alouine asked. "What Man comes next?"

He will be born. From this perspective, Alouine was confronted with the knowledge that the Last Men were failing. Each year, a higher percentage of their few spawn were born flawed and defected, to be cast aside as useless flesh. New children of the Last were scarce. Already prepared to go to the most extreme depths of depravity to hold their power, the Order had grown desperate.

Alouine's situation was at the apex. Shorn of her political power by the death of her father, she went from being a princess to having only her own blood—her genetic code—left to her.

The several hundred-billion credits she owned amounted to very little. She had no influence, no Circle of peers, and few allies. To make matters worse, she found herself in the crosshairs of Carver Delano, her father's most brutal vassal and likely his killer.

There are the Outlands.

If they could be called anything, those inhabiting the bruised and broken spaces outside those palatial enclaves were called Outlanders. The rotting entrails of humankind, left to scratch a squalid existence from the abused soil and to squabble endlessly amongst themselves. Subject to the abuses of violence, rape, and starvation outside the Order's walls, there was also no salvation for them within the Order's Promised Lands.

The Order needed its slaves, and for an Outlander to be captured in a raid was among the worst of all nightmares. A chemical or nano-machine lobotomy followed, then a brutal life as a manufacturing slave, tending herds or hydroponically grown crops.

Or, if found physically attractive enough, a body slave. Females were transformed into brood mares for the pleasure and perpetuation of the state, their children genetically purified while still in the womb. Males became eunuchs under the pitiless knife of their new masters, their reproductive ability harvested for the Order's use in genetic catalogs.

All human flesh on earth reduced to nothing but commercial product for the service and pleasure of the Last men and women of the Order.

The woman felt an unfamiliar sensation in her consciousness, but could not place it. *A schism*, the Observer reminded her. *Man was once whole.*

The current state of affairs did not happen instantly, in some horrific cataclysm. It had been planned that way from the beginning, an agenda that had been implemented incrementally over centuries.

The Earth is abundant, but finite, the Eye observed. *More for some is less for all others. All for some is none for all others.*

She knew that the Last Men were power-mongering sorcerers, working together and bound by pact, oath, and family. They had manipulated the world into handing over everything to them, using whatever means available: at first, the most ingenious schemes of lies and fraud; then, by exerting their powers over invisible, insidious, inhuman forces; and later, the threat of open mega-death, starvation, disease, and murder.

That threat eventually became the culmination of centuries of military development, and the earth could not bear the devastation the Order unleashed.

"If the useless eaters and breeders had contributed, we would not have to starve them out of existence," Alouine thought. "We are in control of human destiny, not them. They have nothing to offer aside from their bodies, and even those are disgusting and weak. An Outlander cannot have a will of its own. Otherwise, it would be one of us."

This Order is not new. It is a the ultimate evolution of the old

Order, the aristocratic, feudal oligarchy of privileged elite gazing down from their ivory towers at the huddled, sickening masses— their slaves. Their victory was complete. As long as there were humans, there was the Order, always striving to be the Last Men and Women on earth.

The strange sensation intensified for the woman. It was a pressure, pushing down on her, forcing her away from the Observer and the Eye. She struggled to maintain her focus.

You cannot stay.

The revelation came, vivid and brutal. There was no method of averting her impending disaster from within the Order. She had to leave the Order of the Last. She had to get away from Carver Delano; he was admittedly too much for her. She needed time to plan. She could not simply run off to another Enclave. He would find her there, and she would never be able to stand the indignity of cowardice.

She needed to enter the Outlands.

Alouine's eyes shot open, her meditation abruptly ended. She understood with frightening clarity the sensation she was feeling. It was shame. Cold sweat fell into her eyes and she blinked it away. She was a divine being. For what reason could she possibly feel this wracking guilt? How would she avoid this horrid sensation in the future?

There were too many things to do at once. She needed to prepare for her journey into a place she had never been before. Alouine knew it would be cold, and that warm clothing was a must, but she was otherwise at a loss.

What kind of supplies and equipment would she need? And when would she leave? She did not want to give away her intentions to anyone, and if she was caught leaving the Enclave, someone would certainly alert Carver.

Rising quickly from her meditation mat, she headed to the door. Only Thaira could help her figure everything out, and only her friend would keep her secret.

SEVEN

The assassins never stopped coming, and never would. Harrow would never stop killing them, either. The lack of proficiency in their approach never ceased to amaze him. They were sloppy, poorly trained—if trained at all—lacking in even the most basic discipline or tactics. Some were willful or brave, some even dedicated, but they could not approach him.

At the upper reaches of the performance envelope, there was no room for halfwits or morons. Here, a place where only the peerless could exist in peace, one must be pitiless, a death-dealing machine. The feeling parts of the body completely closed off from the registering parts of the mind. No pain existed within him, no hunger, no thirst. There was nothing but empty-minded, numb coolness.

How these fools continued to track him down was a mystery, and one that Harrow did not usually bother to try to solve. The bounty could not have been much. It was probably only just enough to illicit a response from the desperate, the starving, the hopeless. The promise of a few ounces of gold under his picture on a wanted poster, or perhaps entrance to one of the Order's controlled zones was enough to ensnare any outsider with a gun. Most of those people were at the end of their rope anyway. Hooked in by the promise of death, or a new, better life. It was pathetic.

There were eight of them, this time. It was far from enough. Typically, he killed or maimed half of those sent after him, and the others fled. The survivors always chose their lives of self-imposed degradation and horror over the idea of rotting away without a burial.

Harrow activated his Software: Integrated Maneuvering and Orientation Node, or SIMON. Interfaced directly into his brainstem, the program took in all the data from his senses, compiling and categorizing it, coordinating his movements, providing him with accurate spatial relations, computing trajectories and projecting its vital findings directly into his visual field.

SIMON supercharged his fast twitch muscles, turned his nervous system into a quantum data stream of unimaginable speed and power, showed him exactly where to aim, calculating distance, elevation, wind, and countless other ballistic factors.

The processing power it lent his mind quickened his reactions to lightning speed and made him a brutally efficient killer with whatever weapon was available, including his bare hands. He invested years collecting the components and building and installing the SIMON within his own body.

The Artificial Intelligence was entirely of his own design. Even the mind-boggling processing power of the Order's fastest supercomputers paled in comparison to Harrow's great creation, interfaced as it was with the awesome power of the human brain. SIMON was another reason the Order wanted Harrow dead, joining all the other reasons in that long and ever-growing list.

Despite the great agency that SIMON allowed him, it was not Harrow's most supreme creation, nor his most powerful weapon, his trump. That was the soul fire, but these cretins did not rate the use of such a draining exertion. He reserved its use for truly trying circumstances, not a simple battle with fools. He used it only when he was forced to.

The appearance of these assassins came like clockwork. Every time he did not die, it renewed his enemies' determination to kill him. Some force was behind the constant attempts, and Harrow meant to get to the bottom of it. Perhaps, just this once, he would attempt to capture one of his antagonists and ascertain the value of their visit, to satisfy his curiosity of how much his corpse was worth.

It was a low priority, however. Whatever the sad state of the world, Harrow loved his life and did not wish it to end. If he had a golden rule, it was to never underestimate anyone. Merely because he had always tested himself against every foe he could find and found them wanting did not mean it would always be the case.

His name and face and mythos had grown because he approached every encounter as though it were the last, the final culminating battle of his life. It was only fate that none of the battles he had fought thus far were the one to grant him an honorable end.

The eight men shuffled along beneath him, in single file. He observed them from a hidden perch atop what was once a shipping container and had become nothing but a rusty steel box, tracking the movements which led them, warily, to the place where Harrow had spent the previous night.

A bustling, urban port area at some point in the distant past, that place had become a decaying graveyard. The spines of rusted cranes rose high into the air like fossilized bones of some ancient and fantastic creature. His father had taught him the name of this ancient ruin long ago, but now no one could remember why it was so named. Three generations, or possibly four, had passed since anyone knew anything.

Just northeast of the center of the Order's military capital and exclusive zone, the city's rusted corpse of iron and concrete had seemed a good place for Harrow to hide, just under the nose of his enemy. It appeared, however, that there was not a single place where his notoriety did not precede him. No matter. The Order had made it their business to kill him. Harrow was in the business of staying alive, and business was as good as ever.

He would have liked to have a more efficient weapon to deal with the current threat. There was only his father's rifle, a cherished memento. But that did not matter. A true warrior knows to go for the heart, and is measured by his aim, not his arrow.

From his perch, Harrow let out his breath slowly, catching and holding the last third of the air in his lungs—restricting the movement of his body, his pulse rate, everything. He lay on the cold, hard steel surface, his belly coated with rust and grit. Preternaturally still. Eyes gifted with almost freakish 20/10 acuity appeared dull, almost lifeless. His targets were less than one hundred meters distant, moving slowly. SIMON provided an aiming point, accounting for the downward slope, the slight breeze. He settled in. He could slip away at any point. Make his escape. None would be the wiser.

If he started running, he'd never be able to stop. There was no reason to change tack now.

The rifle he held was centuries old, he guessed, but it shot true. A bolt-action Remington from the late twentieth century, it was a solid firearm that had been lovingly cared for. He held on his target, the rearguard man. Filthy, dressed in rags, holding some kind of ancient revolver. The bearded figure leaked sweat despite the cold, and scanned around, his wariness palpable.

Every creature has an instinct for the moment of its death. This one was no different. The would-be assassin knew, deep in his guts, that he was within a killer's crosshairs.

Five rounds of hand-loaded .308 Winchester were all that the antique weapon would hold. Harrow might have to manually reload the old firearm during the battle, from the loose cartridges in the wide pouch on his belt. He doubted it.

Holding target, the SIMON made its final adjustments. The four pound trigger broke like a glass rod and reset with no creep. It was a perfect, practiced shot, one that Harrow could have made in his sleep.

The report from the rifle sent legions of crows into the air and one man to oblivion. The bullet struck him in the cervical spine and spattered the following man with a misty red spray. Harrow saw his victim stiffen, and then buckle.

He drew a new breath and threw the bolt, chambering a new cartridge, then drew a bead on the next target. SIMON was, as always, a microsecond ahead. Matching the scope's crosshair to the tiny red aiming dot in his visual field, Harrow drew a new breath and exhaled, catching and holding it once again on the way out. The rifle cracked again. The bullet tore through the man's left shoulder blade and exited the right side of his chest with a puff of red mist. He pitched forward, dying. The first foe had yet to hit the ground.

The remainder of the bounty hunters threw themselves wildly to whatever cover they could find, but they appeared to have no indication of from where Harrow was shooting. It was not fair, but Harrow never much cared for fairness. Life was not fair.

He walked the crosshairs of the scope from one man to the next. These fools were inept and incompetent. He would likely get nowhere by interrogating any of them.

The third shot he placed precisely into the ear canal of a prone form. Sparing not even a full second to observe the full-body twitch indicating that man's certain demise, Harrow was up and moving, simultaneously working the action of the rifle. Even against an outclassed enemy, he made it a habit to never take more than three shots from the same location.

Leaping silently from one container to the next and pattering eastward, he moved into a position from which he would rain enfilading fire on his adversaries. Of the five remaining, only one managed to reign in his adrenaline-fueled fight-or-flight mechanism. He attempted to communicate with hand signals to his horrified comrades.

This is a man with something to prove, Harrow mused as he maneuvered to a more advantageous position. That hint of conviction only made the signaling man a more conspicuous target. Dropping prone once more and ignoring the protests from his elbows and the tweaks within the muscles of his forearms and calves, he lined up and took the shot.

The copper-jacketed lead missile took the man squarely in the back of the skull. The remaining four men stared, horrified, at their dead leader for a moment, and then took off running as fast as their ill-nourished legs could carry them.

Chambering his last loaded round, Harrow swiveled slightly and shot another man in the right buttocks, destroying the hip and sending the man pitching forward to crash into a heap amongst the maze of oxidized metal.

Taking a few careful moments to reload his rifle, sling it over his shoulder and draw his pistol, Harrow climbed down from his perch to solid ground. The three unwounded men would likely run until they were completely breathless. There was little point in giving chase or trying to shoot them as well. The message Harrow had meant to send seemed clearly received.

Maintaining vigilance and extending his senses, the rifleman made his way to where the final wounded man leaked his fluids onto the surface of his grave. His blood gleamed in the faint light. Satisfied that the threats had abated, Harrow moved in closer. The man was barely breathing. He would be dead very soon.

There was a rusty pump-action shotgun discarded near the fallen man's left arm, so Harrow kicked it out of reach, then patted around the man's clothing for other weapons. Finding none, he stood straight and coolly regarded the growing puddle around the wound.

The dying man let out a shuddering, weak breath. "God . . . damn you," he gasped as he pawed at his ragged wound.

"Let him try," Harrow replied. Stoic faced, he gazed down without malice. "I'll kill him, too."

Silent moments passed. With no hope of answers and content to let the man die alone, Harrow turned and began to walk away.

"Why do they want you dead so much?"

Harrow stopped but did not turn to face the man again. "Because I refuse to live in their shadow. Had you been stronger, you would have refused as well. How much was killing me worth, to you?"

"We weren't paid to kill you," the dying man gasped, "Only to find you."

Brows furrowing, Harrow set his teeth and looked straight upward, to the sky.

A thin, red stream of laser light had been focusing on the top of his head; a targeting laser for a satellite-mounted, directed energy weapon, he instantly realized. The assassins had fought and died for only one purpose: to get Harrow into the open, under nothing but sky—a sky his enemy owned.

He activated his quantum engine and spun the tiny, gyroscopic counter-spinning components to seven hundred thousand RPM, enough to create a nigh-impenetrable electromagnetic field around his body. It was a taxing prospect, as the intense heat generated by the machine required equivalent electromagnetic insulation to keep it from burning his body, which consumed hundreds of calories. He thought of the process as feeding an internal soul fire—like stoking a white hot flame, a crucible—the heart of a star.

The near-microscopic machine spooled up to the necessary speed just as the laser-induced plasma channel formed around him. A mere fraction of a second later, a powerful electric current was sent down this conduit in the form of a lightning bolt of catastrophic power. A billion volts of raw energy poured onto him from the heavens and the crack of the air exploding ripped through him in a shockwave.

Falling into a crouch, the Outlander dialed his device in to exponentially increase the power of his own magnetic field, shaping it into an improvised Faraday cage. He squeezed shut his eyes as the brilliant arc of electrical energy cascaded all around him, directed harmlessly into the ground. Harrow covered his ears with his hands to shield his eardrums from the sonic boom released by the expansion of boiled air which split the night wide open.

Silence reigned again, only challenged by the crackling of tiny fires and the bubbling of boiled asphalt. Rising once more from his crouch, he surveyed the scene around him. The fallen man who Harrow had shot was a cooked and smoking skeleton, and the ground around him was scorched black in a wide radius, with the exception of the un-marred, six foot circle that the warrior stood within. He shivered from the residual electricity still crackling in the atmosphere, and his ears rung despite his precautions. The smell of ozone invaded his nostrils.

Glancing upward once again, Harrow directed a mocking smirk at the eyes watching him from the sky. "Enjoy your delusions of godhood while they last."

— — —

Carver Delano sat in his plush leather chair deep in thought. His screen showed a satellite image from seven hundred kilometers up, magnified and with full spectrum analysis. On it, a man walked away from what should have killed him.

The polished oak desk, the fine porcelain plate holding his filet, and the antique bourbon swilling in his glass did nothing to distract him from his most recent failure. Only the memories of the flesh, concealed deep within his weary muscles could waylay him from his duties.

Though nearly fifty, not nearly as spry as he once was and possessed of several genetic diseases, he rarely abstained from red meat or alcohol. His health was as under his control as the climate or lighting of the room. A constant infusion of medicinal nano-machines into Carver's bloodstream ensured his continuing health. The Order's mastery of technology would give him at least fifty more years of active life in the flesh.

Soon enough, he would be back in the warm sun, under a blue sky. That stint in the Third City was growing tiresome, despite all of its advantages. Unlike many of his compatriots, he enjoyed the outdoors, albeit only in moderation and only under the correct circumstances. A warm, faraway beach called him home. The pleasures of the flesh tugged at him. Soon, he would smell the sea air and pliant young bodies would writhe under him yet again. First, he had business.

Counting each day of the ten years he served the old vulture, Carver had served the High Circle Chairman (and himself) assiduously. He schemed himself into the ideal position, and Morningstar's daughter hung before Carver like a ripened fruit, easily plucked whenever he wished it.

He knew the woman could kill him with a touch, the technique honed on countless Outlanders. But he coveted those superior genes that made her a deadly weapon for his own children.

Her mental, spiritual and physical power, combined with his own razor-sharp Machiavellianism, made the perfect alchemy to create the next High Circle Chairman. He had already made it widely known that he intended to take Alouine for his own. It was recognized as a potent match in nearly all Circles, and having staked his claim, none would attempt to stand in his way. He terrified the entire Enclave, or at least, the raw savagery of his Lictor did; with only one exception.

His thoughts wandered to the petulant woman. She was acting childish about the whole affair. Even if she despised him, which she clearly did, she could certainly see how pairing with him would benefit the Order, could she not?

But then, the foolish female could do nothing against him, and she knew it. Carver was immune to her weapons. His star was rising. His contributions within the Third City made him practically indispensable.

Carver had one more duty to attend to in the Third City, aside from obtaining the Morningstar woman, before he could again immerse himself in the power mongering, luxury and unending pleasure he was accustomed to. However, this duty was proving a difficult task indeed. The despicable Outlander continued to defy him. It simply refused to do what Carver desperately needed it to do: to keel over and die.

A commandment issued from lord to vassal extended beyond death. Until he completed this duty, he could not move on, and the High Circle would not let him forget it. The ghost of Gerald Morningstar haunted him still, now three weeks removed from the old man's death.

Carver had tried many tactics and strategies. As the chairman of his own Circle, he had set the entire group of members to task at solving this one crucial problem. To fail so many times was unheard of. He bribed the other Outlanders to kill the man with ever-increasing bounties, offering huge supplies of food, liquor and other drugs, and even gold, though he wondered what the filthy savages would do with the precious metal. None had yet even tried to claim the bounties, even deceitfully.

He sent his own trusted lieutenants, hardened cyborgs with military training and weapons, and never heard from them again. He ordered extermination raids and airstrikes on the slightest rumor, and the momentary endorphin rush of victory was always eventually crushed by a new sighting, a new damage report.

Even when the wretched man was found, he shrugged off satellite-based, electro laser-focused lightning as though it were nothing but mere drops of rain.

The Highest Circle would not tolerate these incessant breeches in protocol, not for a mere one man. It was insulting to the intellectual elite to be outmaneuvered by a despicable, singular vermin.

Carver thought that the Outlander's name, 'Harrow', was apt. He had, in the past three months, murdered High Circle members, stolen valuable technologies, crops, and livestock, and evaded every attempt at capture or assassination.

There were whisperings coming down from the highest of the High Circles that the man was powerful and charismatic enough to lead an Outlander uprising. Carver scoffed at these claims. The Outlanders were as likely to revolt against the Order as cloned cattle were to revolt against the practice of eating filet mignon.

More than that, Carver had actually seen Harrow once, in person, nearly a month before. He was in attendance at the second techno-research facility that the Outlander had raided. The man had killed seven lobotomized human guards in that one raid alone, destroyed at least as many robotic sentries, and stolen just enough components to complete the construction of a powerful AI program for himself. Had he faced the marauding terrorist himself, Carver had no doubt that he would have died, and that . . . well, that was completely unacceptable.

The automation of the facility, and indeed, most of the Order's production and industry, was proving to be a vulnerable underbelly, exposed to penetrating attacks by Carver's arrogant and upstart antagonist. There were no clues as to the underlying purpose of the raid or the AI, either, as Harrow had somehow managed to burn out all of the data before he escaped.

This Harrow was wily and cunning and possessed a powerful intellect. Carver had already begun to see that efforts to end the man's life were not only doomed to failure, but misguided in the first place. There was no one on earth that the Order could not turn to their own uses. This Outlander had a price. Everyone always did. Finding that price was the true difficulty. More than that, it was an immense presumption to figure on cornering the man long enough to make him an offer, and would he even listen at all?

Indeed, to kill Harrow would satisfy the duty placed upon Carver by his Circle. But to instead capture him was an extremely intriguing prospect. To enslave the man and force him to become a servant of the Order, Carver's servant, willingly or unwillingly; that would exceed the High Circle's wildest expectations and place Carver ever more firmly in the spotlight.

Carver's thoughts were interrupted by the soft tone of his cranial Comm unit. He mentally activated his data link to connect the call. "Yes?"

"My lord, the men and equipment you requested have arrived," replied the tinny voice of Heid Acheson, Carver's favorite vassal. The sniveling, simpering minion was highly irritating, but he still possessed many uses to Carver; among them, his incredible scientific mind.

He responded with a disinterested snort. "Tell them to stand by." Sending these new men and machines to death and destruction at Harrow's hands would only be a further waste of resources—resources that cost Carver valuable prestige and influence.

No, there had to be a better way. Carver had no doubt he would find it. First, he needed to know more about his erstwhile enemy. Then he would attack everything Harrow valued in life, until the Outlander was forced to submit to Carver's terms.

Draining the bourbon in his glass with a smooth and satisfying gulp, Carver began to formulate his strategy. Chess was the Order's game, and to master it, a member had to exhibit infinite patience, a keen sense of timing, intimate knowledge of his adversary, and the willingness to make any sacrifice for victory. Carver always believed he possessed these traits, but now was the time to put that belief to the test.

He would have to leave the Enclave, personally, and track down this man, Harrow. He would have to uncover his hidden motivations, discover his values and weaknesses, and convert him. People like Harrow and Carver were one in the same. Carver never put much stock in all the eugenic propaganda that the Order presented. The applications of those sciences were useful, but Carver's Circle was mystic and esoteric; more interested in the occult secrets and the mystery religions of the ages than genetics or cybernetics.

It had cost Carver many things, his leaning toward the mystical rather than the technological, including many opportunities to advance to higher Circles. Still, his study of dark knowledge gave him insight into how to defeat problems like Harrow and other obstacles to the Order's complete control. Secrecy and deception were powerful weapons, both against the Order's ancient enemy, the Outlanders, and against Carver's rivals within the Order.

A witness to the power of spiritualism and a committed follower of the Order's mystery religion, Carver calculated the best time to begin his new venture. The ritual of the Cremation was in a few hours, and he had been chosen as the head Acolyte to the High Priest. It was an auspicious time for him already, and he felt that very soon, his plans would come to fruition.

— — —

Her chiming data link rushed Alouine as she wracked her brain, trying to decide what she would need to survive the hostile wastes of the Outlands. The Cremation was going to begin in just under an hour, and she had to hurry. Already, she wore layer upon layer of her warmest clothing, topped by her most practical coat, and she was sweating.

Stuffing personal items for survival and hygiene into her large, rip-stop canvas satchel, she made her way quickly around her personal quarters—plenty of socks, a small healing kit; her toothbrush, hairbrush, a small pouch with items for her menses, a small, self-sharpening knife.

Foil-wrapped nutrition bars and a supply of capsules containing concentrated doses of red, green and brown algae would provide emergency sustenance, though Alouine suspected that taking whatever food could be found from Outlanders would be the primary source of her diet.

She grimaced, disgusted with the idea of eating rubbish like the filthy savages doubtlessly consumed; or worse, having to hunt whatever small animals might be out there for her pot. *You have no choice*, she reminded herself.

Into her belt, she placed her sheathed, steel stiletto spike, an elegant weapon, one with which she was very well-versed. The sheath itself was a tiny factory devoted to the production of a powerful neurotoxin, and its neodymium-ion magnet would provide power for well over fifty years. With it, Alouine felt very well armed and confident. One way or another, the weapon would soon be stained with blood. Eventually, she promised herself, it would find its way to Carver's despicable, tiny heart.

She was thankful for knee-high waterproof boots, a gift from Valdemar; lightweight and supple enough to leave her movement and fighting ability unrestricted, but firm enough to support her ankles and arches. With care, they would last for the entirety of even her extended lifetime.

With a final glance around the room, she prepared to leave, knowing that she would not be able to return for a long time.

Her eyes fell on the portrait of her father and herself, which called to her from the bedside table. They looked happy together. In the picture, an old fashioned photograph that was a testament to her father's love of all things antique, Gerald was seated and Alouine stood at his side. Her favorite picture of them together; she briefly considered taking it with her. No, it would do more good where it was. It would give her the strength to return one day and reclaim it.

The entire population of the Last Men and Women of the Third City were congregating at the great Pyramid-Temple of Understanding, and Alouine would have to move quickly if she were to find and meet with Thaira before she and her father joined the rest. Brushing past her servants and valets, whom she had banished from her rooms while she prepared for her journey, she headed immediately to the East Wing of Morningstar Manor.

Bowing and retreating before her, none of the servants so much as made a peep about her current state of dress or her anxious-looking demeanor. She crossed the atrium in wide strides and found herself in front of the door to Thaira's chamber. With no time to waste, she mentally activated the door chime with her data link.

"Come in," was her friend's reply, echoed through the panel's speaker.

The door slid open vertically in the manner of a portcullis, and only a scant few meters into the room stood Thaira in her red robe, hood drawn up and hands folded at her sleeves. She did not immediately glance to Alouine but was engrossed in her full-length mirror, picking at imaginary lint which threatened to disturb the occasion.

"Thaira, I need to talk to you," Alouine said with what she hoped was enough gravitas to give her wonderful, but occasionally dense friend some pause.

"All right, but let's do so on the way. We can't be late," Thaira admonished, intent on making clear her own desire to be well seen as a valued and contributing member of the Third City. Alouine knew that a sense of belonging was important to Thaira; that the younger woman intended to make the Third City her permanent home so that they would always be close to each other, and the thought that Alouine's impending escape of the Enclave might be seen as a betrayal grasped her heart with icy fingers of fear and squeezed.

Finally, the younger woman turned and blinked. "What are you doing? Where's your robe?"

Alouine took a breath and plunged in. "I'm leaving the Enclave, and I need your help."

"What? What are you thinking? We can't be late for the Cremation. Do you have any idea how bad that would look? They seal the doors in half an hour and we need to claim a good spot!"

"I can't stay. I'm so sorry Thy, but I don't really have time to explain, either. It won't be forever, I promise, but I have to go before the ritual is over."

Thaira's eyes threatened to leak. She finally took in Alouine's garb with her gaze. "This isn't . . . You're not going to one of the other Enclaves, are you?"

"No."

"The Outlands?" she screeched, tears streaming and ruining her cosmetics. "What could possibly possess you to want to go out there?"

"I know," she said, pulling the other woman into an embrace. "I know," she repeated. "I don't want to. Please, Thy, don't make this harder than it already is."

"I won't let you!" Thaira gasped. "We're sisters, aren't we? You're leaving me? Leaving the Order? That's just crazy!" She locked her arms around the older woman as tightly as she could. "Why is everyone leaving me?"

"Thaira, please. Just trust me. I will come back." She grasped Thaira's face in her hands so that she could look straight into the other woman's eyes. "I will come back, I promise. But I have to go, and I know that you were helping your father on the Security Renewal protocol. Please, *please*, I need to know the best way to get out."

"You want me to *help* you?" Anger now filled Thaira's voice.

"I *need* you to help me."

Taking long moments to respond as she sniffled and huffed, Thaira finally spoke. Her voice cracked. "Sub-avenue 8. It's in grid L 12. Father said it's the highest risk area in the city. They used to use it to herd slaves in, but it's never patrolled anymore and there aren't any sensors down there. It leads past the hydroponics areas."

Pulling her tightly in again, Alouine squeezed, putting some of her prestigious strength into the embrace as if to imprint the feeling of her friend's body on her own. "Thank you," she whispered. "We'll see each other again, Thaira. I swear it on my father's grave. Now go to the Cremation."

Thaira looked pitiful, but there was little Alouine could do about it now. When she did return, she would make it up to her, but for now, she needed to show strength and resolve. When Thaira whispered "I love you," however, it all threatened to shatter and slip away.

"I love you, too." Only with extreme force of will was she able to pry her body away from the other woman's grasping, clutching hands, and she propelled herself out of the room before she had the chance to change her mind.

As she ran down the corridor, orienting herself and implementing her escape plan on the fly, Alouine decided that since she could not punish the object of her rage, the first Outlander she encountered would pay dearly with agony, humiliation and death for the heartbreak here inflicted.

Until then, the Order's Death's Head guards would have to suffice, and she would happily exercise her Kali'prana on each one of them who questioned her or sought to block her escape.

EIGHT

Maintaining his veneer of implacability and confidence, Carver recalled the indignity of having to appear before the Lords of the Highest Circle, a meeting which had taken up the majority of his morning. He still carried their rebukes in his mind as he made ready to play the conquering hero. Those barbed insults stuck with him, and there were many.

They summoned him shortly after the Cremation ritual had ended. Everyone else in the Enclave had kicked off the five days of festivities with ritual orgies, human sacrifices to dark entities, and incredible spectacles of bondage and torture—a celebration of the Order's permanent domination over their subhuman slaves.

Each moment of the malefic wonderment robbed of Carver was another needle plunged into his heart. He had looked forward to the magnificent display with relish for the entire year, as did all Last Men. The great feast was his birthright, a grand opportunity to gain the favor of powerful spiritual entities and enslave them to his will as bound familiars.

Instead, he was forced to stand before the black-robed High Circle, while dressed in the fine red robes that signified his place within the cabal. Carver was forced to answer for his repeated failure to kill or capture the Outlander. Being made to bear their torments during the Cremation festival, when all other Last Men were at the height of ecstasy, brought him near his breaking point.

They sat at their circular, marble table, making him stand in the hollow middle as they rained insults and heaped abuse, hooded in their robes, faces concealed by darkness. He stared into the empty seat where Gerald Morningstar once sat.

There were now twelve of the Highest Circle. No one yet had tried to claim the empty Chairman's seat, but Carver was certain that each one of the dozen old crones was eying it jealously. In their view, he was an upstart, a rogue, a vassal, who did not warrant consideration. He would show them. For now, he was still in their thrall.

"You are a fool or a traitor," Lord Stamp droned from under his hood. The vast marble chamber echoed.

"It must be one or the other," Lord Russell put in.

"We grow tired of your incompetence," Lord Hesse remarked.

These insults were all the more stinging by the heights Carver experienced at the ritual. After all, he had been given the title of Amerced of the White Flame, and chosen as the lead acolyte of the High Priest, and charged with lighting the pyre at the grand ceremony itself—a great honor. Carver's entire Circle watched with unmitigated jealousy as he took his place next to the altar.

He had glanced about for Alouine, the brat, to lord his enviable position over her, but he did not see her in the sea of red robes which crowded around to watch a human roasted alive. The pitiful slave, strapped nude to the Altar of Burnt Offerings, begged for release or a quick death, and Carver, with cruel pleasure, had consigned him to be slowly burned to ashes and bones.

For a small, young Outlander, the slave had screamed auspiciously for several long minutes, and Carver reveled in the cries until they died away.

Then, not even an hour later, Carver was bound to a pyre of his own.

"Who are you, son of Delano?" Lord Rhodes taunted. "Are you worthy of calling yourself a Last Man?" Never before had Carver been so shocked and embarrassed. The High Circle threw his failure in his face, rubbed his nose in it as though he were a dog. "We have doubts about your commitment to our Order."

All he could offer them was vague promises. "If I must, I will kill the Outlander with my bare hands, or die trying." He did not expect the High Circle to believe him. He did not even believe himself.

"The fact remains that you cannot fail again without severe repercussions," Lord Wallenberg warned. "Your liege has left you a duty which even death may not annul."

"My task will prove more difficult if I cannot renew my pacts at the festival."

Lord Palmerston cut in with his harsh croaking. "We have decided that your familiars shall be held in trust, to be released to you as necessary to complete your duty. You will submit requests, and their use will be vetted here. When you can prove that the Outlander is dead, they shall be returned to you in full."

Lord Carver Delano swallowed hard, choking down his rising fury. Harrow was the rock he was chained to, and each day he could not escape those binding iron fetters was another day the crows would come to peck out his eyes and liver.

"I bow to your wise judgment," Carver forced himself to say. If they wanted to take his disembodied servitors away, so be it. He would succeed without them. It was simple. Find a man. Kill a man. Simple did not always mean easy, but saying so would not aid him.

"Now, get out," Lord Rhodes threw out as a final snub.

Storming out with teeth and fists clenched, Carver left the High Circle Chamber and was greeted again by his Lictor, Armiluss, whom he had bidden to wait outside. There was no sense in adding another witness to the degrading crucifixion Carver had suffered. The master swept past his man, not even acknowledging as the beastly figure dropped to one knee in servile supplication. Rising quickly, Armiluss hasted to catch up.

Unlike other Lictors, Carver never forced Armiluss to wear an explosive or electrical slave collar to ensure his loyalty. He had manipulated the servant so thoroughly, had shaped his mind with such precision, that the Lictor's motivations mirrored his own. Certainly, the creature was a fearsome combatant. That he was also a thinking being, capable of some initiative, made him more dangerous. It was a risk that Carver was very willing to take; the reward was well worth it.

The hulking beast of a man stood two and a half meters tall and tipped the scales near two hundred kilograms, a product of every cybernetic and genetic enhancement Carver could lay hands on. His long legs required a slow pace to stay alongside and slightly behind his master as they walked away from the meeting, down the long marble corridor which led from the High Circle's grand council chamber, and back to the hive of offices where Carver did most of his work.

Carver fumed, not bothering to hide the waves of hurt and frustration.

"The council does not understand what you've sacrificed," the vassal spoke. The repeated genetic and cybernetic augmentations had the inadvertent effect of disrupting the speech center in Armiluss' brain, and the cybernetic corrections had skewed in his voice. Unable to properly utilize his vocal cords, he spoke through speakers implanted in the sides of his thick neck, causing a booming, yet tinny, robotic sound.

"They don't care, nor should they. Results are everything."

The pair walked on in silence for another thirty meters. "If you would but allow me to leave the enclave, my lord," the Lictor tried, "I could be back with the Outlander's head by week's end. I shall make him suffer, as you have suffered, and—"

Carver snorted, stopped walking and turned to face his vassal, who froze mid-step before retracting his leg, and, showing the deference he had been taught, retreated to his master's shoulder.

"I understand you wish to prove your loyalty and capability, but I have invested too much time, effort and material in you to send you off to die like so many goons before. Your place is here."

"Master, I assure you—"

"I know, but it is not the right time. The council does not trust me, nor should they. But you must, my young friend. To win here, we must maneuver. You are my trump card. One does not deploy a powerful weapon out of desperation. The circumstances are not yet so dire. Don't worry, we will find a way to put your unique talents to work, have no doubt of that. It will be a bold stroke. First, we need information, and I will provide us with that myself."

He activated his data link, summoning his Circle to attend him, who haltingly and reluctantly complied. Carver shut off the data link and cursed them out loud as whining sons of bitches, but sharing the agony of losing out on the party was actually making him feel better already. Shit flows downhill, and the old saying was true: misery did love company.

They wore their displeasure openly on their faces as Carver met them in their chamber, a half hour later. Heid Acheson was there first, but his expression clearly indicated that he had pleasure on his mind, not business. "My lord, while I respect the urgency with which you have summoned us, I humbly ask that we be allowed to conclude whatever matter needs our attention with brevity."

As Chairman, Carver's voice was the voice of the law. "That is my intention, Heid. Now, be silent and I'll tell you what I need from you."

Heid blinked and shut his mouth tightly.

"Your lab is working on a miniaturized, extreme-low-frequency pulse emitter," Carver continued. He read the look of shock on

Heid's face, and inwardly smiled. "Yes, I know all about your *secret* project. Have it brought here at once. I'm going to need it."

Heid exhaled a long-suffering breath from his nose, only daring to match Carver's expectant stare for an instant. He mentally activated his data link. "The device is on its way."

"Good. I suspect that since your successful test three days ago, you've ordered the parts to manufacture another one?"

Heid merely nodded.

"Excellent. I'm unlocking the Circle's shared funds to you. Make one more of the devices. Keep a replacement for yourself, if you like."

"The rest of you must see to the following tasks," Carver continued, addressing the other Circle members. "First, arrange a blanket of comprehensive satellite surveillance, to extend for one hundred kilometers in all directions from the Enclave. Do whatever it takes to put a full array of sensors in geosynchronous orbit over my Mark. Second, I require a kill team from the Death's Head battalion, with a full extermination load out. I want no less than three rotor lifts."

Grumbles from the Circle met this latest demand. To acquire that amount of the Order's soldiery would be very expensive, in wealth, resources, influence, and political capital.

"That will be hugely expensive," blurted James Savoy.

"Your commentary is unnecessary, Lord Savoy," Carver chided. "Please keep your penchant for stating the obvious under wraps."

"May I inquire as to the object of these tasks?" Heid asked.

"I have an outstanding duty to perform concerning a certain Outlander. Were I to be distracted from business of this nature, were I to fail to do all that the High Circle required of me, I could not, with honor, continue to call myself Chairman of our Circle, could I?

"Gentlemen, I will see to it that this Outlander dies one way or another. I will look upon his lifeless corpse even if I must follow him to the grave to do so. If it costs me your lives, well that is the price our Order will pay to see this scum dead.

"Bankrupt our Circle, if you must. Bankrupt your personal accounts, if that is what is required, for I will do the same. Otherwise, I will know that your dedication to our Circle is lacking, and I will rectify the problem."

The heavy footfalls of Armiluss carried the huge Lictor to stand behind Carver's right shoulder in a clearly implied threat. "You have twenty-four hours!"

"That's enough, Delano. This Circle is not your personal plaything," Savoy growled. "We are not the vehicle for your personal duties and ambitions."

Carver rounded on the other man, his eyes electric. "That is exactly what you are."

"Not for long. I call for a vote of no confidence in your chairmanship, by secret ballot." The other members of the Circle, stunned, did not move or even breathe.

The Circle's chairman blinked. His skin flushed and sweat began to bead under his arms. Still, if Savoy expected his Circlemates to back him, he was a fool. The other Last Men appeared to sit the fence and wait. "It is my right to veto such a motion," he snarled.

Savoy took a deep breath. "Then we must resort to a Trial of Lictors."

Carver inwardly smirked. He was sure that he held every advantage in a proxy duel. "Very well. Our Lictors will meet in single combat, one day hence, to decide this issue."

Savoy nodded curtly, turned on his heel, and strode out of the room.

Watching him go and glaring daggers at his back, it took a

moment for Carver's rage and hatred to subside. The other members of the Circle cast their glances about to avoid meeting his gaze. "I am still the incumbent chairman. See to your duties."

The Circle fell into line with a chorus of "It shall be done, lord," and "By your leave, Lord Delano." Bowing, the men retreated.

Alone, Heid lingered. "James is a fool to throw away his Lictor. He would cut off his nose to spite his face."

I might do the same if our positions were reversed, Carver admitted to himself. "He knows nothing of the meaning of obligation. We must see this task through."

Heid nodded. "Our personal losses will be made good when the threat is destroyed, I expect."

Carver's narrowed eyes locked on the skinny man. "Just do what I tell you, and your continued existence will be reward enough!" The younger Last Man trembled from the violent rebuke. Carver dropped his voice an octave still. "If you help me kill that trash-eating scum, we will broach the topic of recompense at the appropriate time!"

Lord Acheson, humbled, bowed and retreated as well. Just then, a servant arrived with his pulse emitter, and the miserable look on Heid's face as he handed it over to Carver was priceless.

— — —

The border between the Order's exclusive controlled zone and the wasteland beyond was not what it used to be. Only ten years before, it presented a challenge even to Harrow to navigate the automated firearms, the computer-assisted infrared targeting software, the motion-sensing lasers and overlapping minefields and constantly patrolling dupes made of flesh or metal.

In the intervening years, the Order had grown arrogant and lazy. It cost them valuable attention to maintain those defenses, attention that could be better spent on their own pleasure. That was all the opening that Harrow needed. It took him months to probe the crumbling walls, but he eventually found a path which appeared completely unguarded.

The avenue before him resembled an ambush, a cruel hoax designed purely to entrap and punish those foolish enough to trust their senses. Harrow did not trust anything, even the evidence of his own eyes.

Success meant patience. He reminded himself to be careful and intelligent, to reconnoiter the best way in, and to painstakingly plan his strike on the Enclave, sketching out a mapped route in his mind. He felt that he was nearly ready. Another few weeks of planning and training, and he would enter the unholy city of his enemy and slaughter everyone inside. He would take them with such surprise that they would have no chance to resist him.

It was a tight alley, dark and confining and running for hundreds of yards into the gloom. He followed it with caution, eyes in constant motion, eternally vigilant, always aware of threats.

Eventually, his way was blocked. Ahead of him in the murk of the alley was a humanoid form. There was no space to move past without exposing himself to an attack, so Harrow drew up ten feet away and stopped.

The smaller figure stood before him, arms crossed. Vaguely female in form, a veil-like scarf hid most of her features from view. Coupled with a sleeveless, poncho-like cloak which covered her from shoulders to knees, it was difficult for Harrow to gauge her physicality. She appeared slight, but not waif-like. However, her eyes were magnificent even in the scant, indirect light. They were beautifully set and no less pleasing for the sheer and unyielding power they exerted. A truly formidable soul gazed from behind those dark, shining, hooded, and fantastic eyes. The visible curves of her shapely brows arranged themselves bemusedly.

If she was a member of the Order of the Last Men, she did not show it. Notably, she did not turn and run wailing into the night at the sight of him. That fact alone gave him pause.

However intrigued and puzzled he might have been under the surface, Harrow was not one to be easily awed or distracted from the task at hand. "Stand aside," he snarled, his voice thick, and cut with the deep Outlander accent. *Fate speaks in a voice of encounters*, he thought, *but I must still be myself.*

The clear and precise voice that issued from the darkly clad stranger was indeed feminine, and colored with a smattering of haughtiness and no small amount of righteous indignation. "I will not." Her inflection was so perfectly tutored that he could barely understand her.

To brook that kind of arrogance would be unbecoming of the would-be Next. All the same, he did not wish to fight the creature before him. She did not appear armed, and, if she knew who he was, then he had no doubt that she would have attacked already, or sprung her trap. A final warning, he decided. There would not be a third.

"It's not in my nature to brutalize women, but I'm not above it." He had never struck a woman before, or even touched one. His hands shaped themselves into their most familiar configuration, but he left his fists at his sides. Still, if she were foolish or stupid enough to face him, he would give her a thrashing she would never forget.

She crossed her arms more tightly over her chest, and, from the slight wrinkle at the corner of her left eye, Harrow could infer that her mouth, behind its veil, was cocked into a mocking half-grin. "If you think you can." Her taunting, sing-song voice, implied that the impending confrontation suited her perfectly.

The explosion into violence was abrupt. Harrow closed the distance between them in a blink. He lunged forward and his left leg crossed behind his leading leg as he angled his body to the left to gain speed and momentum. His right leg lashed at the woman's chin with a thrusting heel kick.

The potent cocktail of frustration, surprise, and relief was almost enough to give him pause as his deadly powerful kick found nothing but empty air. He pressed on, planted that kicking leg, and whirled for a spinning, backhanded punch. The instant he took his eyes off of her, he lost his target.

She snapped punches at his face and groin from blind spots in his vision, from angles he could not have conceived an attack. She rode his hip, tucked herself into his armpit, lashed at him from beneath his own chin. He was steel, fighting her water.

The speed with which she moved astonished him. She flowed around him, as if a specter. Twenty centimeters taller and half again her mass, he never lost confidence in his own deadliness. She was simply untouchable. Her blows brought with them a distant acknowledgement of pain, but they did not damage his ability to fight or shake his confidence. They excited him.

Something within Harrow began to respond, a curious sensation of a long wait that was finally over. He barely blocked a strike with his forearm, aimed at his face but seeming to come from behind him, and kicked his leg around in a low arc to sweep his opponent from her feet. Taking the battle to the ground would be all in his favor, owning as he did all the hardness and ferocity.

Again, there was no sensation of contact as Harrow kicked the air ineffectually, his boot brushing up a semi-circle of grit and trash. A smile threatened his emotionless façade.

Her toes glided over the filth in the alley, taking the cavorting pair apart once more. The damnable woman gave ground but remained in Harrow's path. For the briefest of moments, he suspected that her arrogance was slipping—that she had expected to easily thrash him and was, if not shocked by his ability to absorb punishment, then at least caught off guard by the obstacle he presented.

"I prefer to take my fisticuffs after introductions," she remarked. She sounded obviously pleased yet completely at ease, as if discussing favorite drinks or unseasonably pleasant weather. Harrow knew she stalled to give herself time to cogitate what she had learned of his fighting patterns and formulate new tactics. He decided to play along; he could use a moment, himself.

He straightened but did not slacken his guard. "I have time for one, not both."

"You are keen to fighting, I gather." All the while, the lady's eyes twinkled merrily. They flashed, playful and deadly at once.

He offered a derisive snort. "Move aside or I'll go through you."

"I'll permit you to pass if you tell me your name."

"To permit is to control," he replied dryly, "and I'll have none of that."

"This road, and land, and everything I set my gaze upon belongs to me by birthright. Ask me to move or tell me your name. That is the price of walking here." The sheer, unbridled arrogance of her tone and the audacity of her ultimatum was a more painful jab to Harrow than the physical ones she had previously rendered.

"Who are you to demand my name and block my way?"

The female set the tilt of her chin regally. "I am Alouine Morningstar of the Pure Blood, Princess of the Royal Seed."

"The pure blood? Ridiculous racist, your Order's blood is the most polluted thing on earth."

"You dismiss my claim. That does not surprise me. You are, after all, descended from apes, no matter the airs and pretense you project." A perfect beat of silence punctuated her remark. "Do you have a name, or should I simply call you 'Ape'?"

As much as he intended to deflect her barbs, and outwardly show no emotion, her thorn had caught him. "I'm called Harrow," he hissed through clenched teeth. "It is the last thing you'll hear."

She tried it for herself. "Harrow." Her eyes flashed. "Harrow . . . you can't kill me."

"Then I'll settle for watching you bleed. Or you can stand aside."

"I block your way because you are of the monkey race. I owe you nothing and you are beneath me. Also, it amuses me." She held out the bait. He accepted it happily. He knew how to foil an ambush: by assaulting through it. Faced with a trap, he dove in and destroyed it.

Wasting no more time, Harrow again launched into the attack. A storm commenced of blows, punches interspersed with kicks, elbow strikes, and chops. Each duelist weathered the gale, intercepting or evading, in a driving harmony of measured but tumultuous vehemence.

Her willowy wrists flowing along and around his steel-coated forearms, the two parried, lunged and jockeyed for position. She was faster, a fraction of a beat ahead in the rhythm they tapped on one another's arms, ribs, shoulders, thighs and faces. She hit him more often, but even his glancing blows hit her harder. For as thin as her bones felt against his, they possessed every bit the sternness of his, and he could never seem to land a solid strike on her maddeningly ethereal form.

He backed up his experienced style of contention with brutally efficient, streamlined, muscular power. Her natural talent and dexterous skill were every bit as formidable. Merits played to flaws in equal measure on both sides.

Alouine's hood fell back, her dark hair spilling forth as liquid tendrils of blackness. Her scarf unraveled, revealing full lips pressed into a thin line. Those terrible, beautiful eyes cast cones of intensity, the severity of a child engrossed at play. She was enraptured in battle, a bloodthirsty, avenging spirit.

Beads of sweat formed on Harrow's brow, his nostrils flaring as the bellows of his lungs pumped air into his molten core like some ancient blast furnace. Here was life, this amazing, infuriating female he sought to push to her limit.

Their physical testing of one another further accelerated its pace. Alouine's small, diamond-hard hands and feet were precise weapons, gouging into the soft flesh of pressure points, nerve bundles and organs. Harrow showed no pain, or perhaps felt none. Disconnected, as he was, from all thought but putting his upstart opponent in her place.

The experienced Outlander was used to life-and-death struggles, and even if his technique could be described as mere 'brawling', he was happy to give the high-born woman a dose of real-world brutality. What he lacked in formal training, he made good with his intensity and precision.

Still, she was maneuvering him, and Harrow knew it. He was not being defeated, but could not steal the initiative from her, either. She guarded it fiercely, holding it just out of his grasp with her speed and fluidity, and would not relinquish her lead.

What frustrated him more than anything else was that he could anticipate her moves with his simulation matrix, and thus, should have been winning; he plainly was not fast enough. Simulating full seconds into the future, Harrow witnessed his death as he barreled toward it at breakneck speed.

He did not want to engage his quantum field engine. That the woman forced him to do so was a testament to her deadliness. He wondered how long he could last against her without resorting to using his soul-fire. In a duel like this, using quantum power to alter reality felt like cheating. He wanted to test himself, see just how far he could push his humanity against hers before one of them cracked.

Though they whirled, snapping and defending blows faster than the eye could track, the stranger had actually led Harrow as though pulling him around by the belt. He identified that stage in the sequence where the pattern would reach its utmost complexity before collapsing, upon which point she would find a vital spot and deliver the final, telling blow.

Knowing he was on death's door, Harrow nevertheless stepped in to deliver the next punch, already aware that his attack would not land, but instead, would leave his body fatally exposed. She ducked under his outstretched fist and time froze.

Her terrible eyes locked on his unguarded chest and the pair reached the inevitable outcome that the faster female warrior had funneled the battle toward from the beginning.

And yet, he twisted so that her shot, delivered with fingers pressed into a cone, glanced off his sternum rather than be driven directly into his heart.

The blow was perfect and should have killed him and Harrow knew it, and he escaped only by spooling up his quantum device, forcibly altering the laws of probability and, in essence, shunting himself forward a single blink in time. Harrow felt Alouine's shock when she missed him. Her breath hitched as he instantly and inexplicably caught her up, making the time gap between the two contenders disappear somehow and emanating a tangible wave of wrongness in doing so, evading death yet again and clawing his way back into the battle.

Still, her fingertips were harder than steel and cracked into his ribs with great velocity, like an armor-piercing bullet. The attack ripped through his chest in a wave of pain which threatened to blast apart his spine. He refused to let the agony register on his features as he roughly shoved it aside and flung himself onward.

Racing neck and neck now, Harrow finally struck her a sound blow with his elbow, thrusting it into her with a hard stabbing motion just below her solar plexus, impaling her diaphragm and making air whistle through her teeth.

The unique bond of expert combatants established, he felt her begin to buckle. In the same instant, one of her sharp knuckles, protruding farther from her fist than the rest, found his kidney like a dagger, in the precise spot where it lay uncovered by rib or pelvis. Another focused blast of her internal energy tore through the soft tissue of the organ, sending a deadening sensation shooting from his shoulder to ankle.

The revelation was there, coming upon them both. Aim for the heart. They slipped, each of them, into the near mystical, no-mindedness of champion warriors, trusting that indomitable spirit, that inherent genius, to guide them subconsciously to victory.

It could not go on. Harrow could not afford the delay or the physical punishment she inflicted. He did not want to dig deeper into his reserves of willpower. His struggle for dominance over this woman made a change of tactic not only necessary, but inevitable. He would try anything to throw the female off rhythm and tilt the scales in his favor. Losing carried a deadly penalty and he would not settle for a draw. His foe, too, showed every sign of willingness to fight to the death.

Harrow tried something he thought his antagonist would never expect. He leaned in and kissed her.

Alouine simultaneously made use of the same tactic.

Terrible in its suddenness, the power of that collective, unconscious will caught them both utterly off guard. Alouine found her hand gently holding Harrow's face. He found that his own hand had caught her wrist in a grip depleted of malice. Full counts passed and the pair did nothing, caught immobile as though exposed to a live current.

She tasted him with her tongue.

He sampled the smell of her face and then exhaled the intoxicating aroma of witch hazel and mimosa through his nose again, pushing it out as if it were poison. He was satisfied to taste a hint of blood as well, but he could not be sure if it was his or hers. Remembering, clarity rushing onto them as a flash, this too became a contest. Mere ticks later, they were again engaged in an escalating conflict, each demanding submission of the other but unwilling to give it.

Heat exploded in various nodal points on Harrow's body. The sweat and flush of his exertions provided convenient cover for how utterly vulnerable and clumsy he suddenly felt. His emotions roiled and he felt dizzy. More than anything else, he did not want to stop kissing her.

Alouine put an end to it. She locked the impossibly sharp point of her artificially hardened elbow into the inside corner of Harrow's jaw, cranking his head to a tilt, and, with her forearm across his exposed throat, heaved him against the wall of the alley.

"Don't test me," she warned breathlessly, her own face bright and chest heaving.

He waited patiently for the three seconds it took for her grip to slacken, counting on the endurance of his own muscles to outlast the explosive, fast-twitch quality of hers. Craning his hand into the crook of her elbow, he levered it away from his tender windpipe. Slamming the cruel edge of his own armored forearm into the junction of her clavicles, he wrenched upward against her creamy throat and growling, slammed her back into the opposite wall in turn.

"And you should not test me," came his rasping, gravelly reply.

"Amusing," she whispered, her lips parted, mouth seeking his. "And fascinating."

He surprised himself. The woman wanted more, and he gave it to her. Harrow's mouth descended on Alouine's once more, nipping and probing.

The Outlander marveled at the sensation, the taste. The way her perfume wound through his nostrils.

It was too dangerous and could not continue. She was one of

them, one of the Last, trying to use her femininity to do what her fighting skills could not: to break him, subjugate him. Pleasure and pride warred back and forth for long seconds.

Harrow's pride won out. When he abruptly drew back, he was unsurprised to see her eyes once again hooded and dark as shadows conveniently leapt to her service as a mask. Desire and indignation swirled in her expression. She locked her eyes on his mouth rather than meet his gaze.

"Yes. Fascinating," he replied, his voice little more than a rumble from his aching, wounded chest. He lifted away from her and said clearly, "Excuse me." Her eyes widened. He was withdrawing, conceding. The victory, hollow as it was, stunned her.

Harrow began to berate himself in an instant. She was not his equal in pure, violent power. She could not hold a candle to the world-shaping power of his quantum machine. Still, he was retreating.

It was too unfamiliar, too unexpected. He had to put it behind him, so he pivoted on the ball of his foot and strode away on his original course, showing his back to her.

Alouine watched him go, saying nothing. Most surprising to Harrow was the unfamiliar juxtaposition he sensed within himself, oscillating between feeling relief and longing.

NINE

Carver felt like a hero as he made his way, alone, to the border of the exclusive zone. It was unheard of for Last Men of any rank to leave an enclave of their own volition, to dwell for even a moment among the Outlander vermin. All the Order members he passed, their servants and vassals, gazed upon him in confusion or awe as he marched to the gate.

He had shown up to the battle arena for the Trial of Lictors dressed as he was now, in brand new synthetic gear for his mission to the Outlands. James Savoy had been thoroughly insulted by the idea that Carver's Lictor would simply wipe the floor with his counterpart and the Chairman would continue with his plans. The thought gave Carver intense glee.

His data link disconnected from the Enclave network to ensure secrecy, Carver had beckoned Armiluss to crouch down so that he could whisper in the giant's ear. "Ensure that this insubordination never occurs again. You know what to do."

The warrior slaves fought nude in a wide, circular area to ensure that they possessed no hidden weapons. Otherwise, the battles barred no holds and lasted until one Lictor went limp, or as the rules stated, was 'disinclined to continue'.

That had not taken long. Armiluss had backed his opponent to the wall and bludgeoned his smaller counterpart to death in less than a minute, caving in the other slave's skull by dropping his knee, and the hundreds of kilos of body weight behind it, onto the other Lictor's temple.

James Savoy was disgraced, his Lictor was dead, so he made arrangements to leave the Third City and travel to another Enclave. Carver found the weakening of his Circle regrettable, but then, Savoy had been a weak link in any case, one who lacked conviction.

Armiluss would have to stay behind, to ensure the continued cooperation of Carver's Circle. That he would need to post the ghoulish abomination as a nanny, to coerce his Circle-mates into following his instructions, was yet more proof that Carver had much higher to ascend within the Order of the Last Men. Soon enough, he swore, his commands would be heeded as the highest law in the Enclave.

Heid Acheson's pulse emitter fit over Carver's left forearm and hand like a metal gauntlet. The actuator lens filled his palm and prevented him from closing his hand entirely. Nonetheless, he felt assured by the extra security it provided. The high-intensity microwaves which the device produced could thoroughly cook a grown man alive in seconds.

The prospect of ending a life with the mere wave of his hand made Carver giddy with excitement. He resolved to test the device on some unfortunate soul, regardless of need. Combined with the anxiety of leaving his life of security and pleasure, for even this short furlough, the nervousness made him feel somewhat faint. His mouth went dry.

"Sir, this is the border of the enclave. I have to advise you to turn back." A slave in black fatigues stepped forward, an automatic rifle slung before him, his hand raised.

"I understand that. Open the gate." Carver let a smug, satisfied smirk drift over his features as the man's eyes widened in shock.

"I've been ordered to never open the gate for any reason."

"I am ordering you to temporarily disregard that order."

The gate itself, a steel bulwark, ten meters high and two meters thick, was coated in a layer of rust from disuse. The locking mechanism was so thoroughly seized with oxidization that Carver feared he would have to summon servants to destroy it with plasma torches. Fortunately, after several tries, the guard managed to turn over the equally ancient, but powerful electric motors and, with flakes of rust grinding into powder, the gears turned and released the lock. Then, with a horrific and shuddering groan, the gate crunched and plowed its way open along a track that was buried in the gravel.

Swallowing down his rising trepidation, Carver stepped out of the Enclave.

He had left the Third City frequently to vacation in other parts of the world. But he had never gone outside its precincts on foot. He travelled in luxury at thirty-thousand feet in pressurized cabins, aboard powerful, scram-jet-equipped aero-planes.

But, at that moment, he put one booted foot in front of the other and walked into the decay and destitution of the Outlands.

By everything the Order held sacred, the Outlands were ugly. The Enclave was bright, clean, sterile, and geometric. Just outside its walls, anarchy reigned—not merely in the lack of social structure but in the very aesthetic of the place. Flattened heaps of churned earth and ancient building materials lay wasted and neglected and overgrown by only the hardiest species of stunted, twisting weeds. Carver's eye could not glimpse even one straight line. He held still for a moment, trying to overcome the vertigo and fear of such an alien world.

The guard said something as he passed, but Carver ignored him, and after he had gone about fifty meters, the gate reversed its previous path and ground shut once more. The crusty clack of the lock as it seated itself in place once more echoed behind him with finality.

Rubble and ruin spread before the Last Man for untold kilometers. He activated his data link and set up a cellular communications channel. "I have left the Enclave," he announced mentally, sharing the thought over the airwaves.

"I see you, lord," Heid Acheson reported on the other end of the channel, from his seat in the Circle's command center. "All nine satellites are functioning nominally." The vassal had six monitors active at the station before him, and he observed from a top-down perspective as Carver casually walked through the broken, debris-choked lane.

"Good. Plot me an intercept course to the Outlander. Let's get this over with."

"The computers are compiling data, my lord. It is taking some time to lock onto the man's electromagnetic signature. However, the initial report is that he is actually entering the Enclave at this time."

"He is doing what?" Carver spat.

"He is raiding the Enclave, my lord. His vector of ingress is sub-avenue 8, Grid L-12." He sent Carver a digital map of the Enclave with his own position, as well as the approximate location of their target, highlighted.

"What's down there?" Carver demanded.

"Hydroponics. It's a food production area."

"Send a kill team immediately to flush him out, and direct me to intercept him when he leaves."

"With all respect, Lord Delano, he'll be long gone before we can get anyone down there. The production facilities are all automated, and they're twenty kilometers long. "

Carver growled with frustration. The damnable Outlander was outmaneuvering him at every turn. "Send them anyway!"

"Yes, my lord."

Glancing at the map image projected into his visual field via data link, and getting his bearings, Carver set off in a brisk walk toward a spot close to where he imagined the Outlander vermin would emerge. The rat could not stay in the larder forever, and Carver would be there upon his escape.

After a moment, Heid's voice again emerged. "There is something else, Carver."

The Chairman was already huffing from the exertion of physically propelling his body in the direction of his foe. That Heid used his first name was another indication of something going terribly wrong. "What?"

"A faint trace of a Mark account, sir," the vassal said.

Carver ground his teeth and, though sweating, picked up his pace. "What? With the Outlander?" Was there a traitorous member of the Order of the Last Men working with the scum? Was that how the Harrow was managing to stay alive?

"Yes, in the same area. I only picked up a faint trace with the sensors. It was there, and then gone again."

"Run down the entire database of the Enclave! I want every member's location in two minutes!" Panting hard, he hastened to pick his way through the maze of Outland debris.

— — —

Harrow could ill-afford the distraction, or the wounds that Alouine had left with him. She had been the sternest test in his life, and to his great dismay, the only one he had not managed to overcome with triumph. He ached, on many levels, hating the fact that she was able to wound him so severely, that she could come so close to ending his life, that she was so beautiful and intriguing.

Try as he might, he could not put her completely out of his mind. Her apparition tracked along with him, refusing to leave him at peace, like the nagging memory of work unfinished.

The hydroponic growth facility was guarded by a single man, a pathetic slave, bred and raised for that purpose and no other, and effectively lobotomized by pharmaceuticals to accept and even welcome his servitude.

Waiting, canvassing the area for traps, he found nothing to indicate an ambush. For a lone wolf like Harrow, it was the equivalent of guarding the sheep with another sheep.

Harrow watched the man make his rounds for almost a full hour, noting his exact routine before making his move. The sentry, a low-ranking soldier of the Order's Death's Head battalion, was a blank canvas, an empty shell. When not patrolling, he simply stared at the wall, all higher brain functions absent.

He seized the man from behind in complete silence. Grasping the guard's chin with his left hand and wrenching upward, Harrow pressed the point of his single-edged and well-honed, nineteen-centimeter dagger into the hollow above the junction of the collarbones and plunged it downward. Guiding the blade back and forth in a vicious sawing motion, Harrow severed the man's upper airways and set him noiselessly free from his life of slavery.

Holding the dying man's jaw tightly shut by the chin, Harrow waited several moments as the guard's spasms and jerks faded to twitches before finally ceasing. Gently, the Outlander lowered the slave's lifeless form to the floor. He paused for several moments, extending his senses, but was met with only the hum of fluorescent lights.

Satisfied that he was alone, Harrow took stock of what he had won, slinging the new rifle over his back and stripping away all the full magazines from the dead guard's web gear.

"Why did you kill him?" spoke a soft voice from behind Harrow's crouching form.

Immediately, Harrow threw himself into a roll to the left, to upset the aim of anyone targeting his back, and drew his pistol. The wounds in his chest and back protested with waves of agony. Coming up on one knee, he put the front sight of the pistol on target—center mass of a teenage male who, for his part, appeared utterly unconcerned.

The boy's arms were at his sides and held no weapons. Harrow's finger tensed on the trigger. He had never been taken by surprise before. He hesitated, his right index finger on the cusp of supplying the total poundage of force needed to send hot lead into the youth.

The boy did not seem to note that he was in the line of fire at all. He was rail-thin, perhaps fifteen years old, with the darkened, weathered skin of a life exposed to the harsh elements. Set between his arresting, almost hypnotic eyes was a large, clear crystal. Though the boy spoke softly, there was something about his voice which commanded attention. "You could have easily knocked him unconscious," he stated. "Killing him seemed really . . . I don't know . . . wasteful."

Judging from his dark, tattered clothing, dirty face and unkempt hair, the boy had to be a fellow Outlander. But how had he gotten the drop on Harrow so successfully? "Who are you?" he demanded.

The teenager smiled. "Quintain," he answered. Walking over to the corpse, the boy's smile faded. "Let's not change the subject, though." He looked down at the still-warm cadaver and the growing puddle of blood. He stooped to close the dead man's eyelids with his fingertips and mumbled a short prayer. "This man didn't deserve to die." Glancing back at Harrow, who was still pointing the pistol at him, he added, "Neither do I."

Harrow let the pressure on the pistol's trigger slacken but did not lower the weapon. "That remains to be seen. What's that man's life, to you?"

"I wanted to rehabilitate him."

"Impossible. He was chemically lobotomized. There is a capsule under his skin, which was filling him with poison. I did him a favor."

"I could have removed the capsule and healed much of the damage it caused, but I suppose we'll never know for certain now, will we? You shouldn't be dismissing things as impossible, anyway. Impossibility is relative. For some people, impossible is merely improbable. We're Outlanders, inside an Order Enclave. To anyone else that would be absurd."

After a moment, Harrow nodded. He finally relented and lowered the pistol, rendering it safe and then returning it to its holster. Indeed, the pair were having a civil conversation and keeping the weapon up struck him as impolite. He stood up straight. "Is that why you're here, to rehabilitate a pitiful slave?"

"Well, no. Apparently, I'm here to meet you. I came for the food, but fate put you here, too. I was going to give the poor man his life back as a bonus to having a full belly. God gave me you and a corpse, instead." The boy looked Harrow up and down. "You'll do, I guess, although I'm not going to have you killing more innocent folks in my company."

Harrow's brow twitched. The boy broached the topic of sharing company; Harrow had not, and had no intention of doing so.

"Anyway, you have a name as well, I presume?"

"I'm called Harrow."

A flash of recognition crossed his face, and the strange boy turned away to hide his satisfied grin.

He began to walk away from Harrow, farther into the facility, but said over his shoulder, "Well, Harrow, since that guy is dead, I doubt he'll need any of this food. Since we're the only ones around, I guess it falls to us, huh?"

Harrow was genuinely puzzled for the first time in . . . thinking back, he could not remember ever being thus. "Help yourself," he muttered.

Quintain grinned. "Ah yes, the old Outlander motto. It's a wonder that there are any of us left, with that kind of attitude." From inside his coat, the boy produced a canvas sack, and, walking along the unending rows of the hydroponic farm, began to stuff it with potatoes and cucumbers. He selected a gorgeous, ripe red tomato and bit into it, messily and with no preamble. Soon, Harrow began to join him in the harvest.

Filling his own cloth sack with potatoes from the growth rails, Harrow caught up to the impetuous youth. "I have to ask you, Quintain, how you managed to sneak up on me like you did. That kind of thing does not happen."

"Magick," the boy mumbled around a mouthful of fruit. He swallowed and continued, "It's pretty easy to direct people's attention away from me. Although I get the impression that if you had been facing me, you would have noticed me. You're different. Some folks, like that poor bastard you opened up—I can stand right in front of them without being seen."

"Magick," Harrow repeated skeptically.

"Sure. It's the simplest word for it. You can call it 'tugging on the threads of Fate', if you want. 'Physical change in accordance with the Will' is another way to put it. I just say 'Magick', though."

"That sounds preposterous."

The teenager laughed heartily. Tomato juice ran down his chin. "That's rich, coming from you. I mean, you might not know the lingo or the ritual of it, but you're quite the magician yourself. I can tell. In fact, you might be more talented than me . . . just maybe not as educated."

Having stocked his supply of organic treasure to his satisfaction, Quintain lingered alongside Harrow, watching him closely with unguarded curiosity. The older man did not reply, so Quintain pressed on.

"I have to use it ceremonially. But you . . . your actions are magickal in an intuitive way. In fact, I'm pretty convinced that I was led here because I knew you were going to be here, too. The convergences were just right."

"I'm pretty convinced that you're mad," Harrow muttered.

The teen grinned. "Good. Anyway, we should be going. No doubt the Order is already sending more men down here to kill us. Besides, there's another person close by that I have a feeling we should meet—another magician."

"There is no 'we'. You and I will go our separate ways now." Harrow mustered his dignity and put an air of finality into his voice as he slung his bag of food over his shoulder. Quintain chuckled, and stepped closer.

"Don't you see that there is no difference between 'we' and 'you and I'? So, there really is no such thing as our 'separate ways' anymore?" The boy leaned in and squinted. "Hey, why is your face all bruised? The guard didn't hit you. Few people could, I'd bet." His eyes widened. "Wait, you've already met the other one!"

Harrow immediately thought back to the infuriating Alouine.

"You did!" the boy exclaimed. "I can see it in your aura. What was he . . . no, wait—*she*, like?" As Harrow turned to face Quintain, the younger man's brows arched. "Oh . . . she was pretty. You were frustrated by her, and . . ."—his voice dropped an octave—"aroused."

Harrow spun on his heel and walked for the exit. The boy had unbelievable insight, far beyond a series of accurate guesses.

"Aw, don't be embarrassed," Quintain hollered as he rushed to catch Harrow up. "If she's pretty enough to make you blush, I can't wait to meet her!"

"Feel free to do so," the warrior told the boy as he stepped back outside, into the cold. "I suspect she will not want to cross paths with me again."

"It's the nature of powerful people to test one another."

"Indeed."

Quintain crossed in front of Harrow, and when the larger man did not stop walking, he fell into step beside him. They walked down the narrow alley in which Harrow had fought Alouine only an hour before.

"In all seriousness, I'm going to need both of you. It's a bit of a conundrum. If I leave to go meet her, and you won't go with me, I'll just end up having to chase you down again. To be perfectly honest, I've been hoping to meet you for months. But I need to meet her just as badly."

Harrow's eyes narrowed suspiciously. "Why have you been looking for me? And what exactly do you need me for?"

"To help me destroy the Order, or perhaps to somehow sublimate it into the true meaning of the Earth. I'm not entirely sure, yet. Maybe we should just oppose it however we can, and see what happens? I tend to think of it as a cancer and you and I could be like surgeons."

"I've already been attempting that."

For a beardless youth in his mid-teens, Quintain showed intelligence and ambition. He reminded the older warrior of himself at that age—physically less imposing perhaps, but clear-eyed and with purpose.

"I know. I can tell. What you've done is important. But it's not on the scale I have in mind. Like it or not, you're going to need me just as much as I need you."

Harrow gave a snort of disapproval. "I don't need anyone. The strong are strongest alone. You don't seem to be offering much in terms of a partnership."

"What you say may be true. But in fighting all these monsters, you've started to become monstrous yourself. This task that we take upon ourselves, whether we do it only for ourselves or for the sake of the entire world, isn't one that can be seen through by a hardened killing machine who has no friends. That's what I'm offering.

"You obviously don't need a partner. A partner would slow you down, get in your way, and possibly get you killed. But it's equally obvious that you should have a friend. You deserve one. Give me a chance and I'll be the best friend you'll ever have."

"I do not appreciate attempts to humor me. However, you may do as you please. That is my doctrine."

"So I may also offer you suggestions and advice?" Quintain asked, cocking a brow.

"I will listen. As for heeding, I make no promises."

Quintain nodded. That seemed simple enough to him. "The woman you fought with, I need to speak with her. If you'd rather not accompany me, that's fine, but I'd like to know where I could meet back up with you."

Harrow was forced to make a decision of whether to trust the younger man, and was finding it surprisingly easy. The boy did not have a trace of guile or deception. Every word, each expression, was sincere and genuine. Like Harrow, the boy wore no mask. "There is a village called Mason-Dixon. I will wait for you there."

"I'm sure I can find it." The teenager paused. "Anything I should know about this woman before I go to meet her?"

The warrior exhaled through his nose as the pair reached the end of the alley. "She said her name was Alouine, and that she was a member of the Order of the Last. A good fighter, though she was also arrogant, insufferable, and possessed her share of eugenic bigotry. Prepare yourself for condescension beyond your wildest imaginings."

Quintain smiled slyly. "And who won the fight?"

Walking away, Harrow murmured, "It isn't over. We shall find out when it resumes."

— — —

A weak and sickly sun rose over the horizon, illuminating the skies with streaks of pink slashing through the constant grey. Alouine washed her hair in ice-cold water from a leaking, rusty pipe that carried it to the nearby Order enclave. Had she stayed within the Order she would bathe in steaming hot, clean water, assisted by a cadre of body slaves, perfuming and pampering her flesh with fragrant chemicals and exotic oils. Here, there was only cold water, pregnant with minerals and chilling to the bone.

Her thoughts were elsewhere. She still had not caught her breath or managed to calm the hammering of her heart, though an hour had passed since her duel. Despite herself, she could focus on nothing but the Ape man. Despite her attempts to blast away the memory of his touch with the frigid spray, the fire with which he battled her and the heat of his mouth on hers would not leave her.

Horrid bruises had already surfaced on her abdomen and throat. The act of swallowing produced a fiery pain that refused to subside, and she had quickly realized that she was a hair's breadth from having her windpipe crushed and the bones of her neck broken.

Her hands and forearms were raw, swollen and tender, and she was grateful for the frigid water despite how otherwise unpleasant it was. The damage was severe, more than she had experienced before, and while her body contained numerous organs, bred into her specially for regenerating damage to her body, it would still take her hours to heal completely, and perhaps days before the soreness faded.

A pitiful Outlander would doubtlessly be incapacitated for weeks with the same injuries; however, Alouine was certain that Harrow, suffering though he might be, was not beaten.

She had just left the Enclave and had already met an Outlander she could not defeat in battle. Her adventure was not starting off well.

"How dare he be so audacious?" she snarled to herself as she roughly ran her numb fingers through her tangled, sweaty locks. *How dare I*, she wondered. To allow that filthy monkey to touch her, to submit to his kiss, it was all highly unnatural. The taste of him clung to her lips no matter her attempts to wash it out.

"An ape. A filthy, low, base ape . . . How dare he touch me

without permission? How dare he order me about as if he had the right! To tell me what I will and will not do!"

She growled in her impotent fury, sending her echo bouncing over the sound of the falling water. The action caused more pain in her throat, which she massaged with her cold hands. Even Carver, the vile scum he was, had at least made an attempt, condescending and thick with threats as it was, to let her believe she had a choice. Harrow had given her no such opportunity.

She wrung out her wet hair, careful to keep her damaged neck straight as she whipped it about and wrapped her long scarf around it to dry. Alouine was teased by a small voice within her at her frustration. The ape, Harrow, had gotten to her, gotten under her skin. She knew that she would need blinders to deny it. It was a far different sensation than those of bitter disgust and resentment she felt for Carver.

He might have been descended from apes, but his power was unmistakable. He had managed what no Outlander could have done, to fight her to a draw, to contest her will and walk away alive.

She was easily his better in all ways that mattered. Her genetics were far superior. Her ancestors were gods. His were slaves. She was a daughter of the Morning Star, had been raised within the Highest Circle of the Order, and with an education that exponentially exceeded what that mongrel Outlander could have possibly learned on his own.

But, he, too, was a force of nature, she thought. *What is this feeling, this sense that he is closer to the meaning of the earth than I am?*

He certainly makes Last Men look like pitiful, clumsy oafs by comparison.

The high-born woman ground her teeth. She understood well the need for a hierarchy of beings. Those of the monkey race were weak, their lives pitifully short. They existed purely to serve her kind, and, left on their own, they degenerated quickly to a cesspool of savagery, or, at best, developed a herd mentality that reached the deepest depths of stupidity. Huddling together for warmth, they damned themselves with their meekness.

Yet, that pretentious fool had spit in the face of the natural Order. He had spit in her face. It burned her, not merely scorching her pride, but everything she held true about herself. She sensed none of the typical perversions of his race within the man.

He was an arrogant, insufferable, and violent brute, certainly. However, she was forced to admit to herself that he was also honorable, noble, and, worst of all, handsome. He'd been in possession of great power and considerable pride, and had not been similar in any way to the slaves and groveling servants she had known her entire life. His presence radiated supreme will, clarity, and tenacity.

I had him! His life had been mine to take, dead to rights, and somehow, he turned the tables. It was the most galling thing to have ever happened to her. More galling was how it made her forget, temporarily but entirely, her reason for escaping the Enclave to begin with. She could think of nothing else but the Outlander.

She expected to encounter Outlanders almost immediately, but not a wild and powerful man like Harrow. There she was, leaving the Enclave for the first time in her life. There he was, entering into its sacred precincts with an audacity which seemed almost a routine for him.

Alouine coughed viciously into her palm, retching spasmodically, and was disturbed to find a fine mist of blood when she withdrew her hand, gasping for breath. Unaccustomed to pain, she found it distasteful beyond measure and heaped more scorn on the warrior Outlander. Still, she could not but reserve some for herself. She had failed to defeat him.

And he stole my first kiss, she thought with more misery. *I'm no romantic, but that was not how that was supposed to be.*

Groaning with disdain and anguish, she staggered away from the water. The heat of her fury and agony warred with the pervasive, insidious cold, and she cursed that, too.

She was uncomfortable despite the warmth of her specially designed coat. Lithium-ion panels in her bodysuit kept her blood warm as it circulated through her body; still, the crisp, near-freezing air irritated her nostrils and throat and managed to penetrate into the joints of her fingers and toes.

Accustomed to breathing the warm and scrubbed air of the Enclave, she trusted in the medicinal nano-machines to bolster her immune system. Her body was already working overtime to manufacture the stem cells needed to repair her wounds.

Puzzled, exhausted, bloodied, and frustrated, she sat on a jutting slab of ancient concrete and wrapped her arms herself tightly about herself as she struggled with the question of what to do next.

Her pride flared, and demanded a rematch. She would heal first, and then she would find that man and kill him, if his arrogant foray into the Enclave did not kill him first.

TEN

It had taken Heid much longer to accumulate an accurate list of each and every member's whereabouts than the two minutes which Carver demanded. Many of them had strong privacy encryptions over their Mark accounts which took precious time to override. Finally, after nearly an hour had passed, he made his report.

"My lord, there are two members of the Third City Order who are not currently within the precincts of the Enclave. One of them is you."

Carver rolled his eyes. "Yes, yes, and the other?"

"Alouine Morningstar, my lord."

He stopped walking. "Are you certain?"

"I went over it twice. Aside from you, she is the only member missing from the Enclave and otherwise unaccounted for."

Bewildered, Carver wandered to a nearby ruin of a wall and leaned on it to catch his breath. He had certainly intended to intimidate the stupid woman, but he did not expect her to drop everything and flee to the Outlands.

The Last Man chewed on the inside of his cheek. She did not merely reject his advances, which might have stung enough. The damnable brat had actually chosen a sojourn in the wild wasteland, the abandonment of her people and her property, over being with him.

"Are you all right, my lord?" Heid's irritating voice scratched within Carver's mind.

"Yes, yes. I'm resting. When was the last time *you* walked for miles through the wastes, Heid?"

"I'm not judging you, sir."

Carver snorted his disbelief, and Heid fell silent again.

He might be able to salvage the situation, but Carver forced himself to admit that it was taking a strange turn. Altogether, it did not matter, he supposed. Nothing had really changed except her physical location, and if she continued to refuse him, he would have Armiluss amputate all of her limbs before he had his way with her. Carver favored simple solutions.

"I will deal with betrayals and traitors at a later time," he announced.

"Should the High Circle be informed?"

"No, keep this quiet. We have no proof of any wrongdoing. If I'm not mistaken, it is not a punishable offense to leave the Enclave on foot." Carver growled. He struggled to rein in his emotions. "I'll make sure she pays for this," he grumbled.

"What was that?"

"Nothing," he sighed. "Back to the business at hand."

Another hour of hiking, with guidance from Heid's eyes in the sky, brought Carver, increasingly bedraggled and exhausted, within view of the Outlander. He tried to stay out of sight but admitted to himself that he had no talent for stealth. He fell in behind the warrior and struggled mightily to close the distance from three hundred meters to two hundred, then one hundred.

The cursed Outlander moved effortlessly over the broken terrain, but Carver fell once, then again, scraping, bruising, and abrading his skin on unyielding rocks. He was keenly aware of Heid watching him from above, and Harrow's appraisal of his presence from ahead.

Finally, an hour after the sky had gone too dark to see and Carver was forced to use a pair of light-amplification goggles simply to navigate from one step to the next, the impossibly enduring man he tracked finally stopped to rest in a ruin and built a fire.

Harrow chose his campsite well, hunkering down within a heap of rubble shielded from the sky, where even the glow of his campfire was concealed. Carver approached cautiously and lifted the goggles from his face, packing them away once more. The small fire cast enough light to see, and it illuminated his antagonist as he approached.

Built solidly and possessed of physical grace and presence, Carver had no illusions about how dangerous Harrow truly was. He had observed the man for hours through a screen, but having him mere meters away was something else entirely. He pushed these thoughts to the back of his mind as he summoned his voice, clearing his throat softly from the ingress of the ruined house. "May I share your fire?"

Harrow did not look up from his gazing into the flames. "Do as you please."

Gratefully, Carver entered the broken dwelling and slumped onto the floor, huddling close to the fire but carefully keeping it between himself and the Outlander. "My thanks," he mumbled.

The Outlander did not comment on Carver's appearance or obvious exhaustion, or the known fact that he had been following Harrow for hours. "Can you tend the fire and ensure that it does not go out?"

"Yes," Carver replied. He spied the small stack of wood fuel which Harrow indicated in the corner of the room, if the space could be called that. *This must be a cache*, he thought. He wondered how many scores of other stockpiles the Outlander might have, scattered throughout the Outlands.

"I will return," Harrow told him, before rising once more and heading off into the night. Carver hoped he was telling the truth.

Long minutes passed and the Last Man took his best guess at

when to add fuel to the small campfire. It did not gutter, so he supposed that he was doing it right. He had to admit to himself that the combination of the cold and dark, with the presence of his known enemy, had raised his hackles and made his hair stand on point. He shivered and cursed the fool's errand he was on.

Carver bit into the tasteless organic hunk of his nutrition ration. It was a far cry from filet mignon, but it would combat his gnawing hunger, and, he hoped, give him the strength to keep up with his newfound traveling companion. The pace was exhausting, even if fear had pressed that exhaustion to the back of his mind.

Harrow had hunted, and returned with the small animal—a rabbit, Carver was sure, though he had only seen one through an encyclopedic computer screen. The Outlander did not seem to be willing to share his meal, which he skinned and roasted over the open flames. He took raw vegetables from his pack to round out his supper, and he offered Carver nothing but healthy amounts of suspicion and space.

The two sat in a vast sea of silence for quite some time, with only the crackling of the tiny fire to ground them to the physical plane. Not that Carver could hope to feel the other realms there, in that constant, wretched cold.

The shivering made him tired and irritable, and all the while, the Outlander sat stoically, unaffected by bland food, poor company, howling winds, and even the obvious wounds he carried on his rugged features. The man was an animated statue. Carver finally grew entirely frustrated by the blanket of empty solitude Harrow had spread over the dismal camping ground. The evening passed by, taking the odd duo close to midnight. "Do you not feel pain?" Carver asked softly. His interest was sincere, as much to satisfy his own curiosity as to build a working knowledge of his adversary.

The Last Man surreptitiously snuck glances at the Outlander here and there, taking mental notes. Not immediately apparent to a less perceptive man, the warrior was heavily wounded, though he did a remarkable job of concealing his injuries.

Carver was there on a mission, nonetheless, and secretly he began to use Heid's pulse emitter to biometrically scan Harrow's body with magnetic resonance imagining. It helped that the warrior remained almost completely still.

Harrow replied, flat and terse, "Of course."

Pursing his lips in frustration, Carver pressed on. "You look as though you were beaten to a pulp. Combined with the cold, I'm surprised you're not writhing in agony over there."

The killer's eyes found their way to lock onto those of the Order mastermind. "That is the difference between you and me. I love my life. I love all of existence. Pain is a part of it, so I love that, too."

Carver blinked several times. He found it difficult to hold fast to Harrow's gaze for very long, and was taken somewhat aback by his strange mode of thinking. "You love pain?"

Harrow's brow twitched in bemusement. "I do not long for it. I simply love it when it comes."

The would-be chairman could only nod. "I suppose that makes sense. Is it because it's familiar?" He cracked a half-smile that he hoped was disarming, and quipped, "A kind of 'love what you know' sort of thing?"

"You're mistaken when you think that because I became a man without fine china or body slaves that I don't know anything about comfort or pleasure. Imagining those things is not difficult. A man is fated for luxury, or he is not. The difference is insignificant to me."

The Outlander surprised him. There was no hint of jealousy evident on the other man's features. He was placid and appeared at peace with himself.

The idea that he could have nothing which the other man wanted infuriated the Last Man. "Perhaps *you* are, and your fate has merely not led you there yet."

"Perhaps." Harrow's eyes narrowed slightly. "I have my doubts, though. The world you came from is diametrically opposed to mine. One of us is going to kill the other, eventually."

Carver scratched his head nervously. "Well, I'm in no hurry to get that underway. If you'd care to satisfy my, ah, morbid curiosity on the subject, however, I'd like to ask what you're waiting for. You may never get an opportunity like this again."

Harrow almost laughed, judging by the miniscule twitch of his lips. "Try not to twist my arm too much."

Carver grinned, as much in anxiety as amusement. When Harrow did not elaborate or continue, he licked his dry lips and pressed onward. "Do you know who I am?"

"I do not know your name, but I know where you come from."

"Yes, well, my name is Carver Delano. I am pleased to at last make your acquaintance."

"I am called Harrow, but you knew that already. I do not allow others to follow me, but in your case I have made exception."

"May I ask why?"

"You have a part to play in my destiny. It speaks in the voice of this very encounter. So many other men have come to me seeking death, whether they knew it or not. They came to kill me. That is a death sentence. You are obviously seeking something else."

Carver forced himself to remain calm and his voice to remain even. "Do you know what I came to you in order to seek?"

"Most likely, it was to enslave me to your Order." Harrow's reply fell like a guillotine, or perhaps the severed head which was the machine's produce. Tense seconds passed, and then he added, "I welcome the challenge. You had better be up to it. I will be moving again in a few hours. You will need rest if you expect to keep up."

Carver blinked. "Enslaved?" he asked, projecting an air of puzzlement. "I understand that your upbringing may leave you with some resentment toward me personally and my Order on the whole. But that is not what I am seeking."

"I am certain that you have personally attempted to have me killed or tried to arrange my death on many occasions. Failing that, I would guess that enslaving me would be the next best thing. Better, for you, perhaps. Otherwise, why would you be here?"

"That goes without saying. Violence is quite the problem solver, as I am sure you would agree. However, I have also sent you bribes and solicited diplomacy. I have never once attempted your enslavement. Besides, a man like you would be resistant to it. No, sir, I do not intend to bribe or solicit, much less enslave you. Rather, I came here in person hoping to come to a simple agreement."

"That is why you are alive. You are willing to offer much, and coming in person means you either trust your ability to lie implicitly, or are willing to make an honest deal; as honest as those like you are capable of. I will listen." He stretched out on the unrelenting ground, insultingly at ease, considering the proximity of a mortal enemy.

Carver schooled his features. The Outlander's speech took him aback, but he pressed on. "I would prefer to be the listener. The only thing I desire is for you to stop attacking my interests. I know nothing of what you want."

"Humanity is divided; I would mend it."

"Humanity will never change. It has always been 'haves' and 'have-nots'. Things can change for you personally. I can arrange for you, and even a number of people you know, to live in luxury forever. Your life can change. You sleep in crumbling ruins and ditches, and eat . . . whatever that thing was." He looked Harrow in the eyes. "All of this fighting and clawing and shooting can stop anytime you want."

"Peace and luxury are two things I do not desire." Harrow

looked at him, and Carver wondered if that look in the man's eye was as close as he would get to a smirk. "You'll have to do better than that."

"I wish I knew what you wanted. But in any case, haven't you killed enough people already?"

"Your slaves are just as expendable to you as they are to me."

"They may be pawns, but they are not inexhaustible. It has cost me something, all these dead ones. You have stolen a great many things from my people, as well. But I am above petty revenge."

"Your people cannot be impoverished by me."

"Certainly not, and that is why I am so willing to bribe you into an accord. Is there nothing you want, aside from continuing to murder and pillage?"

"Do you speak for the entirety of your Order?"

"Where it pertains to you, yes."

"Can you command them to release all their slaves and accept Outlanders as equals?"

A thought of Gerald Morningstar leapt unbidden into Carver's mind. "That task is rather beyond one man, I'm afraid." *Not that I would even attempt it, especially for your sake.*

"Then I fail to see how we can reach an agreement."

"Yes," Carver agreed. After a moment, he said, "Your altruism is discouraging and unfortunate. I did not really expect it of you. Is that all you are? Wounded pride?"

"You and your Order are in my way. Earth is humanity's earth. It belongs to the Next Man, not the current one. That is all."

"That little village of yours, the one you are going back to— is that your little Garden of Eden?"

The Outlander blinked, and inwardly, Carver celebrated. *Ah, struck a nerve, have I?* He pressed on. "Since our negotiations aren't going well, I must inform you that we are under satellite surveillance and I have already issued orders for that village to be annihilated, if," Carver smiled, "you decide to conclude things with hostility."

The crackling flames of the campfire reigned for a beat.

"Harming you is not my intent," Harrow said. "I'll show as much honor to this negotiation as you will. You are free to leave at any time."

Carver nodded gratefully. It galled him how much he actually trusted the other man to keep his word. There was no guile in his voice, nor any subtlety or attempt at manipulation.

Heid Acheson's voice broke into his thoughts, via data link. "The scan is complete, Lord Delano."

The Last Man rose again to his feet, and Harrow stood as well. To Heid, he mentally sent instructions. "When the data is compiled into a file, flag it as 'Do Not Open' and place it behind a triple wall of encryptions. I will look over it when I return." To Harrow, he spoke aloud. "A shame we could not reach accommodation. Things could have been very different."

Harrow's hard gaze bored into the Last Man's eye sockets. "Things *will be* very different."

Turning his back on the Outlander, Carver left the camp. For a moment, he expected the sharp pain of a blade to enter his back, but it never came. Satisfied, he set out toward the Enclave.

"Send a patrol to pick me up."

ELEVEN

When he found her in the early morning hours, she was meditating next to a stream. The filthy, polluted water, so thick and dark, crawled along the narrow, grey, rocky banks, just under the broken-down stone bridge which spanned the small waterway.

Quintain approached her silently. The woman sat in the lotus position, the backs of her hands resting on her knees. He noted that her face was serene, unlined by worry, and lit from within by a strong inner life. She was intensely attractive to him. He knew it was a cultivated effect—to project an aura of awe and dignity and even lust, so that she could exert control over others. He knew he would have to be careful.

Still, she was clean, and Quintain gave that alone a high mark for beauty. He could actually see her skin. Her hair was un-matted and hung like a shining sable curtain; her brows cultivated pristinely, her shapely lips slightly parted in relaxation. It played havoc on the young man's hormones. Outlander women typically could not afford to focus on hygiene when survival was so often at stake.

He took a cleansing breath and reminded himself that his purpose here was not merely ogling. Focusing on her aura, Quintain saw a skilled practitioner who possessed a clear and strong focus. She knew how to attune her inner self to the Eye of the Cosmos. He had never before witnessed someone make use of the Order's strand of Magick, and it fascinated him. Her methods differed subtly from his.

Silently, Quintain zeroed himself in, using secret breathing techniques and practiced internal methods to alter his consciousness and attain his own mystical state. When he encroached on the woman's meditation, it was in a spiritual, ethereal way. He used this process as a foundation of his Magick, and in a practical sense it meant that no spirit saw him as a threat. Thus, he could usually walk unnoticed among the average, spiritually blind people around him.

"You seek the concept of Nil," he said softly, so as not to startle her. Her focus remained, though Quintain was sure she could hear him. He continued in a droning monotone. "Do not make the mistake of thinking that it is a condition of indifference, apathy, indolence, or neglect. It is not any of these human inadequacies. Nor is it mere unconsciousness, a sleep-state or self-hypnosis. It is impossible to be conscious of nothingness, but all consciousness proceeds out of a Zero state. It is a state to be achieved by becoming it, and unbecoming all else.

"It is utter and absolute freedom in the true sense of its meaning—a transcendence of every possible limitation. Nil and Absolute are identical to each other."

Quintain had no trouble telling a complete stranger about the very foundations of his magickal theory. Meeting another practitioner was an honor, and Quintain hoped to exchange as much information as possible. If he could find out more about how the Order performed Magick, it might also give him an advantage when the inevitable confrontations began.

Alouine slowly, lazily opened her eyes to look at the body providing the voice which encroached on her meditation. The peaceful look of her deep meditation had yet to leave her features. She said nothing, but simply watched the boy.

"Humanity is like this bridge," Quintain said. "On one side is the abyss of the animal man, its terrors and materialism and primal urges. On the other side is Heaven, divinity, all-that-can-be."

He gestured to the ancient structure, its stones cracked and slipping, its façade wearing away under the weight of the elements and neglect. "See how this bridge is a symbol? It is broken down. It can carry no weight. To make the journey from one side to the other, humanity must be rebuilt. Do you agree?"

"My own meditations have led me to similar roads of thought," Alouine said. "You seem to know a lot."

"For an Outlander, you mean."

"I did not say that."

"You did not have to. The idea is there, all the same. Voiced or not." He stepped closer to the sitting woman. "See what we have made of this earth," he said, gesturing to the murky stream. "The pulse of it fades; its blood is thick with poison. One must be like a great and bottomless ocean to receive such a polluted stream."

Alouine followed Quintain's gestures. "I suppose that in your eyes, this is all the Order's doing?"

"Neither side is blameless. There are no innocents in this world, save for children."

The teenager sat in front of Alouine and began putting himself into the lotus position, mirroring her to put her more at ease. "Though even they have a responsibility to the earth, both Order and Outlander alike. This is humanity's earth."

Alouine smiled forlornly. "I have seen both sides of the coin, now."

"Yes, but you do not recognize the side of the coin you are currently viewing as a human one."

"I can tell you are a talented Outlander, but I have seen many talented slaves. You said yourself that the Outlanders are to blame as well. They must be subhuman to accept this, their lot in life. Why can they not rise to the level of the Last Men and take what you believe is theirs? If you are equal to me, why don't you prove it?"

The boy frowned. "The Outlanders did not do this to themselves. Even an animal would not willingly degrade the quality of its own life. Their flaw is in the fact that they allowed it to happen. They were victimized by something outside of themselves—something cruel beyond description, which devastated the old empire of the Roamers and turned it into what you see now."

Alouine did not have a rebuttal.

"It was not weapons or brute force that made a ruin of a once great empire. You know as well as I do that, at their core, the Order of the Last Men is not composed of fighters or brutes."

"That old empire could not sustain itself and it collapsed," Alouine answered. "The Last Men are the only remaining keepers of the sacred flame of knowledge."

"You are repeating an age-old lie, and you know it. You use the weakness of the victim to excuse the perpetrator. You can feel this, deep within your chest."

Alouine swallowed hard, sending another signal of pain from her bruised throat. That despicable, squirming feeling had returned.

"Lies are a powerful language, and they make possible a great number of things. I learned to understand this language long ago, because I learned that decisions we make, based on lies, are often of more direct and lasting consequence. This is a true law of humanity.

"The most powerful lies are those told about the law: that 'the only way humanity and civilization will survive is in the hands of a permanent, non-elected, hereditary structure, who self-select from their own number'. That is a lie! It is a lie that the earth cannot sustain the blooming flower of billions of our race!"

"I do not claim to know what the earth can sustain, but I am afraid that in some respects, I have been living a lie." She cast her gaze downward, into her lap.

"We all have done so. As infants, we are spoon-fed the lie. 'The wind is cold; you are limited to what your body can do' and 'all of our suffering is meaningless'. These are all lies. Some are lies that we convince ourselves of. But the wind does not have to feel cold to us. Clearly, we are not limited to what we can physically accomplish. Our suffering does not have to be meaningless." Quintain paused, and then emphatically added, "We are not destined to be slaves." He let that thought hang in the air for a breath. "Your Order is not merely the people in it. It is a system, a structure, which enslaves its members as readily as it enslaves my kin."

Alouine took a deep breath. The guru before her touched something buried inside her. Having missed the great festival of the Cremation, a festival she had experienced every year since birth, she felt a thick veil being lifted from her sight. There were many more lies in her life than she expected to see, as Quintain held a mirror to her consciousness and allowed her to see herself more clearly than she ever had alone. Alouine had never had a great appetite for cruelty, but now she felt nothing but disgust that she had once reveled in it, that her people, the Last Men, had taught her to embrace it.

"Repairing this bridge is my great work," the teenager said. "This is the grand destiny I have chosen for myself. I keep it holy, as my highest hope."

The woman swallowed but could not clear the lump in her still-sore throat. "Yes, that is quite grand," she said softly.

"Perhaps you would like to assist me?"

Alouine sighed. "I understand that the world I came from was not . . . right."

Still, an egotistical part at the core of her resisted; her pride barked and she heard it clearly. "However, I don't really see how much I can help you in your endeavor."

"You are a scion of the Order. You know the Enclaves; you know the secrets of their brand of Magick. You are capable, since you fought Harrow to a draw. The fact that he meant to kill you, and could not, is downright astounding."

The woman snorted. She hated the idea of being measured against the other warrior. "You know that demon?"

Quintain shrugged. "We crossed paths recently. His is a legend that has only begun to grow in these parts."

"Of course he couldn't kill me," she grumbled. "I told him as much. The stubborn fool insisted on trying. He is a mindless brute. That he is some kind of Outlander folk hero does not speak well for your race."

The boy chuckled once. "That's a bit harsh. I don't know the man well, but he is honorable in his own way. He is very violent, I'll grant that. It is a product of his environment, though. Those who are obedient and subservient to your Order are rewarded with the means to live. Those who are rebellious are starved to death and branded as outlaws—Outlanders. We are targets, all of us, for anyone who wishes to kill us. You can't imagine what this turmoil does to the human mind."

"You would be surprised what I can imagine," Alouine said. "That man is a monster and anything you say that lessens his responsibility is simply an excuse."

"I'm not surprised he managed to hurt your feelings. There is no difference between his thoughts and his words."

"Hurt my feelings? I'm sure he wishes he could."

Quintain gave her a queer look and held it. "Come on," he droned, incredulous.

"He did offend me," Alouine allowed. "Regardless of that, I don't see why I should help you. Circumstance forced me to leave the Enclave. Once I figure out how to remove that circumstance, I will return and reclaim my rightful place. Things will be different then."

"Until that time, you are here," Quintain replied. Alouine cast her gaze around, taking in the bleakness and desolation of her surroundings. She shivered noticeably.

Quintain rose and stepped closer to the still-seated woman, crouching down right next to her. "It really is not so bad," he said softly. "You have an opportunity now, whether you see it or not. You've left the world of the liars and entered into the world of the lie they have told, but that is the only way to see the truth."

"That makes no sense. The only way to see the truth is to live in a world of lies?"

"A world of lies or a world of liars, it makes no difference. Here, at least, you can learn what determines if a life is happy and fulfilled."

"Are you? Happy and fulfilled?"

Quintain was unashamedly evasive. He smiled. "I know that if you duck out of a challenge, that challenge will return to you in a different form. I know that we draw toward us what we fear most. I know that if we choose an immoral path, we will pay for it. The spirits make sure of that. I know that positive belief transforms what is believed in." He extended his hand to help the woman to her feet. "And I know that holding on to what we love requires letting it go."

Alouine took the boy's hand and rose. It was warm but gentle, with a firm grip.

"Come with me," he said. "We live in a fallen world, full of sickness, and we are all sick within it. Myriad spirits seek to destroy us and the fabric of our lives, most often at the behest of your people. But there are other spirits who seek to help us grow and evolve. All illness can be healed. The soul regenerates. To heal, you must face all the traumas you have repressed."

— — —

They walked for tens of kilometers. She could feel the strain in her ankles, knees, and hips, the burning in the muscles of her calves and thighs. Despite the comfort of her boots, her feet ached.

Even in the peak of physical condition, which she considered herself to be, she was unused to the constant, repetitive motion of putting one foot in front of the other for so many hours at a time. Even with a full day of walking, the pair had only covered what Quintain estimated was a third of the distance required to reach the "village" he spoke of.

They camped for the night in relative silence, each eating from their personal rations. Alouine inquired about a fire to keep them warm; Quintain put more value on stealth.

The following morning, Alouine found out why, as they passed a trio of mostly decomposed corpses lying by the side of the trail—yet more Outlanders slaughtered by violence and left as carrion for crows and foxes. Quintain stopped to pray over them and lamented that they lay unburied.

Alouine was accustomed to watching Outlanders die. She had never felt any compunction or emotion, as for so many years, she had not considered the Order's slaves to even be human. In the end, she found them good for nothing to her, and kept a few only because Thaira enjoyed having them.

Yet to see the boy praying over those skeletal remains so sincerely, taking time from his journey to lament the passing of people he never knew—it contrasted starkly with her memories of her father's funeral and all of the empty, plastic sympathy of her own kin.

This Quintain, like that demon Harrow, was a different story altogether from her experience of Outlanders. They were nothing like those slithering sycophants, some of whom had even willingly enslaved themselves to the Last Men. Neither Harrow nor Quintain had any desire to please her, or treated her as their rightful master. They chose instead to fight the natural hierarchy, damning themselves forever in the process to lives of struggle and pain.

They chose lives of anguish and conflict rather than simply bow to their superiors. In a way, it demonstrated to her the nobility and willpower each of them possessed. They were not like most of the lowly, broken-down slaves Alouine had encountered, and even broken herself, over the course of her existence.

Harrow's presence radiated with supremacy and tenacity. He did not seem to be a common monster. Still, he was unrelentingly violent, and Alouine had no interest in lowering herself to engage in battle for some Outlander's amusement. Quintain possessed an insight that was possibly in excess of her own. As much as it pained her to admit to herself, he had something she utterly lacked: empathy.

By mid-afternoon, Quintain indicated that they had almost arrived, and there was a twinge in Alouine's chest. A familiar, damnable shiver ran up her spine. She clenched her eyes shut at the sensation, and cursed in a growl.

Harrow was nearby, the murderous scourge; she felt him, felt his powerful aura marauding through the countryside. It sent her psychic senses ringing like a bell and set her chakras blazing.

She ground her teeth, but did not cease in following Quintain to the tiny hamlet.

Alouine swallowed hard. Her throat, chest and arms were still sore from the wounds he had inflicted; still, fate had sent her to this demon, and she would do what was necessary to defend herself.

Steeling her mind, she let her eyes roam the surprisingly fertile countryside. In most areas, the grey and brown colors of death and decay filled the landscape, interrupted only rarely by patches of green where life struggled through. Here, green was commonplace and only in some small places was the ground dead. What she saw when she gazed into the wide meadow caused her to skip a step.

A child in the grip of adolescence ran with delight through grass dotted by occasional flowers, all grown nearly as high as her waist. Her bright and healthy but tangled blond locks streamed out behind her, and the girl's overjoyed, tittering laughter wafted on the wind to where Alouine approached. The woman's confusion grew when she saw who the girl was running toward.

He was like an abscess in the very material of the earth, a dark blight in the meadow. Tall and strong, dressed in black, his powerful hand touched the girl briefly on the head before withdrawing.

Alouine's eyes widened. Harrow was standing on the edge of the meadow like a king surveying his kingdom. The child looked up at him with an expression of adoration. Abruptly, the young girl sprinted from his side, running once again through the swaying greenery.

Before Alouine could wonder what had caused the girl to run off so quickly, the child launched herself in the air and landed in the soft grass, rolling around and giggling. Her voice rang out. "Harrow, look," she squealed as she cart-wheeled about.

She blinked in double-take. What insanity was this? Alouine could not grasp how, or why, the girl was not afraid of such a man. A child should be able to instinctively realize that this man is capable of casual and callous murder of anyone who crossed him.

"Nina," he spoke gently, surprising the high-born woman again. "It's time to return to the village."

The girl sat up and regarded him. "Please, Harrow, not yet. Can we stay just a little bit longer?"

There was a long pause, and Harrow responded, "All right."

Alouine was utterly bewildered at the tableau playing out before her.

Suddenly, Harrow's dark head turned slightly toward her. She swallowed hard once again. Even from her considerable distance, Alouine could see that his fierce eyes had narrowed.

"Nina, stay here." Harrow closed the distance in a few seconds at a full sprint, ignoring Quintain utterly and reaching Alouine almost immediately. She stopped walking and her body unraveled, loosening and ready to respond to anything in an instant. "Leave," he said, the single word a deep growl from his chest. He held his fighting dagger in his right hand.

She was quiet for a moment. "You do not wish to do battle in front of the girl."

"That means nothing to me. I do not wish to battle you now. Leave. You don't belong here."

"Are you responsible for her?"

"I told you to leave."

Alouine's silence was heavy as her eyes searched the man's face, looking for some hint of an explanation but finding none. She nodded slowly. "Of course, Harrow."

Still regarding him in unabashed curiosity, she backed away and continued on her course to the village. She saw the look of astonishment on Harrow's face at her quiet acquiescence and departure, and his frowning chagrin at watching her enter into the village.

Quintain led Alouine through the palisade and into Mason-Dixon town, if it could be called that. Behind her scarf, the Order woman's nose wrinkled. How could these creatures live in such filth? It appeared that their very homes were held together by excrement. Primitive, shoddy, and cobbled together from every sort of material, she imagined that a stiff breeze would scatter the whole lot of them across the plain.

The boy was comfortable, and immediately struck up conversations with several of the villagers, asking nonchalantly if he could barter for some hospitality. He offered a meal in exchange for shelter for the evening and it struck Alouine as highly bizarre that though he was likely a complete stranger, the folk of the village welcomed the teen with open arms. He radiated a pure and trustworthy feeling that his fellow Outlanders accepted instantly, just as she had.

She struggled to follow the words being carelessly tossed back and forth, as the Outlanders had their own dialect and the language was so strewn with slang words and local idiosyncrasies that she felt she was on another planet. Was this how all Outlanders lived?

"Come on," Quintain said to her, breaking her away from her thoughts. "This family has offered to shelter us for the night. You're going to have to help me make dinner for them."

"They're going to trust us that easily?"

The teen gave her a hard look, the first one she had received from him. "No, they're going to trust me that easily. They don't know what to make of you. But I vouched for you, and I doubt you'll make me a liar."

Her brows knitted. "I mean them no harm."

"These people have a keen ability to discern that. It's the only reason they haven't killed us yet."

A large male Outlander led them to one of the buildings. Alouine pushed her disgust deep down into her gut. She almost preferred sleeping under the stars, even if it did mean that she'd be exposed to the wind and cold. An evening of rotten company, including lice and other parasites, was in her future, she was sure.

The interior of the dwelling was dark, but Alouine could make out the forms of some eight Outlanders squatting in it. The furnishings were near non-existent, but the floor did have a thick and relatively clean carpet of unknown origin. The brood of the man, Sharles, was not nearly as filthy or despicable as she anticipated, and though the smell was not by any means pleasant, it was not overpowering.

Sharles announced to his extended family that the pair of travelers would be welcomed as guests in that clipped and degraded Outlander speech which, in her mind, barely qualified as language. That family ran the gamut of ages and genders, from a pair of wizened old gaffers who must have been grandparents to a teeming mass of small children.

Quintain was open and friendly. He told them his name, and then said, "This is Alouine. We're going to make something tasty to eat, okay?" The younger Outlanders crowded around, and Alouine, upon prompting from Quintain, pulled down her scarf so that they could see her face. One of the children commented on her 'pretty' hair, but Sharles, and what Alouine assumed was his wife, corralled them, and the travelers went back outside to prepare the meal.

"Don't worry," Quintain said. "It's only for the night. I doubt Harrow will want to stay here for very long."

"With me around, you mean?"

"In general," he replied, untying the sack he had carried slung across his back. "But yes, especially with you here."

"This is ridiculous. Outlanders are suspicious of me. I don't know if I should find this insulting, or hilarious."

Quintain dumped a dozen potatoes out of his sack, along with what appeared to be pre-packaged salt and pepper in a series of paper packets.

"If they're anything like an average Outlander village, they've been raided for slaves repeatedly over the course of generations. Their children have probably been taken from them. Their loved ones were likely shot dead if they tried to interfere." He looked at Alouine's bare face and seemed satisfied to see her sober somewhat. "They have a right to be suspicious. You don't exactly fit in, and you could easily be a spy."

He handed her a small knife, produced from one of his many pockets. "Here, cut these up. I'll get water."

She nodded, sat, and settled in to the task. Unused to menial labor as she was, she found that she had to truly focus on it, but her thoughts tended to wander. When she had quartered one of the tubers, she set it in her lap rather than placing it back on the ground, and started on the next. A skinny, shaggy black dog startled her by walking right up and helping itself to a few pieces. She stopped to look at it for a moment, having never seen one in person, before it beat a wary retreat.

Exhaling, she took pains not to cut herself with the sharp little blade, but was grateful for the monotonous activity and chance to be alone. She thought back to the episode on the way into the village.

She knew that Harrow was a powerful man, and that alone made him dangerous to most. That he could be casually deadly was not a surprise.

Then, to see that small girl run to him, so clearly full of happiness and youthful exuberance; that certainly was surprising.

Quintain's voice found her mind again, telling her, *he is honorable in his own way*. Unbidden, her mind vaulted back to the feel of Harrow's fingers on her wrist, the insistent force of his mouth, and the sensation of his hair fisted in her hands.

She made a guttural sound in the back of her throat and picked up another potato.

Quintain returned with a pot of clean water, and built up the fire. "Hey, you're doing a pretty good job," he observed, glancing at the pile in her lap.

"What Outlander delicacy are we preparing for tonight, anyway?"

"Potato soup. I'm sure you won't like it, but around here it probably is a delicacy."

"It will be just fine," she grumbled. Quintain chuckled.

"It's not all bad. In fact, if I remember right, there's something akin to a hot spring close by. It's private, and there's no reason you shouldn't take advantage of it." He leaned in to give her hair a mock sniff. "In fact, I can think of a reason or two that you should."

"Oh? And when was the last time you were within a hundred meters of soap and water?"

Quintain shrugged. "At least my conscience is clean. Do you want to know where to bathe, or not?"

"Yes, I do," she grumped.

— — —

Evening fell on the village. After it had stewed for some time, Quintain was ready to serve the meal. The Outlanders ate messily from clay bowls. Spoons were apparently unheard of, Alouine guessed, with the exception of the ladle which Quintain had used to slop the thick gruel into servings. She decided the wait for her bath until late, when she would be less likely to be disturbed.

"It's hot," the young man said, warning the small children he served. "So be careful."

Alouine tasted the concoction warily. It was a bland mush and she did not care for the gritty texture, but it was edible, and she did not want to seem rude; not that the Outlanders were well-mannered. In fact, none of them possessed what she considered manners at all; loud slurping ensued which made her blanch, and, strangely enough, there appeared to be more dinner guests than the pair's host family for the night. The promise of free food had brought several more of the savage eaters out of the woodwork.

Quintain took it in stride. He had made enough of the soup to feed half the village. When all who had gathered had at least one helping, he sent some of the children to ask around for anyone else who wanted some of it. Indeed, the meal rapidly became a gathering of most of the villagers, some of whom brought their own fare to lend.

Harrow did not show himself. The little blond girl that Alouine had spied with Harrow earlier did show up, however. The Order princess snuck glances at her as she bounced over to Quintain and his vat of stew, proffering a handmade earthenware bowl, likely of her own design, and a gap-toothed grin. The teenage chef said something offbeat that Alouine did not quite catch as he filled her bowl. It concerned the bravery of the diners to trust such a skinny cook, and brought a chuckle from those in earshot.

A woman, behind the child, admonished her. "Say thank you, Nina."

"I know, I was getting there," the girl groused, embarrassed. She thanked the slightly older boy quietly. Alouine guessed the difference in their ages could not exceed three years. She could see no small amount of sympathy play on Quintain's face as he fought a blush himself and tried to play it cool.

As the weak sunlight faded to night and the crowd thinned, Quintain's cooking fire was built up and those Outlanders who stayed huddled closer to it. A few of the adult males passed around a jug which certainly contained some kind of rotgut alcohol. Nina, and the girl's guardian or caretaker, or nanny perhaps, had remained behind at the girl's insistence.

Alouine marveled at Quintain's ease. He regaled those around him with tales from the roads, joined in on their songs, accompanied atrociously by a man playing a tiny, box-shaped wind instrument, and even led them in a rendition or two. Clear-voiced and comfortable, the young man had a pleasing singing voice as he crooned an ancient song about 'knock-knock-knocking on Heaven's door'.

Alouine did not know any of the songs, so she simply observed. The older woman who seemed to watch over Nina was so dark-skinned that it was uncanny, and Alouine could not help but stare. When the flames flickered just right, the woman disappeared in the dark save for her teeth and the whites of her eyes.

She caught Alouine looking at her several times, much to the Last Woman's chagrin.

Finally, the woman appeared to have enough. "See something you like, sugar?" she asked, during a lull in the music.

Alouine blinked at being confronted. "I don't mean to be rude. I'm only curious."

"About what?"

"Your skin. Do you mind if I ask what happened to you? You don't look as though you were burned." Alouine had been trying to puzzle out the mystery on her own for better than an hour, so she figured that the only way she would know would be to ask.

The woman was obviously taken aback. She opened her mouth to reply, but then closed it again, and with a tight, incredulous smile, merely shook her head.

Quintain cut in. "You've never seen a black person before?"

Alouine shook her head. "Well she certainly looks black in this light, but I would venture to say that it's more of a brown color." Quintain blinked, started to say something, and cut himself off. Several of the other Outlanders, including the dark-skinned woman, fell into chuckles.

It was quite consternating. "Fine. Keep your secrets."

After she had collected herself, the woman finally answered. "Honey, nothing happened to me. I was born this way. There aren't many of us, but I'm not the only one."

Alouine nodded slowly. "I see." To all others in attendance, she clearly did not; the blond girl, Nina, whispered something to her guardian.

The woman stood and made her way closer to the spot where Alouine sat. "I'm Joanna," she said in introduction, extending her dark, rough hand. Alouine stood to shake it; at least it was a gesture she was familiar with. Joanna's grip was firm; Alouine noted her strong, calloused fingers. She put a little more into the squeeze, which seemed to satisfy the other woman.

"Alouine Morningstar," she replied. Though she was proud of her royal genetic inheritance, it struck her that stating it aloud was unnecessary and the Outlanders would probably think it highly pompous of her.

Joanna did not let go of her hand right away. "Listen here,

salt block," she said. "We come in all shades here in the Outlands. You'd better get used to it."

Not knowing what else to say, Alouine replied, "Very well." That drew another chuckle from Joanna.

"On that note, it's time to turn in. Nina, get your things. It's bedtime." Collecting the young girl with an arm around her narrow shoulders, the two of them walked off toward their home. Alouine could hear them continuing to giggle as they walked.

The episode broke up the gathering in a hurry as the other Outlanders excused themselves with murmurs and smirks, bidding each other a good night and parting ways.

"See? You're making friends already," Quintain remarked. The crinkles at the corners of his eyes told Alouine that he had found the spectacle intensely amusing.

"Oh, shut up."

TWELVE

Harrow had holed up in Joanna's hut while she and Nina met the new arrivals, but he had gotten a full report from the exuberant girl upon her return. The Outlander told himself he did not care, but still listened with rapt attention as Nina recounted the evening's events.

"And then when they shook hands, it looked like the lady wanted to check to see if any of the 'paint' rubbed off on her," the girl said. "It was pretty funny."

Harrow did not find Alouine's racism nearly as amusing, and said so.

"Relax, tough guy," Joanna said. "It was ignorance, not hatred. I can deal with ignorance." Wedged into her cushy chair with an open book on her lap—an ancient owner's manual for an extinct automobile—she was utterly nonplussed. Harrow decided to let sleeping dogs lie.

Twenty minutes later, Nina was curled contentedly next to the fire. When he was sure she was fast asleep, Harrow rose from his seat.

Joanna glanced over at him, pausing in her reading, but he cut off her questioning.

"I will return."

"Tonight?"

"Yes."

"You're not looking for trouble, are you?"

"No." Clamping down on his annoyance, Harrow strode away from the woman, leaving the comfort of her cozy hovel. He stood outside, deeply inhaling the chilled night air. Extending his senses, he spotted the village patrol on their rounds at the palisade. Otherwise, there was no one outside.

Harrow respected Joanna for her skills and valued her services. He came to her for her most ambitious work and paid accordingly— he loved to challenge her, and the canny woman relished it.

The warrior had known that the artisan was infertile since they had met; females in the Outlands did not stay unclaimed by men if not for similar factors. That Harrow had brought her a daughter to adopt had only drawn them closer together.

Harrow knew that there were murmurs in the village that he and the blacksmith were lovers, but he dismissed them as faux drama created by sedentary people. Joanna had needed Nina, and Nina had needed her, and Harrow had brought them together. The thought inwardly gave him intense pride; he drew much strength from it.

A low growl of irritation formed in the back of his throat. Harrow never expected Quintain to be so remarkably bereft of common sense as to lead an admitted Order member to a place where she could prove catastrophic for innocent Outlanders. He had been extra careful and taken a winding, confusing path back to the village, not wanting any of his numerous enemies to see Nina, let alone to associate him with the child. It was not acceptable for Alouine to get the idea that he might have a weakness, and he dreaded nothing so much as putting Nina in harm's way.

Harrow made his way out of the village, pausing only to let the bleary-eyed patrol know that he would be coming back within a day. Alouine's presence had quickly become an annoyance to him. He loathed the fact that she had the ability to mock him, to stand before him, to oppose him and yet live, but the very idea that she possessed that kind of power sent a dizzying rush through his veins.

Kissing her had not left him with a thirst for battle or a desire for blood. Instead, it had left him with the single desire he had nearly acted on. Once his hand had clasped around her wrist and he had felt the warm throb of her pulse under her skin, he had nearly lost his legendary sense of restraint.

Harrow felt his lip curl as he recalled the way she watched him, laughed at him. Of course, he hadn't expected any less.

He needed to be alone.

The would-be Next arrived at the spot after ten minutes of walking.

The spring was not naturally occurring, but it was hidden by foliage and underbrush. A malfunction with the Order's overly redundant and highly automated electrical power-generation grid at that substation kept the water from a broken pipe hot, but not scalding. It ran by the tens of gallons into a fold in the land, forming a steaming oasis. The rugged terrain was inaccessible to most of the villagers, and they had learned since birth to distrust anything built by their enemy. Harrow preferred that place over any other.

He began to disrobe.

— — —

Alouine's steps stopped short of where Quintain had told her she could find the place. She could already see the mists from the hot spring. She inhaled the clean scent of water and dense vegetation and savored it for a moment. The place was easy to find, following the power lines. She moved carefully and silently, making her way around an outcropping of rocks before coming to the water's edge. Her movements came to a sudden stop and her eyes widened in shock.

Only fifteen feet away, Harrow stood in the pool up to his waist. He dove under and swam a short distance before resurfacing again and bringing his hands to his face to wipe away the excess water. Alouine could see the faint scars that crisscrossed his shoulders and hands. His beard was newly trimmed; she glimpsed a tiny mirror and a pair of shiny, steel scissors on a nearby rock.

Among Order members, the wearing of a beard was a barbaric practice. However, she learned that, among Outlanders, the presence of facial hair was the difference between being a man and being a boy.

Groomed and cropped short as it was, Alouine did not find Harrow's beard as repulsive as the undoubtedly insect-ridden, matted and unruly manes she encountered on the faces of the adult males in the village. She doubted that Harrow was grooming for the sake of appearances, however. He was nothing if not efficient. She saw the tactical sense of keeping it short.

Harrow's clothing and weapons sat in a neat pile, including the steel bracers and greaves which explained the hardness of his extremities. Her wrists and forearms still felt tender from the impact of that armor.

The man ran his fingers through his hair. She did not move or speak but remained firmly rooted to the spot to watch.

Until he began to float on his back; then she had the decency to turn. Somehow, her cresting wave of embarrassment gave her away to him.

— — —

Harrow righted himself in the water, furious that he could be surprised yet again. He had not expected anyone else there, of all places, and had dialed SIMON's sensitivity down to its minimal setting in order to relax.

His sharp eyes found her quickly, skulking behind a rock, yet— the set of her jaw, her turned-away head—she looked away not in disgust nor a misplaced sense of decency. To Harrow's strange relief, she averted her eyes in embarrassment. He discomfited her.

His heart contracted against his will. She indicated warring emotions by the look on her face and the set of her body. Something inside her was rife with conflict at seeing his nude form. The thought was pleasing, but more than that. The woman—damnable, insolent, intolerable as she was—something about her called to him, not with words but with something outside of language.

Still, he swam closer to where he had laid his clothing and weapons. "You've caught me off guard twice today."

She crossed her arms over her chest but refused to look at him. "By chance, I assure you. I won't rely on petty chance in order to defeat you," she said. "I came here for the same purpose you apparently have, and no other. . . Though I am starting to think that my being here was arranged."

He said nothing. Of course Quintain had arranged it by telling the woman where she could find a hot bath, suspecting that Harrow would be there. Still, he was impressed that Alouine was able to adapt so quickly to the Outlands. It could not be an easy transition. The Outlands tested the sternness of the soul, and she had not starved or frozen to death as yet.

Alouine smirked, likely realizing the boy's deviousness herself. "In the spirit of mercy," she said, breaking the moment's repose, "I'm prepared to offer you an armistice for the evening. By all means, attend your business. I will return when you are finished."

Harrow scoffed. "Mercy, is it? Keep your 'mercy'. I hadn't planned to leave until morning." In truth, until that moment he was undecided as to where he would spend the night.

She clenched her fists and the heat of indignation burned on her cheeks. He watched the disappointment and annoyance curl her lip into a sneer.

I have her, Harrow thought to himself. "You seem a bit out of sorts. Maybe you're surprised to see an 'ape' in a bath."

"I admit my shock. It seemed more likely to see you wallowing in a shit field or a mud hole."

"Yet, I am not," he said as he walked through the water toward her. As he did so, he climbed the shallow slope and his body rose from the steaming pond. "I'll have you admit something else," he murmured.

She clenched her jaw and did glance at him, just as his narrow waist left the water. Her blush deepened as she took in his shoulders and chest, honed for throwing punches. "What are you doing, fool?"

"Look at me and admit that I am as human as you are." Harrow lifted his knee and stepped completely out of the water. Steam rose from his flesh. The light of the moon and stars struggled through the incessant clouds and illuminated puckered scars, which ran over his form in a tapestry of years of abuse and strife. The cold air gave him gooseflesh and hardened his nipples.

To Alouine's credit, she kept her eyes level with his. Her outrage was palpable; nevertheless, Harrow pressed on.

"What you see is a man. You spoke to me before of airs and pretense. Here, I have none, not even the mask of clothing to hide myself. On the other hand, you've worn a mask each time we've met." His gaze hardened. "Your so-called 'civilization' is a mask. Your bigotry is a mask. It hides who you truly are as much as your veil does. No matter what you pretend, you are what you are, and nothing more."

Alouine matched the stern look in Harrow's eyes. She refused to back down, but his words hit a nerve and she flinched.

She tried to turn the tables, and changed the subject. "What about the mask you wear in front of your daughter? To anyone else, it's obvious that you're capable of any amount of violence at any time. You're a marauder, a pirate! How can you pretend to be a doting, caring father after everything you've done?"

Harrow's face became bland. "She isn't my daughter."

The woman's brows knitted into a frown. "Then what is she to you, some kind of sick pet? Or are you her glorified nanny?"

He turned around, giving Alouine a showcase look at his backside as he walked back into the water. "Nina is a butterfly, and needs no excuses. Besides, children need time for play to be happy."

"It's hard to imagine you as a child, let alone engaged in play."

"Do I strike you as happy?" the Outlander asked, over his shoulder.

He realized that he was showing her the large bruise she had inflicted on his lower back. His kidney would need a week's healing, still. He had nearly forgotten it, but to his irritation, her presence reminded him.

After a moment, Alouine remarked, "Butterflies are all but extinct, you know."

"Innocence still exists."

Glancing over his shoulder, he let her observe him and see with her own eyes what he willingly endured for the future of his people. Nina was his one cherished window into what was good in life. There was not an inch of his original skin on his back, so crossed with scars from cuts, abrasions, punctures and burns. His life was indeed one of agony and struggle. Yet, he could regard a small child, one who was not of his own blood, with tenderness. No animal could do as much. He let her ruminate on that. Nearly a full minute passed as the woman regarded the man.

"You chose to be what you are," Alouine said softly at last.

"As only a human can," Harrow replied, before submerging and surfacing again, facing her.

Dropping down into a squat, Alouine visibly digested his words. He saw it pained her, but to her credit she said, "Very well. You are no ape. Does that validation please you?"

"Whether or not it pleases me doesn't matter. However, it does mean that as long as you do not repeat your attempt to stand in my way, I have no desire to fight you again."

"I did not appreciate your sneaky, underhanded tactics in our first duel anyway. It was an ending to the bout utterly shorn of honor."

"You kissed me, didn't you?"

"What? I certainly did not!"

"There's no need for modesty. You're resourceful. I admired that."

"You admit that it did affect you."

"It was the first time anyone attempted that maneuver on me. I have the good fortune of possessing a steep learning curve, though, so it won't work a second time. All the same, it nearly turned the fight for you."

He had caught her. There was nothing to say. If she took the compliment it would mean admitting that she had initiated the kiss. Her pride fought her, desperately.

"Whatever you are, you are a cunning creature. But you started it. All of it, the fight, the . . . where it led—everything."

"Again, modesty."

Satisfied that he was safe from attack, at least from her and for the moment, he slowly began to allow the hot water to seep into his joints and muscles. Tilting his head back, he let his eyes slide shut and slowly began to open what he imagined was a valve in his body, in order to let some of the tension of constant warfare trickle out.

Alouine watched him for several moments as he gave up all fear or suspicion of her. She fumed in irritation, which pleased him. Scoffing, she seemed to call his bluff and began stripping away her scarf and unzipping her coat.

"There is room enough," she mumbled just sufficiently loud for the man to hear. "I'll not have you keep me from this opportunity."

"You're free to do as you please." He made his way back over to the edge of the pond nearest his possessions, refusing to even glance at the woman as she became nude and slipped into the water, hissing softly as her skin, grown accustomed to the cold, was forced to adapt to the heat.

She sighed her pleasure. "Thank you," she murmured as she submerged herself to her chin.

Harrow asked, "For what?"

"Allowing me the peaceful use of your pond."

"I don't count this place among my possessions."

"All the same, you were here first, and you are sharing."

Harrow decided not to belabor the point that he could not share what he did not possess. The pond felt even warmer now that they were both nude and within its waters. He forced his mind to fix on something other than the proximity of her naked flesh, and internally granted that the task was difficult.

Alouine tucked herself into a ball under the water. She glanced over at him as he rested his arms on the rocky ledge behind him. Head back, throat exposed, he watched his surroundings through heavy-lidded eyes.

She attempted to relax as well. Still, she was not yet prepared to sink into companionable silence. "This place is wonderful," she observed. The sound and smell of clean, flowing water and the haze of steam, combined with a chorus of nighttime insects. It was a lush place, unique in the Outlands, packed with life and warmth.

"Indeed." He was not feeling especially loquacious, and for good reason. The woman's voice was among the most beautiful things he'd heard, when she was not using it to express arrogance or condescension. There was a gripping sensation in his loins that he was utterly unaccustomed to.

"A shame that I had no opportunity to pack thoroughly before

I left," Alouine remarked in hindsight. "What I wouldn't give for a bar of soap."

Harrow sat up slowly, his dark hair hanging in his face. "The Outlands aren't completely bereft of luxury." He turned and began rooting through his pile of things. From a wax paper packet, he produced a small lump of soap, stolen weeks ago from the kit of some Order outpost. Using his dagger, he flensed off some shavings and, holding them in his palm, he offered them in Alouine's direction, all the while not looking directly at her.

She blinked and swam toward him, walking along the slick surface at the bottom of the pond. Her fingers were forced to touch his palm to retrieve the offering; a jolt ran through him at the tiny contact. "You have my thanks," she said softly as she backed away.

He nodded, eyes closed.

Alouine quickly made use of the soap and Harrow's decency as she exposed her body to the cold air. Perhaps it was rather his stubbornness; he had not snuck a glimpse at her, even once. He was certainly not asexual, but he lived by will alone, refusing all else.

"You accuse me of too much modesty, yet you won't even look at me. Are you secretly shy?"

"I don't have any interest in voyeurism," came Harrow's measured response.

"But it's only voyeurism if you let it excite you," Alouine blurted. She immediately shut her mouth again.

"Then you'll understand why I choose to mind my own business," Harrow muttered, with what he hoped was an air of finality.

Alouine would not let it rest. "You are attracted to me."

"That goes without saying."

"The feeling is mutual," she said in a voice just above a whisper.

Harrow said nothing for several moments. The pleasant sound of nocturnal life reverberated through the surroundings as he tried his damnedest to figure out what to say. She was only confirming his suspicions, he noted. It was not as though she was inviting him to . . .

"Forging a peace is enough for one evening," Harrow said. "I'm going to retire for the night." He climbed out of the water and gathered his things. A taunting growl from the deepest corner of his heart rattled its chains and berated him for cowardice—a woman, of all things, chasing him away yet again.

THIRTEEN

Finally safe again within the Enclave, the exhausted Carver could do little more than throw himself onto his couch and snooze. He ordered Armiluss to guard his door and shut off all channels through his data link, after leaving instructions to be woken in an hour by a servant with coffee.

Finally, groggily, he rose and swallowed a large gulp of the liquid, banishing the serving girl and reopening his channels. "Has the file been screened?" he asked Heid Acheson, via data link, with no preamble.

"It has, my lord," the vassal replied.

"Very well, transfer it to my server." Sliding a panel back from the top of his desk, he revealed the holographic projector embedded beneath. With a slight tap on the screen, he transferred the file through his own data link to the server.

Despite the instantaneous download, Carver dallied. His muscles were sore from his trek, and the area between his shoulder blades throbbed. An ache stretched up from that knot of muscle through the back of his neck and reached into his cranium. The business was becoming physically painful, in addition to its frustration and stress.

"Now, you will delete all copies," he ordered.

"They are gone."

"They had better be. I will be making sure of that." With a few mental exercises, he summoned Armiluss into the room. "Heid,

I'm closing this channel again. Once the device is analyzed, you will be required to build a working model. Prepare the facilities to do so."

"Yes, sir," the resigned voice of his vassal replied. "There is one more matter to report."

Carver rolled his eyes and pinched the bridge of his nose to stave off his annoyance. "What is it?"

"The traces are faint, but the Bureau of Informational Awareness reports that a Mark account signal has been triangulated to the," he could not disguise his distaste, "Outlander warren, the one indicated in Operation Order Six. Its RFID signature is identical to that of Lady Alouine Morningstar's Mark."

"She's in the village?" Carver asked himself softly, unintentionally projecting the thought by data link.

"It appears so."

This annoyed Carver further, but he pasted over his surprise an unconcerned façade. "Very well, I will deliberate on this. Stay available."

He closed the channel and rubbed his face tiredly. She was so desperate to escape his clutches, the petulant woman had run from the Enclave and her people. That was no small insult.

His lips pursed as he considered. She had undermined his scheme; she belonged to him, and her sojourn in the wilderness was, in Carver's mind, akin to theft. If she would not go along with his plans and bend to his will, she was useless to him.

That did not matter. If he could not have her, no one would. It accelerated his original plans but was no great loss. Alouine was a traitor and a fool for spurning him. Soon, she would be utterly meaningless and he would be a living god.

His mind made up, he summoned Armiluss to his shoulder and wordlessly commanded the desk projector to display a three dimensional image of Harrow's brain-augmenting microcomputer and the reality-defying quantum device which capped it. Carver was no master of mathematics, nor was he possessed of engineering or technical expertise, but he recognized immediately the brilliance of the design.

Armiluss stared at it, his expression blank and eyes hooded.

"Soon, my young friend, our ambitions will be realized. It's time to go over the next phase of my plan."

"Yes, master," the Lictor murmured.

"This device is a ten-terabyte per second computer, which our foe has designed and built for us. It allows the enemy to bend reality at the quantum level. We shall steal this power from him. What he believes to be his personal triumph will be the very thing we use to destroy him. First, we will construct one of these devices for you, and then, one for my use. When the time comes, you will use its power to remove all the impediments which keep us from what is rightfully ours. After that, I will use mine to take the next step."

"The Incarnation Matrix," Armiluss filled in.

"That's correct," Carver said, tired but pleased. "We will shatter the ceiling of glass that stifles our ascent to immortality. The High Circle members are old and weak, choking on the dust of their traditions. While you use this device to destroy them, and the Outlander, I will use my own to decipher the key to incarnating and reincarnating at will." He paused for effect. "Infinite bliss will be ours, Armiluss. Even if we tire of it, we will be able to create new bodies and manifest physically as we please.

"I cannot think of a more fitting reward for you, my friend, for your untiring devotion and loyal service and your unyielding endurance of the pain mandated by your unfortunate and mean birth."

Armiluss was born as nothing. It was only the constant assaults and degradations which made him useful. *In a way, this is the highest blessing a Last Man can bestow on a despicable slave: a purpose.*

Armiluss maintained his blank stare. "I am forever your servant, Lord Delano. My only fear is never being able to repay your kindness."

"It was been a long and dark road for you, son. The light at the end of this bleak cavern is finally coming into view." He turned his chair to face the much larger man. "We must achieve the promise of apotheosis, together."

"Yes, my lord."

"First things first." He reopened his data link channels, broadcasting to his entire Circle and Armiluss. "Heid Acheson, issue Operation Order Six to the Death's Head teams, and proceed with Plan A. I want that whole area to be the wasteland it is supposed to be, within an hour. Tell them to wipe out every living thing within five kilometers"

"What about Lady Morningstar?" Heid prompted.

"I will not repeat myself."

"Yes sir," Heid said softly. "It will be done."

— — —

Quintain slept in a fetal ball on the floor of the sheet metal and adobe home. The youth was vitally connected to the world, especially in his dreams. Before he had welcomed the familiar embrace of unconsciousness, he had performed a ritual designed to free him from earthly attachments, and to open the portal between his waking, conscious mind and his deeper, subconscious one. He focused his mind on the vibratory frequency of matter and began the exercises to slowly tune in to ever higher frequencies. Eventually, his consciousness broke free of his body with a snap and the keening hum faded into the background of his immaterial surroundings.

It was his way of securing the area. The astral realm was one of malleability, a subconscious world into which the young man projected an etheric image of himself. The spirit form, radiating a soft, peach-colored glow, stood over his sleeping, physical body. Quintain's projection smiled as he looked over the similarly sleeping forms of his Outlander host family. They were safe and warm and well-fed. The shelter they offered was paid for.

A silver thread extended from the top of the projection's head—an extra-dimensional anchor which kept Quintain's consciousness tethered to his physical body. Without effort, he wound out some slack, and floated through the wall of the dwelling. He was free, and walls could not hold his spirit. Because of that skill, Quintain feared neither imprisonment nor even torture. On the astral plane nothing physical could touch him.

His body rested from its labors, but Quintain's spirit never tired. The etheric world reflected the physical one, as if a thick fog had descended over everything real. It possessed its own dangers, but the young man had been astral projecting for years and knew how to defend himself from hostile intelligences, such as those which the dark sorcerers of the Order employed.

During his patrol of the village, he found none of those demonic spirits preying on the sleeping people. So instead, he searched out individuals whose minds and spirits were plagued by turmoil, the malevolent beings of their own design. With these, he would do battle until dawn, unknotting the emotional and psychological issues that afflicted his fellow humans.

Quintain did it with no thought of reward or even recognition. He was happy if just one person was able to wake with a feeling of clarity or a new sense of purpose.

A particular ease permeated the sleeping forms of Harrow's friends, Joanna and Nina, as he visited their dreams. Harrow had an intuitive ability to drive away the same kinds of demons and nightmares Quintain labored against. These two women slept soundly, knowing that Harrow was near and that he would destroy anything which might seek to harm them.

Satisfied, Quintain followed his silver cord back to his sleeping body. However, a feeling of nausea crept over his astral form.

It could only mean one thing. Trouble was coming. He concentrated on the convergences of astral energy and prepared to jump across time and space.

— — —

Harrow dried himself of excess water and dressed, then girded his body with armor and weapons as Alouine continued to enjoy the bath. She wondered at his actions. Was he arming and armoring himself as a matter of course, or was it a psychological shield against what could have become intimacy? He could not often have an opportunity to enjoy a secluded interlude with a nude woman and she marveled at his iron bonds of self-control. Strangely, she even found herself trusting him. The way that Harrow's word of honor meant more to him than his life— to say nothing of petty physical urges— reminded her of her father's steely resolve.

When he had finished strapping on his armored bracers and greaves, and packing his possessions into the innumerable pockets and pouches which covered him, he turned back to the steaming pond to excuse himself and bed down.

She was utterly relaxed, leaning backward, the water lapping at her breasts. Even now he did not gaze directly at her, but eyed her with his peripheral vision. He opened his mouth to speak, but was cut off.

A softly glowing apparition appeared, floating just over the pool itself. Alouine started slightly, and out of reflex, sank into the water to her chin. It took both of them a moment to realize that the ghostly phantasm subtly mirrored Quintain's form. The boy cast a gentle yellow-orange glow over the pool. His arms were extended, palms showing, and a thin thread of silver wire connected his head to the sky, touching something neither Harrow nor Alouine could see.

"My friends," the apparition spoke, "I have sensed a powerful and hostile intent toward us. Something terrible is happening which can never be undone. Please return to the village."

Harrow locked eyes with Alouine for a single moment, but otherwise neither wavered nor hesitated. In a flash, he was gone, leaving her to marvel at the speed with which he passed through the rugged terrain in a full sprint, not crashing roughly into the underbrush, but moving at top speed. The trees and vines almost scrambled to get out of his way, swept aside by some unseen force, and his booted feet found firm purchase on treacherously rocky soil. Whatever power Harrow had used to bend the laws of reality to turn the tide of their duel, he made use of again—that time more blatantly than the last.

Left behind, Alouine rose from the water and hurried into her clothing. "What is it? What exactly did you feel?" she asked Quintain's etheric projection. Though the image was watching her dress, she did not feel self-conscious. In that ghostly state, separated from his physical body, Quintain projected an aura of saintly innocence, far removed from the desires of the flesh.

"I do not yet know," was the spirit's reply. It sounded far away, as though Quintain were calling to her from a great distance. "Something awful is coming. Please hurry." He did not sound anxious or frightened, but insistent.

Alouine pulled on her boots and glanced to the spot where Harrow had disappeared as she fastened the tabs over her shins. "He rushes off to battle without thought or hesitation."

"Harrow fights for humanity's sake. We must do no less. Fear is failure, Alouine, so be thou fearless. Those who tremble at flame, flood, and shadow hath no part in the almighty power of God."

She closed her eyes for a moment. The path was before her, and she would do her part.

"Where he goes, all of humanity will follow," Quintain's spirit projection mused, before disappearing with the soft glow.

Quieting her conscious thoughts, she focused her psychic energy and began to run, following behind Harrow and leaving a dark, steaming piece of paradise behind her, echoing with unvoiced feelings and promises.

— — —

In their hut, Joanna and Nina awoke to a strange vibrating sensation.

"I love thunder," the girl mumbled, still half-asleep. "It reminds me of Harrow."

"It isn't thunder." Joanna shook Nina's shoulder roughly. "Something is happening." Pulling the sleepy young girl up to her feet, she tugged her wobbly form to the door.

When she opened it, her worst fears were realized. Three of the Order's tilt-rotor-driven military aircraft approached from the south. She knew from experience that each carried a platoon of soldiers—if the Order's murderous, merciless thugs deserved such an appellation. They raided the village once again. One of the aircraft was bad enough; she had never seen three of them at once.

One of the helicopter/airplane hybrids flew in low and fast over the small collection of huts. Each one had multi-barreled rotary cannons in a semi-spherical mount, like an inverted dome, under the nose. Because of their fixed wings and dual-tilting rotors, they were very fast but also maneuverable and capable of hovering.

The Outlanders referred to them as 'Dragons', and Joanna had always thought it an apt, if inaccurate, description. They flew, spat fire, and spread terror. But the metal beasts were unthinking and had human pilots, gunners, and crew.

Their noise vibrated the walls of her home with a deep thumping, but some noise-dampening technology allowed them a measure of stealth. Nina was right—they were reminiscent of distant thunder. The Outlanders of the village lived in constant fear of those metal behemoths, in no small part due to their ability to appear out of nowhere and with no warning.

As the planes buzzed the village, one came around and its cannon opened fire, its five barrels blazing at over one thousand revolutions per minute. The bright orange stream of hot projectiles poured out so fast, it resembled a solid line. Hundreds of shells fell on the palisade, rending it, sending sparks and glowing fragments careening into the night, and chopping the nighttime patrol into tiny gobs. Nina began to scream, and Joanna clamped her powerful hand over the child's mouth.

Joanna knew that the pilots of those ships could not have possibly heard Nina's cry, but they responded as though they had. She threw the child onto the ground just outside the door and collapsed on top of her as that deadly hail of bullets zipped through her house and workshop. Hot sparks and tiny, sharp pieces of the metal roof ate into Joanna's back, making her clench her teeth and eyes, and grimace from the burning pain. Something was different. The Dragons had never fired directly into an Outlander dwelling before.

It was not a slave raid. They were here to exterminate everyone.

— — —

Alouine knew how to move fast. Using her ancient psychic arts, she could change her center of gravity automatically, to root her feet to the earth or glide across the ground as if weightless.

Still, she could not close the distance to Harrow as he sprinted toward the village. His head-start notwithstanding, the warrior ran with like a champion athlete, but his sheer strength could not account for the raw speed he attained.

Some irresistible force impelled him, as if the hand of God or some spirit of the wind pushed him from behind. She vaguely wondered if he would burn up all his strength in the run and not have any left for fighting when he arrived.

She watched as he leapt clear over the palisade, a wall nearly three meters high, and disappeared from sight for a few brief moments. Following, she ran up the side of the rough, rusted barrier. Human legs alone could not account for such a leap. His ability to cheat the laws of physics could not explain the explosive power needed to propel Harrow to such a great height. The trail he left from the pond almost seemed as though the Outlander had rockets strapped to his boots.

"Impossible," she muttered to herself. The feat left her stunned, set her mouth agape, and brought her all-out gallop to a haltering trot.

The palisade was easy for her to climb. Still, it cost her several long seconds hopping from foothold to foothold over the chaotic wall of metal.

When she reached the apex of the wall, the scene which greeted her took her aback. Several of the structures in the tiny hamlet were burning, thoroughly raked through with automatic cannon fire. Three tilt-rotor aircraft circled like horrible birds of prey, two of which appeared to be coming in for a landing, the third taking up a holding pattern to cover the others.

The weapons and equipment of the Death's Head battalion were more Thaira's forte than hers; still, she recognized immediately the direful situation.

Part of her tugged her backward, crying out for her to run, to flee into the wasteland and leave the Outlanders to their fates.

Then she caught sight of Harrow again. He had changed course and had blazed a laser-straight line to the first airship in his line of sight, approaching it from behind, tearing free an assault rifle slung from his back. The wide ramp at the back of the aircraft lowered as the ship made a slow descent in order to deliver its cargo of ruthless soldiery.

A heavy machinegun's tripod stood bolted to the ramp itself. Alouine blinked in disbelief as the insane warrior charged directly into its line of fire.

The machine-gunner did not expect anyone to leap into the back of the aircraft, descending from five meters up. The superhuman feat and Harrow's hostile, alien appearance gained the Outlander a valuable advantage.

The young gunner panicked and pushed down on the back of the gun, forcing the barrel upward, as he tried to match the muzzle of the weapon to the shocking new threat. However, Harrow stomped on the long tube of metal, caught it in the high arch of his thick-soled boot, and forced the muzzle back down to the floor.

The long weapon swiveled once again on the fulcrum of the tripod. The top of the trigger assembly smashed hard into the young soldier's chin and he fell backward.

Harrow's thumb toggled the rifle to the fully automatic position. SIMON projected a swath of red into his visual field in an arc which took in the entire cavernous hold of the aircraft, and seating the butt stock of the weapon against the junction of his shoulder and chest, he pressed and held the trigger.

The weapon blazed, spitting fire and thunder and jacketed lead. The noise was incredible in the confined space of the Dragon. Harrow's ears rang. Still, he kept shooting, walking the muzzle of the gun from one enemy to the next. The machine gunner was first. His hands on the gun put forth such grip that the bucking, vibrating machine was an extension of Harrow's own will, braided with his arms, welded to his shoulder.

He let it rip, all thirty rounds in a few seconds. The enemy wore armor on their torsos. Hitting them in the face required a steady aim—not a viable option at six hundred rounds per minute. Harrow could only point the weapon and guide its muzzle along a rough track. The long full-auto burst was intended to freeze them in place and steal their ability to fight back. The key to fighting a Dragon was to fend off its talons and fangs long enough to get your blade into its heart.

These men of the Death's Head were not soldiers in the traditional or normal sense. They were utterly emotionless and possessed infinite wells of artificial sang-froid. To do their fighting for them, the Last Men created the ultimate design—a chemical soldier. Unfeeling, robotic zombies in battle dress.

Still, the spraying bullets knocked the soldiers off their feet and put them off their stride.

The lead projectiles slammed into bodies and bulkheads and careened off, flattening or breaking into tiny whizzing fragments where they struck a sloping surface. Many of the missiles slammed into the metal partition which separated the cockpit from the hold. Where the rounds struck it, they punched through, leaving small, neat holes.

The conscious part of Harrow, the human part, that part of him which could appreciate beauty, untangle the knots of mathematics, or engage in civil conversation, disappeared. He separated and banished it. If he survived, he would find it again. Drawing KA-BAR from its sheath, he lunged to the attack just as the metal Dragon lurched hard to the right.

SIMON read the tide of battle as Harrow maneuvered through the listing body of the aircraft, the gleaming edge of his long dagger flashing in the red light.

The Death's Head men had ice in their veins and were precise, each one a finely tuned and carefully honed instrument of destruction. As capable at hand-to-hand combat as they were at tactics and marksmanship, they moved as one, presenting the Outlander with a ring of tungsten-steel fighting knives, and cruel, serrated bayonets affixed to the muzzles of their guns.

They lacked Harrow's fury and complete, overwhelming intensity. He was only one man to the soldiers, to be slain before moving on.

The soldiers were everything to Harrow. Nothing in the universe mattered more than killing them there and then. He stabbed men through their eye sockets, batted their blades aside with his armored sleeves, cut their throats, slashed through the flesh of their thighs, and opened their internals to the air. The very idea that this area was once a transport vehicle, he dispelled by his will and replaced with his own reckoning—a charnel house. Harrow wanted to sow the aircraft with a feeling of inescapable doom, of being trapped in a metal coffin.

Gore slicked KA-BAR's handle and he nearly lost his grip of the weapon while pulling it free from a soldier's face.

No more could he even conceive of himself as Harrow. He was now *Slayer of Enemies*.

Blood washed over him, the sacrament, and the power over life and death that only the fates and the man at war can command. One long scream of fury pounded in his already ringing ears, and the last tiny spark of a thinking being wondered vaguely if he was imagining the bloody shout, or if, in the catharsis of unrestrained bloodletting, it actually issued forth from his throat.

The ship's pilot lacked armor. Hit by a stray bullet in the back, spasms rocked him as he died. Before the copilot could react, the man's body slumped onto the airplane's controls, sending the entire metal monster listing toward the earth. Warning claxons howled as the vehicle careened from its flight-path and the metal airship became a barge to the underworld.

Synthetic webbing hung from the walls and ceiling of the aircraft's passenger compartment, and the instant Harrow received the sensation of falling through the soles of his feet and his inner ears, SIMON sprung his legs like coils. He vaulted for that material suspended on the left side of the hold. Grasping it with all the strength of his left hand and the flat of KA-BAR's blade, he pulled his body to it and held fast as the entire airplane fell like a meteor from the sky.

FOURTEEN

Alouine ran into the village proper and searched for Quintain while the first Dragon fell from the sky. Harrow had only leapt into it moments before, and she could see the long, strobe-like muzzle flash from the inside.

She mentally berated the Outlander warrior. For anyone else, his actions would be foolishly suicidal. Indeed, as the plane tilted to the side, those actions appeared to have a real and imminent chance of claiming Harrow's life. He must have killed or grievously wounded the pilot already.

Her level of calm surprised her. Indignant and offended that the people who only hours ago had offered her hospitality and shelter were now bleeding and crying, she nonetheless held to a certain kind of surety. Harrow seemed to know exactly what to do. When the best option was to attack, he attacked suddenly and with all the impetus and ferocity he could muster. When the *only* option was to attack, the warrior's incredible strength and fury multiplied exponentially.

The aircraft banked hard to the right, the tips of its rotor striking the earth and cleaving large furrows into the rocky soil. It hung in the air in that fashion for a moment, the other rotor threatening to flip the entire plane onto its top in an almost comical pirouette. Just at its zenith, the left rotor engine gave out. The ship collapsed onto its belly with a groaning wallop, throwing soil and debris in all directions.

Indecision washed over Alouine, and in her frustration, she wished it were manifest so that she could strangle it. Morbid curiosity warred with a keen craving for self-preservation.

This is not my fight, she reminded herself. *Still, I have to know if that man will survive.*

She stepped toward the wreckage. A chunk of metal, twenty centimeters across, whizzed by her, missing by a mere meter as it skipped over the landscape, thrown by the force of many tons of steel impacting the earth. If Harrow was alive, she felt as though she should try to extricate him from the twisted hulk. His act of valor demanded nothing less. However, as she forced the will to move into her feet, a voice invaded her mind.

"Stop, please," Quintain's thoughts spoke to her consciousness. He sounded desperate and pleading, even in telepathy. "I feel that Harrow is alive. Others need your help far more. Please, help us!"

Alouine stopped, and Quintain gave direction. "Head to your left, forty meters beyond the two houses you see there. Hurry!"

Sparing a final glance at the smoking airplane crash, she spun left and ran.

Both houses she ran past were smoking ruins, thoroughly perforated with holes. A smallish man or woman lay in a doorway—a disfigured heap of bloody flesh—the cannon rounds having torn it to ribbons of smoking gore.

Revulsion turned Alouine's stomach. She smelled feces and burnt, meaty, metallic blood. The stench was unbearable. She had killed before, but never a mechanistic, slaughterhouse rendering.

More fire rained from the sky a hundred meters distant. Alouine tore her gaze away from the corpse and ran on.

Quintain, Joanna and little Nina were frantically trying to uncover something buried under the collapsed roof of the artificer's workshop. A heavy support beam, chopped through by cannon rounds, had fallen across the canvas-covered crate.

Whatever it was, the Outlanders held it of the utmost import. Alouine crossed around Quintain and Joanna from behind. "Move over," she demanded.

Chakras blazing with psychic might, she whirled to build momentum, then kicked the beam with her heel, driving it out of the way. It crashed to the floor and took the canvas covering with it, exposing a long, olive-green box. The entire structure lilted violently but did not collapse. Flipping the latches and throwing the lid open, a hand-held artillery piece emerged in Joanna's grasp.

Blinking, Alouine could only watch with dismay.

"Harrow isn't the only one who can hunt Dragons," Joanna remarked as she positioned the tubular device on her right shoulder, grimacing under its unwieldy weight. "Grab that case, there," she told Quintain, and he picked up a wooden box from within the crate.

"Where did you get this?" Alouine asked.

"From Harrow. It's a recoilless shell launcher he found in an old armory. Your Order once used these to wage war on our kind. It's time to return the favor."

The woman kneeled at the corner of her hut and positioned the weapon to face one of the remaining Dragons.

Alouine took several large steps back. Caught in the middle, she desperately sought a way to avoid choosing a side.

"We have to hurry before they see us," Joanna growled to the boy, and began to sweat profusely despite the bitter pre-dawn cold. "Get a shell out of that box."

Quintain gingerly handed her the projectile, which had '84 mm HEAT' in yellow letters stenciled onto the metal casing. "Do you know what you're doing?"

"I know how to use it in theory. In practice? We'll see."

Joanna dropped the shell into the breech, shut and fastened the latch, and tapped on it to ensure that it was closed. She hoisted the weapon again to her shoulder with a grunt and peered through the illuminated sight. Joanna tried to line up her shot to the nearer of the two hovering metal beasts.

"Don't stand behind me!" she shouted, and Quintain, Alouine and Nina scrambled to get out of the way.

Taking another moment to re-sight the weapon, she placed the aiming point directly onto the hovering aircraft, then touched the trigger switch. There was a loud whoosh, and Quintain and Alouine covered their ears. The tremendous bang sent Alouine's heart into her throat.

Nina pressed her face into Quintain's back. The concussion from the back-blast was intense and nearly knocked Joanna off her feet.

Time froze. A droning buzzed in her ears. Adrenaline from the thump shook her bones. The blast made her chest feel hollow and set her head spinning.

She watched the trail of the missile in the sky. It passed harmlessly under the hovering aircraft and exploded with a faraway snap, two kilometers behind it.

Joanna snarled a curse. "Quick, the other one!"

She mashed her cheek to the now-warm barrel as she dropped back to one knee, then tipped the weapon forward to place the steaming muzzle on the ground. Quintain placed the other shell into her outstretched palm as she reached behind her. Raising the elevation of her aim by a single degree, she loaded and fired. This time, she could not trace its progress against the dark sky. A bright orange spark lit at the precise spot where the right wing met the fuselage.

The hovering monster bucked in the air as the wing caught fire, and Alouine imagined it as a horrible creature, rearing its nose back and roaring in outrage. Then the wing broke off and the terrible airplane spun around the axis of its remaining rotor and plummeted to the ground, trailing orange-gray smoke as it fell.

The quartet hurled themselves flat to the ground as the remaining Dragon countered with a long burst of rotary cannon fire. Shells ripped into Joanna's home, tearing it to glowing, metallic shreds and kicking up a massive dust cloud.

— — —

The pain fed Harrow. He nursed on it, drew it into the molten core of his soul, and consumed it in that fiery reactor as fuel. When he opened his eyes, all he could make out was a haze of acrid smoke. He had blacked out on impact. SIMON was rebooting.

The crash had strained both his shoulders to the point of dislocation. His hamstrings burned as if they would snap at any moment. The muscles of his abdomen felt shredded. He flexed the fingers of his left hand; at least two of them were broken.

Still, he rose to his feet within the twisted, metal hulk. Deafening silence pervaded the crash. Nothing moved and no one lived, save for the Outlander. Thick smoke hung in the air and billowed from the rent beast.

Desperation and loathing combined to a potent cocktail. Wounded and alone, Harrow knew his chances of survival were slim. Explosions rocked the hull of the crashed transport and the sounds of ongoing cannon fire echoed from the smashed maw of the plane's cargo-loading ramp. Strobes of light from the continuing assault flashed through the crumpled opening, squeezed nearly shut by the impact of the crash. He located an area still large enough that he could squeeze through.

If survival was in doubt, the odds of actually being able to influence the battle were even more so. The warrior racked his mind, searching feverishly for some kind of trump—a grandstand move he could make that would leave his enemies defeated and his allies safe.

Ultimately, it did not matter. His hated foes were within his grasp and he could not conceive of escaping without offering battle, and so he swallowed his agony and crawled out of the wreckage.

Agony and hate swirled in double helix. There was no other method to achieve victory; weapons alone were useful and good, but the courage to drive a blade into another man's guts was the ultimate factor here, and Harrow possessed that in droves.

More squadrons of soldiers remained—dupes, pawns, puppets of the Last Men. Harrow disdained them, felt contempt and loathing pouring streams of broken glass through his veins. He wanted to feel them die. Boiling with hate, he set out to do exactly that.

— — —

Alouine watched with anxiety as the final Dragon came about and began to descend at the outskirts of the village. Though they had lost the other two aircraft, the Order's troops continued their assault.

A round from the Dragon's cannon had torn through Nina's forearm midway between the wrist and elbow, breaking both bones and leaving her hand attached by little more than ribbons of flesh. Joanna worked feverishly, tearing off the handkerchief she wore on her brow and cinching it tightly just below the elbow.

The girl's face was alabaster white and she was mercifully unconscious from shock. Unless Joanna could stop the bright red blood from pouring out of the wound, Nina would soon expire. She bore down as hard as her powerful hands could grip the cloth, and the pumping liquid slowed to a steady trickle.

With nothing to stop them, the final Dragon descended and lowered its ramp in mid-air. The troops aboard ran down the ramp and fanned out as soon as the landing struts made contact with the ground. As soon as all had disembarked, the aircraft lifted off again and sped away.

"We have to leave," Alouine said to no one in particular. "This battle is lost."

Quintain stood from where he had been kneeling next to the wounded girl. "No it isn't. Harrow is coming. Look!" He gestured to the east and the women's eyes followed.

They had to squint through the smoke to track the blurring form as it maneuvered across the broken ground, but the Outlander warrior was indeed making his way toward his foes.

Alouine swallowed dryly and blinked once, then again. The vision meeting her eyes was not of Harrow, but something else. A warrior, clad from head to toe in bronze armor. She shook her head to clear the vision, but it remained. She could see the same awe and wonder she felt within herself on the teenage mystic's face.

No gap was evident in the form-fitting, gleaming armor the figure wore; its sculpted, polished plates glinted in the dim firelight. A cuirass of bronze scales covered the warrior's torso, inlaid with numerous shining stones of jade, turquoise and agate which punctuated the engravings of ancient runes and hieroglyphs encompassing the whole.

The front section of the tight helm was a smooth faceplate, featureless save the single, subtle vertical ridge which bisected it from top to bottom. It did not possess a vision slit, or holes for the eyes, or any other gap or perforation, which made it seemingly impossible to see through. The top of the helm had dual crests set at diagonals, from which a plume of four feathers projected, two from each. In the figure's gauntleted right hand was a weapon. It could only be described as a lance, four feet long.

The blade resembled an elongated arrowhead and accounted for half of the weapon's total length, while the haft was a deep, rich mahogany and constituted the remainder of the odd, deadly-looking spear. A hefty bronze pommel completed the item, to balance it against the thick, steel slab of its warhead. The metal looked nearly four inches wide at its flaring base and an inch thick along the spine of the double-edged blade.

"What am I seeing?" Alouine softly wondered aloud.

"Knowingly or not, Harrow has invoked a spirit of some kind," the boy beside her explained in a faraway voice.

Alouine rubbed at her eyes in disbelief. "Is it real, or in my imagination?"

"Both," Quintain whispered.

With murderous intent, the apparition ran toward the Order's soldiers, kicking up hard, frozen soil by the impetus of its churning legs. Alouine and Quintain watched as the lead soldier found the charging warrior with the sight of his rifle and opened fire, exhorting his comrades to do the same.

Whether or not they consistently missed their mark, neither onlooker could tell, but the frightening, armored fighter neither faltered nor paused. He barreled into their ranks, scattering them like frail, dead leaves in a gust of cold, winter wind.

Blood and limbs sailed through the air as if tossed by a frenzied pack of predators. Here, the armored figure used its weapon as a sword, chopping off a soldier's arm completely through the meat of the bicep and hardness of bone, or cleaving his rifle completely in twain, steel barrel and all. The metal showed a glow where it fell in two halves, as if cut through by intense, focused heat. There, the weapon was a proper spear, driven into the abdomen of the enemy through a vest designed to stop bullets and reinforced by an impact-resistant ceramic plate.

It twisted the weapon to open a gaping and horrific wound, and then physically slung the dying man off of the blade and over its armor-plated shoulder. The bronze-coated fighter leapt from one Order pawn to the next, rending and tearing with inhuman severity. Pitiless, the machine-like vision of war committed fully to the labor of sawing open their throats, cleaving into their skulls even through the high-tech, woven armor of their helmets, and stabbing them in the genitals to savor the anguish of forcibly taking their manhood from them. It carved their bodies into constituent parts but did not stop there. It vandalized their very identities with the horror of steel and bronze, erasing what made them distinguishable individuals.

Quintain could not continue to watch the terrible scene. As Alouine glanced over, stricken-looking, the young magician performed a short ritual prayer. He closed his eyes and vibrated, in a deep pitch, the words, "Thou art the Kingdom, the Power, and the Glory, forever; so be it." As he did so, he touched his forehead, chest, right shoulder and then left before clasping his fingers over his heart. These words Quintain utilized because they constituted an ideal method of equilibrating his personality and raising his mind to the contemplation of higher things.

He brought into operation his ideal self and awakened the dynamic center of his consciousness, extending his mind to the horizon. Liberating himself from the compulsion of instinct, he made ready to overcome the prospect of facing the terrible warrior spirit that had subsumed Harrow's personality. He imagined with eyes closed that his height increased enormously until reaching the semblance of a vast figure, with head reaching into space and feet resting securely on the earth.

From that exalted point of view, the earth appeared as a small globe beneath the feet of his towering astral body, and the feeling was accompanied by incredible ecstasy and a heightened awareness. Quintain's belief held that the nature of man was transcendental, that the essence of mind was infinite. He embraced all things, since all things were within his nature. His mother's words echoed in his mind: 'Increase thyself to immeasurable height, leaping clear of all body and surmounting all time, become eternal and thou shall know God. There is nothing impossible; deem thyself immortal and able to do all things.'

Quintain's spirit form expanded in a swiftly moving wave which passed through and encompassed Alouine, the others, the entire village, and the world for as far as could be seen.

"I shall return Harrow to us," he vibrated from his throat in aside to Alouine, though his lips did not move. When he opened his eyes once more, they glowed briefly with a blue-white light.

Completing the transposition of what he imagined into his waking visual field, Quintain drew a series of imaginary pentagrams into the air with his mind. To the east, he placed the air pentagram of glowing yellow and mauve, saying "Before me, Raphael." To the west he placed the water pentagram of blue offset with orange: "Behind me, Gabriel." To the south, he placed a fiery pentagram of scarlet with flashes of emerald: "On my right hand, Michael." To the north he mentally traced the banishing earth pentagram of olive and black: "On my left hand, Auriel."

"For before me flames the Pentagram, and behind me shines the Six-rayed Star," he murmured, finishing his preparations. His every molecule, every cell, astral, etheric, mental and physical felt energized and grounded as centers of spiritual force. Each constituent part of Quintain's psycho-physical make-up was its own small universe; his mind and body were not two separate things, but dual manifestations of the same unit. He strode fearlessly to intercept the spirit of battle and destruction who was still violently waging war on the men of the Order.

— — —

The wave of slaughter had reached its peak and crested. Few of the soldiers still offered resistance to the armored monstrosity. Some fled, some still fought for their lives to no avail. The blood of the slain drenched the demonic form of the figure's armor. It ran in rivulets down the smooth, solid mask of the helm, sank into the engraved runes of its bronze scales, and dripped freely from the spear-sword weapon that the mighty warrior still brandished. As the young magician made his way toward the scene of carnage, he was forced to step on ground sodden to mud with the hot, scarlet fluids of the fallen.

The monster still hunted. After slaying a man, it slung the lifeless bodies effortlessly through the air into the pile with the others, to land with sickening thuds. It raised a mound of cadavers, as an ancient army might do after a battlefield victory. If it noticed Quintain, it did not respond.

The teenage mystic planted his feet in front of the hulking, steaming figure. The armor it wore gave off intense heat—whether a kind of etheric force or physical energy, Quintain could not tell. Finally, it ceased its labor and faced the young magician. Whosoever remained of the enemy ran and did not look back.

Quintain knew instantly that the spirit possessing Harrow was an ancient and exceedingly powerful one. Had he tried himself to call this being forth from its extra dimensional abode to act as a servant, to extend his personal power and execute his will on earth, he might have found the task beyond him. Even treating with this entity carried enormous risk. Losing vigilance for a moment would subject Quintain to the spirit's wiles. Despite his preparation, the young magus knew that he could be possessed, obsessed, or even destroyed by its power.

Quintain determined that the spirit was of infernal variety. It related to the subconscious stratum of the human psyche. Spirits inhabiting these regions would be personifications of powers or energies buried in the subconscious mind—qualities of human consciousness that had been disowned as too potent or terrible for waking thought.

Before he could try to convince the spirit to leave peacefully, it spoke. Its voice boomed with metallic quality, backed by the sounds of thunder and fire, in a dialect beyond Quintain. It demanded something. Quintain held fast.

Fluent in the tongue of angels and spirits, the teenager tried this. It was a guttural, almost barbarous-sounding language, communicated from the stomach in a force akin to shouts. "Dooain ils, Gah," he spoke. *Name thyself, Spirit.*

"Ol Anhur, t umd Onuris," the figure roared. Its voice was as pressurized, superheated gases escaping a metal vessel. *I am Anhur, also called Onuris.*

Continuing in the angelic tongue, he told the spirit, "I have deemed your task complete, Onuris. Return now from whence you came."

Onuris took a step forward but was stopped in its tracks as the multicolored pentagrams flared to life at the four cardinal points around Quintain. "You may not compel me," it intoned with the sound of groaning metal. "I am Slayer-of-Enemies. My pact is eternal."

"And so it shall remain. This battle is over. Be gone to rest in your realm, and return when you are needed once more."

"You do not command me." The spirit sounded aggressive, offended and hostile.

"Not yet. But I shall discover your sigil. Do not force me to banish you now, for if I do, I shall summon you myself, in chains, and subject you to punishment."

The spirit laughed a horrible sound. "My sigil is carved in metal and stone and shall last ten thousand years. You cannot threaten it. The one who bound me to this pact rewarded my service in advance."

Quintain fought the urge to frown. "If the one whom you possess dies, your pact ends."

The spirit paused to consider this. "I care not for this one's life."

"If he dies, you may never be summoned to battle again. Leave now or I shall find your sigil and deface it. I shall strike it from the face of the earth forever." Quintain meant his threat with every fiber of his being.

The spirit growled in frustration. The sound struck even at Quintain's magically armored heart with daggers of fear, and the vibration resembled a quaking of the earth. Finally, it relented.

"Very well, young one, I will depart. But, under the terms of my pact, I shall return."

Where the armored warrior-spirit stood, Harrow appeared, and immediately crashed to the ground. His clothes and hair smoked as he pitched face first into the bloody mud. He clutched his dagger KA-BAR in a death grip within his right fist.

Smoke billowed from the back of Harrow's skull. Quintain blinked once, but quickly pulled himself together and fell to his knees next to the wounded Outlander. He wrestled with Harrow's limp form to flip him over onto his back. Then, with a palm on his forehead, he pressed the rear of the warrior's skull into the cold earth. Steam hissed.

FIFTEEN

Quintain watched as Alouine kept Nina unconscious by manipulating her chi, using the ancient secrets of the Order. The high-born woman touched the wounded child's forehead and chest and slowed her heart rate to a pace that was near death. The circuit of blood was broken, and if the child's heart continued pumping at its normal rate, it would soon spill all of the life-bearing liquid out of the child's ragged wound.

Quintain soaked a convenient grey blanket in cold water from one of the village wells and draped it over Harrow to keep him cool as he wrestled and fought with the warrior's unconscious form, dragging the leaden man back to the spot outside Joanna's ruined home where the two women were concentrating on saving Nina's life.

Horror clutched at him and turned his stomach as his eyes swept over the village. The dwellings were chewed up, smoking ruins, and the dead and dying lay littered throughout. In the south field, where Harrow had fought the final battle, the churned-up ground was soaked with blood and heaped with corpses in a ghastly display.

He stuffed his nose into the crook of his elbow to fend off the smell of smoke and cordite, feces and blood. Glancing down at the brutally wounded girl, the teenager forced himself to blink away his tears.

"What are we going to do?" Joanna asked.

Breathing heavily and sweating despite the cold winds, Quintain swallowed dryly. "First, we have to stabilize these two and get them ready to move since we can't stay here." He locked eyes with the older woman and said what all were thinking and none but he would give voice to. "Her arm is ruined. We have to amputate. Heat up some iron, and try to find something that'll go through bone cleanly."

Joanna cursed and grimaced. It was a hateful idea, to remove Nina's right hand—she wore it plainly on her face. The loss would cripple the girl for life.

"Better a one-armed girl than a dead one," Quintain sighed as he scrubbed his hands and arms.

She nodded automatically and stoked the fire in her forge.

Alouine nearly killed Nina several times in keeping her anesthetized, but using the sharpest tools from Joanna's ruined workshop, cleaned to a shine and disinfected in fire, the trio cut and peeled back the flesh just above the wound. They sawed away the jagged splinters of bone, and with a smell that would never fully leave them, sewed together the stump. Quintain was careful, precise and compassionate throughout the procedure. It had been years, but he had seen his mother perform similar work before.

They used copious amounts of antiseptic, and diminished the supply of items in Joanna's orange canvas medical kit to nearly nothing. The remainder of those supplies they applied to Harrow. His burns, bruises and scrapes did not seem life-threatening, but the moment Quintain was satisfied that he had done all he could for Nina, he moved on to the warrior.

Exhausted from the stress of his labors, he slumped onto his rear after checking Harrow completely, feeling for internal bleeding or broken bones. He looked over at Nina. "How is she?" he inquired tiredly.

"Alive," Alouine replied. "Her heartbeat is weak, but steady.

It'll be a miracle if she can escape infection." Joanna cradled the poor girl's head in her lap and said nothing. "What about him?" Alouine asked.

Quintain ticked off the list of Harrow's ailments on his fingers as he spoke. "He's strained nearly every muscle in his body and has two, maybe three broken ribs. He broke a couple fingers on his left hand, probably during the crash. I set and splinted them already. I think his shoulder was separated, too, but he popped it back in on his own. Something in his head overheated. The burns are nasty, but it's really the potential brain damage I'm worried about. It could have cooked the inside of his skull. There's no way of telling until he wakes up," he said, then added, ". . . if he does." The two women digested this news in silence for a long moment.

"We have to get out of here," Joanna said softly. "The ones who ran could come back, or there could be more on the way. The pilots of that last Dragon have already radioed back to the Enclave by now."

"We can't carry one of them, let alone both," Alouine said.

"The village tractor survived," Joanna replied, gesturing to the west. Partially covered by its canvas tarp, the hulking metal vehicle was untouched where it was parked next to the smoldering ruin of a house. "We'll hitch a cart to it and carry them in that. But we should hurry and get as far north as we can."

Quintain sighed. "We can't go north."

"What? Why? We have to get as far from the Enclave as we can," Joanna argued. Alouine seemed inclined to agree, nodding slightly.

"I need to get Harrow to the place where I was born," Quintain replied. "It's to the south."

"Look, I'm grateful to you for helping to save Nina's life, and for bringing Harrow back. But the Enclave is almost straight south of here. They'll find us. A single Hawk will kill all of us." Joanna referenced the unmanned drones which constantly patrolled the skies around and above the domed Enclave.

Quintain set his jaw. "I'm asking you to continue to trust me. We have to go to my home. There are things there which will make all this pain and loss worth it, I promise."

— — —

Joanna drove the tractor, keeping a slow, trundling pace for efficiency. The vegetable-oil fuel which powered it would last for twenty kilometers and no more. She constantly scanned the grey skies for the threats of Dragons or Hawks which might dive down on them at any moment.

Quintain and Alouine rode in the wide, open wooden cart, with the wounded forms of Harrow and Nina stretched out between them. Joanna's launcher and the two remaining shells, along with every tool and piece of equipment the older woman could salvage from her shop, were packed in every available space.

They stuffed as many blankets and coats as they could find around the unconscious Outlander pair, to cushion their journey and keep them warm. Harrow's bolt-action rifle had miraculously survived the repeated assaults on Joanna's hut; after checking to make sure that it was unloaded and safe, she laid it across Harrow's chest. She stripped weapons, ammunition and hand-thrown explosives from a few of the Death's Head corpses but refused to approach the ghoulish mound Harrow had raised.

The young magus felt terrible. He had sensed near sixty Outlanders in the village the day before. Though he was sure that some few had run off and escaped into the surrounding hinterlands, the Order's raid had ended the lives of the rest. Wanting to stay behind and see to the burial of not merely the innocent victims of the battle but also the soldiers of the Order, he was disappointed that he was forced to leave them where they lay.

Those villagers did not deserve to rot under the sky and become scraps for crows or vultures, and unlike Joanna and, he imagined, Harrow, Quintain held a certain kind of sympathy for the duped, black-clad soldiers of the Order's Deaths Head battalion. Ensnared by hostile manipulations of the most despicable sort, those men, too, had given their lives, only in pursuit of a misguided goal.

Still, they were human, and Quintain held that even a moment of love in an evil man's life held the power of redemption. Those men were given no such chance at salvation.

The first hour of the journey passed almost completely in silence as each of the strange trio digested the events on their own. Joanna lost all of her friends, clients and neighbors. All the people who respected and loved her for who she was and what she could do—dead or scattered to the winds.

Quintain stared at Harrow. Even in sleep, he did not look at peace, with brow furrowed and a permanent grimace etched onto his features.

Finally, Alouine could no longer bear the silence. She reached across the cart and touched Quintain's hand as it rested on his knee.

"Will you explain to me what happened back there?" she asked softly, only forcefully enough to carry her voice to him over the exhaust of the tractor's engine.

Quintain did not respond with anger or dripping sarcasm but said, "Many people died who did not deserve to." He wore his despondency on his face.

"Yes, and for that I am sorry." She squeezed his hand again. "Truly, I am," she insisted when he met her gaze once more. "That was a shameful display, and I have never had any respect for the Death's Head. Unless I miss my guess, the raid could only have been arranged by a single source."

"You know who caused all of that to happen?"

"I have suspicions. But in order to understand what I should do about it, I need a better idea of where I'm coming from. Can you help me?"

Quintain sighed. The noble woman had a point. "I'll try."

She nodded. "What happened to Harrow back there?"

The teenager ran his fingers through his greasy, unkempt hair. "It depends on how you look at it," he said tiredly. He considered his words, and Alouine gave him the time to do so. "I don't know much about what Harrow has done to himself. The machine in his brain is something I'd like to find out about, but as for how it works . . . I can only study the effects.

"As for the demon—in magic, it is called an invocation. In psychology, it can be considered a voluntary psychosis, a temporary schizophrenia. The unconscious mind contains thousands of archetypal figures. It's a realm where the difference between man and universe is very indistinct.

"In the magical system I study, rituals are used to come into contact with these entities for various purposes. To my best guess, Harrow used the power of his augmented brain to spontaneously and intuitively invoke one of these archetypes. In certain terms, it can be called 'sympathetic magic'. Perhaps he epitomized that spirit so thoroughly that he, for all intents and purposes, became it."

"You made a series of prayers and gestures," Alouine prompted.

Quintain nodded. "The banishing ritual of the pentagram, to protect myself. There is always a chance that dealing with such massive psychosis can be dangerous. Potent psycho-spiritual forces can infect an unprepared person and even destroy a fragile psyche."

"How did you speak with him in that state?"

"The spirit had complete possession of him. Make no mistake, the conscious mind we call 'Harrow' did not exist, or at least, was completely subsumed. In his place was another entity altogether.

It said its name was 'Anhur', but it seemed to want me to call it 'Onuris'. I can guess that it was a spirit recognized, or maybe worshipped, in some ancient land far away, and because I am not of that land, it wanted me to use a title for it that was appropriate for a foreigner."

"What was that strange language you spoke?"

"It was Enochian. Many centuries ago, it was discovered as a way to communicate with spirits, or archetypal forces, if you prefer."

"How do you know these things? I mean, where did you learn all of this?"

"I'll explain more when we reach my home. It'll be easier there."

— — —

It was a dark place, hidden underground. Alouine, accustomed as she was to flying spires and the breathtaking quality of height, felt as though she was descending into some cavernous, hellish pit, or the den of a filthy, burrowing animal.

Quintain had arranged Nina's comatose form on his back and taken her down into his lair first, then returned so that he, Joanna, and Alouine could all wrestle Harrow's similarly limp form through the twisting passages. He lit the crystalline lamp, the small jewel in his forehead, which shone brightly with clear, white light, and carried Harrow's legs under his arms as the two women struggled under the weight of his powerful upper body. Joanna grimaced with effort, while Alouine frowned at the menial work.

Finally, they arrived in Quintain's inner sanctum and, having placed Harrow on the floor, tried to calm their labored breathing. The teenager disappeared for a moment, taking the light with him. After a loud clack which reverberated in the dark, some soft, yellow electric lamps came to life, none higher than knee level. When he returned, Quintain brought with him two jugs swishing with liquid.

The chamber was a massive, circular affair, and nearly every available inch was crammed with books. They formed stacks, pillars—mounds of them, from moldering paperbacks to leather-bound, priceless editions. In their thousands, the vastness of his collection loomed large over the weary travelers. There was a system to the tidal wave of bound paper as the two curious women soon found. A single subject made up a stack of books, sometimes twenty, sometimes forty in total, often with an open book balanced on top. Each stack leaned on others precariously. A wrong nudge here or there would cause an avalanche of epic proportions.

"This is," Alouine began to say in a whisper, but her voice left her as she gazed around, wide-eyed. She noticed an ancient Holy Bible in its huge, ox-skin covering, balanced precariously on top of a similarly time-lost Quran. Both were easily a millennium old. Either item was among the rarest thing on Earth; to Alouine it was mind-boggling to find them here, in the trash-heap den of an Outlander rat.

"Amazing," Joanna finished the thought.

Quintain poured water for the two thirsty women and handed it to them in ceramic cups. "I like print media," he said before gulping thirstily from a cup of his own. "But it takes up too much physical space. There's a thousand times more information stored digitally over there." He indicated a nook, seemingly built from the surrounding tomes, which contained an ancient monitor atop a desk, with interface equipment before it. Underneath and to the left, three computer towers, which had to be centuries old, hummed away.

"How did you come by all of this?" Alouine asked. The water was amazingly clean and clear and tasted better than any she had sampled before, especially in the Outlands. It was superior to even that which she found in the Enclave, and after a few sips, her thirst disappeared and she felt refreshed.

"My mother left it to me," was Quintain's reply. He tucked blankets under and around Nina to keep her warm, and stuffed another under Harrow's head to cushion the injured man.

"It's an impressive collection." Alouine was accustomed to hand-held digital displays but recognized the bound tomes for what they were. Quintain shrugged, dismissive to the awe with which the two women beheld their surroundings.

"Being educated is only the first step to being enlightened—not that I'd make any claims to that myself. But the mastery of altered states of consciousness, the experience of the spirit world, is far more useful, I've found, than centuries of knowledge or received wisdom handed down from generation to generation. No body of text or teaching can replace practice—real, direct experience of other realms, attained in deliberately induced, altered states of consciousness. It is one thing to read endlessly, and entirely another to actively enter the other realms and deal with the intelligences there, for the benefit of humanity."

Neither woman knew quite how to respond to that. They passed several long moments in silence, cogitating.

"I see you've tapped into the Order's power grid," Joanna finally observed.

Quintain shook his head. "Nah, that's not necessary. I don't like to take chances with anyone finding this place. The Enclave is lazy about policing their energy infrastructure, but no one can claim that they're stupid or incompetent, and I don't like to rely on my enemies' laziness. Besides, generating power is easy. The parts are stolen, I admit, but I built the torus field generator myself. This place had wiring already, so my mother and I just patched the output on the generator to make it usable electricity. Of course, there's massive overflow that I've been trying to figure out what to do with, since I'm only running my computers and lights. Oh, and the heaters. I like the place nice and toasty.

Anyway, all that stuff is a breeze for a torus field with stable vector-equilibrium."

Joanna stared at him. "You're saying you create your own electricity?"

Quintain blinked. "Sure. It's easy. Like I was saying, I've got more than I can use."

— — —

Harrow floated in blackness as though it were water, utterly submerged. There was numbness and silence and nothing besides. He was thankful for it, grateful for the respite. The pounding he had taken passing through flames of agony that licked over his flesh and disintegrated his bones was over—at least for the moment. Harrow suspected that he would eventually have to go back. But he was so very tired.

It was a voiceless voice that spoke to him. He felt rather than heard it. Ears did not matter, nor did words; it was simply a feeling, an outside pressure.

"You are breaking," it hissed. He could not escape the wave of thought, threatening to crush him from the fore. He cursed. He wanted to be left alone, to escape, to lick his wounds in peace. He could not summon any resistance against the ardent desire to go on feeling nothing. Why could he not just sleep forever? The aching was far away. That damned, wretched cold in the faraway distance, exactly where he favored it. He did not want to go back.

"Is this your grave, maggot?" that voice groaned. Harrow grimaced. He tried to turn away as one who clings to a pillow too long in the morning, and so shield himself from the unwanted intrusion, the light and sound. "You are the shit of the earth. I expected much of you—too much, perhaps."

Harrow finally parted his swollen eyelids. He was suspended, nude, in the dark, which stretched into infinity. Before him loomed the being—the god, the archetype of struggle and war and unrestrained violence. The bronze-armored warrior, blazing with heat and light and indomitable aggression, stood hundreds of feet tall. Harrow's tiny form was held immobile before its massive, armored chest, subject to the distorting waves of energy given off by the molten, almost solar surface.

"Leave me alone," the Outlander croaked, exhausted. He began to feel once more. The great furnace of the terror before him cooked him. His moisture, The Water of Life, the last vestiges of vitality evaporated away.

Waves of mocking, horrid laughter, reminiscent of the marching footsteps of a million armored men, battered Harrow's naked form. "I am bound to you." It ducked down swiftly, to put its smooth, solid, uncaring and featureless faceplate before the man. "I am you!" The roar sent tremors plowing through the tangible sea of black, shaking Harrow to the bone.

"I never wanted . . ."

"Principles have no regard for petty desires. You will do as you must!" The voice was so booming, it threatened to deafen the Outlander's mind and soul, to shake him to pieces, to disintegrate him completely into constituent molecules. He nearly wished it would. He almost wanted it to break him down to atoms, to end him completely. "It is your choice, mortal. Will you have pain, or Lethe? Peace or War?"

He considered. In that place, there was no pain. Without pain, his rage and hatred abated. The earth was beyond his concerns. The young magician would carry on the fight, with or without him. Perhaps the reforming princess would assist him, and together they would find victory.

"To go back will mean more fire and blood. You will suffer until you die. The lives of many more men will end on your blade."

Harrow choked, his body racked with spasms. His hair caught fire. His skin boiled and peeled. What possible reason could there be to return to that life of agony? It was over. But there, in the distance, he caught a glimpse, between devastating coughs.

A feather of blond hair flashed in his vision, and then a grin full of teeth too big for the small mouth which contained them. He welled with some instinct, something deeply ingrained in his humanity; something he had fought to tightly control. Something he thought was a curse.

"Do you have something to protect?" the god, Anhur, asked him. It was cold and cruel and matter-of-fact, but almost taunting, as though it knew the answer already.

It was an instinct that crushed self-preservation. It was not a curse. It was a blessing he had inherited. The father's instinct to protect, passed to him from his own father and inherited—unbroken—down a line of ancestors which stretched back to the beginnings of humanity. The feeling was a passionate, starving flame. Its fuel could be only one thing. "The girl," he murmured. "Does she live?"

"She does."

"Then I choose War," Harrow announced, resigning himself to his fate.

The spirit held aloft its weapon, the sword-spear, as though offering it to the man. "Fight," it commanded, and Harrow complied.

— — —

Little Nina woke up first but had trouble opening her eyes. It was strange because she usually had a lot of energy after sleeping, and even though she felt like she had slept for days, she could not shake the fuzzy, awkward feeling, as though her whole body was stuck in mud. She was tired beyond belief, even beyond that day when she had nearly died, the day when Harrow had carried her home.

She winced. There was a throbbing ache shooting up her arm from her right hand, and she drew her knees up and around it to protect it. She must have hurt it badly, so she tried to put it between her thighs to give it a gentle squeeze. When she attempted to curl her body around the aching appendage, she could not feel it with her legs.

She felt strong hands on her back, adjusting her. They pulled her into a familiar-feeling lap and a tight embrace.

"Oh, sweetheart," whispered a cracking voice in her ear. She recognized it as Joanna's voice, but had never heard her sound so sad. "Sweet child." She could smell tears and felt strong fingers brush her long, blond mane back.

"Joanna," she whispered. Her diminutive voice was raspy from thirst. "What's wrong?" The older woman sobbed once, then again. It became uncontrollable. She buried her face in Nina's hair and cried.

"I'm so sorry," she bawled, her voice hitching over and over as welling emotion, which felt like wails, only left her as exhausted whimpers.

"It's okay," Nina ground out. She felt as though she might suffocate under the weight of her beloved caretaker's stifling sorrow, so she tried to shift, to wrap the woman in an embrace of her own. That is when she saw it.

There was no small, thin hand where there should have been, only a bloody stump wrapped in gauze and cloth. The little girl stared at it and frowned. Then she blinked several times, trying to make sense of it, her eyes tracking from the wound to her own shoulder and back again. When she focused her confused gaze on Joanna's face, she found all the horror of red eyes and streaming tears. That confirmed it for the girl—what she faced was reality. Silently, her own tears began to fall. Joanna tried her hardest to offer the girl a smile through her gasps.

"I'm okay, Joanna," the girl said. "It hurts, but I'm okay." She wrapped her arms tightly around the woman's neck and hugged her fiercely. "Don't cry."

They held their embrace for a long time before Nina looked around. Her mind whirled; she wasn't able to make much sense of their surroundings. There were many books, many more than the few that Joanna had at home. She saw the boy with the shiny rock on his head and the pretty lady from before.

A line of worry creased the girl's forehead as she remembered. "Are the Dragons gone?" she asked.

"Yes, baby, they're gone," Joanna said. Nina could not tell if the woman was laughing or crying. It sounded as though she was doing both at once.

They must have chased the Dragons away. The boy cried, too, but the pretty lady just swallowed and looked away guiltily when Nina glanced at her.

"Can I have some water?"

"Yes, of course you can," the Outlander woman replied. She filled her cup again from the jug, and offered it to the girl, but another sob escaped her when she saw Nina reach for it with both arms, but only one hand. She frowned, sheepish that she had already so easily forgotten. Her missing hand felt as though it were still there, still attached and hurting badly. Joanna helped hold the cup to her lips and she drained it quickly.

Quintain unapologetically wiped his cheeks, unashamed of the display.

Alouine stood up. "I should get some air," she mumbled, and left the way she had entered. Joanna did not make any indication of having heard her, and Quintain did not attempt to stop her.

"Where is Harrow?" Nina wondered sleepily. Joanna gently turned the girl in her lap so she could see the warrior, laid out and still, a few yards away.

"He was hurt, so he's resting."

"Maybe I should rest, too."

"I think so, too," Joanna said gently, as she helped Nina lie down again, and then covered her with a blanket. "Just sleep, baby," she crooned. "I'll wake you for supper."

Nina whispered, "Okay," and mercifully, she fell again into sleep.

— — —

Quintain knelt on the floor at Harrow's head, which he lifted and placed on top of his touching knees. Taking cleansing breaths, he focused his mind and entered into a meditative trance, attuning himself to act as a channel for healing on physical, emotional, mental and spiritual levels.

Matching his subtle body with Harrow's, Quintain channeled the healing energy of the universe through the man's physical form, focusing on his wounds in turn and starting at the older man's head. He guided the flow of energy through the meridian energy lines in Harrow's body, releasing the muddied and distorted kinks and cramps which clogged Harrow's chakras. After slipping further into this trance, the gem set in Quintain's forehead began to glow.

Quintain placed his hands directly onto Harrow's numerous wounds in turn, despite having his eyes closed. With the use of his astral sight, he made quick work of setting a foundation for Harrow's recovery.

The young man thoroughly enjoyed healing others. He brought Harrow's form back into a state of equilibrium and programmed the man's body with a suite of protocols that it would automatically follow to facilitate a return to wholeness.

He had laid his palms on Harrow's temples and directed the energy through the man's head, when the warrior's bloodshot eyes shot open. Harrow cast his gaze about wildly for a moment, utterly uncomprehending, before finally he focused on the teenage face looming over him.

"What are you doing?" he croaked. His voice was weak and

thick with the effort it took to speak from a parched throat and desiccated lips.

"Don't move," Quintain ordered, his own voice reverberating with the echo of astral power. Harrow complied.

Wrapping up his efforts with a short and muffled prayer, Quintain carefully and gently placed the warrior's head back onto the folded blanket which served as a pillow, and opened his eyes. The glowing of his forehead gem gradually faded, and a satisfied smile lit his face. "How do you feel?"

Harrow groaned lightly. "Is there any water?"

The boy shifted to pour a cup for the wounded fighter, then, cradling his head, helped him to drink it.

"That's good," Harrow murmured.

"I aerate it with ozone," Quintain replied. "Drink some more, it will help balance your system. I'll attempt further healing tomorrow."

Harrow swallowed more of the liquid greedily. After a long pause, and in a gentle whisper, he said, "Thank you."

The boy just smiled and nodded. "I'm sure you want to get back on your feet as soon as possible. I want the same thing."

Joanna cleared her throat to gain Quintain's attention. "Did you just heal him with your mind?"

The teenager cocked his head a little. "I don't think that's possible. What I did was more like facilitating his body's own self-healing by aligning with and acting in accordance to the universal energy of nature."

"Oh," the woman replied. "Sure. Blah-blah, accordance, blah-blah nature," she mumbled, shrugging. "Got it."

"Tell me what happened," Harrow gasped. "Where is Nina?"

"She is here, sleeping," Quintain responded soothingly. "She was hurt, but she'll live. You were more worrisome. I think you invoked some kind of intelligent, spiritual entity—an extremely powerful one."

"Yes," Harrow sighed. "That is my conclusion." He grimaced, as though remembering. "What happened at the village?"

Quintain glanced away. "You killed or drove off the raiders, but . . ."

"What is it?"

"The village was destroyed."

Long, tense moments followed, and the magus watched Harrow's aura as his emotions swirled. Eventually, he managed to steady the labored, erratic breathing that whistled through his clenched teeth.

He took a deep breath. An exhausted resignation echoed in his voice. "I'm glad you're alive," he said. "You, too, Joanna."

"Likewise, tough guy."

"What about the princess? Did she escape?"

'Escape' implied that Harrow still harbored suspicions of Alouine, that somehow she bore, in some measure, the blame for the raid. Quintain could hear it in Harrow's inflection and intended to put that to rest immediately.

"Let's get this straight right now," he said boldly. "I have not once sensed any hostile intent toward any of us from Alouine. I believe that she had nothing to do with the raid. She was in the wrong place at the wrong time, just like us, and she did help us to fight back. Much of the credit for saving Nina's life is hers. She is outside, taking some time to herself."

Harrow absorbed this in silence for nearly a full minute. "All right."

"You are in my home, so I'll ask you to respect my wishes. That woman already feels a great deal of guilt and shame, and she doesn't need any more of it. A certain amount is natural; it enables us to orient ourselves. Let that be enough."

"Very well. I'll not broach it."

"Good. Like it or not, we're all in this together now."

Harrow sighed and fell into another round of cogitation. Joanna stretched, her joints popping.

Quintain granted the other man a measure of peace to come to grips with recent events, then asked, "Can you describe the nature of the machine you've installed in your head?"

Harrow took a breath. "In basic terms, it is a torus field generator, which utilizes a tiny, sixty-four tetrahedron crystal. As you well know, the universe is alive, and its infinite energy can be tapped by aligning properly with it.

"The concept is understood by the Order and provides for all of their energy needs, so it made the design easy. I only miniaturized it. Coupled with my own body's personal electromagnetic field, it interacts with the environment on a quantum level.

"As you are likely aware, matter is simply energy condensed into a vibration at a perceivable frequency. Qubit-driven computing power is capable of handling the intense data load, but it required isolation from the electromagnetic radiation and extensive filtering. Overcoming those issues was the hardest part. Everything else was simple."

"That's brilliant. I should have thought of that."

Harrow glanced away. "Just because something is possible does not mean it should be done," he announced, his voice sinking an octave. "I didn't want to do it. I was forced to."

"What do you mean? Who forced you?"

Harrow exhaled. "The Order did. Not directly. But I knew that if I was to wage war on them, I would need to do something drastic to have a chance at success. I wasn't born this way." He nearly seemed ashamed. "I've vandalized my humanity and become something else."

Quintain stared at the floor. The older man had a point. The teen remembered their first meeting. He had accused Harrow of becoming monstrous. But the other Outlander had already known what he was doing—saw how twisted it was making him. For a moment, neither man spoke.

Quintain cut into their repose. "Harrow, why is battling the Order so important to you?"

The other man blinked, taking a steadying breath. "I suppose I inherited this war, much like you did. My father showed me how corrupt and insane the world is. He gave his life to try to make it right. I can do no less. Besides, you can see for yourself how evil they are. They took Heaven for themselves and left only Hell for the rest of us. Someone has to end this. It's just the right thing to do."

Quintain grinned. "I knew you were the right man for this."

"Right or not, I'm the only one doing it."

"Not anymore."

SIXTEEN

Quintain approached Alouine from behind. The woman lingered near the remarkably well-hidden entrance to the Outlander's den. From any angle of approach, the entrance was camouflaged and nearly impossible to spot.

She sat atop a jutting hunk of concrete in a classic thinker's pose. One knee was drawn up, elbow resting atop, and chin supported by the back of her hand. He could see in her aura that several of her chakras were muddied with doubt.

"You're considering leaving us," he said.

"He was right. He said that I don't belong here," she muttered. "This wasn't what I envisioned when I left the Enclave." Her voice gained ferocity and no small amount of virulence. "It's time for me to return, and do what I should have done. I'll kill the man standing in my way, and damn the consequences."

"Guilt and shame should never compel a human to do anything. They compel us to cease an action, not to engage in another."

She rounded on him, her eyes glinting. "This isn't my world."

He climbed up next to her. "The world is the world. It belongs to everyone."

"You know what I mean."

"Well, sort of," he said. He made his voice gentle and even. "I don't mean to pry, but didn't your people cast you out?"

She snorted. "They don't do that. The Order does not have to ostracize anyone. If a member proves too much of a nuisance, death is the only prescription. I left because of circumstances. It's not as though they shunned me. I shouldn't have run. I'll figure out how to remove that swine, and then this will all be like a bad dream. They'll welcome me back with open arms."

"You think so?"

"There are still people there who love me."

"There are people here who love you."

Alouine sighed. "They hate and fear me, and for good reason. And you don't count; you love everything. It's not the same if I'm just a part of a package deal."

"Harrow loves you." He stated it as a fact. The woman couldn't do anything but blink for several moments as her thoughts roiled. Quintain watched her, utterly impartial. Finally, she shook her head.

"We're not— I mean, we don't—" She seemed unable to form the words properly, and blew out a frustrated breath. "Just because we're no longer *deadly* rivals doesn't mean we're no longer rivals."

"He loves you. Neither of you know it yet, but he does. You need each other." He paused, chuckling, and added, "You deserve each other."

"You are clearly delusional," Alouine put in, managing to portray again some vestige of dignity.

"We see the truth in three steps, Alouine. First, it is ridiculed, and then violently opposed. Finally, it is accepted as obvious fact."

She ground her teeth and glared at him. "You cannot be serious!" Her fists clenched.

He just smiled back at her with eyebrows raised, and slightly— *sagely*—nodded his head.

She slapped her forehead with her palm and snarled inchoately. He let her battle it out in her mind for a full minute.

Finally, after he observed her taking a few calming breaths, he gently spoke. "Alouine, you are everything that Harrow desires in life. Love which you deny will become pain you feel inside."

"He hates me."

"Honestly, do you think his war with the Order is entirely about venom and hatred? No. Harrow is a proud man. His pride dwarfs even yours. He wants to be accepted for what he is. The Last Men cannot do that, and that is why Harrow's battle with the Order takes on the image of such a violent struggle. If they will not accept him, he'll destroy them."

The noble scion stared into the distance, cogitating.

"A human life should have ample opportunity to thrive. We should all have opportunities to share in life's pleasures, surrounded by abundance. Harrow forsook that entirely. You've known it from birth.

"Your Order has done a superlative job. Nearly all of their agendas have been crowned with success. They have poisoned Outlanders, manipulated them, robbed them of all knowledge and valuables, disarmed and corralled them, and have essentially broken their communal spirit.

"However, they made one costly mistake. They did not wipe us out completely. We're worth more to them as slave stock than we are as corpses. Had they eradicated our kind, they might not have had to contend with Harrow, and myself.

"Our duties are twofold: to defend, and to heal. We must defend our race, safeguard the helpless, oppose aggression, defeat the wicked, and be righteous in the face of evil. We must heal the land, the geomancy of the Earth; heal the mind, the body, the soul of humanity.

"This is the crux of the world Order: where the nature of earth is holarchy, the Order creates hierarchy. Hierarchy is the only outcome of the Order's undying hubris. It is the main root, from which warfare, social violence, sex-repression, child abuse, and deception spring.

"My enemy is well-known to me—those self-appointed elites,

the technocratic and esoteric cabal that calls itself the world Order of Last Men. And their plan, formulated for millennia, has come fully to fruition. To achieve their coup, it was necessary to remove the minds of men from individualism, from loyalty to family traditions and national identification. It is this policy of 'un-earthing' men, dividing them from themselves and the world-that-is; to enforce hierarchy and rivalry with every other group or sect. First, get the future slaves warring with one another. Then send your own minions to conquer the remainder. To supplement physical anarchy, it is necessary to create a kind of anarchy of the mind.

"To revolt is a natural tendency of life. Even a worm turns against the boot that crushes it. The vitality and relative dignity of a human being can be measured by the intensity of his or her instinct to revolt." He glanced over pointedly to the woman, her eyes downcast as she listened. "No matter what you choose, you're welcome here, with me. You have time to come to a decision. Why don't we go back inside? I have to talk to everyone as a group."

Alouine nodded slightly, rose from her perch and followed Quintain back into his lair, apparently willing to further hear him out.

— — —

"You are all welcome here for as long as you want to stay," Quintain said, after everyone had gathered together again within the confines of the den. Nina still dozed in the corner, which suited him just fine. The girl needed the rest. He wanted to attempt to rehabilitate her wounded arm and, more importantly, her undoubtedly wounded psyche. He pressed on.

"I have a few favors to ask, though." For the first time, the young man felt the scrutiny of his elder audience. It had been three years since his mother had gone and he had not shared his home with anyone in the interim. He felt sheepish and keenly aware of having been alone for far too long in his own private space. "Well," he said, cocking his head to the side, "it's kind of," his tongue tangled and for a moment he felt nonsensical.

"Spit it out," Harrow ordered.

"All right," Quintain gasped defensively. "Look, I don't know how to feed all of you, for one thing. For another, I haven't had any women here for years, and there's the, uh," his voice became a bit smaller, and though he willed his ears to stop burning, they would not. "The small matter of, you know," he tried, but the words came out abashed and mumbled, "sleeping arrangements, and," his face burned with embarrassment, "hygiene."

Joanna barked out a chuckle, which only drove Quintain's embarrassment deeper.

Things were easier when he flitted about without his clumsy body and its preposterous hormones weighing him down. *In times like these, I wish I could leave it behind for good*, he thought.

Alouine cut in. "I am certain we will make suitable arrangements." Harrow did not seem to disagree and Joanna only seemed bemused by the spectacle of a teenage Quintain fussing over propriety.

"There is actually more space here than it appears," Quintain fumbled. "We can move some things around and create partitions—you know . . . for privacy."

"An excellent idea," Harrow murmured.

"There's access to plenty of water," the boy continued, happy to put that topic behind him. "Food is an issue, though. I grow some things, like fungus and a few vegetables in the adjacent caverns, but it'll be meager if we have to split it so many ways."

"No one will starve," Harrow said. "I will see to that as soon as I am . . ."—his voice trailed off, and he softly added— "feeling better."

"All right, then," Quintain spoke. "There is the matter of plans for the future."

No one responded immediately. A sadness locked on to Joanna's face as she was reminded again of being bereft of purpose and the tools of her trade which she had spent the better part of her life acquiring.

Again, Harrow spoke first. "I speak only for myself, but there are battles yet to be waged and I intend to take the fight to my enemy."

"More raids on the Enclave?" Alouine taunted. "You'll only be an annoyance."

The warrior gritted his teeth and pushed himself up onto his elbows to glare at the woman. "No," he growled. "No more raids. I'm going to invade. At the village, they came for our blood. I'll see them drown in their own."

"So what? Your great plan is a suicide charge into the teeth of your foe? You are as arrogant as you are foolhardy. You'll die. That is the only certainty."

"It doesn't matter. I'll limp on crutches in the afterlife if I must!"

Quintain stepped between the pair. He planted his feet firmly and summoned his most commanding voice. "Now, look, I have to agree with Harrow, which is to say that the Order's predations have gone on for far too long. On the other hand, while I am willing to give my life to see this done, I'd prefer that as a last resort."

Harrow ground his clenched teeth.

"When you march to battle, you won't be alone," the boy promised the man. "I'm going, too. But we have preparations to make first. Your body needs time to heal. We should train ourselves for this—and each other."

"I don't need any help," Harrow spat. "My entire life was training enough, for this."

Quintain turned on the man. "Not needing help isn't the same as not accepting it when it's offered!" he yelled. "Your stubborn pride has a use, but not here, and not now!" He blew out a breath and tried to calm himself. "You have my help," he repeated. "To cast it aside would prove how arrogant and foolhardy you really are."

Harrow slumped back onto his pillow, defeated, and sank into a sullen silence. The younger man pressed on. "All warriors throughout history have been aided by the thought of a home to return to. You have that." He gestured to Nina's resting form, unsure if the girl was still asleep or not, and suddenly thoroughly abashed at having raised his voice. The turbulent warrior relented and closed his eyes, fuming, but beginning to cool. The teenager then rounded on Alouine.

"Lady Morningstar," he spoke in a pleading, placating voice. "You know that I'm not too proud to ask for help. We need yours. You can return to your home. More than that, you can conquer it and make it yours, and right the centuries of wrongs that have been perpetrated in the name of your people!"

Alouine sneered. "Yes, that's what I've always wanted: to rule over a pile of corpses!" She flung a gesture in Harrow's direction. "This fool means to destroy it all, to murder all of my kin, and you mean to help him! And I'm supposed to assist you? Not on my life."

"If you were to help us," he said quickly, before Harrow could snarl any grave promises about Alouine's life, "I'm certain we could reach some kind of accord. In exchange for information and assistance, I'm sure Harrow would be very willing to reign in his desires for revenge and reserve them only for those truly deserving." He glanced back to Harrow. "Am I correct?"

He did not immediately respond, but eventually ground out, "You are not wrong." Finally, he seemed to come to terms with his roiling emotions.

"You're utterly insane," Alouine sighed. "Hundreds of the Last Men make their homes in that Enclave. Each of the males owns a Lictor bodyguard that would laugh in your face as it pulled you apart. Not to mention the garrison of the Death's Head, and all of the security AIs, much less the Vigilant Panoptical.

"To do what you mean to, you would need to get inside the Temple of Understanding. Every inch of that building is pre-sighted and guarded with automated firearms. The plaza around it is patrolled by the Triary—the most hardened and elite of the Death's Head. Even the land around the Enclave is watched by a hundred satellites in orbit miles above. Without an active, functioning Mark account, you'd be walking dead men."

"Quintain and I have been inside the Enclave before. I've snuck in myself no less than half a dozen times. There is nothing there I cannot handle."

"Same here," Quintain put in. "Though my own trips inside were confined to the underground food factories while still in the flesh. No camera or AI or Death's Head dupe can detect an etheric projection." He paused to think for a moment. "The pyramid structure—the Temple of Understanding?"

She nodded, bidding him to continue.

"It's guarded by more than just men and machines. A host of demonic familiars swirls about the place. For me, they are my only true obstacle. Your home is a nexus of evil, Alouine. The spiritual adversaries of humanity are gathering there for an assault on the future of the earth. They must be stopped."

Alouine ground her teeth. She resisted the idea of truly throwing her lot in with Outlanders, no matter how capable or competent they were. The difficulty wrote itself plain on her face. To do so meant turning traitor on everything she had ever known.

"If anyone can succeed at this, it's us," Quintain said. "Let us help you create a new Order—one you can be proud of, instead of ashamed."

"Very well," she finally murmured. "If you are committed to this folly, I will not try to stop you, but only on the condition that you honestly seek to change the policy of the Last Men." Her gaze fell on Harrow, and she held it there. "I will not abide a murderous rampage."

Quintain spoke up, satisfied that he was on track to brokering a deal. "Good. We agree on that, at least."

Harrow did not argue, but neither did his silence bring the others any comfort.

The boy tried to put the issue to rest. "Now I strongly suggest that you rest and recover for the night while I try to find some answers."

— — —

Etheric projection had always been so easy, but the kind of 'mind-diving' he was about to attempt always made him slightly nervous.

Quintain felt his spirit tear itself free from his body with a snap. Instantly, he was elsewhere, standing in the Experiential Archive, his spirit form propelled there by his mother's technique. His mother had referred to it as the Akashic Record or the Spirit Library, but it was the Archive to him. By any other name, it was still what it was.

No matter how many times he repeated the exercise, he still found it impossible to describe the Archive to anyone who was not a soul traveler. It wasn't really a place, as far as he or his mother knew. It was more of a communal image, a mental construction that reached through time. Yet it felt so real that Quintain could reach out and touch the stones around him, feel the drip of water and the movement of the air.

Its origin dated back to a supposed better day, when the Old Ones had walked among men.

The teen had his doubts on that count, but he'd never voiced them to his mother. She had a kind of blind faith that Quintain lacked in any form, tending toward the skeptical despite his vast accumulation of esoteric knowledge. The spiritual and the scientific were one and the same to him. He did not dismiss either but checked one against the other. Still, any story was probably better than no story at all.

Besides, his honored mother was family and family was allowed its quirks.

The inside of the Archive was dark and curved in an organic fashion. It looked much more like the handiwork of a sadistic breed of giant, black, resin-extruding wasps than the stone that it was formed to resemble. The walls curved away in the warm darkness, covered with veins that pulsed in the damp heat.

There was a musk there that could assault the nose. It was a scent that almost no one unprepared could stand. The smell was something that spirits exuded when frightened, as Quintain found out when he'd surprised his mother while she was summoning and binding one day. That experience, he supposed, had given him enough wherewithal to counteract the dizzying and noxious effect of the pheromones.

His spirit walked down the bone-shaped corridors, listening. The Whispers were quiet. Normally, they were almost clamorous in that place where they were closest to the world of Men. But, at that moment, Quintain could feel the silence like a weight on his shoulders. It was the quiet of being ignored for something of greater importance, and it was a sensation he knew well. Something, or someone, must have gained their attention. It was the first time he was aware of that happening.

The sinking feeling in his stomach grew. He picked up his pace to reach the central core before the vision faded. Knowing that his time in that corner of the Spirit World was limited, he pressed onward. No magician, not even teams working together, could stay there for long, as his mother had wisely appraised him before his first visit, and this was especially true if one did not have the aid of the Whispers.

The many irregular corridors of the Archive converged on a single hub like the spokes of a giant wheel. Each tunnel emptied into the massive domed structure, bigger than anything men had built in the history of the earth. Then again, men hadn't built that, either; the Old Ones had.

Quintain paused at the doorway, drawing the signs of acceptance in the air with his hands. There was no physical challenge, but a subtle pressure eased off of him, and he could pass through the arch into the dome itself.

The bony, ribbed floor sloped downwards in a gentle fashion to stop at a perfectly circular and mirror-smooth pool in the very center. The diffuse, pale-blue lighting of the Archive cast shadows on the pool—the Archive itself, in a sense. It was the place where memory and perception were stored among the People. It was the source of the living library that stretched through time and space, separate from it all.

His mother had told him stories of those who had encountered long-lost relatives in the Archive—ancestors or distant descendants. The laws of temporal paradox held no sway. The future was not hidden here; it was laid out.

The only problem with the Archive was that he could be buried beneath the weight of the information it possessed. It had swallowed up the souls of people stronger than he, who had asked the wrong kind of question.

Crossing the half-mile radius of the dome to the pool and kneeling down beside it, the magus folded his etheric body into lotus position and closed his spirit eyes in concentration.

Quintain's mother's side of the family had a very distinct set of hereditary quirks, passed down for longer than any of the earth's incomplete histories could record. He knew that in the ancient time stretching back to the beginnings of humanity, there had always been keepers of secrets.

The Order was simply a continuation of those cults, the hoarders of the secret of flame, the first priests of the earth and the first kingmakers of humanity. According to the lore, fire and light were the ancient symbols of intellect and evolved consciousness. The Last Men and their descendants carried these secrets over the course of millennia and used them to rule over the ignorant masses.

The final straw came when the humans discovered the arts of summoning and binding spiritual or archetypal forces as familiars, a practice which he was well-versed in theory. All spheres of existence in the universe are essentially the same, from subatomic particles to entire galaxies; from the microbiotic to the macrobiotic. God's creation spanned a great scale of vibratory frequencies, with humanity's consciousness oscillating in only one tiny area of the spectrum.

He was aware that all of existence contained underlying and overlapping consciousness and intelligence. Quintain abstained from doing much summoning of those extra-dimensional entities, and he was very hesitant about binding them to his soul.

His mother had frequently reminded him that they were inhuman intelligences who cared nothing for the welfare of humans. Many were diametrically opposed to the spiritual evolution of the human race, and would gladly corrupt and destroy a human soul.

The exceptions to this self-imposed ban were those spirits which his mother had introduced to him; spirits of angels, the keepers of the four corners, necessary for the banishing ritual of the pentagram and the six-rayed star, and other Workings. God had set Man above those spirits and ordained them as messengers, guardians and servants of humanity.

He was being distracted again. As much as the origins of humanity fascinated him, Quintain had other information to seek. Again, he acutely felt the absence of the Whispers. Those guiding voices had always helped him stay on track.

Redoubling his efforts to concentrate on his task, Quintain humbled himself and went through the steps required to enter into a meditation within a meditation, armoring his psyche for the images and feelings he would be exposed to. He summoned his guardian angels and put them to task.

Gazing into the pool, he pictured Anhur, the god-form or archetype bound to Harrow's soul. As the mighty, bronze-coated warrior took shape in his mind, a reflection of the being coagulated into place within the rippling pool.

Extending his awareness, he projected his desire to learn about the being he set forth. The Archive responded by flooding his consciousness with waves of raw, unfiltered data, and Quintain struggled to keep up with the torrent.

He was able to snag key pieces as they shot by. Anhur was an ancient and powerful spirit. Like most, it was a fragment of a more commanding over-soul. The teen was reminded that, just as human souls were tiny fragments of the cosmic creative principle or God, the other spirits of the universe were likewise made of components. Like a mosaic, each spiritual fragment, combined with others of its ilk, gave rise to a larger picture.

From abstract, ideal principle to manifestation, the layers of spiritual forms laid on top of one another in spirals which rose from the material earth to the divine heights of the astral world, a spectrum which human consciousness simply could not reach. Quintain grasped that this Onuris was a first tier spirit, an angel—as close to manifestation as a disembodied intelligence could be. That explained why it had been able to manifest into the physical world, using Harrow and his reality-warping brain augmentation as a channel.

The god-form itself was a specific aspect of a more general principle: conflict. Tracing its lineage up the spiritual hierarchy, the magus found that Anhur-Onuris was an aspect of Oriphiel, the terrible archangel of wrath who purifies mankind with an unforgiving hand.

Of course, humanity had worshipped gods of war and battle for millennia by scores of names. Some shared aspects with other fragmented spirits, as gods of thunder and war, gods of strategic thinking, gods of destruction and unrestrained bloodletting.

Onuris, Slayer of Enemies, the Solitary Warrior, represented strength and power, and was associated with gods of the sky and salvation and protection, but also freedom and victory. As spirits went, it was less severe than most of its violent, domineering ilk. Having spoken to the being, it was apparent that the spirit cared nothing for Harrow's life or psyche and would consume both with its desire to act, to have its presence felt on the earth. That was the primal yearning of all spiritual entities. Onuris was no different.

Whoever had bound such a spirit to Harrow had done so with a great deal of diligence and intuition. Quintain shifted his focus to search the Archive for the summoner responsible for binding Onuris to Harrow's soul.

The image of a man coagulated within the pool, and he was shocked to notice that the pictorial representation of the man resembled Harrow almost exactly. Larger than Harrow by a slight margin, and with longer hair and beard, the figure could have been a picture of the Outlander warrior from the future.

Stranger still, he felt a sense of epiphany at beholding the figure which went beyond mere echoes of intertwining fates. Nagging emotions clawed at him, but he pushed them away. Tangents were dangerous and time was against him.

The Archive also showed Quintain a sacred grove, somewhere in the Outlands, marked by a gigantic carving of Onuris' spirit sigil, constructed of metal and stone. Surrounded by elm and oak trees, the massive dais was at least four meters across and shaped with incredible precision; the lines were laser straight and possessed no flaws in their curves. He committed the image of the sigil to memory, a hard and angular symbol constructed of thick lines and sharp angles.

Carving a physical representation of a spirit's sigil, its signature and a symbol of its power, was often offered by human summoners as a reward for loyal services rendered. In this instance, the god-form was paid, generously, in advance.

Was Harrow's father responsible? What kind of man would use his own son to perpetuate such horror on the world? Quintain sighed. Without the Whispers, the guiding librarian spirits of the Archive, he was at a loss.

He hated the very idea of calling his mother's residual memories forth, to question the vestiges of her spirit. She deserved to rest in peace. Still, he had not disturbed her in the years since she had died, and he pushed the thought away as a final resort.

Her cares were over, and these knots were Quintain's to unravel.

SEVENTEEN

His data link chimed incessantly, but Carver muted it. The High Circle would expect a report, an explanation for how he had managed to 'misplace' two tilt-rotor aircraft and three full companies of Death's Head soldiers.

The Last Man ducked them. He had not expected the soldiery to accomplish the impossible and actually kill Harrow themselves, but exterminating that village served duel purposes—it robbed the Outlander of a safe base where he could supply and rest himself, and it also sent a clear message. Carver had threatened to do it and did not want his threats to appear empty.

If some minions, who would otherwise merely be kicking their heels, had to pay the price for that, Carver was fine with it. He had paid—generously—for their services, having deposited a massive amount of credits into the Temple of Domination's coffers. The pawns were his to do with as he pleased.

What would otherwise be the point of maintaining such monopoly of power by so tiny a minority? He scoffed. In the Enclave, hundreds ruled thousands, but only a dozen men had real power to do as they pleased. The High Circle no doubt viewed it as yet another egregious and ignominious failure, without realizing that it was merely one step in a multi-phase plan.

Carver and Armiluss walked along the corridors of the Temple of Understanding to the laboratory space provided to Carver's Circle, passing through the checkpoints and biometric scans. As the automatic doors slid open, they stepped into a room so gleaming with sterility and cleanliness that it irritated the eyes.

White walls and floors and a glowing, florescent ceiling cast harsh light on stainless steel furniture. Machines and measuring devices of all types and descriptions littered the room at varying intervals. Metal arms with probes and cameras, replete with tools of all kinds for gripping and cutting and drilling, projected from the walls and ceilings regularly. It was a den of clinical materiality, a world that both man and Lictor were sure they did not belong to.

Armiluss did not show it, but his master knew that he was frightened by places like this. The Lictor's body and mind had been disassembled here, broken down to constituent parts and rebuilt to Carver's liking. The process had been agonizing. Yet, there was more to endure.

The Last Man had been nothing but forthcoming and candid when it came to that room, carefully explaining what was to be done and how much pain it would cause. In this particular case, he assured Armiluss that he would be unconscious for the implantation and that there would be no difficult, frustrating, and debilitating rehabilitation required, as there had been so many times before.

Carver spotted Heid on the far side of the room and picked his way through the space. The scientist stood before a transparent, cylindrical containment device with a holographic tablet in hand, feverishly checking various measurements and attending other minutia.

"Well?" the chairman said.

"Finished. It's a remarkable design that addresses every conceivable problem. Brilliant stuff, really." Carver huffed, annoyed. "Of course, it's far from perfect. I mean, it is very simple, for what it is. I'll have to purpose build some tools, but the design will benefit from some sophistication." Heid rambled, as he often did when nervous, and shut his mouth.

"Very good. Prep it for installation."

Heid blinked. "The design can be greatly improved."

"Yes, you said as much. It will be, I'm certain. This particular one, however, is going into Armiluss' head; the sooner the better." He glanced back at the looming Lictor. "Go into the surgery theatre and hand yourself over to the orderlies there." The bodyguard trundled off.

"I can make adjustments and build an updated version, for implementation by tomorrow evening," Heid spoke, when he was certain the Lictor was out of earshot. "In fact, the surgery time will be quite short. Two hours, by my reckoning. The procedure is delicate but simple."

"Tomorrow . . . That won't do. We'll need to keep Armiluss under until then. There's no sense risking the handing over of such power to a slave until I have a device of my own capable of trumping it."

"You don't think he would . . ." Heid's voice trailed off, unable to finish his thought.

"Oh, certainly," Carver said. "Armiluss would happily kill us all."

Heid closed his mouth and glanced away, and though Carver had said it just to frighten his vassal, he was sure that it held at least a grain of truth.

— — —

Quintain could not believe the vast difference between his thought process and Harrow's. Sitting beside the bed-ridden warrior and grateful for the chance to hash things out in private, he gazed at the older man sternly. "No one thinks that they are evil," he said firmly. "No one believes that his own actions are motivated by evil. We humans always know, *always*, which is the right way, and which is the wrong way. The wrong way often feels better or takes less work, so we may justify it to ourselves—we rationalize it, we justify it, to feel better for having chosen it!"

Harrow did not look away, but he did close his mouth.

"It is a simple matter of human nature, these justifications. Everyone does this, including me. So, it is a great mistake and fallacy to brand others as evil. We can perceive the result of their actions to be evil, but those people do not see it that way!"

"Yes, the results of their actions," Harrow said. "Right use is the rule of all possessions."

"But no one wakes in the morning with a mind to do evil! A wise man once said: 'Judge not, lest ye be judged'."

"Nonsense. They just had their grand festival, their high holiday, consecrated to the ideal of annihilating their own compassion and empathy! How can you defend them?"

Quintain sighed. "I am not defending them. This Carver Delano is a horrible person and the world would likely be far better without him and his ilk. Is more murder really what this world needs? And if we present ourselves to the Last Men in that light, do we have a chance of convincing them?"

"I do not require them to be convinced. I require them to die."

"Harrow, wiping out our enemies is not the right use of the abilities you possess."

The older Outlander snarled. "Your pacifism will be our downfall!"

Quintain set his mouth in a firm line. "I'm no pacifist. Defending others is one of the highest callings of man. No one feels more shame at having failed the people of that village than I do! It's a course of events that has repeated without end! Our brothers and sisters are mutilated and scarred and terrified! How do you think that makes me feel?"

Harrow sneered but looked away.

"Those Last Men are no different than you or I," Quintain said. He felt on the cusp of penetrating Harrow's hardened heart and doubled his effort. "They are repositories of sacred knowledge and secret teachings, and they must be persuaded to share what they have with the rest of the world. Even if you *could* wipe them out, is that what the world really needs? Centuries of abuse and degradation cannot be healed by genocidal revenge!"

"They will never see us as anything more than subhuman slaves."

"You know that isn't true."

"Alouine is an exception to the rule. Even a blind dog finds food once in a while."

"We must prove our worth to them, as we did with her! If we are good and they are evil, why would they listen to us? No, we have to change the way we think—*all* of us—and cease fighting with each other. My friend, my brother, there are things which must be passed on to you. But first, you must begin examining yourself, your agenda, and your mission! Who are you? What do you believe? Is it true?" Quintain's dark eyes shined in the dim light. "Are you helping to divide the world, or are you helping to bring it together?"

Harrow held fast with his piercing gaze. "There are only two languages on this earth, boy— violence and reason. I am fluent in the one and you are fluent in the other, but I'm warning you: there are those among the Last Men who will not respond to anything but violence. I will speak in the language they understand. So you deal with those who might listen to reason, but I think you'll find them in short supply. There will be more violence, and lots of it."

Quintain remembered something he had read long ago. "Only the dead have seen the end of war. Is that it?"

Harrow's ice-blue eyes flashed. "Until the last of the Order is strangled with the guts of the last Lictor, yes."

The magus considered Harrow and all that he had seen the other man do. He had slaughtered that guard in the food production facility without hesitation and, albeit in the thrall of a spirit-bound psychotic episode, had waded into the carnage at the village without reservation.

Quintain tried to assume the role of the aggressor within his mind. He considered the choice of Harrow's weapon. Most likely, the long fighting knife was simply the best object at hand for the task, an 'up close and intimate' tool of brutal mayhem. It necessitated closing the distance to the adversary and violently stabbing and slashing him to ragged bits. The thought made the young man queasy, turned his stomach, and made his hair stand on end.

A firearm, like a pistol, carried with it a sense of detachment, he imagined. Certainly, there was a proper stance and posture, but the physical action of shooting someone involved far less intensity, fewer muscle groups, and the mere squeeze of a trigger. No, a dagger is as personal, vicious, and brutal a way to cause harm as it gets.

What kind of mindset does this entail? Closing with the target hard and fast, using deception or surprise, or simply a committed and determined pouncing, one must be filled with rage. The dagger-wielding warrior knows that he must get it over with quickly. His attack is a frenzy of murderous intent, and demands total commitment.

He does not even begin to slacken or disengage until his blood lust has been sated, and his mark is stricken from the rolls of the living. There is blood, much of it, coating everything, spurting into his eyes and nostrils. To kill a man with a dagger is to taste his blood without gagging.

Quintain swallowed dryly. He forced himself to face facts squarely. The mentality was foreign, alien to his senses, and horrifying to explore.

"There are other ways," he stated, pale and haunted by his thoughts.

"You are not prepared to do what it takes to win this war," the warrior said bluntly.

"You refuse to see it as anything but a war! The wars of men have always been for the profit, control, or racism of a few. The very concept should be disgusting to human sensibilities." He closed his mouth for a beat, considering that he might have stepped too far. Still, he was angry, and pressed on. "This may be your personal war, but it isn't mine. There are other ways to reach the end we both envision. Your wounds have blinded you. You can't see the truth."

Harrow blinked and glanced aside, as though remembering.

"Wherever we seek discord, we injure ourselves. You are living proof of that. Wherever we seek perfection—that is where we find healing."

"I think you just want to see the good in people, even when it isn't there."

"All natural things are benevolent, unless they are abused. The world is in harmony when we are. I have no doubt that there will be those who reject redemption, but I have to trust that we can protect ourselves from any negativity that does not arise from within us! We can't be corrupted by others unless we surrender our integrity!"

The older Outlander frowned. "Is that what the spirit bound to me is? A corruption?"

"Yes."

"My father bound it to me for a reason. You saw what happened. I'm going to need its power again."

Quintain smiled. "There are always other ways. There are other spirits who are not as selfish and uncaring as that one. It is using you, whether you realize it or not."

"It is a weapon. My father gave it to me in order to destroy the Last Men."

"What if it destroys you first?"

— — —

The hardware itself was a step on the road to godhood, but down a different path than the one Carver Delano desired to travel. The ability to project a quantum field was amazing in itself. The counter spinning components generated enormous amounts of raw energy and fed them into his body's own magnetic field. Using the device lit every nerve in Carver's body with white-hot power. He sent a ripple of quantum energy through every atom of his body, accompanied by a surging feeling of supremacy and puissance which welled up inside him.

No wonder the Outlander is so arrogant, Carver thought. He could feel why Harrow thought he could oppose the Order. Unfortunately for him, Carver turned the ape's trump, his 'triumph', into the key to his own victory.

He felt invincible, with complete control over anything that came within arm's reach of him. He still had Heid's pulse emitter, as well.

But it was the operating system, the software, which truly fascinated Carver. This "SIMON" was, by itself, an incredible technical achievement. Quantum computing power, Qubit-driven—the pure data processing ability was staggering.

Armiluss could handle the manipulation of physical things with his older, now-obsolete copy. Carver would rely on him to handle the Outlander. Not to satisfy his duty—Carver scoffed at the thought—but because the man would continue to oppose him one way or another, and demanded removal. Along with the High Circle. But, that was another matter, and would have to wait.

First, Carver focused on theory. The Order of the Last Men had been working on a God Machine for generations, and with his newfound ability to process untold amounts of data and run vast numbers of simulations in seconds, Carver would be the one to finally complete a design.

While the hard data of untold years was locked away from him, since only the High Chairman of the Enclave was allowed unrestricted access to such a secret project, Carver had memorized many of the schematics he had seen while in that old buzzard, Gerald's, service. It gave him the crucial foundation he needed, while the interfaced computing power he stole from the Outlander provided the necessary impetus to carry the design through.

He knew that electromagnetic fields were the key to preserving consciousness beyond the dissolution of the body. All matter proceeded from thought, and the only thing Carver had to do was reverse this process.

"Heid Acheson," he transmitted via encrypted data link.

"Yes, my lord?"

"It appears as though I'm going to need neodymium— twenty kilos at the least. I'll send you detailed schematics."

It took a moment for Heid to respond. "The circle's funds are depleted. There is no way we can afford this. Also, are you certain that the Highest Circle will allow you to pursue this course?"

"I don't care how it is obtained. I will produce an order for the Techno-Research division to hand over to you the materials needed. Just go and pick them up."

"But only the High Circle can authorize—"

"They will," Carver snapped. "I will see to it."

The Highest Circle's encryptions would have taken years upon decades to crack, even with the brute force of the Order's most powerful supercomputers. But Carver had already used SIMON to decipher them in an evening. He issued to Heid a standing production electronic order for the supplies he needed, authenticated with the personal seal of Lord Stamp.

"It is a convincing forgery, my lord, but if the High Circle finds out about this, it will mean both of our lives."

"By the time they find out it will be far too late for them. Do as you are commanded, Lord Acheson. The time is nearly upon us."

EIGHTEEN

Five days passed while Quintain supervised Harrow's recovery. The grasping power of the warrior's injured left hand was diminished, but he could stand and move—gingerly at first, but with increasing vitality. His strained hamstrings hobbled him, and every tweak of his shoulder made him grit his teeth, but, everything considered, Quintain supposed that it might have been far worse.

Life fell into something of a rhythm. Quintain was busiest of all, rationing out the scarce resource of his personal time amongst the others, yet still managing to meditate for hours on end.

His first task was to rehabilitate Harrow and Nina. The big warrior was a phenomenal athlete to begin with, and his body possessed an incredible natural inclination for rapid healing. So, aside from assisting him with stretches and checking on the splints which kept his injured fingers immobile, Quintain could do little.

However, Nina had acute problems: the psychological trauma of losing her hand, the phantom limb pain, and the constant threat of septic infection. It was all Quintain could do to keep the wound clean. Hypnosis was the easiest method of dealing with the trauma, but he was not keen on using invasive techniques. The thought made him uncomfortable. Human psyches were such fragile things.

They spent two hours together every day. He gently took her stump into his hands, feeling the roughness of the scabbed-over wound. When Nina winced, Quintain mirrored the reaction. "Sorry."

Nina patted his arm with her hand. "You don't have anything to be sorry for."

The older boy felt wistful for a moment, and thought to argue, but he decided to just accept her kindness. "Everything looks clean," he said, carefully and gently rotating her arm to inspect the wound. "Let's let it breathe for a little while."

"Sometimes it feels like my hand is still there." She put on a brave face, but Quintain could see her eyes well up.

"That will probably continue," Quintain offered lamely.

"It isn't a bad thing," Joanna put in, circling around from behind a wall of books. "I'm going to try to fabricate a prosthetic. Your body's natural motions may help you to learn to use it more easily."

"You mean a fake hand?"

The older woman nodded. "Don't get your hopes up too much, baby. I need to find materials and a place to work first. And," she added in a mumble, "I never knew how much I . . . didn't know. We have a lot of reading to do."

Quintain resisted the urge to sigh and roll his eyes, as he had essentially become a librarian for Joanna, who had thrown herself into learning as much as she could from the massive stacks of books. He was happy to have a guest with a thirst for knowledge which rivaled his own. However, while the woman could read, she did not know how to research or investigate. Her unrelenting questions had begun to seriously annoy him, and he was forced to arrange a pile of books for her and place a dictionary and thesaurus on top.

"I take it you've finished the stack I set up for you?"

Joanna nodded again. "The Roamers really knew everything, didn't they?" For the past three days, she had delved into the collected knowledge of biomechanics, chemistry, electrical engineering, physics and metallurgy as a drowning woman gasping for air.

"Not everything," Quintain remarked quietly.

He reminded himself that for all of the Roamers' knowledge of science, their civilization had still collapsed. Eventually, he figured that Joanna's awe and yearning would wear itself out, but for now, he indulged her. She would have to face the traumas she had suffered and even this newfound well of learning was an opiate, a way for her to focus on something other than her pain and grief. The woman barely slept, and when she did, it was with an open book in her lap. It was not healthy.

There were moments when he would catch her staring, haunted by memories of things she had seen. Quintain sympathized. He too had been utterly unprepared for the carnage and cruelty he had witnessed at the village.

He rose from his seat on the floor. "I'm going to see about rustling up some lunch. I'll bring something around in a little while."

The girl and her mother thanked him in stereo, and he left them alone, pausing long enough to see Joanna push an open book into Nina's lap.

He walked to the adjacent chamber where Harrow had made his quarters to ask if he was hungry, though he knew the answer would be affirmative. The man was a bottomless pit as far as food was concerned. Quintain supposed that he had the good excuse of his injuries. A healing body needed more nutrition than a healthy one, but he suspected that Harrow's physique and lifestyle— if it could be called that—demanded a ravenous appetite in the best of circumstances. The man was eating him out of house and home.

The antechamber was sparse and dim. It contained only Harrow's bedroll and his pile of weapons and armor. He and Alouine had squabbled over this particular area, closest to the lair's entrance, for its easy access to the outside. When he stated in his succinct fashion that he was responsible for Nina's security, and to a lesser extent, Joanna's, Alouine ceded the point. She removed herself deeper into the underground warren.

Harrow cranked one-handed push-ups when Quintain rounded the partition that separated his space from the more communal area. "Is your left arm still bothering you?"

Harrow merely grunted. A drop of sweat fell from his nose as he hoisted his body weight upward on his good right arm.

Quintain watched for a moment. "You're so much like a horse, it's incredible."

At this, Harrow stopped. He caught himself, gingerly with his left hand and rotated himself into a seated position. "Just what is that supposed to mean?" he asked breathlessly as he settled in to punish his abdominal muscles with crunches.

"A horse, from what I understand, was an animal that had no conception of conserving energy. It could not grasp the idea of waiting or being patient."

"Indeed."

Quintain only shook his head. "You're not an animal, are you?"

Harrow lowered his back to the floor but did not begin another repetition. Silence reigned for several moments.

"I'll return with food. For God's sake, just rest. You'd think I was running a shelter for lunatics. The only sane one here is the youngest!"

Harrow chewed on that thought. "Agreed," he mumbled quietly to himself, just loud enough for Quintain to hear as he walked away.

— — —

Three more days and Harrow felt his health had recovered. The first step toward proving that he was significantly healed was a successful hunting trip. Deer were plentiful nearby, and he managed to bring down a fat doe in the early, pre-dawn hours with his father's rifle. The fifty-kilo beast felt light across his shoulders.

He was satisfied that his strength had returned and his soreness abated.

He settled into the ruined basement of a nearby building to hang the creature from the mostly collapsed roof girders so that he could bleed and clean it. Working proficiently with KA-BAR to take the hide, he laid it over a wire while he butchered the animal.

The scent of blood was thick in the air, but he still sensed Alouine's approach. She had taken to wandering in the morning, despite Quintain's warnings to stay close to the lair.

"Well done," she said flatly. Harrow merely nodded. "You're going to eat this?"

"If butchered properly, it will feed all of us for some time."

Alouine stepped closer, though her nose wrinkled. Harrow's arms were coated in blood to his elbows. She watched him work.

He took the heart and the liver and discarded the other internal organs, then set to work removing meat from bones. He stopped on occasion to work his blade on a whetstone.

"Why keep the heart?" she asked. "Is it edible?"

"Seared in a pan, it is. I find it harder to swallow raw." The woman blanched, and Harrow responded with a tiny smirk. "At least I won't have to split the lion's share." He wrapped his prize, along with the rest of the meat, within the deer's hide tightly, bundling it with twine.

Leaving the remainder to scavengers, he threw the bundle over his shoulder. It was a good twenty kilograms and the thought was satisfying. The first flies began to appear, buzzing around the carcass, so he had finished just in time.

"This needs to be hung in a dry place so that it can be preserved," he said, and without any other preamble, he set off back toward the lair.

The woman fell into step beside him. "I'll help you."

"It's a simple process. The weather has been cool, so none of it should spoil."

Alouine scoffed. "That is not what I meant." Harrow glanced at her. "I was speaking more," she paused, "generally."

Harrow did not say anything as the pair worked their way along the rubble-strewn paths back to Quintain's lair.

She picked up on his tacit consent. "Despite what you might think, you and I have goals in common. I left the Enclave because things there are changing, rapidly."

"What things?"

"There is a man who has gone completely drunk with power and ambition. My father was the Chairman of the Highest Circle, and . . . he was the leader of the Enclave. One of his subordinates murdered him and intends to take his place."

Harrow digested this in silence. The Last Men had killed both of their fathers. It was a sobering thought.

"He also intended to take me for a mate. I couldn't bear the idea."

"Why not kill him? You're nothing if not capable of that."

"It is a complex situation. He has too much influence, too much political power. Believe me, I wanted nothing more than to feel Carver die, to watch his eyes roll back and to savor his last gasp in this world. But he comes from too large a family. I would never know peace."

Harrow's lips pursed. "Carver Delano."

Alouine blinked and nearly missed a step. "How do you know that?"

"I've met the man. We share a common enemy. I believe your Order has tasked him with killing me. He has tried many times. Before we met again in the village, he sought me out. I should have known then that he would make good on his threats."

"So he *was* behind the raid on the village." Alouine seethed, her fists clenching. "Wait. You mean to say that you've actually met him in person?"

Harrow nodded. "Only a few hours after our first meeting. He followed me for a few klicks after I left the Enclave. It seemed strange; I allowed him to catch me up, so I could hear what he had to say."

Her eyes bulged. "Just how reckless are you?"

"He was alone. I had no doubt that we were being watched from above, but," he paused, trying to convey his thoughts in a way the woman would understand. "I respected his bravery."

Alouine hopped over a large stone in her path. "I could call that man a great many things, but brave is not among them. What could he possibly have to say to you?"

"He tried to bribe me."

"That makes more sense."

"I did not expect that we would reach an agreement, but I am not beyond honorable negotiations. He threatened to have the village destroyed if I attacked him, so I let him leave."

"You should have killed him on the spot."

"In hindsight, yes. But the same can be said of you."

She nodded, grimacing. "Still, something doesn't sit right about this. I've never known Carver to risk danger or even discomfort. He must have been up to something beyond trying to grease your palm."

Harrow blinked. "Grease my what?"

Alouine sighed. "It's an expression. I think his trying to bribe you was merely a front for something else."

That made Harrow's mouth form a grim line. Ascribing honor to his foe was proving more and more difficult. "All we did was talk," he said. "He wore a weapon of some kind on his right hand, which he kept pointed at me, but I assumed it was because he was afraid. It was like a metal glove with a lens in the palm."

"That could have been anything. He has a very capable and inventive scientist under his thumb."

Harrow nodded and the pair walked on, consumed by thoughts.

"I might have brought it up to you before, but," the Outlander's voice trailed off. "I was suspicious of your purpose and intentions."

"I don't blame you. When we first met, it was my anger with him that made me so ready to fight you."

"Still, I was wrong."

They hiked in silence for several minutes. Harrow broke it by saying, "We both want this man dead."

Alouine nodded. "That is far easier said than done. He has a Lictor, a bodyguard, who is the most imposing brute I've ever laid eyes on. Present company included."

Harrow's eyebrow twitched, but he had no rebuttal.

Alouine pressed on. "If he dies, my main obstacle to seizing power in the Enclave dies with him."

"What would you do with it?"

"With the Enclave? My father wanted to reform the Order, to end the senseless cruelty. There was too much inertia, too much weight of tradition. Now, the Third City is at a tipping point. Carver will make his move soon, if he has not already. The turmoil and upheaval he creates might be the best chance to effect real change."

Harrow took a moment to absorb that. "You believe he will attempt a coup?"

"I have no doubt. The man is every bit as reckless as you are. He's a murderer with no sense of his own limitations."

Harrow let this pass, preferring to let his actions and not his words defend his pride.

— — —

Alouine followed along until they reached a deep ravine, created by the collapse of the ancient street into the sewer underneath.

Harrow set down his bundle. "Toss this to me when I reach the bottom," he requested, before acrobatically descending, hopping nimbly from jutting rock to snapped girder to broken pipe. His feet had just reached the bottom when he felt the air move behind his head. Reacting without thinking or looking, he caught the twenty kilos of butchered animal. His brows furrowed.

"Your reflexes are as good as ever," Alouine called down to him, with a smirk gracing her lips. She took a half step back and leapt down the entire distance in one bound, slowing herself in the air before gracefully touching down beside the larger man. She stuck the landing with a flourish.

Harrow shook his head in disapproval. "You call me reckless?"

Alouine smiled. "I call you a good bet."

He shouldered the burden once again. "I understand that you're using me. You have everything to gain if I succeed."

The woman sighed. "You don't have to look at it that way. I'm betting everything on you, don't you understand that? It's why I'm still here. I know full-well that you expect me to betray you at the earliest opportunity, and there doesn't seem to be any way to convince you otherwise. But I have no reason to lie to you. We are in this together and I intend to follow it through to the end, whatever that may be."

Harrow clenched his jaw, seeming to war inside himself as to whether he could trust her.

"Quintain trusts me," she offered, as though she had a window into his internal conflict.

"He is a boy. A naïve one," Harrow said.

"Not my strongest argument, I admit," she replied. "Still, his judgment must count for something. Regardless, I'm relying on you. I want you to know that you can rely on me as well."

"Why?"

Alouine blinked. "Because there are good people at the Enclave, people I care for, and I don't want to see you try to murder them." She took a breath. "Your rage runs deep." She looked into his crystal blue eyes. "I think you're right to feel it, Harrow. There has been a great . . . injustice done, and it does need to be set right. You do deserve a measure of revenge on behalf of your people. I do want to help you. All I want in return is for you to spare the ones I love."

"People you care for," he echoed softly. "Ones you love? Correct me if I am wrong, but did you not just partake of a ritual designed to sever you from your compassion? Didn't you watch an Outlander burn at the stake so that you could destroy your sense of empathy?" He rounded on her, his voice steeling. "I know all about the Cremation and what it means to your Order."

Alouine raised her hands defensively, palms open. "I did not go to this year's festival. It was my opportunity to escape while everyone else was there. I know that does not excuse my participation in past festivals to you, but it is a yearly ritual for a reason. The effects of it, they wear off." Though it was true, it sounded a hollow excuse. "There is no way to atone for what my people have done. I've learned a great many things, Harrow. I've learned to regret a great many things."

The righteous blue flame of anger stoked itself into a raging inferno in the man's aura. "Your Order revels in the horror and suffering of my people. They should suffer the same fate they have consigned to others, so they can understand the pain of death by fire." She could see in his eyes a vision of the entire Enclave burning.

"You are no stranger to violence," she reminded him.

"I do not savor it! I do not take pleasure in what is merely necessary!"

"When we were in the village, and you channeled your familiar, you mutilated the Death's Head men you fought. You defaced them. You castrated them."

Harrow clamped his lips shut. "I was," he murmured, "not aware." There was a brief grimace of abashment on his face that should have satisfied her, but had the opposite effect.

"Some part of you is always aware," she responded softly. "We have all done things for our convictions that we only come to understand later."

"Judge not, lest ye be judged," he mumbled.

"Something akin to that."

They walked on in silence for long moments, nearing the underground lair at last.

"What are you thinking?" she asked, stopping short of the entrance.

Harrow continued walking inside, leaving her by saying, "That we have come to an understanding. I can only trust fate that I won't regret it."

— — —

The exposed coil of the heating element glowed red-hot, and Harrow found it more suitable than a fire for his purposes. He had shut the machine off and dragged it to an unused side chamber, along with a large bucket of water.

There was a convenient marble bench along the length of the room, a ledge that ran along the wall, and it was perfect. The room, dark—save for the indirect light bouncing in from outside—had only one entrance. The far wall had begun to crumble under the weight of generations, leaving deep cracks in the floor at one end of the room. Designed perhaps as a reading nook, the warrior repurposed it as a sauna. Those same cracks would provide a place for water to drain into.

He had not bathed since before the battle at the village and began to stink to his own nose. He imagined that to others, he gave off an unholy stench. A thick layer of dried blood, crusted sweat and caked soil matted his hair and made his clothing stiff.

He would need to beat out his coat like an old rug, and do it outdoors— the clouds of dirt would be thick.

To rectify the situation, he had gathered the heater, a pile of suitably porous rocks from outside, and the water. Careful not to burn or electrocute himself, he laid several of the rocks on the exposed element until they were hot enough and, with clothing removed, stacked them into a pile, using KA-BAR and one of his steel armored sleeves.

Trickling water onto them until the room was filled with steam, he reclined on the marble bench and let the vapor cleanse his skin and seep into his clothes, particularly his undergarments. He would launder everything properly later. For now he simply bathed to remove the film on his skin. Sweat poured from his pores and condensation beaded on the walls.

Twenty minutes of peace followed, and a comfortable numbness crept through his muscles and bones. He wiped the moisture from his eyes and swapped out the cooling rocks for freshly heated ones as he heard Quintain wander in from the corridor, "What in the world?" The boy poked his head into the room thick with fog. "I hope this does not ruin my books."

"The steam will condense long before it reaches them," Harrow mumbled. "The water will eventually collect in the cracks in the floor."

Quintain nodded. "You never cease to surprise me."

"You can join me, if you want."

"Why not? It seems to beat washing cold."

"My sentiments exactly," Harrow sighed.

"I'll get towels so we needn't air dry."

With eyes closed, Harrow listened as the teenager left and returned moments later, then disrobed and plopped down a respectful distance away on the marble bench.

They sat in silence for several minutes until Quintain chuckled. "What is it?"

"Nothing," the boy murmured. A beat of silence reigned before he giggled again.

Harrow grumbled, "Out with it."

"It stinks in here," the boy blurted with a chortle.

A slow, lazy smirk crossed the warrior's lips. "Indeed." The steam was doing its job, releasing every drop of sweat and every particle of dirt and funk from the skin and clothing of the two Outlanders.

"Ugh. It's like a man stew. Is that you, or me?"

"It was less bad before you arrived."

Quintain broke into an open laugh. "Probably."

"On the bright side, when the others discover what we're doing in here, they will almost certainly want a turn, and at least we were first," Harrow mused.

"Good point."

Both men considered this, a smirk on Harrow's face and a mischievous grin on Quintain's. After another few moments, Quintain segued, "We should talk."

"Now is as good a time as any."

"I think I've found a new workshop for Joanna in my etheric travels, but I need to go there physically to make sure. So I'll need to leave for a few days."

"How far is it?"

"A few miles to the southeast. I want to give myself enough time to thoroughly case the area."

Harrow nodded. "Would you like me to go with you?"

"I don't think so. You should stay here and continue your rehab. You and Alouine seem to have come to terms. The two of you should begin training together. If the place I'll be searching for actually exists—and isn't just wishful thinking— it'll be a good step in the right direction. We'll be able to start preparing for a showdown with the Order."

"All the more reason I should accompany you."

"Well, like I said, the place might not actually be real. Searching the astral planes is not the most objective exercise. Sometimes you get caught up in your own desires and see something just because you want to. I'll go, quick and discrete. You have the valor part down, but I don't really trust you on the discretion part. No offense."

Harrow almost laughed. "None taken." Standing, he moved to the water bucket and poured some of it over his head and, splashing it over his skin, rinsed off his flesh. He made sure to leave the bucket half full for his companion.

"Good God, that feels better," the boy remarked. He handed Harrow one of the towels. They smelled musty but were clean. "There's a good place to hang our clothes to dry. I'll show you."

The pair wrapped the towels around their waists and gathered their clothes. They walked out of the still-steaming room, but they were stopped dead in their tracks by three female forms gawking at them from the corridor.

Alouine had her hands on her hips and looked mildly perturbed. One of Joanna's eyebrows threatened to climb up her forehead to her hairline, and when the men emerged from the fog, she clamped one hand over Nina's eyes. The girl had her remaining hand to her mouth and managed to move her head enough to peek past her guardian's fingers.

"Finished, are you?" Alouine asked dryly.

"Help yourselves," Harrow replied, his face blank and voice even. Quintain had to hide his face in his clothing as he hurried past, while the larger Outlander male strode by at a leisurely pace. He felt three pairs of eyes tracking him and rolled his shoulders once so that they could watch the muscles of his back ripple. He heard Alouine pretend to scoff.

The two were hanging their clothing on a line when they heard Joanna exclaim from the makeshift steam room.

"Damn, it stinks in here!"

Quintain fell into gales of hilarity and even Harrow cracked a genuine smile.

NINETEEN

Alone, the teenager walked through a frigid, windswept wasteland of bombed-out rubble, overgrown with grey-green vegetation. Nature, wounded and starved, struggled to break through the thick layer of pulverized bricks and cinderblocks, and grow in what little sunlight penetrated the grey pallor above. There were animals—rabbits and squirrels and the occasional chirp of a bird could be heard in the post-dawn light. Soon, those animals would hibernate for the coldest months, but for now they were still active, doing their best to fatten up for the lean times to come.

Also, there were Outlanders.

They watched him from their hovels, which were literally holes in the ground, as he walked down the center of the decrepit road. The only building materials at hand were stacks of rocks and bricks, haphazardly piled over pits dug in the earth. The homes were indistinguishable from the surrounding landscape to the uneducated eye, but Quintain could pick them out as he strolled along.

Cave-dwellers, louse-colonies, people who had no conception of washing, no real language skills—it broke the boy's heart. What could a man think about, who only lived moment to moment? What could he innovate when he could not read, and put the knowledge of the past to use?

Human beings reduced to the level of feral swine, living and acting only from base instinct and savage nature. It filled the young man with a raging sorrow; that miserable existence in stinking, filthy, muddy, lice-and-flea-infested piles of rock—grey and hopeless.

He knew they tracked his every movement. Careful to project an aura of harmlessness but also extreme poverty, the last thing Quintain wanted was to be seen as prey. With the animals about, he didn't think anyone would actually want to eat him, but he knew they would attack and kill him if he showed anything worth taking.

Closing his eyes, he felt that he was nearing his destination, and strode on using astral sight to find the treasury of machines he sought. Even with his physical eyes shut and his ethereal eyes open, he could sense three souls emerge from the ruins and begin to track along behind him. After another hundred meters, Quintain stopped.

Three young men approached from behind him, and, for a moment, the teenage magician's heart clenched in his chest. He did not want to fight, and did not relish the idea of being chased. So he turned to face them and waited, reminding himself that regardless of how degraded they were, they were still people—his brothers.

The first young man in the chevron of boys was exactly in the middle in height. He was flanked by the taller one on the right and the shortest, youngest-looking one on his left.

Plastering a smile on his face which was as genuine as he could manage under the circumstances, Quintain extended his right hand, palm up. "Hello," he said, a little too loudly.

The young man in front of him resembled a mud creature, only human in his eyes and so caked with dirt and filth that his features were near unrecognizable. He spared only a glance at the outstretched hand. "Ain' seen yoo b'fore," he drawled.

"I'm Quintain. It's been a few years since I was out this way."

The boys broke into a semi-circle around the young magus, hemming him in. "I'm Vol. This is Stringer," he said, gesturing to the taller boy, "and Mite," he finished, hooking his thumb at the short, stunted-looking youth on the other side. "Wha'cha doin' here?"

"I'm looking for something," Quintain responded, taking a half-step back so that he could smile at each of the accosting youths in turn. "It's good to meet you guys." He hoped that it wasn't merely wishful thinking. None of the trio seemed violent, only suspicious, and that was to be expected.

"T'ain't nothin' t'find," Vol said. "Best t'move along."

"I wish I could, but this is too important to pass up. Perhaps if you fellows would help me, I could find what I'm looking for that much faster."

"Ain't no free women and no food, here."

"Good thing I'm not searching for either of those. There is a place around here that has machines in it. It might be partially buried."

Stringer nudged Vol and leaned down to whisper to him. The boy nodded. "We know th' place," he said, "but there ain't no point. Nothin' works."

"That's all right," Quintain said easily. "All things can be repaired."

Vol scratched his head through his thick cap. "You one o'them machine priests?"

Quintain thought about that for a moment. He did not consider himself a 'machine priest', though he got the gist of what the other boy meant. Any answer he gave would likely lead to further suspicion, so he decided that bluntness was the best policy. "Yes, among other things. But I've come here for an even more powerful machine priest. Actually, she's a priestess. I'm supposed to find machines for her to use."

Vol appeared to consider this. His taller compatriot, Stringer, just stared at Quintain hard, his eyes locked on the shiny jewel embedded in the magician's forehead. The other one, Mite, had already lost interest and was gazing off to the horizon. "We ain't had a machine priest since I was a little kid," Vol said. "Wha'd ya mean by 'other things'?"

"I guess I'm more of an 'all-priest'."

"Wha's that mean?" Vol's brow furrowed, and Quintain could see that the other Outlander was suspicious, and that he assumed he was being tricked.

The magus sighed to deflect some of the suspicion. "It just means that I know more things than just machines. Things like people, and spirits."

"Yer fulla shit," Vol spat. "You don' know nothin' 'bout me."

Quintain took a deep, cleansing breath and let his eyes sink closed. His third eye gem lit with a soft, blue-white glow. The other Outlanders hastened backwards a step. Their auras were muddied with the poison of doubt and fear. In this state, the magus could read them like open books.

In the faraway, vibratory voice of his astral-gazing trance, Quintain intoned, "I know many things, brother. I know that you are an honest and caring young man. I feel the weight of responsibility you bear for your two friends. You lead them because they are dear to you, but sometimes the burden of doing so casts you into despair, and in dark moments you wonder if you are better off alone."

The boy stared at him, slack-jawed. He glanced at his two companions and stuttered the beginning of an argument, but the magus cut him off.

"It is not wrong to doubt, but be without fear. Your friends are loyal and love you for what you are," he rumbled from his chest.

Turning the glowing gem toward Stringer, he said, "You are worried that your height makes you a marked man, and that your size means equally large expectations. You are afraid that people, especially Vol and Mite, but also your family, will rely on you and that you will be unable to meet their expectations. Be without fear, brother, for your mind will grow to fill the house it inhabits."

The tall boy mutely stared at the ground as Quintain rounded on the last youth. "Poison has robbed you of your health since birth. Others fear that you are too simple to be good for anything, and secretly hope that you leave before becoming a further burden. But be without fear. The gates of health and happiness are not closed to you; you need only a teacher who understands your plight."

The stunted boy just grinned dumbly. Quintain could see the glow of his gem reflect in the other boy's etheric eyes. He left the trance and reopened his physical eyes.

Vol would not meet his gaze. "You are a priest. You need t'meet th' chief. Come on, we'll take ya."

They led him through a camouflaged little town. Last Man's eyes would see the wasteland they supposed it should be. However, the magus saw trading posts and guard bunkers, grain storage, chicken coops and rabbit warrens. Occasional pairs of eyes peered out at him from the shadows as Vol led him in a practiced, calculated route, following underneath a crumbling overpass to keep them hidden from the sky.

An ancient underground complex, which had once been used by the Roamers to transport large numbers of people via long carriages which moved on steel tracks, had been repurposed as the center of the Outlander community. The chief claimed the largest series of chambers as his own. Protected by concrete and earth, it was a palace and a fortress in one.

Multiple tunnels beneath the earth intersected to form a massive, underground colony. Quintain saw near two hundred Outlanders in that section alone, and he knew that transport tunnels like these ran for miles. The Roamers had called this the Subterranean Way, or 'Sub-Way'.

The derelict of the Roaming Empire was a natural habitat for Outlanders, much like his own home, but that the community had grown this large surprised him. His mother had never taken him here before.

The chief himself was elderly by all Outlander standards. His fiftieth year had come and gone. He sat on throne of cushions piled up against the far wall, surrounded by what passed for his court. His numerous wives and daughters, a dozen in all, flocked around him in small groups, gathered around various low tables, and played parlor games involving cards or boards with tiny pieces.

Quintain, led by Vol, approached the man who summoned them forward with a wave of his hand. He was of stocky build, with thick forearms and fingers like stubs. The teenager had never seen a fat Outlander before and still could not claim to have done so, but this man pushed the envelope.

His middle was wrapped in a pudgy band of flesh which served to advertise his position of power. His meticulously groomed and braided beard stood out proudly; it was clasped by jewelry made from a Death's Head soldier's signature emblem.

The magus wondered briefly if there was a war-trophy and, if so, if it had been personally won or gifted to the man. It was not the only mark of his authority. Bangles hung from his wrists and ears and beside the 'throne', a long string of scalps.

A hatchet-like weapon was propped up close by, the haft of which was intricately carved. He had a well-cared for pistol, the same issued to Death's Head soldiers, tucked into his wide belt, and as Quintain and Vol neared him, the magus spotted more armed Outlanders sitting close enough to spring to action.

They also wielded weapons taken from the soldiery of the Order, as well as similar hatchets tucked into their belts for close action. They were likely the chief's picked men, his bodyguards, and possibly also his sons or the husbands of his daughters.

Vol made a strange submissive gesture of bowing his head low and showing the chieftain his open hands. The magus just stood there.

"Make your business quick, boy," the chief spat dismissively, his voice a low, thick rumble.

"Found this priest, sir. He's f'real."

Quintain pursed his lips slightly. *Quick indeed*, he mused to himself as he stepped forward into the light.

The chief appeared as though he was going to upbraid Vol for wasting his time, and perhaps have his men throw the boy a beating. But he leaned forward and, squinting, beckoned Quintain even closer. "I know you," he said softly.

Quintain blinked. "I— Wait. You do?"

"Oh, yes," the man said, his rumbling growing louder. "You don't remember me, do you?"

The teenage magician arched a brow but said nothing.

"My name is Crate. I remember your mother, boy. She was a great moon priestess, a powerful witch and the best thing to happen to Outlanders in generations. Hell, she helped deliver my four oldest children! She fixed my arm when it was broken and healed an infection in my son's eye." The man stood, and all of the other conversations in the great hall ceased. "We still use much of what she taught us here. I'm in her debt forever!"

"As am I," Quintain said softly.

The chief, Crate, nodded vigorously but let silence settle over the room. He stepped down from his cushioned platform at the top of the stairs. "Her death pains me still," he said. "It was my greatest defeat."

"And mine," the boy agreed.

"Where have you been? I searched for months for you, to see that those devils hadn't ended you, too. It's been years. Three years now, am I right?"

Quintain nodded. "I was laying low." *Perhaps too low*, he thought. Those people probably could have used his help. He felt guilty knowing that he was missed, but at the time he hadn't been ready to step into his mother's shoes.

The chief returned his nod. "Yes, I see." He walked right up to the boy and did not have to lean down very far in order to closely inspect the gem in his forehead. "That is your mother's mark, as sure as I'm standing here. I'd never forget that. I want you to know that you've always had a place here. Even if you're only half the priest your mother was, I'd offer you my protection and just about anything else I have."

"I fear I might never become even half of what she was."

"Ah, but she trusted you, enough to pass on her secrets, I think. Maybe you were wise to hide for so long. I did a fair share of that myself, in the wake of your mother's death—rest her soul. But now the danger has passed, yes? And you've returned to take your mother's place among the people?"

"Begging your pardon, but no one can take the place of my mother. Each of our lives has a Great Work and I have my own to fulfill. Besides, the danger has hardly passed."

If anything, it has intensified. Harrow saw to that. His life's mission was to escalate, to push things to a conclusion, to any conclusion.

The thick man brushed off Quintain's comment. "Where are my manners, anyway? You've been travelling, you must be tired." He clapped his ham-sized hands twice. "Bring some food and drink for my guest. We'll talk more once you've eaten, yes?"

Quintain swallowed and nodded. He had wandered into a delicate political situation, and felt keenly that he would need to summon every shred of diplomacy he possessed in order to avoid angering or disappointing the man.

He was led to a more private, adjacent chamber where a

large table was set up—the chief's room for dining, but also, he suspected, a room for meeting with his top men. Water and a bowl of what smelled like rabbit stew were set out for him, along with a tall glass of wine, which he did not touch.

Crate, who sat across from him, chuckled. "The witch never touched alcohol, neither."

Quintain let the comment pass. He wasn't hungry, but he had slurped down the contents of the bowl anyway. Outlander custom demanded he eat whatever was put in front of him and compliment the chef no matter what. Truth told, the dish was quite good. "The food is delicious. I thank you for it."

"Certainly, certainly," the man murmured, patting the table. "There is more where that came from. We should hold a feast to celebrate your return."

The magus held up a hand to stave off the bigger man's excitement. "Sir, it's not my desire to disappoint you, but I have business to attend, and that is the only reason I've come here."

Crate fought a frown. Quintain could see it on his face; the chief did not want to anger the young priest and especially did not want to drive him away, but he also warred hard with himself to reign in his excitement and expectations. "All right," he mumbled, "what's this business?"

Quintain cleared his throat. "It is a bit of a story," he warned.

"I trust that you will keep me interested."

The magus took a breath, and launched in. "Before she passed on, my mother handed down a prophecy. She told me about a hero, or a group of them, who would rise up to carry the fight to our enemy. I didn't know whether to believe her then. She was weak and didn't make much sense. But now I've found the warrior she spoke of. I'm convinced that this man, the Harrowing Rain, is the best hope for defeating the Order and conquering the Enclave."

"The Harrowing Rain," the chief echoed, "he's just a legend, a tale that spreads itself like sickness among the ignorant." Quintain watched his aura carefully. The idea that there was a hero set to overthrow the Order appeared to satisfy him, but he could tell that the chief was insulted that this hero was not him.

"That is what I thought, too. But I tracked him down. He does exist, and he's more powerful than even the stories say." He paused for a moment. "I realize that sounds a bit crazy. But it's true. We're going to attempt to get inside the Enclave and bring it down from the inside, but we're going to need help."

The chief gazed at him thoughtfully. "I urged your mother to let me attack the Last Men over and over again and she never agreed. She did not think violence was the answer."

"I am not my mother," Quintain said, his voice turning flinty for a moment. "She was correct, back then. The situation has changed; the Last Men are at war with each other. There is dissention in their ranks. The time to strike is coming."

"How do you know this?"

"I have an ally, a woman who was one of them. She lived in the Enclave for all of her life until recently."

Crate stroked his beard. "So you have a traitor who is willing to help you? You realize that is exactly like the kind of elaborate trap the Order enjoys using, don't you?"

Quintain nodded. "Yes, I considered that. Harrow thought so, too. Trust me, if this was a trap, I would have sensed it by now... It probably would have sprung, by now." *There have been ample opportunities.*

The Outlander chieftain fell into a cogitating silence. Finally, he asked, "So what would you have of me?"

Quintain considered how to word his response. He had so far only told the man that which the Order already knew. If the chief turned traitor to the enterprise himself, it would not harm anything. He did not know anything about what Quintain, Harrow and Alouine were doing that the Last Men did not already know or suspect. Now came the decision to fully trust Crate or not. His mother had, but that had been years ago. Ultimately, someone his mother trusted had betrayed her to the Order, and Quintain was still not sure if Crate was that someone or not.

"We will need safe passage through your lands, to begin with. And I came here seeking machines. We have with us a powerful machine priest. Her tools were destroyed in a battle and I am seeking replacements for her."

Crate nodded. "There is a machine temple close by, but it was also ruined in battle shortly after your mother died. My fighters and I clung to it for two weeks before the Death's Head drove us out. Then they used explosives to collapse the roof. All of the machines inside are buried."

Quintain grinned. "That won't stop men like us."

"Yes, you're right," the chief agreed. "If it is machines you need, then it is machines you will have. Come with me. I'll show you what you are seeking."

— — —

"I found it!" Quintain exclaimed as he jogged back into the central area of his lair. Breathless and shivery, the excitement poured off of him nonetheless.

Harrow sat, leaning against the wall, his father's rifle disassembled before him. Joanna chewed thoughtfully on a piece of deer jerky while her hands, idle for too long, braided Nina's hair. The young girl sat at her feet, flipping through a picture book of animals she would almost certainly never see in reality.

Only Alouine was absent. She could handle the Outlanders singly or in pairs but during these dog days in the dead of winter when everyone was concentrated in the main living area, she preferred solitude, only emerging to collect a new tome, or at mealtimes, or passing through on her way to one of her long walks.

Quintain had been gone for three days. He had let the women know that he was leaving of course, but he also expected a warmer welcome upon his return.

Joanna and Nina both simply looked up at him; Harrow only flicked his eyes upward for a second before returning to his cleaning.

Quintain swallowed and tried to control his panting as it became obvious that no one else shared his excitement. "Don't you all mob me with questions at once."

Joanna rose to the bait. "All right. What did you find?"

He could not contain his grin. "A machine shop."

"You found a place to trade machines?" Nina asked.

Quintain stripped off his woolen hat and mussed his hair out. "No, no. It's a workshop. Like Joanna's from Mason-Dixon, but with more and better equipment: presses, mills, lathes; precision instruments from the days of the Roamers."

That got Joanna's attention. "Really?" she gaped. "Where is it?"

"Only a few miles from here. The only thing is," he said, glancing away and giving his head an absent scratch, "the, uh, roof has collapsed. So it's a bit of a fixer-upper. But I think most of the machines are in working order or can be repaired."

Harrow's only response was a slight nod. A great deal of heavy lifting lay ahead of him. Joanna's skill set was already capable; and high quality, precision machines combined with her growing knowledge from Quintain's library promised to be worth the effort.

"And it's kind of in an interesting neighborhood," Quintain added. "I've had to negotiate with the locals."

He sighed. In the years since his mother's death, the Outlanders of the area had mostly degenerated back to their savage natures. Crate was doing his best to hold them together, but his control was rapidly fraying. Quintain supposed that he was partially to blame for this, but he never had his mother's talent for leadership and organization. Her death had not only destroyed the only family the young man had ever known but had also ruined a great chance to build a community.

Harrow replaced the bolt in his father's rifle with a smooth clack. "They won't be a problem," he said softly.

"Violence, as always, will be our last resort," the boy said. "I used to know these people. Their chief remembers me."

Harrow nodded vaguely as he usually did when he was only half-listening. His rifle re-assembled, he leaned it against the corner and stood. "When are we leaving?"

Quintain cast a glance at Joanna and Nina. "Dawn?"

Joanna tapped Nina on the behind. "You heard him, squirt. Let's make sure we're ready for the trip." The pair rose to action, compiling food and warm clothing and books. The woman seemed energized by the news.

"I'll find Alouine," Harrow volunteered. He was always ready to move, his weapons and armor and gear either worn or kept within arm's reach at all times.

Quintain nodded. "Yes, I'll go, too."

"She's in her room," Nina helpfully supplied while folding up extra blankets. Her missing hand slowed her only slightly. She was beginning to adapt to the loss.

The males headed deeper into the cavernous lair. The Order princess had strung a curtain across the entrance to the space she had claimed for privacy. Quintain stopped short of it while Harrow slowed only enough to announce, "I'm coming in."

He brushed aside the curtain and Quintain's annoyed glance.

The woman reclined, her head propped up on her bundled outer coat as a makeshift pillow. An open book entitled *The Revolution* sat in her hands. The room was, as in the rest of the lair, quite warm thanks to Quintain's electric heaters, and Alouine had removed her outer bodysuit and unfastened the thin, dark, skintight undergarment to her navel. Designed to trap her body heat, the garment proved a sweaty annoyance in the dank confines of the underground library.

Quintain caught a peek at her dark grey bra and blushed furiously, spinning on his heel and showing her his back. Harrow pressed on, nonplussed.

"We are leaving in the morning," he said. "Quintain has found a new workshop for Joanna and we're going to secure it."

She held up a hand to cut him off. "I heard. Sound travels down here."

Still facing away, the teenage boy said, "You're welcome to stay here in the meantime."

"Nonsense," Harrow replied. "We must all take advantage of every opportunity to enhance our readiness."

"She's capable of making her own decisions."

"No, Harrow is right. This is another piece to our puzzle, and I'll help where and how I can." She marked the page she was on and set the book down, then she fastened up her bodysuit. It left little to the imagination in any case. "I'm decent now. Don't compound your rudeness by haunting my threshold."

The boy slowly turned to take a peek, and supposed that he should be content with the idea that although the garment Alouine wore seemed painted on, her skin was covered. The violent flush refused to vacate his cheeks and ears, but he took two steps into the room to stand beside and slightly behind Harrow.

"Tell me about what you found," Alouine said as she sat up.

"Much of the equipment is in decent condition. I'll take along a toroidal power generator. It may take a week to get everything up and running, but after that Joanna will likely be able to turn out any item we may need in the future."

Harrow interjected. "We should begin laying plans for infiltrating the Enclave. Too much time has already been lost."

"Given up on the idea of a frontal assault?" Alouine asked evenly.

"I have been adjusting my strategy," Harrow replied through his teeth. "An assault would cost casualties that simply can't be paid with the resources to hand."

Alouine nodded and let the man keep his pride. "That is my conclusion. After giving it some thought, I think it may be possible to sneak both of you in. I still have a friend on the inside."

"I am not fond of deception," Harrow sneered.

"Do you want to succeed or not?" she asked flatly. The warrior exhaled his annoyed resignation. "I understand that you're disgusted with the Order's methods, but you are ignoring a crucial fact."

"Which is?"

"They work. They've worked for centuries."

"I am not merely going there to swap out regimes," Harrow said. "This thing we do must be a statement to the Last Men, loud and clear, that Outlanders are no longer toothless puppets and slaves to be abused; that continuing their predations will have terrible and deadly consequences. I'm not afraid of Carver Delano. He is afraid of me, and rightly so. I need only kick in the door and that wretch will flee like the vermin he is, while the whole rotten structure crashes down around him."

"You're still not considering the man's circle, let alone his Lictor. It's not just Carver we have to worry about."

Quintain interjected. "There is ample time to fine-tune our strategy. Can you both be ready to move at dawn?"

Both of them nodded.

Harrow stared at Alouine for several long moments.

"What is it?" she asked.

Harrow worked his throat once and murmured, "Nothing," then turned on his heel and left.

Quintain beat a hasty retreat after him.

— — —

Everything that they took with them, they were forced to carry on their backs, which made even a short walk of six kilometers something of an exercise. Harrow carried the most weight, but all five of them were heavily laden. Stacks of books, Joanna's tools, weapons and armor, food and supplies, materials and spare parts. Fuel for the tractor from the village was spent, so they were forced to carry everything.

Chief Crate and his men had not been idle. They had already begun the laborious task of raising the collapsed roof of the machine shop by levering it skyward with steel beams and clearing out the debris from the inside. The chief and two of the men were squatting in the dust near the entrance, gnawing hard biscuits for their lunch, when Quintain led Harrow, Alouine, Joanna, and Nina to the spot.

It was a squat building, the once clean and professional façade of which was still visible under generations of dust and grime. The long walls spanned nearly sixty meters and appeared to be stable, as did the foundation. Fortunately, the soldiers of the Last Men were not thorough in their demolitions.

Crate stood, and watched the group lighten their loads onto the dusty floor-space that his men had already cleared. Panting and sweating, they passed water back and forth.

Nina collapsed into a seated position on the floor and let out a long whistle. "Let's not do that again for a while," she gasped. Alouine and Joanna leaned with their hands on their knees and Quintain put his hands on his hips and rocked his head way back.

"Yeah, I second that," the magus said, rolling his shoulders gingerly. The straps he had used to lash his bundle to his back had bitten and assaulted his thin bones viciously. It had been a grueling hike for all involved. Harrow hid his pain and fatigue better than the rest.

Quintain was again assaulted by nostalgia. He knew when he had first followed Crate into the building that he had been there before. He felt his mother's ghost still lingering in the place. *Some things do come full circle*, he mused.

His mother did not have the same opportunity that Quintain had, nor did she have the same allies. Still, he insisted that secrecy be paramount. His mother had fallen to a sniper's bullet and he sought to avoid that fate.

When the odd group had caught their collective breath, Crate approached. "Welcome," he said. "I am Crate, elected chief of Shadow Glen. I call friends all enemies of the Order and also all those who call this young priest friend. Since you are both, I call you brothers and sisters."

"It's good to be here," Quintain said. "This is Harrow, Joanna, Nina, and Alouine."

The chief nodded, but kept his gaze locked on Harrow. "So you are the one," he said softly.

"I am what I am and nothing more," the warrior murmured in reply.

"If even half of the stories I've heard are true, you are a champion of Outlanders. I would be proud to adopt you—all of you—into my family."

"With respect, my life has room enough for only one father," Harrow replied. "I will never have another."

It was a sentiment Alouine agreed with entirely.

Crate's mouth made a tight line, and Quintain was worried that he might have taken offense. A moment passed before he even exhaled a breath. Finally, he said, "I am no hound after glory, Harrow. Understand the risk I am taking by opening this place to you. The people trust me because I am their father, I love them as my own children, and I have as much reason to make war on the Order as you do. This is a dangerous game. If those murdering scum find out what you are up to here, they will come back as they did before and drive us out and slaughter my people."

"We can gain nothing if we risk nothing," the warrior said.

"This means, of course, that we'll have to trust each other," Quintain put in. "It's a big risk that we're taking by coming here. But I believe that together, we stand a better chance than we do separately."

Harrow extended his hand to the chief. "We have the same goal," he said. "I will destroy the Order or die trying."

Crate stared at the offer for a moment. "I can do no less," he stated, before clasping Harrow's hand tightly.

They settled in and got to work. It took three days to clear enough space and to raise the fallen roof beams enough to access the machines underneath. Quintain also used that time to study the wiring layout of the building, so that he could patch his torus-coil electrical generator in and tune it to the correct voltage and amperage.

The suites of metal-cutting machines were controlled by a central computer, as Quintain had guessed. He threw himself into the task of repairing the main console with Joanna's help, though mostly the woman continued her reading. She resolved to understand Computer Numerical Control, Computer Aided Design and Computer Aided Manufacturing by the time everything was up and running.

It was a hard, dirty, sweaty week for Quintain. He was happy to see that Harrow was just as filthy from the physical labor of clearing rubble. Stripped to the waist even in the cold, his muscles bulged as he worked, tossing chunks of concrete and cinderblock out of the side door of the building and into a crumbled stairwell. Alouine, too, had taken the opportunity to exercise, her bodysuit peeled off of her upper body and her modesty intact only due to the synthetic grey, halter-style chest binding she wore as her bottommost layer.

The pair looked fantastic—true marvels of human form and athleticism. They invented exercises together, with one standing in the doorway and the other tossing bricks and chunks, slinging them in rhythm so that the other would have to catch them and toss them again. Not only was it an expedient way to clear the rubble, but it was an incredible exercise in hand-eye coordination, hand strength, stamina, and all-round dexterity. They pushed each other but stopped shy of open competition.

Quintain was thankful that he was too busy to watch, but many other Outlanders had volunteered to help clear the space and repair the machines only to get a glimpse of one or the other of the supremely fit pair. Women chattered like hens over Harrow and men nearly slipped on their drool at seeing Alouine. The teenager found it rather entertaining but couldn't really blame them, either. Like gods in their midst, the warrior and the princess stood as shining beacons, examples of the height of dedication to physical fitness.

Vol was close by on a regular basis, wanting to help Quintain as best he could and more—to learn all he could from the other boy. The magus did not have the heart to tell him that he was more hindrance than help. His incessant questions compounded the already endless queries that Joanna pestered him with. The hard-pressed youth occasionally had to drop everything and find a place to meditate in order to keep his patience.

"Wha'cha doin'?" the boy asked. "S'a weird time ta take a nap."

Quintain, folded in the lotus position, peeked at him through one narrow-slit eye. "If you were busy minding your own business you'd be too busy to mind mine."

"Arrite, sheesh," Vol groused, and stormed off.

It only reconfirmed Quintain's suspicions that he was not cut out for leadership. He was not his mother, and would complete his mission his own way.

— — —

Eight days and the computers would finally boot up. The machines were repaired and lubricated. Raw materials were gathered. Joanna felt as though she had been given a great gift. It was bittersweet when she remembered how much pain she had endured and how much carnage and suffering she had witnessed to get to that point. But now she could finally get back to work; and such work as she had never imagined possible.

CAD programming was daunting at first, but once she understood the basics, everything began to fall into place. She marveled at how easy and intuitive the Roamers had made the manufacture of precision metal items. Even an idiot could cut steel to tolerances of less than one hundredth of a millimeter with the aid of robots and computers. It had never been so easy to transform a vision into reality.

She was not a fighter or a leader, but she resolved to make herself indispensable anyway. She stole Harrow away from his constant physical training to take precise measurements of his body. Working late into the night with dozens of books open in front of her, she conceptualized on a screen as she would in her own mind until her eyes burned and she could not keep them open any longer.

She remade his armored bracers and greaves to be lighter but even stronger than before, with contoured ridges added for stability and to focus the impact to a smaller striking surface, for greater effect when the steel was used as a weapon. Padded, studded gauntlets for his hands were only the first step in her creation of integrated weapon mounts along his arms.

Harrow seemed to appreciate the idea of unleashing punches which triggered shotgun shells that were aligned atop his knuckles, so Joanna drew up plans. If the hopes of the Outlander world rested on this warrior, she thought, he would be as armed as she could make him.

She eventually settled on a design of three parallel barrels that were only long enough to hold the shells and extend just past the Outlander's fisted knuckles. Synchronized firing pins could be set to detonate the shells simultaneously on impact from a punch, or triggered from a short distance to spray nearby targets with twenty-seven lead pellets of nine millimeters each.

It was an incredibly short-ranged weapon, accurate only to a few meters, but Harrow had a tendency to find, and fight in, the tightest spots.

The inventive woman included spring-actuated extractors that would automatically eject the spent shells when the breech was flipped open, for ease of reloading, and even shaped thin metal clips to hold the shells together in groups of three so that a new volley could be rammed into each device at once.

When Joanna delivered the weapons, along with thirty custom-fabricated brass shells, Harrow seemed ecstatic in that he smiled a vicious smile. "I don't know how to thank you," he said, strapping the weapons onto his hands. He would practice fire some of the shells to 'zero in' the dispersal pattern and synchronize the data with SIMON, but sacrificing some of the ammunition to ensure that he was not out of battery was worth it.

"Just do what you do, tough guy. That'll be thanks enough. Besides, I'm not done yet."

Joanna knew that the Death's Head soldiers used light-amplification goggles to see in dark conditions, so she manufactured magnesium flares in strips sewn into the palms of Harrow's gauntlets. These were lit by friction induced by pulling a thin metal tab near the webbing of his thumbs, and produced three seconds of dazzlingly bright, white light. She judged this capable of overloading the sensitive equipment the Order's soldiers used. Even in normal conditions, the light could blind or disorient anyone looking directly into it, as the woman found out first hand in testing.

She used scavenged explosive material from grenades and recoilless rifle shells to make two hand-held shaped charges. Those would enable Harrow to blast through locks, or cut steel, or render unusable anything he wished to destroy. She made sure to stamp 'FRONT TOWARD ENEMY' on the devices. "Just remember that the wide part of the cone shape has to point toward what you want to blow up," she told him.

Alouine had lent Joanna her stiletto sheath so that she could study the potent toxin it produced. It was when she broached the topic of magnetically-launched poison darts that Harrow pointed out that she might be behaving somewhat over-ambitiously.

"I'm appreciative of your effort," he said, "but please don't burn yourself out. I have enough weapons now."

His words flipped a switch in her demeanor. She thrust one hand onto her hip and the other propelled her finger into the center of Harrow's wide chest, and her head cocked angrily to the right. "Don't give me that shit. You're not the only one who gets to sacrifice for this. I'm doing my part, and you're going to shut up and like it."

The warrior narrowed his eyes. "Don't mistake me, woman. My concern is for your health. When was the last time you slept?"

She waved her hand in his face. "My health? Oh, no. You did not just go there." Standing on her toes, she pressed her face close to his. "You don't get to stake everything, your life, and ultimately our lives, our futures, on one roll of the dice, one final battle, and then turn around and lecture me on my health."

Harrow sighed. "Do as you please."

"You're damn right I will," Joanna spat. "You just have no idea," she added softly, her voice trailing off.

"No idea of what?"

She exhaled slowly. "How much you mean to us. How much you mean to Nina. Don't you get it? You've given me everything I have; you gave me the courage to work my craft when no one else believed in me! You gave me my precious little girl! I just want to do everything I can to make sure that you get through this in one piece!"

The muscles of Harrow's jaw worked and he glanced away, to the floor.

"We want you to live, you big dumbass. Stop being such a fucking hypocrite and rely on me! I will get you through this . . . I have to," she added in a mumble, her anger having burned itself out. Finally, she had begun to feel the exhaustion she had kept at bay for so long.

"I understand," he said gently, "and I'll gratefully accept all that you give me. But tomorrow is another day. Please sleep. You will need the rest if you're going to tackle another project."

Joanna pursed her lips. The man had a point. "Fine."

He nodded again. "Thank you. For everything."

"Idiot," she mumbled, "I should be thanking you. At least you're tough; it makes up for how dense you can be."

The warrior sighed. "Goodnight, Joanna."

TWENTY

Things finally progressed smoothly for Carver Delano. The rough stretch he had endured lay behind him. For three weeks, he managed to avoid or ignore the Highest Circle's constant demands for status updates while completing the Incarnation Matrix designs. He stockpiled the necessary materials while keeping his overlords in the dark, and fed his newly minted schematics into the Order's automated manufacturing facilities. Given a week for fabrication of specialized parts, construction of the Matrix could begin. It was nearly time to make his move.

The Enclave's central Network, with some coaxing through SIMON, now recognized Carver as a member of the Highest Circle. Without a prompt, the account reader on the High Circle chamber's massive door read his fraudulent data and smoothly opened for him as he approached.

He found the chamber empty. That was no surprise as he monitored each High Circle member's location remotely by data link. Heid Acheson, wearing his white lab coat, followed him inside with clear trepidation, along with a whole team of slaves, assistants, and laborers. Several of them pushed anti-gravity carts loaded to the brim with equipment and materials.

Carver led Heid past the hollow, circular table where the High Circle sat for their meetings, to a small antechamber at the rear of the room. The thinner metal door slid open and revealed a rarely used lounge, comfortably appointed with soft furniture. The vaguely humanoid robotic servant's AI booted itself automatically as the door opened. It greeted the Last Man with a pleasant, feminine voice and asked how it might serve him.

"Clear this room," Carver ordered. The slaves, along with the robot, began the task of removing all furnishings and appointments. He turned to Heid. "How long will it take for you to set up the machine?"

"My simulations estimate a total of ten hours, including the calibration."

"Very well. Get to work. I will ensure that you are not disturbed."

Carver could only wait while the machine was built for him, but since he had installed the stolen quantum computer in his head, it had given him an intense drive and a great boost in vigor and vitality. While he would have been content to relax and let the process run its course before, he was now restless, almost anxious. Perhaps this was how the Outlander, Harrow, felt all the time.

He knew exactly what to do to ease his mind. Standing from his cushy leather chair, he drained the last of the bourbon in his glass and summoned his Lictor. "Come along, Armiluss. There is one matter of business I've been putting off for too long."

"Yes, master," the hulking, rhinoceroid creature gurgled in his tinny speech.

The pair left the High Circle chamber, walking down the corridor to the sky-trams. "Perhaps after you assist me with this, we will head down to the brood pits for some fun and games. Would you like that?"

"You are too kind, my lord."

When they reached the boarding platform, Carver summoned a single-car tram. The information panel on the interior of the lavishly padded transport chimed.

"Please state your destination."

"Morningstar manor." Carver took a seat and gestured for

Armiluss to do the same. With the occupants settled, the AI-driven conveyance took off at top speed, heading east across the Enclave.

"Your pardon, lord, but there is almost no chance of the Morningstar woman showing back up at her home."

"I agree," the lord replied haughtily. "She is not who we are going to visit. Rather, I want to make sure that the despicable little tramp she used to pal around with is not providing her any assistance or information. We will see if there is anything to learn—or anything to take."

The Last Man and his slave departed the tram after ten minutes of riding, arriving unannounced at the Morningstar family's personal platform. The home was vast and reminiscent of a jumble of ancient step-pyramids. Sheathed in slate-grey marble, it was a stately palace fit for a king.

Carver scoffed as he put his patent-leather clad foot on the first mirror smooth paving stone that led to the entrance. Had he not been planning to cast aside his body as so much useless ballast, he might have happily confiscated the property. The God-machine was nearly ready, and so the soon-to-be overlord was content to get some more use out of his flesh in the meantime.

He stopped before the thick, steel portcullis which led to an inner courtyard full of trees and gardens. That kind of nonsensical attachment to natural things made him somewhat queasy.

Glancing to the shiny, reflective panel, he mentally activated the door chime function. Certainly, between him and Armiluss, he felt confident that they could force their way in. The portcullis would not stop his Lictor any more than a paper screen. They would enter with violence, if it came to that, but he preferred to first see if he could enter by deception.

Thaira Landgrave's face appeared on the panel's screen. "Yes?"

Carver nodded in satisfaction, his suspicions confirmed. "Hello, madam," he said carefully. Pretending not to know the face looking back at him through the screen, he announced, "My name is Carver Delano. I've come to speak to one Thaira Landgrave."

The woman's eyes shifted nervously. She recognized him, he could tell. "That is me," she answered. "What is your business, sir?"

"I am investigating a disappearance of one Alouine Morningstar. May I come in?"

Thaira nodded and mentally activated the controls for the metal gate, which slid smoothly open.

"My thanks," Carver offered, before sweeping away from the panel and into the house proper. Armiluss dogged his heel.

They had crossed the courtyard and neared the ornate, brass-and-basalt entrance to the living quarters when Thaira emerged. She was dressed in the standard dark bodysuit but had thrown a flowing white robe over it and fastened it loosely at the belt. Two slaves flanked her, one with a serving tray replete with coffee and tea, cigars and light snacks, and another with a platter which held steaming towels.

"Greetings," she said. "As caretaker of this home, I offer you what hospitality I can. Shall we adjourn to a sitting room?"

Carver waved off the servants. "That is kind but unnecessary. This will not take long."

He could feel the anxiety rise in her chest as she turned and dismissed the servants with a nod. The woman was far from stupid and possessed some intuition; she did not seem to enjoy the prospect of being left alone with Carver and Armiluss. It made Carver intensely happy.

"So, do you have any information on Alouine's whereabouts?" the woman queried.

Carver stepped closer to her, not quite threatening yet, but ready to begin at any moment. He had always been so good at this—intimidating people. If he were honest, it was one of his only skills—*had* been, until he had stolen Harrow's power for himself. He never ceased to enjoy it.

"I was rather hoping you would be able to provide me with that. I see you have made yourself quite comfortable in her father's house."

"This house belongs to Alouine," Thaira said. "She left it in my care while she is away."

"So, she told you that she was leaving."

"She mentioned that she would be away from the Enclave for an unspecified amount of time. That is all I know."

Carver nodded slowly and clasped his hands behind his back. "Alouine did not tell you that she was not going to one of the other Enclaves, but rather, into the Outlands?"

Thaira's mouth formed a tight line. "I do not know where she is," she said, trying to keep her voice firm. It might have been convincing to someone else, but Carver knew better.

"And you have not been in contact with her?" he asked, a sneer creeping into his words.

"Not at all. I wish I could be more help to you."

"Oh, you can. I'm afraid I'm through waiting for that stupid bitch to return," he snarled, dropping all pretenses. "You will have to stand in for what I had planned for her. Armiluss, take her."

The huge Lictor shot forward, but Thaira was neither untrained nor helpless. Her body unraveled into a fighting stance instantly, and she shot two kicks into the monster's flanks, using the balls of her feet as precise hammers and aiming for his smallest ribs.

Armiluss did not seem to notice the blows at all.

Thaira's eyes widened as she scampered backwards. "What do you think you're doing?" she screeched. "I am a woman of the Order, not some slave to be abused!"

Her servants, hearing her distress and trained to sacrifice their lives for those of their masters', came charging out of the same door which they had disappeared into.

Carver spooled up his pulse emitter with a droning hum.

Pointing the actuator lens at the charging slaves, he mentally dialed the device to its most potent frequency. The air popped as a cone of heat distortion burst from the weapon, catching both of the servants as Carver waved it back and forth.

They recoiled in horror and began screaming abruptly, and then ceased just as suddenly as their hair and clothing ignited in a flash and immediately their skin, eyeballs and blood began to boil. Huge, roiling blisters rose and burst on their flesh in seconds, and they withered and crumpled to the ground, dying in fiery agony.

Carver kept up the stream of microwave heat until he heard their bones crack from the pressure of the expanding marrow within. He could not wipe the cruel grin off of his face had he wanted to.

— — —

Thaira made to run into the house, but Armiluss, moving swiftly, cut off her escape. Wide-eyed and panicked, she leapt and spun, aiming a heel kick at the Lictor's clenched teeth, to push him out of the way, if nothing else.

To her horror, she encountered resistance before her foot made contact with the beastly creature's maw. The Lictor spooled up his own quantum field and it reacted with the magnetic field of Thaira's body, repulsing her. Like kicking through a thick mud, the energy field was enough to overcome the strength of her leg muscles and the velocity imparted to her foot by her precise technique. Her foot slowed, and then stopped in front of the Lictor's face. Before the repulsive field could throw her across the courtyard, his hand shot out and grasped her outstretched ankle.

The creature swung her by the leg like a rag doll and slammed her into the hard ground as if her body was a club and her ankle the handle.

Instinctively, she curled her shoulders, tightened her neck muscles and tucked in her arms, but the powerful Lictor imparted such force on her body that when her left shoulder cracked into the ground, her neck formed a pivot and her head bounced off the hard walkway with a sick, dull crack. Nausea whirled through her guts and she blacked out—she woke again a split second later when the Lictor dropped her leg.

Stretching out her right arm to try to drag herself away, Thaira did not seem to notice the Lictor stand over top of her, his legs straddling her body. He drew back his fist, aiming for the base of her skull to dispatch her.

"I said take her, not kill her," Carver said, which gave the Lictor pause. The Last Man circled around, cutting off Thaira's desperate but pathetic attempt to escape. He squatted down next to her prone form. "She still has a use," he murmured sadistically over the crackling of the burned and broiled bodies of the servants. "Hold her up."

Armiluss fisted a hand in her hair and roughly righted Thaira, yanking her clear off her feet. She groaned weakly and both arms shot up to grab the Lictor's wrists to take some of her weight off of her abused scalp.

Carver tore the belt of her robe away and Thaira kicked at him ineffectually as he moved on to the fasteners holding her bodysuit together. With his free hand, Armiluss seized her by the calf of her uninjured leg and levered it skyward, nearly wrenching her hip from its socket.

The Last man finished disrobing the woman as his Lictor twisted and contorted her helpless body. Tears welled in Thaira's eyes as humiliation and disgust roiled in her chest and more waves of nausea turned her stomach.

"Don't do this," she pleaded in a rough slur. Her eyes rolled about in her head. A thin line of drool escaped her lips and ran down her chin, eventually mingling with her tears.

Carver thought she looked beautiful. He shrugged off his coat and undid the front flap of his trousers. "Don't worry. You're just a proxy until I get what I really want," he said, fisting himself hard. "Although if you're good, I might keep you on the side."

Roughly, he entered her with no preparation and she gurgled in impotence, pain and despair, which sent a shiver of pleasure up the man's spine. Pushing hard, he felt a barrier to his progress and with steady pressure, felt it give way. Thaira let out a squeak of agony.

"You surprise me," he groaned, his breath coming in gasps. Grunting, he said, "You always struck me as a much . . . looser woman than this." He caught the scent of blood and it fired his libido even more. Behind her, Armiluss began to pant as he watched. His hot, damp breath blew over the side of her face and into her ear.

Carver noticed that his warrior slave was watching and sneered. His concentration flagging, he reached up to push the Lictor's offending face to the side and doubled his effort.

Finally, when Thaira's rolling eyes took on the glazed, faraway look of complete mental breakdown, Carver reached his peak with a crocodilian hiss. Pulling free from her body, panting, he scooped up her torn robe and used it to wipe himself clean before tossing it nonchalantly over his shoulder. Armiluss discarded Thaira roughly onto the ground like refuse.

"Was it satisfactory, master?" Armiluss asked.

"I suppose," was Carver's dismissive answer as he caught his breath and rearranged his clothing. Just then, his data link chimed—Heid Acheson calling. He opened the channel and mentally sent, "What is it, Heid?"

"The Highest Circle has just called up an entire battalion of Death's Head troops," Heid sent with no preamble. "I thought you would want to know."

Carver nodded vaguely to himself. "Interesting," he mumbled

softly. Louder, he said, "Armiluss, we're finished here." The monstrous slave stepped over their fallen, bleeding victim to stand at his master's shoulder. Via data link, Carver sent to Heid: "What are they planning?"

"The Security Bureau has reported increased Outlander activity. It seems the Highest Circle is going over your lordship's head, and intend to handle it themselves."

Carver smirked. He stretched his arms wide, feeling relaxed and refreshed and still enjoying his post-orgasmic haze. "More power to them. I will be at the slave pits. Alert me when your work is finished."

If they sent an entire battalion away from the Enclave, it would only make his plans easier to complete. As he was proving, no one could stand in his way. Indeed, it seemed that Providence was clearing his path for him.

Last Man and Lictor left as they came in, with Carver setting fire to the flowering plants and trees in the atrium, leaving a broken, unconscious Thaira Landgrave on the cold ground where she lay, surrounded by fire and corpses.

— — —

The young magus quickly became disappointed with the sad-sack, co-dependent state of the Outlanders of Shadowy Glen. The energy vibrations here were mostly negative, low-frequency feelings of fear and distrust, as if the people were collaborating in their own degradation. The web of despair wore on him like a battery in the cold.

He did not know what to do about it, either. To tell these people that love is all they needed, to explain that it was not an intellectual concept or moral imperative but rather a background emotion that exists with an ardent recognition of the unity of all things and a connection to the energy of the universe; it would sound cliché and he would be laughed out of the place by those with the cognizance to even understand.

The truth was that although he was sensitive to the needs of the people, he was not the bottomless reservoir of emotional energy his mother was. Harrow's uncompromising, dualistic stance was not helping matters, either. The warrior was unconsciously reinforcing the very state of mind that Quintain knew would have to be abandoned before real change could occur.

The teen wrestled with these very problems for days at a time, leaving his body behind as he traveled the etheric realm. Unlike Mason-Dixon, Shadow Glen was beset by demonic spirits who preyed on the energies of the people in waves, feeding on their pain, terror, hunger and malaise.

To make matters worse, dark intents marshaled more forces against them. Hostile feelings poured from the nearby Enclave like black lightning, an impenetrable gloom that held against even Quintain's most severe attempts to breach it. Slowly, it built to a fever pitch, a low, throbbing hum that reverberated through all dimensions. The other Outlanders could not see it or hear it, but they felt it. Unconsciously, their terror and intolerance waxed to new heights.

As the malignant will took shape, it was easier for Quintain to interpret. The Last Men were on to them; they gathered their extra-dimensional familiars in the astral world and their soldier-slaves in the physical, to hurl them at the Outlanders and crush them for all time.

Seeking out the now-familiar, signature auras of Harrow and Alouine, Quintain observed them while hiding his etheric presence. The pair of them sparred regularly, training for their impending coup. He studied the interactions of their subtle fields.

It pleased him to see that neither was dependent on the other, but that each had finally begun to recognize what the other had to offer. There was no competition for energy but only a cooled and almost friendly rivalry. They pushed one another, trying to find the peak of perfection.

Panting and sweating, the training partners flopped, leaning against the walls in the room they used for that purpose. It was a convenient place in the rear of the 'machine temple', where the noise of Joanna's constant industrial progress provided a background melody. It was all a bit mechanistic for Quintain's taste, but, he admitted to himself, it was entirely necessary.

Harrow, his hair tied back into a wolf's tail to keep it out of his eyes, wiped sweat from his brow. Alouine's sheer speed and fighting style still stymied him as it did in their first meeting; with the power of his quantum field projector or his spiritual familiar, he could best her with ease, but this was not about that.

Quintain understood that Onuris was a tool of destiny and outside of him as a man. Harrow's pride demanded that he fight her fairly. However, on those terms, the most he could manage was a draw. "You have my thanks and my respect," he muttered.

Red-faced, the woman beamed a genuine smile and Harrow's aura reacted predictably. "A line can overcome a circle," Alouine said, before swallowing dryly, "just as a circle can overcome a line. You charge straight in and attack in direct lines. That is why you are so stumped by circles."

"Tell me where you learned to fight like that."

Her breath whistled through her teeth and her chest heaved. "At first it was computer programs." She took water to moisten her tongue. "And then my father brought in a tutor for me, a very wise and ancient man who completed my training."

"You avoid grappling like a plague," he observed with no small consternation.

She laughed. "What are you, one hundred and six, maybe seven kilos? You're twice my size. I'd be throwing out everything I was taught if I stood still and let you manhandle me."

That thought, of manhandling the woman, burned in his lower chakra until he crumpled it up and threw it away. Quintain watched as he struggled with his feelings. Harrow's skin was already flushed and sweating from the exertion, which had given him ample opportunity to study the woman's body in detail. He tried to keep his analysis as clinical as possible, but her beauty and nearness made his usual detachment a challenge to maintain and his aura bespoke the challenge.

"No," she continued, "it is far better in my case to yield and redirect, to use mobility and flexibility; to avoid and not block, to strike first and fast and repeatedly; to target the enemy's vulnerable places; to attack his pillars and break his balance." She sighed, and added, "All easier said than done with you."

"He must have taught you well. Until we met, I'd never felt your kind of killer instinct in anyone else I'd fought."

"What you felt was the energy of the Death Touch, the Kali'prana. You're the first to have survived it."

"Was that something else your ancient wise man taught you?"

Alouine nodded. "To my knowledge I am the only one alive who has the technique. Back then, I was excited by it. Now I see it as the awful burden it is. He would be disappointed in how terrible my aim has been."

"What do you mean?"

"It was a mistake to have thrown it at you, when my real target had passed in front of me only a day before. I suppose I should apologize for that," she murmured, adding, "eventually."

Harrow lightly scoffed.

"My apologies don't come cheap," the woman said, with a teasing hint to her voice. "Anyway, where did *you* learn to fight?"

"My father taught me to attack and defend when I was a boy. I suppose a decade spent fighting for my life has completed my training."

"Your father is . . ." the woman prompted.

"Dead," Harrow finished, flatly.

Alouine nodded. "I'm sorry." She let a respectful moment pass. "You had no other teachers?"

"Of course," the warrior replied. "Experience and Necessity; but nothing in the way of your formal instruction. Had my father lived longer, all of this might be over by now."

"I believe you."

After another moment, Harrow asked, "Is your instructor still in the Enclave?"

"No, he left. I believe he could feel his time coming to an end. He was dear to me, and his daughter, who is like a sister to me, remained behind, at my side, until I left her, too—to run away." Alouine's eyes cast downward, toward the floor. "Like a coward."

The Outlander nodded slowly, without judging. "You miss her," he said softly.

"Yes," Alouine replied. "But not for much longer, I think. It's time to put things right and erase the mistakes of the past. We are nearly ready." She appeared to draw strength from her memory of the other woman and the prospect of seeing her again. "Shall we go over the plan again?"

Harrow gradually and with much reluctance agreed to expand his plans beyond 'get inside; kill everyone'. "If we must," he replied with a hint of a smirk.

The Order princess narrowed her eyes slightly and shook her head but recognized that the taunt held no malice. She opened her mouth to reply but was interrupted.

As a soft yellow-orange apparition, Quintain appeared to them as he had before, entering their visual fields with a sizzling snap. "That will have to wait," he murmured in the faraway, vibratory drone of an astral voice projecting across dimensions. "Our foe still has the initiative and we must go over to the defensive once again."

Harrow sighed. "What is it now?"

"Unleashed hostility—the like of which has not been seen in

generations," his ghostly projection replied. "Take Nina and Joanna to the underground complex and have the people prepare for an attack. I shall attempt to learn more."

— — —

Harrow took a position, fully armed and armored, near the main entrance to the complex. He watched the pale grey of daytime begin its inevitable fade to black as Quintain reported on the storm on the horizon. The temperature dropped; it felt even colder due to the lack of moon and stars, and night settled onto the Outlands like a blanket used to smother an infant.

Quintain's early warning had allowed the Outlanders four hours to evacuate the surface and bring everything of use into their underground bunker. Crate mobilized ten men to assist Joanna and Nina in moving a portion of the integral parts of the machine temple, but many of the machines were too heavy to move. The building which housed them was painfully exposed to attack; they had not been careful enough in hiding their activities from the Order's prying eyes. Quintain cursed their satellite surveillance as yet another unfair advantage.

The magus kept his astral thumb on the pulse of events the entire time, serving as a messenger. There, as at Mason-Dixon, the Order meant to strike such a blow as the Outlanders could never recover from. Flitting invisibly from the surface to the bowels of the subway station, he gave crucial reports of the tempest of hatred blowing in from the northwest. Ten of the Death's Head's rotor lifts left the Enclave and approached, skimming the earth and in a tight formation.

With his physical body safely stashed in the ancient Sub-way, he told Harrow as much via etheric projection.

"There are ten airships."

Harrow watched the scene unfold from behind the slope of a rubble heap, through the scope of his father's rifle at maximum magnification.

Crate had caught sight of the approaching armada and immediately ordered every one of his warriors underground. He nodded to Harrow and gestured for him to follow before marching inside to batten down.

Harrow exhaled a wary breath. "We won't be able to oppose their landings," he murmured, more to himself than the ghostly figure beside him. "That is the only time they're truly vulnerable."

The metal Dragons, upon disgorging their black-clad human cargo, lifted off and turned about in the air, flying back the way they came with their distinctive, low rumble.

"They're being cautious," he mused.

The transports usually stayed close above the dismounted infantry they had transported, to provide support with precise cannon fire from the air. Having lost two out of three gunships sent to raid Mason-Dixon, the Death's Head appeared to have developed a healthy respect for the Outlanders apparent ability to shoot down their aircraft.

Harrow frowned; the capability to damage the Dragons in the air had disappeared when Joanna dismantled the remaining munitions for her shell launcher and repurposed them. Fortunately, the enemy did not know this. That the Dragons were turning back was a boon, but also an insult.

"The Last Men value those machines more than the men they ferry."

"The airships are less easily replaced," Quintain observed. A heartfelt sadness was evident in his reverberating voice.

From three kilometers away, the soldiers of the Order were tiny, even when magnified twelve times by the powerful optic device atop Harrow's rifle. Even so, he could tell that they were heavily equipped and numerous. He counted twenty men from each airship, each one a company, further divided into two platoons and each of those into five-man squads. Interspersed in the attacking force were what appeared to Harrow to be heavy weapons companies armed with belt-fed machineguns.

Every twentieth man, he estimated, carried a recoilless shell launcher like the one he had given Joanna all those months ago. Other soldiers carried spare shells in cases on their backs. There was a mortar platoon also, with two of the light, man-portable, high-trajectory artillery pieces the Death's Head used for fire support.

One of the platoons, formed from the largest and strongest of the enslaved men, wore even heavier body armor than the rest. Each one of these men had a large, metal cylinder strapped to his back. Harrow could tell by watching them through the scope that these weighed on the troops significantly; using SIMON, he inferred that their weight approached thirty kilograms.

A black, hovering anti-gravity sled, controlled remotely, followed along behind this group, heavily laden with drab-colored cases which could contain even more of the cylinders or perhaps a different surprise altogether.

Both Harrow and Quintain watched their foes as they fanned out professionally, each section covering the others near it as they leapfrogged from cover to cover.

"This could only be worse if their gunships had stayed behind," the warrior muttered.

"The tunnels and caverns will provide bottlenecks," the apparition offered in reply.

"They are prepared for that," Harrow said, thinking aloud. "An attacking force must have a three-to-one advantage to have a chance to succeed. Their numbers are closer to ten-to-one. This complex cannot be held if they attack here in force. If their toehold becomes a foothold, we will have sacrificed Joanna's new workshop as well as the lives of all these Outlanders."

As he spoke, he mentally plotted the likely course of each

element of the enemy army. SIMON calculated their current speed and cross-referenced it with their known tactical doctrine, factoring in the extra caution they displayed in maneuvering around corners and picking their way through the rubble. "They will reach the machine shop in forty-eight minutes, and this location in sixty-four," he announced, his jaw clenched.

"What is to be done?" Quintain asked.

Harrow stood. "I must go over to mobile, hit-and-run tactics. That is the only thing that can slow them down before they get here."

He strode inside, looping the sling of his rifle over his shoulder. First, he wanted one last look at the preparations, so he could at least know there was something between Nina and Joanna and whatever Death's Head men might manage to get past him.

Walking inside, he reached the stairs, where at least the men had the courage to form a barricade with their own bodies, and began to push past the wide-eyed, anxious, dry-mouthed men there. They had piled up rubble and other heavy items and set up fighting positions behind the cover provided by ancient turnstiles and ticket booths, where the Roamers had once purchased transit on the subterranean carriages. Normally, it would be a nigh-impenetrable position, but the warrior instantly sized it up and found it lacking.

Checking each of the tunnels, he found them mostly the same. At least the station was nominally guarded in all directions. These Outlanders knew how to set up a defense; he gave them that. In this instance, against the forces arrayed against them, it would not be enough.

Harrow glanced around at the huddled masses of Outlanders. The men among them, grim-faced, were content to merely guard the entrances to their underground burrow, to simply hold on and bear what was inevitable and unchanging.

He expected women and children to cower and quiver at the nearness of their enemy. The sight of armed, able-bodied men crouched or squatting, cooing and coddling at their loved ones—it broke his heart.

He immediately set out again for the main entrance to the underground complex, striding purposefully through the carpet of whimpering Outlanders. Fuming at the thought that he alone could see Necessity, could hear her dictating what actions must be taken, he set out to make a difference however he could.

Crate planted his bulk in Harrow's path. "Where are you going?"

The warrior locked eyes with the chief, and the cold, murderous glare in his eyes told the other man everything.

The thicker man frowned. "You think we're cowards," he accused in a soft growl, but loud enough for the men—*his* men, to hear him. The warriors within earshot turned on Harrow, glaring daggers.

Harrow snared the man by the lapels of his coat so fast that the man flinched, and he shook him once, sending a shockwave through his arms and into the other man's chest. It was not his intention to embarrass the chief in front of his warriors, but a certain shock was needed. He put his face close to Crate's. "You are cowering in a hole!" he hissed.

Crate blinked, and then blinked again. Any other time, he was certain the chief would have roared at being so manhandled, but Harrow could see that the thought was striking the man more violently—that Harrow was right.

Crate was afraid. He was afraid of the Death's Head, and he was afraid of Harrow; afraid of fighting back even against the other Outlander, though the other man was laying hands on him at that moment. He was afraid of pain, of being hurt.

Still, he had pride. Male vanity was essential in the role of chief, of a leader of others. Harrow knew Crate did what any man would; he rationalized. "Don't throw away your life. There is an entire battalion out there! It would be crazy to try to hold the surface against that." His eyes clouded over and his voice lowered. "I've never seen so many."

Harrow sneered and released his hold on the man. "That is what will make this battle decisive. If you," he said, first to Crate but taking in the others with his gaze, "are what passes for Outlander men, for warriors, I'm ashamed to call myself one."

Crate curled his lip back and clenched his teeth, then opened his mouth to retort, but nothing came. Every eye on Harrow dropped to the floor.

"If you love your fleeting safety more than a battle for freedom and equality, stay here. I don't want your arms, or your lives. Slither in a cave or worse, lick the hand that beats you like dogs. I hope all memory forgets that you were ever my brothers."

His words were harsh, but he desperately wanted to shake these men from their apathy and cowardice. He did not care that they might be angry with *him*, so long as they were angry.

Crate had to decide quickly. Never mind losing face with his people, he had only a heartbeat to resign himself and to reconcile what he saw as a death sentence. Following Harrow meant the possibility, indeed, the probability of having his gut shot out, or being torn apart in an explosion. He knew scrapping and raiding and how to discipline others with a beating, but this was soldiering.

The Death's Head men were robotic, pitiless, more like machines than human beings. They had no personalities. They were warrior slaves who did nothing but train to kill Outlanders. They had access to factory-fresh weapons and body armor and endless supplies of munitions to hone their marksmanship and hurl at their prey. There were two hundred of them, with an efficient command system. And they were all willing to die because their instinct for self-preservation had been scientifically isolated and genetically removed for generations.

The chief and his men had old rifles, what scraps of armor they had stolen, fabricated or repurposed, and a supply of ammunition that was downright paltry. He said so. "Use reason. We can't stand toe-to-toe with them in the open and expect to live. Why shouldn't we let them come to us? We've held this fortress against them for generations! None have ever set foot in here while men like us have guarded it. What will attacking them gain us?"

"Things have changed," Harrow answered. He imagined the Death's Head men filling the entire tunnel complex with poison gas or fire, or using explosives to bury it. "I must keep them as far from here as I can. If they reach this place, they'll destroy it and kill everyone inside."

His own thoughts began to change. He could see the chieftain's point; the other Outlanders were leagues away from being warriors of his caliber. Even without his quantum device and extra-dimensional familiar, the men did not meet his standards.

Once again, others could rely on him, but he could not rely on them. Something had to be done, however. Only by attacking could he ensure the destruction of the enemy. Huddling underground for a siege was not only cowardly but doomed to failure, as the Death's Head could expect unlimited supply and reinforcement from the air. Harrow was sure that they would stay until all the Outlanders were either dead or led away in chains. "Stay here. I will thin their ranks and try to lead them away."

"Wait," he blurted out. "You'll be immediately surrounded if you go that way. At least go around them and attack from the side." He pointed down the east tunnel.

"I prefer victory over death, but I will have one or the other. Will you show me the way?"

"I'm going with you." Like clockwork, his loyal sons pressed in around him, as well as a handful of the other warriors. He began to lose his fear of injury and death. Harrow watched the shift in the chief's eyes. Two dozen men against two hundred, and somehow the odds did not bother him as much; something had changed.

"Let's go reclaim our future."

Crate led the group, passing through the gathered crowd, and Harrow matched his stride. "These men—my sons—they want to live to see that future. Don't throw our lives away."

"I won't be reckless. But we have to mount an effective defense. We'll set up ambushes and be flexible, and if they kill any of us, it will only be after we've killed dozens of them."

A collective, affirmative snarl ran through the group of men. Four trustworthy men were chosen to remain behind and guard the main entrance, with another pair at each other tunnel, but it was more of a concession against panic than a real defense. Nineteen men prepared to follow Harrow out and offer battle to the Death's Head.

"Do you even have a plan?" Crate whispered urgently as he followed Harrow back out into the crumbling husk of a cityscape. They exited the east tunnel where the track emerged from underground and became a raised monorail, each man hopping down to the ground in turn.

"I will soon." Harrow raised his voice to encompass the group. "Remember to stay low at all times. Never give them a clear silhouette to shoot at. We will move from cover to cover. Stealth is paramount. Do not speak unless absolutely necessary. Do not shoot unless I fire first." He paused to allow his instructions to sink in.

"I estimate that they will position their crew-served weapons at the flanks of their battle line." He gestured to the north and northwest with his hand like a knife. "If we can ambush and envelop one of their flanks, we may succeed in drawing them away from their intended targets."

Wide-eyed, the Outlander men gaped at him. He inwardly sighed but refused to second-guess himself. Time was of the essence, but these men still needed something aside from instruction in basic tactics. Their morale suffered terribly. It showed in their faces and posture. He swallowed, and launched in.

"Bravery, the warrior spirit, is made of two parts: the internal, and the external," he began haltingly, not sure if the men would understand. "Our enemies are like rabid dogs. A rabid dog may pose a terrible threat, but it only possesses the external component of bravery; inside, the animal is not thinking. To have complete bravery, you must be ferocious on the outside, but calm and steady on the inside.

"I have always thought that any day is a good day to die," he continued. "That does not mean that I sought out death. I want to preserve life, especially my own; greater battles than this must be waged in the future, and I must meet them. But I have always known that if you go into battle with fear in your heart, you will die or be maimed beyond repair. Only by accepting and embracing the possibility of your death, can you focus everything on the task before you: defeating your enemy.

"Your mind and body, your aim and your weapon, must all work in unison. Be hard and unforgiving as steel on the outside, and as serene as a quiet day with your children on the inside. If you can do this, your bravery will be far more important than your skill or your weapons."

He gave the men as much time as he dared to make peace with what he had said. "Those who are going, the time is now."

Not a single man stayed behind.

TWENTY-ONE

Quintain did not idle while Harrow set out to lead his aggressive defense of the Outlanders. He returned to his body and woke from his out-of-body experience. He opened his eyes and took a moment to focus enough to see Nina crouched to his left, with Joanna behind her. Alouine sat a few meters to his right in lotus position, meditating.

The area they had crowded into was dimly lit and stuffed with other Outlanders, some of whom were softly, nervously chattering.

Alouine opened her eyes also. "You're back."

The boy nodded, sat up, and rubbed the back of his head where it had rested on the bare concrete. "Not for long. I wanted to check on things before I head back out there. Is there anything I can do here?"

"We're fine for now," Joanna said. "Probably not so much if those killers get in here."

Nina cut in. "Harrow won't let them. You'll see."

A moment passed, and Alouine sighed. "I wish there was something I could do. Guns and bombs aren't exactly my forte."

"Still, you are providing a much-needed last line of defense," Quintain countered. "I don't think Harrow could be so confident if you weren't here. He's relying on you. We all are."

Alouine took a steadying breath. She rankled at the idea of being left behind, as though she were some helpless Outlander's wife. Her aura burned with desire to act. Still, the thought that

Harrow trusted her and relied on her seemed to calm her and gave her strength. She would do this, for his sake. She would guard his loved ones and Quintain's unconscious body.

Joanna stood. "Well, I for one can't sit here and sleep through this," she said, giving Quintain a wink. He rolled his eyes. "If nothing else, I can hump ammo or tend the wounded."

"So I'm supposed to just stay here?" Nina asked.

Joanna frowned. "If you know what's good for you, you will. I mean it, girl. If you leave this space, I'll beat you within an inch of your little life."

The girl crossed her arms over her chest and huffed loudly, blowing wisps of hair out of her face. "Fine," she muttered. Satisfied, her guardian stalked off in search of something, anything, she could do to assist in the defense.

When the older woman was out of earshot, the girl complained. "I hate this. I wish I'd just grow up already."

Quintain and Alouine met gazes, and the boy arched his brows in a pleading gesture.

"I wouldn't be in such a hurry to grow up," Alouine said softly. "Times like these can't last forever." Quintain felt her sincerity. "Sometimes the best thing to do is to do nothing."

"That's not what Harrow would say," the girl murmured in response.

"Wisdom comes in many forms," Quintain offered.

"That's easy for you to say. Your mind can leave your body and fly around while you stay here and sleep through it all."

"The danger is the same for all of us. Besides, etheric projection is not difficult. As soon as this is over, I'll show you how."

"Really?" the girl chirped. Quintain nodded, and Alouine let the ghost of a smile creep across her lips.

"For now, though, I have to get back to it. Just like their ancestors from ages ago, there are brave men fighting in the face of defeat. As then, blood of heroes will stain this land. But they won't be alone. I'll do what I can to protect them." He lay back down on the hard floor. "Be safe and without fear." With that, he closed his eyes and set himself into the leaving trance, breaking free of his body again with a snap and leaving the Outlander girl and the Order princess gazing at one another.

I am a world unto myself, living a thousand lives, who keeps the secret of all times and ages.

Careening at high speed through the tunnels, Quintain's disembodied spirit accelerated at speeds no material being could touch until he burst out into the open sky.

He only thought of Harrow and instantly snapped into astral being near the man.

Dusk surrendered to night and an oubliette of black murk fell over the earth. The thick carpet of clouds and moonless night were another curse that seemed to emanate from the Enclave. The Death's Head men had numerous technological innovations to offset darkness, thermal optics and infrared spotting scopes among them.

The would-be Next Man led the others in single-file through a rubble-choked depression which had once been a street. Crate stuck close behind him and all of them walked with a hunch, ready to throw themselves flat at a moment's notice.

"This route should keep us out of their direct line of sight," Harrow whispered. "In two hundred meters, we will separate into two groups. You will lead one," he murmured to Crate, "up and onto that overpass." He pointed out the area he had in mind. "Take the men who are the most crack shots with you. From there you'll have complete defilade and a clear line of fire into the street."

"What's defilade?" the chief asked flatly.

"Cover. You'll be able to hit them without being exposed to return fire."

"Why didn't you just say that?" Crate hissed.

"Never mind," Harrow grumbled, and pressed on. "I will set up the other group on ground level. Then, I will attack the enemy and lead them into the ambush. The ground level group will fire first, and your men will need discipline to not give away their position. Hide well and wait. The Death's Head will take cover and move to flank the men on the ground, and that is when you will kill them."

The chief swallowed but nodded. "Got it."

The disembodied magus floating above them could see their auras. With the exception of Harrow, the nerves of the group were already strained. For a moment, he worried that the task was beyond them.

Then he saw them—the demons, spirit familiars of the Order preying on the Outlander warriors. Dark, misshapen forms, blights in the otherworldly fabric of the lower dimensions. They nipped at the souls of the men, weakening them. They were not naturally occurring thought-forms arising from within the minds of the men. Harrow's expansive aura had already banished the internal fears of the other Outlander warriors. These spirits were selected and enslaved by the Last Men to sow despair among the Outlanders.

They would be easy enough for Quintain to deal with. He performed the banishing ritual of the pentagram, mentally marking out the space around the slowly moving team of men, and set his own powerful, spiritual familiars to work.

Four mighty devas, kings of the cardinal directions, blazed into astral existence at Quintain's beck and call. The vaguely human-sized and shaped flames, burning in their various colors, set upon the servants of the Order with a righteous fury. They scattered the negative spirits, casting them in panic to the far corners of the cosmos.

Harrow stopped abruptly, which almost caused a pile-up of the single-file men behind him.

"What is it?" Crate asked.

"The magician, Quintain. He is watching over us." He turned to face his fellow Outlanders. "You all know what to do. We can win this. I'm counting on you."

The chief and his men nodded. Somehow, all present found that they were breathing easier, as though a weight had lifted from their shoulders. Even Harrow's expectation of them was not the burden it might have been. It appeared to energize them. They stood straighter, had stiffer backbones and tighter legs.

Crate put words to the feeling. "We won't let you down," he whispered. Reaching out, he took the man behind him by the shoulder and nodded. That man repeated the gesture, and on down the line. Half of the group peeled away, following their chief. They had a difficult climb to the overpass ahead of them.

Harrow looked at the remaining men and was pleased to see steel in their eyes. "This way."

— — —

The warrior set the men up in the ruined ground floor of a building at the south end of an open plaza. Cover was scarce in the area ahead. It was as good a place for an ambush as he could hope for. The overpass was two hundred meters to the right and gave the elevated men with Crate a tremendous position from which to enfilade the Death's Head soldiers with plunging fire.

He put the men in a line abreast, deep into the cover of the building so that they were hidden, and then jogged out into the plaza to make sure that he couldn't see them at a glance. Satisfied, he ran back.

"Keep your nerve and stay hidden," he said. "I'll be twenty minutes or so."

"We'll be here," one of the younger braves told him, and he nodded.

"Just don't shoot the first thing you see, because that'll be me,"

Harrow murmured with a smirk, which drew chuckles from the other men.

"Good luck," the same man said.

Referencing SIMON, he set off to intercept the easternmost force of Order soldiers. He estimated that the section tasked with guarding the battalion's flank lay some four hundred meters away, across several blocks of the ruined cityscape.

He stalked them as quickly as he could. Stealth counted for less than audacity. With the quantum device spooled to twenty-five percent power, he made prodigious leaps from cover to cover, trying to keep to the high ground. Finally, he found them, sweeping through the city in single-file, each one of their weapons pointed in a different direction. He moved to cut them off.

Posting up at a crumbled building's corner at his right shoulder, Harrow waited until the muzzles of the lead soldiers peeked around the edge of the building. The Death's Head men checked corners with two of their soldiers, one crouching and the other standing. Harrow stomped on the rifle barrel of the crouching man to force it down and away, and grabbed the barrel of the standing man with his left hand, yanking it toward and past him with all his strength.

The standing Dog-man pitched forward and tripped over his crouching comrade, and Harrow kneed him hard in the chin. He heard the man's teeth break. With the same leg, he stomped down on the crouching soldier—now buried in a tangle of limbs—and caught him in the nose with his heel.

As both men reeled from his assault, Harrow reached out and plucked a hand grenade from the load-bearing vest of the man he had kicked. As those behind the leading pair scrambled to clear the corner and get him into their sights, Harrow tore the pin from the small bomb and tossed it underhand to the first soldier he saw.

The trooper tried to swat the smoking device away with the

muzzle of his weapon while wind-milling backward. The soldier behind him shouted "Grenade!" and threw himself flat, followed by his other comrades. Harrow ducked behind the corner again as the bomb exploded with a sharp, deafening crack, sending bits of metal and chips of concrete hurtling in every direction.

He made sure the soldiers could see him running away while they were still too stunned to fire. As predicted, they immediately gave chase. Harrow began to lead them on a running battle to the place where the other Outlanders were waiting.

— — —

When he neared the ambush zone, he sped up to give himself a few more seconds to set up properly, sprinting to the finish. Crossing the plaza, he cut to the side as soon as he was sure he was out of sight of the soldiers chasing him, and crossed to the building where the Outlanders had set up.

Harrow had done his part—the remainder rested on the men with him. A victory here would belong to all of them together. He took his father's rifle back from the man he had left it with.

"Get ready," he whispered, "but wait until I fire first." He had pushed in between two of the men, both of whom were hunkered behind their rifles which rested on the crumbled wall. It was a solid firing position. "Stay low." He glanced to his left. The younger brave there breathed, deep and steady, and only blinked when a drop of sweat sank through his eyebrow and fell onto his eyelashes.

The Death's Head men did not come charging around the corner; Harrow did not expect them to. Two of the soldiers peeked around, night vision goggles in place— one kneeling and the other standing in their standard manner. Breaths hitched in the chests of the Outlander riflemen as merely catching sight of their foe gave them a rush of adrenaline. Harrow dared to issue a low, warning hiss to steady them.

Seeing nothing, the enemy soldiers communicated with hand

signals to their comrades, who jogged past the pair at the corner, the sights of their rifles in line with their eyes as they moved, mating their muzzles to their gazes. They were disciplined, checking high and low.

The under-officer ran across the street and Harrow's eyes followed him as he threw himself into a crouch next to the ruins. "Almost," he breathed.

"Fan out," the Death's Head group's leader growled loudly. His voice echoed in the quiet. "Move the machinegun there," he said, pointing to the west corner of the rubble. "Watch your sectors. The vermin is here somewhere."

The two troops carrying the machinegun and its spare ammunition finally moved past the corner and into the kill zone, and as they made their way perpendicular to the Outlander's cone of fire, Harrow placed the crosshairs of his scope on the right eye of the under-officer. "Now," he said, before catching the exhalation. SIMON provided the aiming point and he matched it, holding target and squeezing until the trigger broke.

His rifle cracked and the men on either side of him twitched. The leader of the Order's soldiery went down immediately, a cloud of red mist enveloping his face. The other Outlanders opened fire.

Staccato bursts broke open the night, their sharp cracks taking over for the report from Harrow's rifle. Caught in the ambush and instantly leaderless, the Death's Head men nonetheless did not panic. One shouted, "Ambush! Take cover!" while several of the others returned fire.

An entire cardinal direction erupted on them in muzzle flashes, barking gunfire, and snapping projectiles. Two more of them fell, clutching wounds. The rest scrambled, throwing their bodies to the ground or scrabbling to put something solid between themselves and the screaming bullets.

Harrow threw the bolt of his father's rifle and placed a round into the throat of the man with the section's machinegun, who fell as though an un-stringed puppet, his weapon clattering to the earth. "Pour it on," he shouted over the din as he pulled his own rifle back, slung it over his shoulder, and observed with SIMON.

The Outlanders with him were not possessed of great marksmanship, even with their enemies less than one hundred meters distant. Harrow's computer augmented brain provided instant ballistic data. He stepped back to help direct his comrades' fire.

The young Outlander to his left was firing in a disciplined manner, but Harrow could not see his shots landing as he tried to hit the exposed side of a Death's Head man who had squeezed into cover that could not conceal himself entirely. "You're shooting too high," he said loudly into the man's ear. The brave nodded and adjusted his aim and fired three times more; the first round missed again but hit the rubble. The second shot shattered the man's hip and caused him to slip, exposing more of his body. The third hit the soldier in the jaw, a messy and disabling wound.

Harrow gripped the younger man's shoulder. "There you go." Putting more force into his voice, he shouted, "Let's move!"

He led the Outlanders away from the position just as the Death's Head soldiers who had reached cover drew a bead on the area and began to return fire in force. Panting, the last of Harrow's men skipped around the corner to the alley behind, their designated fallback area, just as the space they had occupied moments before was filled with skipping bullets.

The Order men poured rifle fire into the vacated position, chewing up the rubble into dust. Then the soldiers began throwing hand grenades into it, which exploded with a series of intense cracks as Harrow shoved the brave warriors ahead of him and away, down the narrow, debris-choked corridor. Thick clouds of dust and smoke billowed from the abused building, which groaned and teetered, on the edge of collapse.

Harrow pulled the last man in line straight up and hooked his thumb behind him. "Kill anything that comes after us," he said, and the warrior nodded and leveled his rifle into the haze of smoke. Harrow squeezed past the line of men to the fore, crossing around behind the building.

When he reached the corner, he peeked around toward the overpass and was seized with pride. Crate and the Outlanders with him poured rifle fire down on the Death's Head men who were now fatally exposed to them. "Stay here but be ready to move," he ordered the foremost man, who nodded and passed on the word to those behind.

Drawing KA-BAR, he padded toward the distracted Order soldiers, resolving to finish them quickly before their reinforcements arrived, and to make off with whatever he could grab before leading the brave ambushing force of Outlanders to safety.

Crate's shooters took a deadly toll on their enemies as Harrow spooled up his quantum field device and charged in.

One of the Death's Head, taking over for his dead or dying commander, was speaking rapidly but robotically into his radio headset from his hiding place in a deep ditch. "Cold Hand two, this is Belt Fed one. Fire mission; grid November Victor eight-seven-three-four three, five rounds, fire for effect. Will adjust, over."

Harrow cursed inwardly and, at a full sprint, veered toward the voice, his dagger flashing in his fist as his arms pumped. He could not allow the man to make any such adjustments.

Harrow vaguely acknowledged the Quintain's astral presence as he transported his consciousness to the chief, who was directing fire from the crumbling overpass. "You need to move now," the etheric spirit shouted to the man across time and space.

Crate blinked. "Stop shooting," he hollered. "We've got to move!" The Outlanders gathered their weapons and ran for the edge of the elevated road just as the mortar rounds whistled in on top of them.

Shoving his fellow Outlanders violently, Crate dropped to the hard, cracked concrete just as the first of the shells impacted the overpass only fifteen meters away. With a deafening crash, concussive force and screaming hunks of shrapnel careened over the men, who crawled on their bellies away from the explosions.

Four more shells screamed down from the heavens, three of which impacted the ground below the raised road, sending enormous fountains of dirt and concrete into the air. The fourth hit one of the supporting pillars which held up the ancient structure. It tottered dangerously.

"Cold Hand two," the Death's Head soldier said as he craned his neck over the low rise to spot for the mortars. His message was cut off as Harrow leapt into the ditch. The soldier tried to snap his weapon up and draw a bead on the charging Outlander, but Harrow was too fast. He grabbed the lip of the man's helmet underhanded with his left fist and wrenched it hard to the side. He plunged his dagger deep into the flesh of the man's exposed throat.

Twisting and withdrawing the weapon, the Outlander skipped to the next Death's Head killer, whirling just as the second man got the muzzle of his rifle in line with his chest.

Harrow triggered the shotgun gauntlet on the back of his left hand, and with a tremendous thump, bracketed the man with two dozen pellets from two meters away. Blood and gristle sprayed through the smoke as the trooper reeled backward.

Harrow stepped into the attack, and, pivoting on his left foot, brought his right leg around in a thunderous roundhouse kick. He thrust all the muscles of his hips, thighs and torso into the blow. The ridge of his armored shin slammed into the soldier's head at the bridge of the nose and crushed in his face. His head snapped backwards and bounced off of the broken ground behind him with a wet crunch.

Scooping up the rifle from the dying artillery spotter, Harrow advanced into the enemy midst. SIMON calculated aiming points as he quickly and efficiently dispatched the remaining three soldiers with precise bursts to their exposed faces.

Smoke trailing from his left fist, Harrow dropped the stolen rifle and waved the Outlander men forward from behind the building, where they had watched, wide-eyed. When they jogged over to where he was, he said, "Half of you collect weapons and ammunition from the dead. Take everything you can carry. The other half will come with me. Crate's group may have casualties. Be sharp. We only have a few moments."

The men worked swiftly. Within three minutes, they had regrouped two hundred meters back, wedging themselves deeply into the cover provided by the ruins.

Several of the men on the overpass were wounded from the mortar strike; the tiny metal fragments from the exploding shells had burned their way deeply into one man's chest, entering his body under his right armpit. Another man's foot was nearly taken off by the attack. Both men were unlikely to see the sun rise, though the men had put a tourniquet on the one man's ankle and slowed his bleeding to a trickle.

Crate himself had a semi-circular notch ripped away from his right ear, which bled heavily. His face had swollen badly from another fragment which had hit him in the chcek. Likewise, several of the other men had superficial wounds.

Harrow considered. The ambush had been quite a coup, netting them a prestigious haul of enemy dead, as well as captured weapons and ammunition, for the cost of only two casualties. Still, the Outlander warriors were already exhausted and running low on water, which they sucked greedily from the canteens and jugs each man carried.

"You're tired," he said aloud, "and hurting." The men and their chief looked up at him with heavy-lidded eyes from where they had kneeled, sat, or crouched to catch their breath. "These men," he said, pointing to the two grievously wounded warriors, "won't live without treatment. Take them back to the station and leave the rest to me." He was proud of the brave amateurs who had, in his eyes, demonstrated their worth.

"Fuck that," Crate said, slurring the words because of his facial wound. "You dragged us out here. Let's get this done."

Harrow shook his head. "You've all proven your bravery, and now you have new weapons and more ammo. With any luck the Death's Head are wheeling around to avenge their comrades. We've accomplished our mission and turned them away from their objective. Go back and defend the others."

"If you get killed, we're screwed anyway. Let us help you," the chief argued.

"I said I wouldn't be reckless with your lives. The lessons you've learned here can help you in the future. Besides, if I'm killed, they might stop attacking and go home. They're here because of me. I started this. Let me finish it. None of you have anything left to prove."

"Bullshit. This is our war, too."

Harrow reached the end of his patience. "It's too dangerous for you to stay," he growled, spittle flying from his lips. "I might get lost in the battle. If I lose control, I could end up killing all of you!"

The other men blinked. The young man who had stood beside Harrow during the ambush spoke up. "What do you mean?"

"It's happened before. I have a power in me, and once I unleash it, it can't tell my friends and enemies apart. Now I know that I'm going to need it to win, but I can't use it if it puts all of you at risk."

Quintain's softly glowing apparition manifested in a flash, and the other Outlanders stumbled and reeled backward from it, startled and awestruck. The magus ignored them in favor of the import of the moment. "I must protest," he delivered in his faraway drone. "There must be another way."

"I have already simulated every other possibility. This must be done, or we face annihilation." He took in the group of exhausted, nerve-wracked fighters with a gesture and gave his blunt assessment. "We got what we needed out of these men, but their fighting power is spent."

The ghostly image of the boy-priest said nothing, so Crate swallowed and spoke. "All right," he sighed. "We'll go back." Some of the men with him made to argue, but he cut them off with a raised hand. "If you have the strength to bicker, you can help carry the wounded."

Muttering tired curses, his warriors gathered their gear and carried or helped those comrades who were too injured to walk. The chief stood, pushing the ground away with the muzzle of his rifle.

He locked eyes with Harrow. "Is there anything else you need from us?" he asked as his men stood ready to depart.

"I trust you to protect those I brought with me."

Crate nodded. "Count on it." A solemn moment passed. "You've proven yourself to us, too. Come back alive." He turned toward his men and waved them on, and the battle-weary band set off toward their underground fortress.

Left alone with the gently glowing spirit-form of his young companion, Harrow set his mouth into a tight line.

"I don't like this," Quintain said, his voice sounding closer and more physical than usual.

"Bring me back, after." Harrow said simply. "You've done it before."

"This is not a game. Dealing with spirit familiars is not as simple as you would believe. Onuris has a mind of his own. He might not just pack up and leave as he did before."

The warrior turned his hard gaze on the ghost. "You'll figure it out. I'm relying on you."

The etheric boy gazed back with resignation in his translucent eyes. His astral forehead-gem glittered. "I was afraid you would feel that way."

Harrow clenched his fists. *All depends on me. As long as I live, I will think only of victory. I will destroy anyone who opposes me.*

TWENTY-TWO

Alouine wanted to pace, climb the walls and scream her frustration, but she comported herself with dignity, if only for Nina's benefit. The sharp little girl was a roiling ball of anxiety and boredom, and appeared to oscillate between the two feelings by the second. Only Alouine's constant projection of calm helped the girl avoid a mental breakdown.

They were at first relieved to hear the Outlanders welcoming their warriors back from further down the tunnel.

"Is Harrow—" Nina spat, before Alouine cut her off.

"I'll check. Stay here." Before the girl could groan her disappointment, Alouine added, "I'll bring him right here if he is." She ran down the tunnel to the main chamber.

The braves set the two men with the worst wounds near the chief's cushioned sitting area, and Alouine had to shoulder and elbow her way through the crowd of gathered onlookers. "Make way," she grunted, pushing her way through.

Crate looked up at her from his kneeling position near the man with the shrapnel in his chest. "Where is the priest?"

"He hasn't woken up," she replied. "Where is Harrow?"

"Still out there." He hooked his thumb over his shoulder toward the entrance. "He sent us back."

Nina crept up on the scene and crawled between the legs of the gathered crowd. "You left him out there alone?" She spotted the dying man under her, gasping for breath, with foamy blood bubbling at his lips. "Oh, God," she murmured, reeling onto her backside.

Alouine reached out and snagged the girl's ear, dragging her attention along with it. "Run and find Joanna and bring her here," she said. The girl's eyes threatened to creep back to the wounded man, so Alouine gave her ear a tweak. "Go, now." Nina gave a jerky nod, then rose and ran off.

Diagnosing the man's injuries, Alouine pressed her left thumb to his heart and her right thumb to his forehead. Closing her eyes and focusing her chi, she slowed the man's heartbeat and breathing to a crawl but kept him alive and unconscious.

"His lung is punctured." She grasped the man's coat at his shoulder and pulled him onto his side, so that the blood filling his left lung would not overflow into his right. "He doesn't have long."

Crate glanced up to one of the men who had fought in the ambush with him. "Bring his family," he said softly. The brave hastened to do what his chief bid him.

Nodding in sympathy, Alouine backed away. "Tell me where Harrow is."

Crate shook his head. "He said it's too dangerous," he began, but the woman cut him off.

"I'm not interested in his opinion. I want his location."

The chief sneered. "I'm not telling you. There's no way that men come back and send women out in our stead."

"I'm also not interested in your good reputation," she snarled.

"Listen, bitch, I know who you are and where you come from," he growled, "and I don't owe you shit. The man said it was too dangerous for us. Just what do you think you're going to do out there? You don't even have a rifle!"

Alouine's eyes bulged. She did not wish to be crude, but her control over her dignity slipped. Being called a bitch was one thing;

that the man doubted her abilities was something else altogether. "Tell me where he is, you cowardly bastard."

Crate gestured to the dying man at their feet. "Does this look like cowardice to you?" He pointed to his swollen, bleeding face. "Does this?"

"It looks to me like the going got tough and you ran. What did you expect would happen? You'd brawl with them like dogs and they'd flee with their tails between their legs? They're here to kill you—all of you! And they won't stop until they do exactly that!"

The chief cocked his head to the side and spit a mixture of phlegm and blood onto the floor. "Harrow said that he'd handle it," he offered weakly.

"That's just who he is," she responded, with less vehemence. "Please, tell me where he is." She paused, and then added in a murmur, "I need him."

The Outlanders were depending on Harrow for their lives, but Alouine needed him for something else, something in her heart. She needed to see the battle, to watch with her own eyes and be there for the man as he took the weight of the world onto his shoulders.

Crate gave her a hard look and then sighed. "The last I saw of him, he was heading east along the big highway. If you head north until you reach it and then turn east, it should take you right to the battle."

Alouine nodded and set off. Immediately after exiting the underground structure, she could hear gunfire, occasionally punctuated by the sharp crack of a hand-thrown explosive in the distance. It was as black a night as she had experienced outside the Enclave. Extending the heightened senses her genetics had blessed her with, she navigated with pupils dilated to maximum and ears tuned to the sound of the fighting. Chakras blazing, the woman extended her sense of touch beyond the boundaries of her flesh and slipped over the broken ground like a specter.

She found the highway that the chief had indicated, and, facing east, saw hot smoke rising from half a kilometer away. Putting her head down and pumping her arms, she ran toward it, without even a vague idea of what she would do when she arrived.

A strange nostalgia filled her. Once again, she was chasing after the man who was doing battle with the servants of her people—men bound by iron oaths and devious manipulations of the mind to fight and die for the Last Men without reservation. In the village, she had merely been curious and impressed by Harrow's bravery. Now, she ardently hoped for his victory.

It felt like a betrayal, but she knew it was not. She was not the same person she had been. She had never had any respect for the Death's Head, dismissing them as she did the Lictors. Now, after seeing how they were hated and feared, she, too, despised them.

— — —

The Death's Head soldiers had already reached the Glen Canal, an ancient, ruined waterway which the Outlanders used as a sewer and dumping ground. It marked the border of Chief Crate's territory, and Joanna's machine shop was only one and a half kilometers beyond it.

In the wider, open lanes to the east, the army of the Last Men advanced like an avalanche, with nothing to stop them, and took strong positions around the rubble of what had, centuries ago, been enormous printing and publishing company buildings on the north side of the canal. In an area less than three hundred meters long and one hundred wide, a ferocious battle raged on.

Alouine sought a high vantage where she could see beyond the canal. Every bridge to span it had crumbled away with time. It would take an impossible leap to clear the disgusting brown-black murk which oozed throughout the bottom of the depression, and she certainly did not want to wade through it. She suspected that the Death's Head soldiers would have no such apprehension.

It was difficult to see individual shapes of men as she climbed up and then crouched atop a pile of pulverized cinderblocks, careful not to impale her feet or hands on the rusted rebar which projected from every surface.

She could not spot Harrow, but the black-clad drones laid a veritable barrage of bursting shells between the buildings, presumably to prevent him from getting through them. They used their mortar artillery like a shield, to keep him at a distance, where their firepower could do its work.

Glowing smoke and geysers of earth and brick sprouted up from the impacting rounds, accompanied by interlaced sharp cracks and a kind of dull thump which, even from this distance, echoed in her chest cavity. What flammable material still existed in those buildings burned, sending a pallid, acrid smoke into the night sky.

She lay down on her belly there, having never before had the chance to get such an overview of a battle. Blinking, she forced her eyes to focus on the distant images.

Finally, she spotted the Outlander warrior—only, it was not him. In Harrow's stead, Onuris began the counter-attack. A threatening thunder arose which quickly grew to a roaring hurricane. Like a scythe, the horrid, metallic apparition fell on the Death's Head, carving deep into their forward units.

Tracer bullets resembled confetti ribbons against the red-violet night sky streaked with smoke. They drew their flashing orange lines in the dark in all directions. With Onuris in their midst, the soldiers fired wildly, without concern of hitting their own. Beautiful colors clashed with horrendous explosions and ripping gunfire like acid and oil. A shiver crept across Alouine's shoulders.

She imagined a great scorpion fighting ants, its bronze-clad body impervious to the jaws and stings of its smaller and more numerous foes. It seized one of them in a crushing grip before dispatching it with a precise, powerful thrust of its massive stinger, plunging the spike into and through the helpless enemy before hurling it away like refuse and snagging another. Shadows danced in a strobing, flickering ballet.

It transformed the area into a smoking, seething, fire-and-blood strewn maelstrom, where every second meant horror and death.

She watched, transfixed. The Outlander was doing it. He was winning alone. It was an immense and magnificent and horrifying sight, inspiring in its valor but repulsive in its barbarity.

The foe threw in fresh reserves; the last of them, Alouine guessed. They did not last long. Against the reality-warping power of Harrow's quantum machine and the sheer psychopathic furor of his spirit familiar, the Death's Head could do little. It was like hurling marbles at a stone wall—a terrible, bitter struggle without mercy.

Finally, the gunfire died down and with a few final bursts, ceased completely. The great astral spirit hunted his foes to extinction.

Alouine wavered. There was no telling what the possessed man would do.

She decided to go. Harrow might be wounded or worse, despite all of his power to distend the principles of physics. Though she had no doubt that Quintain was projecting his spirit nearby, she knew that for all his spiritual strength, the young magus could not physically come to Harrow's aid.

Rising and brushing off the layer of dust on her chest and belly, she took a running start and leapt for the far bank of the canal, putting all of her psychic might into the jump. She still splashed in the muck a meter short of the dry bank. Arms out to her sides for balance, she nearly slipped and fell in.

Grateful for her waterproof boots, she waded out of the filth. Still, a grey-green layer of ooze clung to her, reaching up to her knees. It stank like nothing she had experienced, and she fought down a bout of intense nausea.

She crossed the hundred meters of broken, overgrown earth to the largest building. It had once been a three story affair but had crumbled to ruins. Now, it was steeped in fire and smoke, the final death knell of a structure built by the hands of men. Robotic devices had cleared the land and constructed everything within the Enclave she called home. There, men had lain and mortared the bricks with flesh and blood and bone.

Onuris prowled nearby. She heard the spirit's horrific keening, the sound of metal being slowly torn by forces too powerful to resist, and marveled at how greatly this shook her. It found the pit of her gut, already shaken and queasy, and settled there; a lump that seated itself heavily atop her womb.

She swallowed. She wanted to just sit down and breathe, to suck oxygen into her lungs until the feeling passed, and fought the urge to urinate. Her legs turned rubbery and her knees felt as though they had melted.

It was a primal kind of fear unlike any she had experienced before, and which bubbled up from some dark recess of her mind. A child's fear of the nighttime thunderstorm or the panic of a hare ambushed by a wolf. Her bowels tightened and only a supreme effort of will kept their contents inside of her. Madness, a retching horror, and even a bizarre hint of lust pummeled her senses.

A glance at her own mortality, the promise of a glimpse of the thing that might end her life; sheer, perverse, morbid curiosity kept her moving. Keeping low to stay under the smoke, she crept to the corner and peeked around it.

The boy magician, in his etheric form, was wrestling with the invidious, metallic, humanoid form of Harrow, subsumed by his bronze, armor-skinned god-form. Like the terror of the Cremation Festival, she could not peel her eyes away from the smoldering, statuesque figure which boiled and melted the very ground it trod upon.

Beast and boy briefly shouted back and forth in the guttural, nonsensical language which they had employed before. Alouine could tell that the ghostly figure of the boy was trying to reason with the demonic entity as he had back in Mason-Dixon. For its part, the being was apparently in no way ready to relinquish its control.

It threw its head back and released a deafening roar of rage and spite. The very ground under Alouine's feet shook, every inch of her body rattled, and she pressed the heels of her palms over her ears and squeezed. It was as though she were mere meters away from a rocket launch. She was certain that even the Last Men within the domed Enclave, all those kilometers away, could hear it. The furious sound ripped right through her, to the soul, at a resonant frequency tuned to the human psyche. She felt her mind wobble and contort, as glass before it shatters from tone and pitch.

The building on her right began its final collapse, and she did not even notice it over the roar of the creature's scream until dust and debris began to rain all around her. Out of instinct, she bolted.

The roaring cut out, though its echo reverberated to the horizon.

It saw her as prey, and it pounced. Falling backward, Alouine knew she was going to die.

— — —

Quintain threw himself onto the blazing-hot back of the metal monster. He could not think of anything else to do.

Even his etheric body felt the intensity of the demonic being's burning rage as he threw his imagined arms around Onuris' neck and tried, feebly, to hold it back.

Something in the astral dimension popped; the young magician felt and heard it simultaneously. With might that echoed the beast's physical roar, another mighty wail tore through the higher planes.

Enough!

It was Harrow's voice.

The point of that spear-sword, streaked with blood burnt black from its heat, stopped in mid thrust. The fine point of the lance rested on Alouine's chest, pressing into her coat and on a direct axis to her heart. The material it touched sizzled and smoked and drew back.

Like a statue, the warped figure froze, fixed in place.

Alouine scrambled backwards on her palms, pushing furrows into the dirt with her heels.

With a hiss which somehow seemed to contain no small amount of satisfaction, the warrior spirit was defeated in a battle of wills, and relinquished the Outlander's body back to him. Time froze for an instant as reality reconstituted itself, and the heat which the bronze devil-god had emanated dissipated all at once.

Again, Harrow's smoking body crashed to the ground, this time at Alouine's feet.

She blinked and breathed heavily as a kaleidoscope of emotions crashed over her—relief in her mind, unholy terror in her heart, nausea in her gut, and still, somehow, a strange trickle of feeling creeping from the crux of her thighs like an ache.

The psychotic creature could have rent her in twain. Curiously, a nagging feeling in her heart wondered what it would have been like. She banished the morbid thought with disgust.

A moment passed and she could do nothing but sit and pant, wide-eyed.

Quintain's spirit observed, "He is still breathing."

The Last Woman parted her lips to reply but could force no sound to issue from them. She swallowed, wet her tongue, and tried again. "That was . . ." she murmured absently. The image of the faceless bronze, feathered beast still seared itself into her vision.

"Yes, but Harrow needs your aid."

She nodded, still dazed from the experience and shaking from the brain chemicals flooding her bloodstream. Glancing at her coat, she found tiny wisps of smoke still rising from where the god's weapon had touched it. Gradually, her focus returned, and she was able to push her feelings down into the deep recesses of her mind. She would deal with them later.

Checking the Outlander for a pulse, she was satisfied that it was throbbing strong in the large artery of his neck. Aside from a raw redness which covered his skin from the intense heat, he had no other injuries she could see. It appeared that he was better able to insulate his physical form from the devastation than before. His clothes smoked, but his head showed no signs of the terrible burns he had suffered before.

"A moment ago, I was not pleased to see you putting yourself in such danger. Now, I'm glad you're here," the ghostly boy said.

"My sentiments, exactly." She rolled Harrow onto his back. With effort, she stripped him of his smoldering coat and tossed it away.

"I will return to my body and send more help."

Alouine waved him off. "I can carry him." Then she paused, and cursed.

"What is it?"

"The canal," she murmured. The prospect of going in there again was not one she cherished, let alone having to carry a man twice her weight through it. At its deepest, it was at least waist high.

"I will return with others," the spirit-boy said.

"Never mind that. There are wounded men who need your care in person. I will bring Harrow back. Check on Nina and Joanna as well."

Quintain's etheric spirit pursed his lips as he considered. "All right," he said, and with a crackle of bending space-time, he was gone.

She steeled herself and made up her mind; she'd do what she had to and carry the man.

Fortunately, Harrow woke up as she carried him on her back to the bank. "Stop," he groaned. "Put me down."

She happily but gently complied and he collapsed to his back again. "Will you be able to walk?"

He ignored the question. "What are you doing here?"

She bit her lip. "Rescuing you." A smirk tugged at her mouth.

He growled weakly.

"Will you be able to walk?" she repeated.

It took a moment for Harrow to respond. He bit down hard on his pride, enough to admit, "Not yet. Not alone."

"Take your time," Alouine mused. "You've earned it." After a second, she added, "And you haven't seen what we'll have to wade through to make it back."

— — —

"Go wait where it's safe, you stupid brat," one of the guards snarled at her.

"No," Nina argued, her brow furrowed. "Not until Harrow comes back."

The man twisted around, taking his hand from his rifle, and made to cuff the girl backhanded across the ear.

He paused when Quintain, awake and on his feet, appeared over her shoulder. He shot the sentry a disapproving look and said clearly, "Don't do that."

The scruffy, bearded Outlander brave shrugged and spit on the floor. "It's your funeral," he muttered.

"There you are," Joanna hissed as she caught up to the younger pair. Frowning, she glared daggers at the girl. "What did I tell you? You're in for it now, little lady."

Nina pouted. "I just wanted to be here when—"

The man next to the guard nudged him hard on the arm with his elbow. "Heads up," he growled. The line of defenders hunkered down behind their rifles as movement near the station's entrance caught their attention. Startled by the sudden shifting, Joanna wrapped her arms around Nina protectively. Only Quintain remained unfazed, squinting toward the entrance.

Shadowy figures made their way slowly across and around the hastily-erected barricades.

Seven rifle barrels tracked the silhouettes.

When they drew into the light of the fire burning in a large metal drum, the Outlanders still guarding the entrance immediately lowered their weapons.

The bedraggled and reeking pair made their way down the concrete steps of the underground station. Harrow slung his right arm over Alouine's shoulder, and he leaned heavily on the woman. His other arm dangled, useless, his shoulder raw and tender.

Several of them rushed forward to help the injured man. He held up his hand to wave them off with a grimace.

Two of them ran to fetch the chief. They nearly tripped over Nina as she ran and launched herself at Harrow's midsection.

Even through his discomfort, he laid his arm over the girl's back and pressed her closer. She buried her face in his stomach.

"Hello, Nina," he murmured, suppressing a groan. The girl did not respond; she simply clung to him tightly.

Quintain followed her. When he met Harrow's gaze, a knowing look passed between them. Resignation reigned on the boy's features. "Your luck keeps holding out no matter how much you push it," he said tiredly.

"I don't need luck," Harrow replied. Quietly, so that only the boy, girl, and Alouine could hear him, he added, "I have good friends."

The reunion was cut short by Outlanders pressing in all around them. Joanna looked on, proudly. Questions flew in volleys from the gathering crowd so fast that Harrow could not distinguish them.

Crate's booming voice, skewed and slurred from the swollen wound in his cheek, overpowered the din. "Make way there. Give them some space." The crowd fell back as the chief pushed his way through.

He stood, looking at Harrow for several long moments.

"I wasn't sure you'd live," the man finally said.

Harrow nodded vaguely. "We all refused to die today," he replied, his voice soft.

"No. You saved us," Crate said. His words were echoed by Outlanders to the left and right of him, and soon became an anthem, a mantra of acclaim and adoration, rising in volume and unraveling into cheers and cries.

Men and women wept alike. The tension in their hearts and guts and the fear of impending death fled them in a heartbeat. Many fell to their knees as the emotional catharsis unstrung their legs. Others surged forward to touch the man who allowed them to keep their lives.

Taken aback, Harrow swallowed. "Wait," he rasped, though his voice was drowned in the noise. "You saved yourselves. I only did what—"

Quintain, pressed next to him by the crowd, spoke into his ear. "Don't fight this. Let it happen."

"I can't be their hero," Harrow hissed.

"Too late," the boy mumbled. A half-grin spread on his face. "You already are."

For the next few hours, the Outlanders of Shadow Glen feasted and celebrated their miraculous victory over the soldiers of the Last Men. Crate, his face bandaged, oversaw the festivities from his cushioned seat, laughing and drinking with his warriors and playing with his children.

Harrow took one look at the emotional gathering and then limped off to be alone. He did not succeed, as he was soon joined by Quintain.

The tired and sore warrior looked up at the teenager from his seat, back braced against a wall, with heavy lidded eyes. "No lectures now, boy."

Quintain shook his head. "I wasn't going to lecture you. This is a bit over the top, and I don't expect you to embrace it."

"There is no cause for celebration. This wasn't a victory. We merely survived. Tomorrow, I'm going to seek a real triumph. No more waiting."

The boy frowned. "So soon?"

"If not now, when? Our enemy won't take long to grow and program more of their soldiers. I have half a mind to leave now and fully press this advantage. Infiltrating the Enclave will never be easier."

Quintain's brow twitched. "Are you sure your body will hold up? You've aggravated every injury you had."

"You are an exceptional talent with healing, Quintain. If you do what you can with your knowledge and abilities, I believe it will be enough. With that, a decent meal, and a good night's sleep, I'll be ready to face my destiny."

"You do seem to have had an easier time invoking Onuris," the teen admitted.

"This time was different. In the village, I lost control of my emotions and blacked out. This time I was awake. Aware," he added, his voice low, "as if I was standing behind myself, watching. Not directing my body but . . . guiding it."

"What changed?"

"My focus," he said. "There are many things I lack, but a steep learning curve is not one of them."

It took Quintain a moment to respond. He sighed. "All right. We'll leave after you're rested. I'll go find Alouine and let her know. Relax here and I'll bring you some food."

He found Alouine somewhat surprisingly in the company of Joanna and Nina. The trio of females claimed a corner of the massive station for themselves, and sat, chatting. Joanna passed a plastic jug, swishing with a clear liquid, to the other woman, who took a tentative sip. Afterward, she loosed a few delicate coughs.

"It's good, right?"

Alouine smiled genuinely. Quintain found the self-deprecation on her features intensely charming. "That's not a word I'd use for it," she muttered, handing it back.

As much as the magus appreciated that the women were bonding, he knew that Harrow was deadly serious about leaving. He approached them.

Immediately, Joanna offered the boy her jug of liquor in a salute. With a smirk, he passed.

"I'm afraid we don't have much time to celebrate. Harrow wants to press on." He took a deep breath. "He wants to set out for the Enclave at dawn."

Alouine frowned. "He won't be close to being recovered by then."

"There isn't any use in arguing. You know that. He'll do what he's going to do and there's no stopping him. I'll do what I can for his injuries. In the end, he's right. There's no time like the present. Come morning, he and I are leaving."

"I'll be ready to go with you."

Joanna hopped up. "There's no use sitting on our butts. I'll give Harrow's gear another once-over."

TWENTY-THREE

Fed, rested, and the willing subject of Quintain's sacred healing prayers, Harrow felt confident and as physically sound as he could expect.

Breaking fast with Joanna, Nina, Alouine, and Quintain sitting around him, he sensed that this could be the last time that they were all together. Joanna and Nina would stay behind in Shadow Glen. Still, Harrow banished all discussion of death or failure.

"This will work," he spoke softly to the group. "One way or another, it ends today." He took Nina's tiny hand in his own and leaned down to whisper to her. "Be strong and I'll see you soon."

She smiled and nodded and seemed determined that she would not let Harrow see her cry or even worry.

He led the way, with Alouine beside him and Quintain bringing up the rear. It was a long, eighteen-kilometer walk to the border of the Enclave, and despite a few minor setbacks, like the clumsy teen slipping on loose rocks and splitting open his chin, the trio made good time.

Night poured in to fill the volume of the sky. The colossal domed city, symbol of tyranny for Harrow and Quintain and place of birth for Alouine, loomed over the three of them from only half a kilometer distant. They huddled in the shadows of the rubble, as close as they dared to the space where the minefields began, just out of range of the AI-directed, swiveling firearms.

After they rested for twenty minutes, had a snack and drank

water, Alouine said, "Remember, I'll need an hour to put our plan into action." She locked eyes with Harrow. "Do not deviate. I'll clear your route inside, and gather as many of the Last Men as I can at the Temple of Understanding. You have to give me a chance to explain to them." She took a breath. "You have to give them a chance to choose their fate."

Harrow nodded his head slightly. "I agree. Just keep them occupied. Quintain and I will find Carver and the other leaders." His mouth tightened to a line.

"Unless I miss my guess, he'll be in the capstone of the pyramid. And his Lictor, Armiluss, won't be far from his side."

"Once we decapitate this beast, we can consume its corpse and become something new."

Quintain smirked. "Your phrasing is crude as usual, but apt. Just remember to keep your own head. Let's not lose sight of a future for all of us." He reached out and grasped the warrior's shoulder. "*All* of us."

"Don't worry about things on my end," Harrow replied gruffly. "You just make sure that the Order's spirit-slaves don't interfere."

"Count on it," the teen said.

Alouine rose. "All right," she announced. "I'm going."

"Be without fear," Quintain said.

"Or overcome it," Harrow amended.

With a nod, the woman set off into the dark.

After a moment, Harrow drew his pistol from its holster and extended the weapon, grip first, toward Quintain. "I want you to take this."

The teen looked at it, then at Harrow, and shook his head abruptly. "I don't want that."

"Take it anyway. It will be too dangerous inside to be unarmed. I know that violence is your last resort, but I would rather you have it and not need it, than need it and not have it."

Quintain took the weapon and hefted it in his hand.

"Do you know how it works?" Harrow asked.

"In theory."

The warrior pointed out the safety toggle on the side of the firearm. "It's loaded and ready to fire. Release the safety here," he said, demonstrating, "and pull the trigger. If nothing else, it might buy you a second or two. Every second might be precious in there."

Sighing, the boy nodded. He flicked the safety back on and put the weapon in his coat pocket.

"Are you ready for this?" the older male asked.

Quintain blew out a breath. "I think so. In one way or another, I've been waiting my whole life for this. I just wish . . ."

"What?" Harrow prompted patiently.

"I wish it wasn't me here, doing this. I mean, I know it needs to be done, and I know we're the best chance the world has of throwing off the Order's tyranny. I'm here," Quintain said, almost to himself as if reaffirming the fact. "I'll do what I have to. I just wish . . . I didn't *have* to."

"There is no one else," Harrow said. "It must be us, or nothing will ever change."

"I know."

"I'm proud of your courage."

"Let's wait until after it's put to the test," Quintain replied, trying a half-smile.

"There's no need. You've demonstrated it countless times. It will be there when you need it."

The magus huffed once. "Let's hope so," he said, as he settled in for an hour of waiting that seemed to take far longer.

— — —

Cigar smoke curled from his lips as he watched Armiluss wreck another slave. Watching Carver rape the Landgrave woman must have fired the Lictor's libido because he had spent hours rutting with the cheap, cloned human flesh on offer at the brood pits.

Carver played electronic parlor games via data link while half-observing his Lictor, and spent freely from the last reserves of his Mark account. Soon enough he would have no use for the money anyway. The private penthouse suite he had rented reeked of pungent bodily fluids.

Armiluss chucked yet another dead and broken female form over his shoulder, adding to the piled bodies of the previous three. Carver offered him polite applause.

"Well done, my boy, well done." The Last Man checked the time via data link. "We may have time for another, if you'd like."

The Lictor nodded, and Carver summoned the accompanying valet with a wave of his hand. The hook-nosed, ratty little slave appeared in an instant. "Bring another slave and tally up the bill."

After a moment, the weasel-like servant returned. "Apologies, my lord," he stammered, "but there appears to be insufficient funds in my lord's account."

Carver shrugged. "No matter," he flippantly remarked, before turning the lens of his pulse emitter on the man. The air boiled and so did the slave's head; a half-second of a scream was cut off by the bursting of the man's skull as the microwave heat expanded his brain matter explosively. The Last Man cursed and turned away to avoid being showered with steaming gore.

Armiluss simply watched.

Carver dropped his still-burning cigar in the puddle of bubbling fluids leaking from the servant's headless cadaver and began dabbing the dots of hot blood off of his face with a heated, moist towel.

"Let's go, Armiluss. It appears as though you have used up the last of my funds. We have other matters to attend in any case."

The Lictor rose and began to refasten his clothing, and then master and slave left the bordello and its corpses behind, walking out of the casino-brothel without a care.

As they walked toward the sky-tram concourse, Carver's data link chimed.

"The device is finished and functioning nominally," Heid sent.

Carver nodded, his lips contorting smugly. "Excellent timing, Heid. We are on our way to the Temple now. Please vacate the premises." He smiled to himself. "You will not want to be there when we arrive."

"I am leaving now. Acheson out."

Carver shrugged. He was beyond caring about Heid's flippant attitude, just as he was sure that the other man was eager to be rid of him.

Heid knew what he had built in the High Circle's chamber and knew that without a quantum engine like the one Carver possessed, it would not function. The man did not have the courage to lie to Carver, let alone betray him. Everything was progressing exactly as Carver designed.

He issued an urgent request to meet with the entirety of the Highest Circle at the earliest possible time, with the explanation that he had discovered new and pressing information about the Outlanders that was too sensitive to deliver via data link. Many of the ancient men were furious that they were disturbed, but they agreed to assemble in the capstone chamber in one hour, with grave threats that Carver's information had better be worth it, or else.

Carver could barely contain his giddiness. "It is beginning," he told Armiluss. "I trust you are prepared."

"Yes, master," the Lictor droned.

"Very good. The meeting is in one hour, so we can take our time." He climbed aboard the summoned tram and commanded it to head for the Temple of Understanding.

Upon arriving, the pair went to Carver's offices to clean up and change their clothes. Carver savored a final glass of his finest bourbon. Via data link, he arranged for the delayed delivery of a message to his parents and brothers in the Second City Enclave, detailing the situation. The missive would be digitally held in a secure server until dawn, local time; twenty hours by Carver's impeccable calculation. By then he would be his own God, and far beyond reproach for his actions, but he wanted his family to know what a Delano had done in the Third City. He could not resist the chance to gloat his ultimate triumph.

Dressed in his finest suit, he rode the lift to the capstone, his Lictor looming over his shoulder. There was no erasing the satisfied smile on his face.

— — —

Alouine raced along at ground level, following the sky-tram track suspended above her. Now that she was inside the climate-controlled and sterile environment of the Enclave, she stripped her coat and discarded it. Already she was sweating, having adapted her body to the far colder conditions of the Outlands.

She might have summoned and ridden a tram, but she did not dare reconnect to the Enclave network to use her data link. The last thing she needed was for other Last Men to know that she had returned to the Enclave, though she wished she could let Thaira or her servants know that she was on her way.

Activating the radio-frequency identification chip, the Mark account in her right wrist, she knew that all automated doors in the Enclave, at least the ones her account was cleared for, would open for her. The signal it broadcast was simultaneously an IFF transponder. All the Death's Head men would read her as friendly through the heads-up displays mounted on their helmets, and the automated firearms did not register her as a target.

Indeed, she had merely walked into the Enclave through the

same alley in which she had met Harrow. An interested pair of guards was easily dismissed after she had turned the Mark signal on. It took her ten minutes to navigate the unending rows of hydroponic growth vats.

Anyone scanning for her signal would instantly know she had returned, so she had to hurry. Even so, she doubted that there was much Carver could do even if he learned that she was in the Enclave, except sic his Lictor on her; in which case, she was confident that she could lead Armiluss in a merry chase and give Harrow enough time to find Carver and kill him.

An order for the Death's Head to disregard her account signal and target her for destruction would need to be vetted by the Highest Circle, and he obviously hadn't had the influence or inclination to have them do that as yet.

When she returned to the building which had been her place of birth, Alouine hesitated. She decided it would be safer to sneak into her own home of near thirty years. There was a possibility that she had already been branded a traitor to the Order. For one thing, she did not know if Thaira was inside, or if Carver had posted assassins or kidnappers to wait for her return.

It was surprisingly easy to enter the manor. She scaled the multiple exterior levels of the palatial building with acrobatic leaps, and entered through the tram boarding platform.

The first servant she saw as she entered the corridor past the thick and heavy glass doors stared at her in shock and confusion for an instant, before diving to the floor and pressing his forehead to it in supplication.

Strange how in such a short time, she had gone from expecting such behavior to finding it abhorrent. She sighed. "Don't do that," she said but cut herself off, scowling. There simply was not time.

Rushing past the prostrate form, she sped to Thaira's chamber.

At the door, she stopped, breathing deeply from the run. Would she be inside? If so, how would her friend, who she had thought of and longed for terribly, react to seeing her so abruptly? She found that the sweat collecting under her arms and in the cleft of her breasts had spread to her palms.

She bit her lip with nervous energy.

Like a servant without a data link, she manually pressed the door chime.

"My instructions were clear," said a familiar but frail voice through the speaker. "I am not to be disturbed."

Alouine could sense a deep, abiding sadness in the response. She struggled for a moment, and when she found her voice, it could only produce one word: "Thaira."

The door immediately slid open. Alouine saw her friend's form outlined on her bed in the dim light, and she made hesitant steps into the room. "I'm back," she murmured, the sound little more than a breath.

Sobbing ensued at once, and Alouine threw herself the last few meters, sitting on the edge of the bed and gathering the other woman into her arms.

They both wept openly. "I'm so sorry," Alouine whispered. "Let me look at you."

Thaira's hair brushed her face as she shook her head vehemently. "No, don't."

"Lights, twenty percent," Alouine commanded, and the room brightened slightly. Thaira buried her face in her hands, and as Alouine took in her friend's form, she saw the evidence of a sound thrashing.

Thaira's arms and hands were purple and red with fresh bruises. Worse, her right leg was in a stabilizing robotic brace from her hip to her foot. Alouine's eyes widened in horror and fury, and she struggled to keep her emotions in check. After a moment, she managed to ask in an uneven voice, "What happened?"

The other woman continued to sob. "Carver Delano happened," she spat. "A few days ago, he started running amok." She clutched at Alouine desperately. "He killed some of your servants; cooked them alive with some kind of directed energy weapon." She sniffled. "His Lictor did this. He held me, while Carver—" she gushed, before her voice turned to unintelligible blubbering.

Alouine blinked. She felt a blaze of blue-hot, righteous anger bubble up from deep in her guts as her chakras lit with ethereal power. Just as suddenly, the sickly cold of remorse pummeled the feeling back down.

This was her fault. She said so. "I should have put an end to that menace long ago," she muttered, holding the other woman close. Her voice gained strength. "Now is the time to put right that mistake. Carver Delano will be dead by morning, I swear it."

Thaira coughed once. "There's nothing you can do," she said, despondence thick in her words. "His Lictor has some kind of ability to bend reality." Her voice sank to a faraway whisper. "It's like nothing I've never seen. He's untouchable."

Alouine swallowed hard. *Carver is nothing more than a thief and a bully, but he is damnably good at both. The Death's Head have seen Harrow in action too many times. Carver must have copied Harrow's device or had that toad Acheson design one to compete with it*, she thought. Her lips drew back viciously. "It doesn't matter," she whispered. "We have to try. Can you walk?"

"Slowly," Thaira answered pitifully.

"Good enough. Let's go to the Temple of Domination. I want you by my side for this, right where you belong." She helped the other woman sit up and then stand. "Is anyone watching the house?"

Thaira began to dress herself. "Not that I know of. Why? What are you planning?"

Sighing, Alouine launched in. "I've made some allies in the

Outlands. They can defeat Carver, and his Lictor." She nodded to herself. "Yes, I believe they can. But they're going to need help getting into the Enclave, and we're going to give them that."

Thaira shifted her weight anxiously. "Letting in Outlanders to kill Order members is pretty much the highest treason I can think of. Are you sure about this? Even if it works, what happens after? Are they just going to leave?"

"I think that after tonight, the definition of treason is going to change. Come on, we have to hurry."

TWENTY-FOUR

Two white-clad Triary guards were posted at the High Circle chamber's door, and for a brief moment, Carver thought that the elder statesmen of the Enclave had somehow discovered his intent.

His fears were allayed when the pair made no attempt to accost him. He walked up to the door and, with Armiluss looming next to him, broadcast his presence via data link.

The door slid open, and man and Lictor walked inside. To Carver's immense satisfaction, the thick blast door lowered once more, solidly clacking into place behind him.

Twelve ancient, grumpy, tired-looking men glared at him from their spaces around the circular table. Each one had a Lictor of his own standing just behind their chairs.

The display was obviously intended to intimidate Carver, to exert the Highest Circle's authority, and to make clear their disdain and impatience.

High Lord Russell put voice to their intent. "We have gathered at your request, young Lord Delano," the liver-spotted, wispy-haired man croaked. "This had best be important, for your sake. You have only this last chance to impress us."

Carver smiled broadly. "My lords," he said, letting an imperious tinge creep into his voice, "I thank you for this opportunity. Before we begin our business, I would like to say a few words."

"With brevity," High Lord Stamp admonished.

"Very well," Carver agreed. "Indeed, time is short. That is to say that *your* time is short," he amended, his gaze and gesture spreading to encapsulate all twelve men. Offended murmurs ran through his older audience. "It is my duty, and I admit, my pleasure, to inform you that none of you will be leaving this room alive."

Several voices rose in protest, but Carver managed to stay them with his raised right hand. The metal of his pulse emitter glinted in the dim light. "Your mistakes and failures are manifold," he announced loudly, cutting through the indignant mutterings. "But the crux of those resides in the fact that you do not recognize the dictates of Providence. It has long been known that I have eyed that seat," he said, pointing to the vacant, central chair reserved for the High Chairman of the Enclave. "But I have come to a realization, gentlemen."

He began to spool his quantum device. Communicating via data link, Armiluss did the same.

"This Enclave—indeed, the entirety of our Order—does not need a Chairman or a council. No monument has ever been raised for a committee. It needs a Director, a singular man of vision, to sweep away the dust and mold of ancient, corrupt, time-lost creatures like you, and to bring the world into a New Order, one intimately connected with the spiritual hierarchy and committed to the principles our Order was founded upon."

"Your vanity is to become your death sentence," High Lord Rhodes hissed.

"On the contrary," Carver said. "To birth this new Order, I will put your decaying carcasses to one last use, as the fodder from which my glorious reign will grow."

High Lord Hesse growled, and pushing his frail, skeletal palms against the table, made to stand. Carver cut him off.

Voice booming, he cried, "Do not think for one moment that I do not know the deepest secrets of our Order. I know that the ultimate secret is that there is no secret! Any fool can summon a demon. The power you cling to has always been a cynical fraud. Your claim of advanced spiritual mastery is nothing more than parlor tricks and charlatanism, a smokescreen!"

He lowered his voice to a sneering hiss. "It is time for our Order to be revitalized." Using SIMON, he made certain that the magnetic locks of the door behind him engaged with a sharp clack, cutting off any avenue of escape or rescue for the ancient men.

"Enough of this farce," Lord Stamp snarled. He was the nearest of the Highest Circle members, sitting at the closest edge of the table to Carver and Armiluss. Creaking as he twisted in his chair, he cast a glance over his shoulder at the Lictor stationed there. "Kill them both," he ground out.

Armiluss sprang first, interspersing himself between Carver and Lord Stamp's Lictor. Helpfully, Carver side-stepped to assist him as both of their quantized magnetic fields shot invisibly into existence.

Taking on the full force of the charging Lictor, Armiluss enveloped the other slave and stopped him cold with one hand against his chest, like a bullet flattening against armor too hard and thick to penetrate.

With a thrum of power, Carver's Lictor cocked back his gigantic fist, and with a single blow, he utterly unmade the other slave, shattering him into a million pieces, shivering all molecular bonds and hurling a torrent of gore back from whence a man had come. The tidal wave of blood and dissolved flesh washed over a third of the room.

Carver grinned maniacally. Half of the ancient men, wide-eyed in shock, were splashed to soaking by the misty spray. Armiluss began his assault on the other Lictors, whirling and scything through them, pummeling each to death with a single, reality-tearing blow. He took on two and three at once, moving faster than the eye could track. It was a stunningly beautiful ballet of complete destruction, and nearly brought a tear to Carver's eye.

Rather than merely stand and watch, the quantum-augmented Last Man wanted to make his own mark on the scene. His pulse emitter came to life with a pop, and he leveled the weapon at Stamp, the closest target.

The feeble man raised his hands in protest and might have cried out but Carver did not hear him as the air broiled and waves of microwave heat poured through the chamber.

Wisps of silver hair caught fire. The man's robe twisted and contorted and shrunk, and then ignited as well. A horrid crackle of boiling moisture accompanied Lord Stamp's flaming demise.

Flames shining in his widened, wild eyes, Carver advanced on the other High Circle members as they weakly scrambled to get away. Armiluss hunted their Lictors to extinction in a furious blaze of quantum power.

Man and Lictor washed the walls of the High Circle chamber in blood and flame, and Carver chuckled, amused, all the while.

— — —

The two women took a nervous sky-tram ride to the squat, five-sided building called the Temple of Domination. The massive structure, each side over two-hundred-eighty meters long, housed the sophisticated command and control apparatus of the Death's Head, the main network hub of the Order's intelligence gathering and surveillance resources, and a barracks for the elite officers of the Death's Head, the Triary.

Thaira was intimately familiar with the building. She had offices in the inner ring. Alouine had never set foot inside.

"So, what exactly is your plan?" Thaira asked.

"We need to broadcast an emergency signal to all the Last Men in the Enclave and gather them at the Temple of Understanding. Surely, there are already protocols in place for that."

Thaira considered this for a moment, and then nodded.

"Good. After that, we have to shut down the Enclave's automated security. I'll attempt to address the members in the Temple and convince them to stand down while my allies take care of Carver and the Highest Circle."

Thaira was quiet for a moment. "I never expected that you'd be trying to take over the Enclave by force," she murmured. "Much less that you'd be using Outlanders to do it. Is that why you left, to gather up a cat's paw or two? If you had asked me, I would have helped you, even before you left. You didn't need to do this alone."

Alouine sighed. "If I hadn't left, I never would have realized that this is the right thing to do." She thought of Harrow for a moment. "Things would have been far worse. We have a chance to save some of the people here, to help them see reason and reform themselves. Our society, our very way of thinking, is a colossal error. I have to try to correct it before it destroys us all."

"I'm not sure I follow," the other woman admitted.

"One of the Outlanders I'm going to help had been planning to invade the City for a long time. Until I met him, his goal was simply to kill everyone and burn the entire Enclave to the ground. Make no mistake; he can do it. It was not an empty threat, I promise. Fortunately, and thanks to the other Outlander, he's had a change of heart. I believe it's genuine. But I'll have to uphold my side of the bargain. The Enclave can stay only if we release our slaves and agree to share what we have with those outside."

"None of the members will agree to that. I'm not sure I do."

Alouine took her friend's hand and gazed into her eyes. "Please, trust me, Thai. Once you've been in the Outlands, it changes things; changes the way you think. Our Order possesses nothing that it hasn't stolen from the world. We're going to have to start giving back, if we want to survive." She paused for a moment. "When you meet Harrow, and Quintain, you'll understand."

"Why make this devil's bargain just to kill Carver Delano? A few weeks ago you or I could have done it ourselves."

Nodding slowly, Alouine struggled to put her thoughts into words. "At the time, I did not want to insult my father's memory, or risk my standing in the Order. It was a mistake." She folded her hands back into her own lap. "I realize that now. But for as much as I hate that man, as much as he has insulted and offended me, and you, the Outlanders have as many reasons to want him dead. Maybe more." She sighed again. "This isn't about him, though. We have to seek a peace with the Outlanders. A great paradigm shift is coming, and we must shift with it, or we will be wiped out."

The sky-tram slowed to a stop at the boarding platform just outside the Temple of Domination.

"It's time to choose," Alouine said as she rose from her seat. "I can't force you. I can only ask for your trust. Tell me no, and I'll leave without rancor; but if you decide not to come with me, you should leave the Enclave as soon as you can."

Thaira rose also, though with more difficulty. "You've never lied to me. You promised you'd come back, and you have. If you truly believe in what you're doing, I'm going to help you."

It took them only moments to gain entrance to the massive structure. Thaira's Mark account still opened every door and Alouine had turned her own chip off. The Triary guards standing at each entrance and gateway of the concentric building ignored them.

For their part, the women did their best to walk slowly and naturally, even engaging in small, banal conversation to give the appearance of belonging.

Alouine noted each and every presence of Triary soldiers. She admitted to herself that her appearance was odd. She was still wearing her thick, outer bodysuit and grimy, knee high boots; highly unusual dress indeed for a member of the Order. But she wasn't broadcasting a Mark signal anyway, and did her best to cultivate an appearance of one of the Order's assassins, following her master. That females were only rarely used in this way was also a reality which weighed heavily on her mind.

There was also a small chance she would run into a Last Man or Woman who recognized her. Whenever she saw one of the comfortably dressed individuals, she dropped step to march slightly behind Thaira. The limping woman in her robotic leg brace also cast their mission into nervous doubt. Members, especially women, were nearly never seriously injured.

The corridor marked 'Enclave Security' accepted Thaira's Mark signal as well, but the Triary sentries stopped them.

"This is a Class 4 area, ma'am," the white-clad guard on the left side droned. Thaira glanced at the black, dangerous-looking assault rifle slung across his chest. "Unknown persons must be vetted by the Bureau of Security Concerns."

Thaira held her wrist up to the door panel's scanner. "Thaira Landgrave vouches."

The panel's red light did not immediately shift to green. Alouine's mouth formed a tight line. While she was confident that the two Triary members posed little danger to her, especially as close as they were, Thaira appeared significantly handicapped by her injuries.

Incapacitating or killing both guards, completely and simultaneously, would be a challenge. Particularly since Thaira was directly between one of them and Alouine. It also meant the end of the mission. The vital signs of Triary members were monitored remotely. If they failed, the alarm went up and the building would be locked down and on high alert.

Finally, gloriously, the light turned green and the steel barrier before them slid open.

Thaira nodded to the soldiers and proceeded through the door to the next area, with Alouine close behind her. When the door slid shut behind them and locked with a solid clank, both women released the breaths they had held.

"I thought for sure it was all over for us," Thaira said, whispering.

"You're doing well," Alouine remarked. "Keep your nerve."

"We're almost there." Another fifty meters down the otherwise sterile white corridor, and the pair found themselves in front of a traditional oak door with Thaira's name emblazoned upon it in gold leaf.

As they slipped into the woman's office, both of them headed straight for the desk, where the interface for the Order's hardened military computer network awaited. Thaira took a seat in her high-backed leather chair and keyed the controls while Alouine observed over her shoulder.

"I can issue an Enclave-wide alert and summon the members to gather together at the Temple of Understanding under my own authority," Thaira said as her eyes scanned the holographic screen, "but disabling the automated security is going to be more difficult. There are multiple, redundant fail-safes, and the whole system is behind a triple wall of encryptions."

Alouine considered this. "Would it be easier to disarm the security system one section at a time, rather than shut it down completely?"

Stroking the controls, Thaira worked to find an answer. "Somewhat easier, yes," she replied. "I can try initiating a grid-by-grid shutdown for systematic maintenance."

"They'll be coming in through the access to the hydroponic areas. The same place I escaped through."

"I'm on it," Thaira announced as her fingers flew over the softly glowing touch-keys.

— — —

SIMON kept precise track of the elapsed time, and when an hour had passed exactly, Harrow stood up, and then leaned down to gently shake Quintain.

The boy had been meditating for quite some time, sending his disembodied spirit on reconnaissance. He found the Enclave as guarded in the etheric world as it was in the physical. When the vibrations of Harrow's gentle prodding reached him through his silver cord, he quickly followed it back to his body.

"It's time," the warrior said as Quintain opened his eyes. The magus nodded and stood up. "Let's hope that Alouine has upheld her part."

"I trust her," the boy said.

"That will have to do. Come on."

As they snuck down the tight confines of the alley, Harrow was assaulted by nostalgia. When he met Alouine there, for the first time, he had never thought for a moment that, a mere few weeks later, she would be waiting for him inside the place, propping open the door and allowing him in.

They crossed the alley without incident and padded down the stairs toward the underground maze of production facilities. The Death's Head had doubled the guard there, and two of their dupes now patrolled the endless rows. Harrow unsheathed KA-BAR silently, but Quintain's hand on his shoulder stopped him. He sent a questioning, annoyed look at the boy.

Quintain shook his head and pointed to his own chest, and the older warrior rolled his eyes. But, after a moment, he nodded his consent.

The boy sat cross-legged on the floor and went into his trance. Long moments went by. At first, the guards yawned heavily and their crisp, active movements slowed. Another minute later and the men had, apparently of their own volition, laid down on the floor without a word to the other and simply took a nap. Within a few more moments, both were snoring away, locked in the sleep of the utterly exhausted.

"How did you—?" Harrow hissed.

"Those men are wide open to subconscious suggestion," Quintain whispered back. "It was easier to hypnotize them into feeling too tired to stay awake than it would be to convince them to not see you. They were looking for you, after all. I prefer the path of least resistance. I gave them false memories that they hadn't slept in a week. If nothing wakes them, they'll be out for a whole day."

"A useful trick," the warrior mused.

"I'm here to Work," Quintain quipped softly. "Let's go."

The pair of Outlanders snuck by the comatose guards and continued through the area. Harrow wanted to disarm them at least, but Quintain shook his head. It was better to avoid taking the chance of waking them.

They headed for the twisting stairwells, well over a kilometer beyond the ripe and verdant vegetable wealth in the hydroponic gardens, which would lead them to the Enclave's street level.

At the stairs, they arrived at the first area guarded by several of the automated firearm posts. They were mounted high on the walls in the stairwell, one at each floor. Peeking upward, the pair could see that they were at least four floors down.

Harrow was accustomed to dealing with the robotic sentries, but had no idea how Quintain had done so in the past.

"I've never been this far inside," the boy muttered, answering Harrow's unvoiced question.

"Sudden, bright light can disrupt their targeting, but I only have a handful of flares," Harrow whispered in reply. "Now comes the moment of truth."

He leaned into the stairwell as far as he dared. The weapons were pinpoint accurate and opened fire without warning on anything not broadcasting the correct IFF signal. He swallowed. No matter how fast he was, he was certain that if the automatic gun was still active, he was about to lose a hand.

He took a deep breath and waved his hand into the stairwell.

Nothing happened.

He did it again, and the swiveling carriage which mounted gun and camera did not move to track it.

"All right," he murmured. "It appears we're in business. I'll go first. Just remember to sprint to the top. Don't stop." He nodded to the boy and gripped his thin shoulder, giving him a reassuring squeeze. "Ready?"

Quintain wiped nervous sweat from his brow and nodded. "I'll be on you like a backpack," he grunted.

They ran up four flights of stairs, pumping their arms and legs as hard and fast as they could.

Panting, they reached the top after what felt like an eternity.

None of the weapons had fired at them.

A steel door blocked their way at the top of the stairs. Harrow tried to depress the horizontal push bar, but it was solidly, magnetically locked.

Behind them, still as a statue but no less ominous for that, the barrel of the last automatic, AI-directed gun loomed, pointing at their backs.

Harrow considered. The door certainly wouldn't stop him if he engaged his quantum engine, but he did not want to do something so rough. Likewise, he could blow the door open with a shaped charge, but the idea was to be as stealthy as possible.

He settled on trying to use SIMON to pick the magnetic lock.

"I don't like this," Quintain said, indicating the machinegun behind them.

— — —

The smell of broiled meat and freshly spilled blood was actually making Carver hungry. Smoke clung in the air and he waved it out of his path as he walked toward the high-backed chair, stepping over a charred corpse here and a shred of tattered Lictor there. He was careful not to slip in the fluids.

He closed his eyes for a moment, savoring the feeling of sitting where he had so longed to sit. The taboo of it, the utter impropriety, gave him a secret thrill.

My destination is mere steps away. I can almost touch it.

His hands found the controls, and he activated the holographic interface. Mentally, he connected to the console via data link. The meeting of the High Circle was, according to the server, still in session. "Carver Delano," he said aloud, "Mark account number one-three-eight, two-four, eight-seven-six two."

Just as he planned, the network already acknowledged him as a member of the Highest Circle thanks to SIMON. "I motion to be High Chairman of the Third City Enclave." The computer before him accepted the motion as legitimate, and Carver smiled with glee.

"All in favor: aye," he said. "All opposed," he murmured, pausing to glance up at the bloodstained walls and charred, shriveled corpses. Silence reigned. Armiluss looked on dispassionately. "The motion carries, one vote yes, and twelve abstentions."

The system accepted it as legitimate as well. With a few simple keystrokes, Carver was master of the Enclave.

"Congratulations, my lord," his vassal spoke.

Victory had never felt so orgasmic.

"Thank you, Armiluss," he responded demurely. "I could not have done this without you."

"It was my pleasure, master," the giant killer droned.

"Now, to our first matter of business," Carver said. He closed his eyes to concentrate on his data link. "I decree that Alouine Morningstar and Thaira Landgrave are stripped of membership in the Order of the Last Men. Their apprehension is the highest priority of the Death's Head. If they should resist arrest, their lives are forfeit."

Now my very thoughts become the law of the land, he thought, ecstasy welling in his chest.

The order was issued to the Temple of Domination at the speed of a data link. Carver considered what to do next when he noticed that there was an urgent message chiming in his own data link channel. Intrigued, he opened it.

The Temple of Domination had issued an emergency broadcast, summoning all Last Men to the Temple of Understanding. He read the last line twice. "For your safety, do not disregard this summons."

Fingers on the console's keys, he determined to pinpoint the origin of the signal, and was annoyed, but unsurprised, to find that Thaira Landgrave had issued it from her office in the Bureau of Security Concerns. Well, she'll be dealt with shortly, he thought, dismissing it.

But he decided to be thorough. He wanted to see her doing it, and found the camera footage.

There she was: Alouine Morningstar, posing as a servant. Carver stared at her image for several long seconds. Thaira had needed to use her authority to vouch for the other woman, so Alouine obviously was not using her Mark account.

The women seemed to be running diagnostic maintenance on the automated security system. Carver squinted at the screen. That did not make sense to him, unless . . .

They were shutting it down one sector at a time.

They were letting in Outlanders. They were letting in Harrow.

Carver put a stop to the faux maintenance, overriding Thaira's commands and locking her out of the system.

Then he opened a channel to the Death's Head high command, and immediately ordered a company of the Triary to sweep the grid that Thaira had disabled. "Kill everything there," he snarled, "without exception."

TWENTY-FIVE

"Damn," Thaira cursed. "It won't respond to my commands. I'm locked out." She sighed. "I hope your friends are already inside, because I can't keep the security in that sector disabled. It's all coming back on line."

"They're inside by now," Alouine said, hoping beyond hope that it wasn't merely wishful thinking. "If you've broadcast the emergency signal, we should be going."

Thaira nodded and rose awkwardly from her seat.

When she opened the door to her office, two Triary soldiers were already standing there. Both had rifles in hand.

"Thaira Landgrave," the one soldier barked, "you have been stripped of membership by order of the High Chairman. Surrender to us." Simultaneously, they both toggled their weapons to firing mode.

Faster than lightning, Alouine drew and cast her poisoned stiletto spike at the soldier on the left. It pierced the plastic heads-up display of his helmet and sank to the hilt into his left eye.

Before the first soldier dropped, Alouine swung into action against the second, throwing a Kali'prana lance of destructive energy into his chest on a direct line through his heart, stopping it cold.

Both men crumpled, dead before they hit the ground.

Thaira, blinking, turned back toward her friend. "We're in trouble," she declared. She dragged one of the corpses, still clutching its rifle, inside the office, and then slammed the door shut once again. She took the rifle and several extra magazines, and tucked the soldier's pistol into her belt.

Alarm klaxons howled. A metal shutter began slowly descending over the single window in the office which faced the inner courtyard of the building.

"Shoot out the window," Alouine cried.

Thaira, firing from the hip, sprayed the glass on automatic as she waddled toward it, and Alouine dove through first, shattering the window outward and splintering out its wooden lattice. She tumbled to a crouch outside but quickly rose to her feet, turned, and reached back to yank Thaira through after her.

She wasn't fast enough. Thaira squeezed through, tossing her rifle out first, but the metal shield cinched down on her leg before it cleared the window.

Metal groaned and plastic snapped as the robotic brace supporting her injured leg took the weight of a steel shield eight centimeters thick.

Thaira desperately tore at the straps holding her leg in the device, and Alouine assisted her. Bullets fired from the other side of the courtyard snapped past their heads.

The women freed Thaira's leg as the window shutter crushed the brace.

Half-carrying her friend, Alouine scampered to the right, trying to put the gazebo in the center of the courtyard between them and the Triary soldiers firing at them.

— — —

The boy expressed his displeasure with the situation and Harrow agreed. "I know," he whispered as his augmented brain worked. If he could find the right frequency to broadcast through his own magnetic field, he might be able to fool the door into opening. SIMON's vast computing power began to crunch the data as the counter-rotating components of the engine spooled up.

A faint hum behind them startled Quintain, and when he glanced back, a small red light began to blink on the gun-camera's frame.

The device was booting up.

"Please, hurry," the boy whispered.

Harrow snarled. "Change of plan," he growled, as the machine behind them clacked and whirred, testing its pitch and yaw and coming online. The action of the firearm cycled, ejecting a round which clinked its way down the stairwell, and loading a new one.

The warrior destroyed the gun with a crushing wallop from his left-handed shotgun gauntlet, which shattered the camera's casing. Shoving Quintain to the side, he dodged a stream of bullets as they poured from the gun, tearing into the wall next to the steel door and filling the top of the staircase with noise and light.

The recoil shook the weapon free of its broken mounting, and the weapon fell off of the carriage, connected to the swivel only by the wires leading to its firing circuit. For a few seconds, it hung there, still blazing rounds, until the wires snapped and the smoking machinegun tumbled down the stairs.

Harrow and Quintain looked at each other, wide-eyed for several moments. A high-pitched whine filled both of their ears.

The sleeping guards in the production area had undoubtedly heard, and Harrow instantly dismissed the impossible idea of continued stealth. He slapped the two shaped charge bombs Joanna had given him over the hinges of the steel door, gesticulating wildly for Quintain to cover his ears. As the boy did so, Harrow spooled up his quantum magnetic field and used it to cut the magnetic force keeping the door locked.

He triggered the bombs and man and boy were shaken to the core by the incredibly sharp crack.

The thick door fell toward them and Harrow caught it on his shoulder, peeking around it and through the smoke to see what awaited them on the other side.

He saw tall Enclave buildings through the haze but no humanoid shapes.

Just then, more bullets snapped at them from the bottom of the stairwell. Harrow snarled and glared at the boy, who flinched as the projectiles rang off the metal guardrails and took chips out of the ceiling.

Growling, Harrow threw the steel door down the space between the stairs. He did not watch to see if he had hit either of the guards, but grabbed Quintain's sleeve and ran.

Orienting himself to the huge pyramid about a kilometer distant, he dragged the somewhat stunned boy along with him, heading for a lane between two of the precise black buildings.

They disappeared into the shadows there, and crept along the lane to the end of the block, but what they saw at the other end stopped them in their tracks.

Last Men, two dozen of them, and at least ten Women, were walking toward the pyramid along the wider avenue. Harrow roughly shoved Quintain to the opposite facing wall to keep them out of sight.

For each male, a corresponding Lictor trundled along, forming a protective ring around their masters as they moved. All of the Last Men and Women seemed nervous. They must have heard the explosives Harrow had used on the door.

An entire company of Triary soldiers passed the group of Last Men, jogging in the opposite direction toward the area Harrow and Quintain had just vacated.

The warrior was content to let them pass by. The ringing in his ears persisted. Quintain looked as though he wanted to say something, but the older warrior cut him off with a curt shake of his head. Momentarily deafened, neither Outlander could be sure of the volume of his own voice.

They let the band of their enemies move down the street. After several moments, they disappeared from sight and the pair moved out.

They stopped again at the corner of a building, and there, across a wide plaza, was the capital of the Third City, the utterly enormous black pyramid. It rose over two kilometers into the sky, almost scraping the highest apex of the city's dome with its gold-encrusted capstone.

The group of Last Men and their Lictors were herded inside by Death's Head soldiers dressed in white. Alouine's plan was proceeding.

Harrow and Quintain hid as best they could and waited.

— — —

Ripping gunfire tore through the gazebo, an old structure that had been converted long ago into a place for the Last Men and Women who had duties at the Bureau of Security Concerns to snack and drink when they were otherwise unoccupied.

Bottles of liquor shattered and the Triary guards fanned out to flank the two women.

Thaira, the better marksman of the pair, held her rifle firmly, occasionally peering out from around the curving sides of the small building to shoot at any glimpses of white she could spot. "Now what do we do?" she demanded, as she dropped an empty magazine from the weapon's well and replaced it with a full one.

Alouine swallowed and took a deep breath. Valdemar Landgrave's word's echoed in her memories. "There is no difference between physical and mental force," her teacher had said. "The crushing of all opposition must be absolute."

Many opposed her: Carver and all of his dupes and slaves, the spirits of dead Last Men stretching back for millennia, the very structure she meant to turn upside down.

That only reinforced the rightness of her cause. Their opposition was a kind of prayer to her. So, she would give them a miracle to answer that thoughtful worship.

She drew up frightful amounts of Kali'prana energy from the ground in massive gulps, funneling it through her coiled legs and into the base of her spine, where the deadly spiritual power swirled around and through her chakras on its way to her brow.

Upon activating her Third Eye chakra with the sickly cold of this awful transcendence, she imagined her body eroding—dissolving like stone under eons of harsh, grinding winds. Instantly, gale-force gusts of horrid, grey-hued dust issued forth from the crown of her head, swirling with distorted mirages which warped and stretched in random directions and trailed amorphous streamers of stricture, suffocation, and demise.

Knowing deep in her gut that she would pay harshly for what she was about to do, she closed her eyes, drawing these deathly thought-forms taut, and then released them in a hurricane of blight, exhaling through her lips as one who puts out the flame of a candle.

She and Thaira occupied the eye of this etheric storm. All other living beings in the courtyard dropped to the ground, unstrung and snuffed out.

Beats of perfect silence reigned before Alouine fell to hands and knees, pale and shaking, a willing conduit for a current of life-blighting emptiness. Mouth dry, she retched spasmodically.

Thaira shivered. "Did you just—" she asked, before pausing. "Was that—" she tried again.

Alouine's fingers and toes felt icy. Her skin was an ashen grey-blue and her lips had gone utterly white. Valdemar's warnings about heavy use of the Kali'prana echoed in her mind as spasms and tremors rolled down her back and her arms shook under her weight. She could only nod shakily. Even the coldest nights in the Outlands had not filled her with such a bone-numbing, clenching chill.

"Are you all right?" Thaira gazed around at the fallen guards, who had simply collapsed into heaps where they lay. She gathered the other woman close to her. Tiny crystals of ice had formed on her sister-friend's eyelashes and at the corners of her lips.

"No," Alouine exhaled. "But I'll live." She felt enclosed in a block of ice.

Concentrating and drawing forth new willpower from reserves she had never known to tap before, she pictured Harrow's horrid metal spirit familiar, and tried to feel again the all-consuming, seething heat it shed, partaking of the memory of that cosmic fire. A spark ignited in her heart; she could not tell if it was dread or desire. It did not matter; the ice began to thaw.

She gritted her teeth and punched the ground with a thud, and imagined the shockwave shattering the ice on her body as it traveled up her arm.

Rising to her feet and slowly regaining her color, she looked at the still-crouching Thaira. "Let's get out of here."

"There's no way we're getting back out through the building," Thaira replied. "By now, it's locked down tight."

"Then we'll have to go over it. It's the only way."

Long, anxious minutes passed as they climbed up the inner wall of the aged building, with Alouine assisting Thaira as best she could. The pair used window sills and drainage pipes as hand and foot-holds, trading off between using the sling of Thaira's rifle and Alouine's long scarf. Floor by floor they ascended, with Alouine posting at the next handhold and then pulling her friend up. Sweat poured from her in rivulets. Thaira's right leg dangled, useless and painful.

The dread of phantom crosshairs rode Alouine's back, between her shoulder blades. She wondered which would kill her—the bullets or the fall. That brought no comfort, but it distracted her from the numb exhaustion, the ache in her gripping fingers, and the desire to just sleep.

Finally, grunting and panting, blood and sweat in their eyes and tangled hair, they scrambled onto the roof. The Temple of Understanding filled the horizon to the northeast, across the wide, artificial river which ran through the Enclave. Rather than head directly toward it, the two women half-hobbled and half-ran toward the sky-tram boarding platform attached to the east face of the building.

Fortunately, Last Men and their Lictors were still evacuating, and so the pair of women crept their way the last hundred meters across the roof to the platform, keeping to the shadows. Pointing to Thaira, they split up, with the slower, injured woman moving left so as to cut off the tram as it pulled away from the station.

Alouine knew she would have to time it correctly. She silently dispatched the pair of Triary guards on the platform itself with precise stabs of killing psychic energy, just as the waiting group of Last Men had finished boarding; three men, their Lictors, and a woman. Others waited in a queue behind them, seated on cushioned benches. She ignored them and ran at a full sprint for the tram as it began to move.

Surprised shouts followed her as she kicked in the glass of the door, and before the Lictors could rise to their feet to oppose her, she whirled into their midst, planting Death touches with her feet and fists. The bulging eyes and screams of the other occupants were annoying enough; she also had to contend with the sickly feeling that her body was breaking down under the strain of being a conduit for so much Kali'prana energy.

As the tram car passed the very terminus of the platform,

Alouine hooked her ankle on one of the car's handrails and threw her upper body back out through the hole in the broken glass she had just made.

She snagged Thaira's outstretched hand, whose leap could not lessen the strain. Bodily lifting the other woman's entire weight felt as though it would tear Alouine's shoulder from its socket, but she refused to let go, and after several tense moments with the wind whipping at them, she managed to pull the crippled woman completely into the car.

"Sky-Tram monitoring has detected anomalies," the car's AI spoke in its calm, chiming voice. "Would you like to report an emergency?"

Thaira's pistol, leveled at the Last Men, provided an answer.

"No," one of them men stuttered. "Everything is"—he gulped—"fine."

— — —

Long minutes passed, and the ringing in their ears faded. Neither Outlander could see any more of the Last Men approaching the pyramid. The group which had gone inside had doubtlessly progressed far into the structure.

White-uniformed Triary guards, seven of them in total, milled about the entrance. "I don't think putting these men to sleep is going to get the job done," Harrow murmured.

"There are too many of them anyway. The best I could do is to try distracting them," Quintain replied. "Is there no other entrance?"

Harrow shook his head. "The base of the pyramid is two-point-two kilometers wide. I don't want to circle around just to find that all other entrances are guarded like this one." He paused for a moment. "We'll have to fight our way in. You knew this would happen."

"That doesn't mean I have to like it," the boy grumbled.

"Enough waiting. Follow as soon as I've cleared the way." He pushed himself out of the shadows and began stalking toward the nearest Triary soldier, speeding up gradually from a nonchalant walk to a trot, to a loping run and finally a charging sprint.

Before the guard could shout a warning to the others, the powerful Outlander warrior went on the offensive. Both his hands moved instantly. The second soldier to the front was blocking his left-hand dispersal, so he released the right with a sharp swipe of his arm. A pattern of twenty-seven lead pellets blasted the leader with a dull, deafening thump from his right gauntlet.

With one dispersal achieved, Harrow placed his smoking right hand on the ground and pushed against it as hard as he could. He managed a one-handed cartwheel. SIMON's lightning-fast computations slowed his perception as the firing calculation lined up again.

All five of the soldiers were still clumped together. Shot from an inverted position, Harrow released the three-shell spread. A cloud of bullet-sized lead balls bracketed the target group. Five hits, five probable kills.

The shooting of the other two was both instinctive and professional. Four lances of fire struck out at Harrow. Input processed, he twisted his hip three degrees left and bent backwards. His hands touched the ground behind him.

The speeding lead passed within inches of his body; one of them underneath the arch of his back. Any one of them would have been near fatal, if they'd made contact. Harrow could see it coming before they'd even fired. As the third burst of lead passed underneath him, he let himself fall backwards, tucking into a roll.

The two remaining soldiers would have three more shots at him in total, before he could stabilize enough for another attack. SIMON stated that this was an acceptable margin; adjustment was not difficult. Harrow sprang up from the roll and went from standing to a full sprint.

As anticipated, all three rounds went over his head, one close enough to singe his hair slightly. With a brutal enemy right on top of them, even well-trained soldiers shot high. Harrow tore KA-BAR from its sheath and launched into a flurry of stabbing attacks, along the most favorably calculated vectors, aimed at the one soldier who had tried to cross behind him.

The more talented of the two remaining dupes parried two of the thrusts with the barrel and upper receiver of his firearm, but the third skipped over the intercepting steel and buried itself in the junction of the man's left shoulder and his chest. KA-BAR's point found the opening of the man's armored vest and punched deep into his armpit and then high into his chest. He lived another six seconds of excruciating pain.

Left-handed, Harrow yanked the pistol from its holster, slung across the stabbed man's chest. His right hand on KA-BAR kept the impaled soldier propped up as a shield, and he squeezed off four shots at the remaining underling over the shoulder of his dying comrade. Three hit home.

Time came rushing back to Harrow as he fell over with a disbelieving grunt, having defied balance and leverage too far. Combat time elapsed a total of six-point-two seconds. Satisfactory.

With Quintain's help, he pulled himself painfully out of the awkward position of having landed with his leg twisted under him. The warrior smelled the strange odor of his own burnt hair.

The fallen sentry moved away from Harrow, dragging himself with his good arm and trailing blood on the polished stone floor. Harrow looked down at him and exhaled slowly. His muscles were going to pay in pain for his excessive demands in about an hour, but it had been worth it.

"Stop squirming," he said in his most natural tone of voice. He had found that his usual flat, raspy tones did more to disturb people than any display of rage or anger. The wounded soldier either didn't hear or was still deep in denial. He continued to writhe towards the door. With a tired exhalation, Harrow straddled his back and placed the sharpened edge of KA-BAR underneath and against his throat. He pulled up slowly, drawing blood. "You will have a quick death if you give me some information first," he intoned, matter-of-factly. "I only offer once."

"Eat shit, vermin," the soldier ground out.

"That is no longer the fate of Outlanders. How do we reach the top of the pyramid?"

"You've never even heard of an elevator, you filthy savage?"

Harrow cut him off by bouncing his face off of the floor.

TWENTY-SIX

The outer walls of the pyramid were fifty meters thick, Harrow calculated with disdain as the Outlanders crept inside. The structure was incomprehensibly, unreasonably huge. What purpose could something so massive serve, aside from a monument to the egoism of a few?

The halls they stalked were as much museums as corridors, lined with statuary in a cold, post-human style and hung with disturbing paintings and tapestries. Harrow supposed that the abstract collections of colors and shapes were what passed among the Last Men for art.

Occasionally broken up by a framed and captioned portrait of some honored member were various images of human suffering—women in various kinds of bondage and torture, and men crushed flat or dismembered. They passed a façade of an emaciated, nude man, streaming what seemed like real, wet blood from every pore, his skeletal arms spread wide and his hands nailed to a crossbeam at the wrist. Quintain glanced at this, frowned, and shook his head.

Thick doors of glass that appeared to swivel easily on polished industrial hinges blocked their way. Beyond them, the pyramid opened up into a truly cavernous auditorium, trapezoidal in shape. The ceiling of the chamber loomed some five hundred meters above the gathered Last Men below, dwarfing the intimate crowd of some two hundred who milled about aimlessly in the otherwise empty space. Harrow could see a staircase, easily a hundred meters wide, which led to a huge podium on the far side of the expanse.

Some of the Last Men held delicate glasses of bubbly, faintly yellow liquid or small plates with tiny snacks. They chatted and laughed. Slaves carried bottles and trays to refresh them. Triary guards and Lictor warriors ringed the gathered members, facing outward. A man with a holographic tablet was making his way among the crowd. He appeared to be checking to see if all members were present.

The sight bewildered both intruders. They backed away from the glass and posted up against the wall to stay out of sight. It appeared as though the Last Men had no conception of personal danger. A supposed emergency to them was merely occasion for socializing while their slaves tended, not only to the problem at hand, but also to their comfort.

"That can't really be all of them, can it?" Quintain whispered.

Harrow seethed. "You should stay here," he hissed, "and I'll finish this right now."

"Alouine warned us not to deviate from the plan," the boy replied, his hand on Harrow's arm. "She's doing her part. Let's just do ours and find the way to the top."

"Those are the very people who translate the policies and intents, issued from the top of this building, into reality. They're all gathered in one place, and without them, the power of this Enclave is broken," Harrow growled. "We may never get this opportunity again."

Quintain sighed. "I understand. And I'm tempted to agree. But we can't."

"You'll spare this den of vipers on the slim chance that one or two of them have no fangs?"

"Yes," the boy hissed back. "We don't have time to argue about this now. You agreed to the plan, now stick to it. We could be discovered here any second."

Harrow took a few more seconds to consider. Finally, he said, "Fine. We'll go to the top first. Let's find another way around."

The pair wandered the concentric halls at the base of the giant pyramid for another few minutes before they found what they were looking for.

Two sets of double doors with a simple electronic panel demarked the elevator boarding area. "Well, we want to go upward," Quintain murmured, and reached out to tap an arrow pointing that direction on the screen. He paused. "Then again, it might send the lift machine in that direction. What if it's already above us?"

"It wouldn't make sense to control it from down here. That button only tells the machine that people on this floor wish to ride, and which direction they want to travel."

Quintain pushed the 'up' button.

There was a chime from the wall panel they stood in front of, and both warrior and magus could hear the magnetic lift slowing as it descended to them. Quintain glanced up at the lit numerals in a row above the door and watched them tick down.

"I've never ridden one of these before," he said. "Hopefully, there's nothing to it."

Harrow merely grunted.

The car came to a stop and the doors opened. The largest and most ferocious looking Lictor either Outlander had yet seen, a tower of sheer muscular bulk, filled the doorway. The hulking mass of brutality locked his eyes on the intruding pair.

Quintain let out a noise like a whimper. "Let's take the other one," he whispered.

"Wait if you want," Harrow replied. "I'm taking this one."

"Come in," Armiluss said, his deep, booming voice made comically tinny by his speech impediment.

The Outlander cracked his knuckles and rolled his neck, which responded with a series of pops. "I'll meet you at the top," he said to the boy in aside. A quick system check with SIMON and his quantum device began to spool.

Quintain sighed. There was no point in trying to argue.

Harrow boarded the elevator, a metal cube less than four meters on each side. To his surprise, Armiluss even took a half-step to the side to provide him more space to enter the confined machine. Quintain sighed again, nervously, as the doors closed. He moved to the other lift and pressed the button to summon it.

Inside, Harrow and Armiluss faced off. "Well?" the Outlander asked. "Shall we begin?"

"You will be dead by the time we reach the top," the Lictor droned. "And I shall gift your lifeless corpse to my master."

Harrow took up his fighting stance. "It will be your corpse I'll fling at him, before I kill him, too."

The Lictor was all shoulders, thighs and fists. He dwarfed Harrow, just as the Temple pyramid dwarfed all other structures of the Enclave. The Outlander had to crane his neck to see the larger warrior's face; the crown of Armiluss' head nearly brushed the ceiling of the metal box.

Both men were determined to make the elevator into a coffin for the other.

— — —

The huge, grotesque man shot forward with the impetus of a rifle round, extending a forearm as thick as Harrow's thigh, and a hand that could palm his head like a toy. His punch landed with the explosive force of an artillery shell. Harrow had seen it, observing how the Lictor channeled destructive muscular energy up from his feet, through the powerful pillars of his legs and his thick torso, gathered it in his shoulder, and shot it forward in the blink of an eye.

He ducked and the blow crashed into the wall of the elevator, leaving a crater. SIMON read thousands of kilos of force in that single blow. Sweat broke out on the Outlander's brow.

The steel of the elevator wall bent outward, ground against the metal of the lift's shaft and reverberated horrible noise into the space. The machine shuddered and groaned but continued to rise.

Harrow countered with a forearm punch that crossed over the top of the Lictor's arm and smacked into his cheekbone with a crunch. There was no give at all. The Outlander felt all the force of his blow bounce back into his elbow painfully, as though Armiluss had a head made of iron. He tried a knee strike to the Lictor's midsection, trying to put his kneecap five centimeters deep into the huge beast's diaphragm.

It drew only an angry snort from the bigger warrior.

Harrow drew deeper into his arsenal of tricks. Armiluss brought his elbow down in a smashing blow squarely on the junction of Harrow's neck and shoulder. The Outlander tore a strip of magnesium from his palm, lighting the intense flare even as he was driven down to one knee under the Lictor's crushing strike.

Armiluss backhanded Harrow hard across the jaw, sending him reeling backward and loosening several of his teeth. His back bounced off the steel wall behind him, leaving yet another dent in the metal box.

The Lictor pressed his attack, but Harrow lashed out with his fist, from just outside of his shorter reach. Still, having the Outlander's knuckles speeding toward his face caused Armiluss to hesitate for a fraction of a second, in which time Harrow opened his palm and flashed the burning flare into the huge man's face.

Blinking and disoriented, the Lictor took a half-step backward, white afterimages burned into his retinas. Harrow pressed in, landing a fierce, straight-on punch. He discharged his right shell gauntlet directly into the side of the Lictor's head with a tremendous bang, which spattered blood and hair in all directions and left a high-pitched whine in Harrow's ears.

Armiluss did not simply drop dead, but he did reel backward

and clutch his smoking head with one massive paw. It was as though his skull was reinforced with steel. The combined firepower of three shotgun shells merely peeled off a layer of skin and scalp.

Drawing KA-BAR despite his growing unease and discouragement, Harrow pounced. Though he thrust the point again and again, finding all of the targets he aimed for, he could not discover a place on the Lictor's massive, rhinoceroid form where the blade would penetrate more than a centimeter. He reversed to a downward grip to put more force into his stabs, but the flesh he drove into tightened at the point of impact.

Momentarily blinding the Lictor was a small, temporary victory that Harrow could not capitalize on. The Lictor's body was so hard and dense that the Outlander was sure that his blows were hurting his own hands, feet, and elbows more than they were damaging his foe.

He could not stand toe to toe against the much larger, stronger Lictor. Not without being crushed by the superior power, the reinforced skeleton, the skin woven like armor, and the utter indifference to pain possessed by the beast; an indifference to pain that put even Harrow's incredible threshold to shame. The Lictor bled from multiple cuts, all of them superficial.

Harrow activated his quantum device and prepared to attack the Lictor from every conceivable direction, to break all molecular bonds in his body and annihilate him utterly.

The device spooled up to ninety percent power and Harrow unleashed his attack and yet, instead of a blow that reshaped all of reality and made his destructive will manifest, rending the massive being into a cloud of red mist, it was thrown as yet another simple, mundane stab with his dagger.

The Lictor caught Harrow's wrist in his massive palm and squeezed his armored forearm with a vise-like grip. He drew Harrow closer. "It appears our quantum fields cancel each other out."

Wincing, the Outlander swallowed. His mouth went utterly dry. "A shame," he breathed.

Armiluss pulled him forward with a powerful jerk, right into his other fist, which smashed into Harrow's abdomen so hard it felt as though his spine might snap. Every particle of air belched from his lungs and he doubled over in pain, gagging.

The Lictor reared back with one leg, coiling momentum, and swung his knee in a perfect arc to Harrow's lowered chin. Even with steel-covered forearms overlapped to block the strike, he could not absorb the sheer impetus of the blow. Plucked from his feet, and propelled into the air, his skull ricocheted off of the metal ceiling and staggered him. He blinked, and then he was on the floor. The tiny room whirled.

SIMON's data feed momentarily cut out and the system began to automatically reboot. In a vague corner of his mind, Harrow recognized that this meant he had received a brain concussion; hitting the ceiling had knocked him out and hitting the floor woke him back up.

He tried to rise, could not, and settled for simply rolling to the right, which was fortunate as the Lictor's massive boot came stomping down like a meteor on the spot his head had just occupied. The magnetic lift again shuddered under the blow, throwing Harrow's equilibrium into turmoil as a split moment of weightlessness overcame him.

Then Armiluss dropped to his knees and began to pummel him with fists and elbows. Harrow covered up as best he could and curled himself into a fetal position. Thunderous blows rained on him. The Lictor did not aim. He did not have to.

For the first time in his life, Harrow felt helpless. The feeling of an undefended place, devastated from above with no chance of retaliation, pervaded him, and he hated it. Whole payloads of explosions washed over him. The Lictor dumped punishment on him without mercy or reservation.

He bled and his bones broke under the assault. His body was a burning city, limp, powerless, ravaged; a blink from being wiped from the face of the earth. He was hammered against the anvil of the steel floor like some soft, malleable metal, a crushed flat, living form reshaped to a mashed cadaver.

Complete obliteration; he welcomed it. Decades of struggle were coming to an end. *Finally*, he thought. *I did my best. This is as far as I go.*

At once, Armiluss stopped beating him. Another few seconds would have ended it forever. The giant warrior simply ceased and rose to his feet.

Harrow, through the haze of agony, realized that the other fighter thought he was already dead.

You may as well be dead, groaned a familiar, metallic voice inside his skull. *I cannot come to your aid so long as your foe blocks my manifestation.*

Somehow, his lungs found a breath. "I don't need you," the Outlander hissed in the barest hint of a whisper.

Within his mind, Onuris snarled taunts at him. "Inside your heart, you know the truth. Your father believed that you could not win your battles alone. That is why he summoned me. That is why he bound me to this pact. He did not believe in you! He could not conceive of your victory without me! I agreed to the pact because I agreed with his belief. On your own, you are worthless; a weak, pathetic being . . . human. All too human."

Harrow groaned. "Shut up," he grunted aloud. The Lictor gazed down at him.

"Will you prove him wrong?"

Pushing away the floor with his palms, a line of bloody drool connected Harrow's chin to the red-streaked puddle of sweat and saliva under his face. He blew out a wet breath as he struggled to rise.

"Prove us wrong, warrior," the spirit commanded, daring the Outlander to stand and thrusting at the heart of his pride. It extended its spear-sword weapon to Harrow and boomed, "Fight!"

With an unholy growl, he got his feet under him and stood; wobbling, staggered, pulped and leaking like smashed fruit. Armiluss watched impassively.

"Why should I?" he murmured. "Why should we?"

"What?" the Lictor asked.

The Outlander looked up, into the eyes of the looming, bleeding hulk. "Why should we fight each other?" he asked clearly. "Are we both here of our own volition?"

Armiluss blinked, his brows furrowing. "Just be silent and let us finish this."

"No, I won't. Not until I know that this is what we both want. Is this what you want?"

The Lictor began to respond as if programmed. "My desire is irrelevant. Only my master's will . . ." he said, but his voice began to trail off. "—may command me." He murmured softly, as though hearing, and comprehending, his own words for the first time.

"Nonsense," Harrow spat. He reached out and posted one hand against the wall of the metallic cube to support his raw, beaten body. Every breath hurt. Something rattled in his chest. "You have the same machine in your brain that I do. We are masters of everything we can reach. The fabric of reality is ours to command. Why would you listen to anyone else? Can't you make your own choice now, about what is truly right for you? Can't you obey yourself?"

The massive chest of the Lictor pumped up and down as he cogitated; Harrow thought he might hyperventilate. Armiluss opened his mouth to speak, closed it, and then opened it again. "Disloyalty now would make my life to this point meaningless," he muttered, his voice popping from the speakers in his neck.

The Outlander sighed. "We alone give our lives meaning." The mere act of speaking made him tired and dizzy. "Start a new life. Be loyal to yourself first. That is the beauty of being your own man."

Armiluss appeared to consider this for a few seconds.

A pinkish mixture of sweat and blood dripped from Harrow. His body shook with tremors.

Finally, the Lictor spoke. "I am not my own man," he announced sadly. "All that I have ever been has led to this." He raised his fists. "We must continue."

Harrow blew out another breath. "So we must," he whispered.

"Are you ready?"

The Outlander pushed away from the wall and struggled to recover his own guard. He nodded once.

Alouine's words resounded in his mind: *Just as a line can overcome a circle, so can a circle overcome a line.*

Armiluss stepped in and threw a straight, left-handed punch with full extension. It nearly took Harrow by surprise, not by its power or speed, but that he telegraphed it.

Rather than try to block the strike, Harrow made to avoid it. He threw his head backward and side-stepped to his right, and though the Lictor's smallest knuckle still caught him on the chin, the punch glanced off and passed by. The Outlander threw his arms around the extended punch. He clutched the beast's arm tight to his chest and swung his lower body upward, counting on the Lictor's strength to support all of his body weight.

Kicking behind Armiluss' back, Harrow hooked his left heel in the crook of the Lictor's other elbow, and then crossed his other ankle over it, trapping the arm between his knees. Squirming, he slithered under Armiluss' left arm, trapping it in his own armpit.

He arched his back powerfully and clenched his legs as hard as he could, which splayed the Lictor's arms wide as though the giant man were caught on a cruel rack of torture, and Harrow's body was the crossbeam.

Armiluss was not idle. He backed to the wall and repeatedly slammed Harrow's body, draped across his back, into it, denting it again and again. Realizing he could not shake the Outlander off, the Lictor spun and fell backward as violently as he could, crushing Harrow into the floor and causing the elevator to shudder and buck.

The intense impacts jarred Harrow's already pulverized bones, and punished his internal organs, but he held on for everything he was worth. When finally slammed to the floor, he took advantage of the instant when the Lictor's arm was trapped under his weight to free both his hands.

He reached out and grasped the Lictor's head in his arms, his hands cinched onto his armored forearms with all the force he could muster. Squeezing Armiluss' head to his chest, legs locked powerfully around the far shoulder, Harrow leaned backward as far as he could, putting all of the strength of his back into it.

There was no telling how much total weight it would take to snap the Lictor's neck, so Harrow poured everything he had into the grapple. Pain—the body's way of keeping the muscles from destroying themselves—he ignored completely. He felt capillaries burst in his eyes, felt the tendons fray between his shoulder blades. He felt the fibers of his flesh shearing from his bones.

Muffled, the Lictor's voice still reached his ears.

"I'm sorry."

A second later, Harrow heard a loud, wet pop and felt the overstressed bones fail. The Lictor's body went slack all at once. When the Outlander released his grip, his foe's head remained at a lethally unnatural angle.

"As am I," Harrow said softly. He lay on the floor, panting hard and painful, with the dead Lictor still on top of him as the doors of the elevator finally opened.

— — —

The elevator doors opened and Quintain peeked out before exiting. Seeing nothing to immediately threaten him, he rounded to the other lift and looked inside.

He was struck by what seemed a piled pair of corpses. The huge, misshapen bodyguard lay on his massive back, across Harrow's almost-unrecognizable form.

They had destroyed everything within the space. The walls of the metal cube swelled outward in dented bulges, as did the floor and ceiling. Blood and sweat slicked on every surface. It appeared to the boy as though a bomb had detonated within the enclosed room.

He tried to pull the Lictor off of his fellow Outlander, but the huge man was hundreds of kilos of dead weight. He grunted and strained but could not manage to budge the corpse.

"Stop," Harrow groaned, which made Quintain start.

"You're alive," the boy breathed.

"Yes. Just let me rest here a few moments more."

The boy glanced nervously over his shoulder. He didn't hear any sounds, but that did not mean they wouldn't be discovered at any second.

"Why didn't you . . ." he began to ask, but his voice died away.

Harrow coughed. "They must have copied my machine. I couldn't."

"Oh. We're at the top," the boy said, trying to sound encouraging. "Almost there."

"You're almost there," Harrow replied with a wince. "Just go. I've kicked in the door. The rest is up to you."

"But I'm not—"

"You can be," the warrior said quickly. "Fate speaks to you now, in this occasion, this opportunity. Seize this and make it yours."

Part of Quintain dreaded what Harrow said next; another part basked in it. "I'm counting on you."

"What will you do?"

Harrow now gingerly and slowly began to squirm out from under the corpse of his dead foe. "Send the lift back down. I will try to find Alouine, and help her, if I can."

Quintain nodded. "All right. Good luck."

"Find me after."

Reluctantly, Quintain touched the symbol on the wall to lower the lift again, and watched as the doors creaked closed.

He took a deep breath, and crept through the colossal hall, trying to follow the walls. There were six monumental pillars, each shaped like a kneeling man who took the weight of the slanting, pyramidal roof of the Temple's capstone on a shoulder. A single one of the stylized granite men looked to weigh hundreds of tonnes. He tried to stay in their shadows but knew he was likely under automated surveillance anyway.

When he reached the third row of pillars, his keen eyes spotted two of the white-uniformed Triary members guarding the only door in the space. It led, he guessed, to the High Circle's chamber.

He concentrated. The men, considered the most hardened and disciplined of the Death's Head, were still ultimately will-less slaves, and Quintain was certain he could hide his presence from their spiritually blind perception.

Not so for the spirits he sensed guarding the entrance. Astral familiars of the Last Men eternally stood as sentries for the blackest of sorcerers on earth.

There was no other way to his destination, and he could not sneak past. The demonic entities would certainly sense him. In a way, they were a failsafe against the spiritual autism of the physical guards.

Quintain was not sure if those spirits could alert or even

possess the men they shared servitude with, and did not want to find out. He needed to get into that room, however. Hiding behind the massive foot of a man-pillar, the magus sank down into his meditational pose.

He needed the help of the Devas now more than ever, and hoped they could hear him in such a discordant and vile place.

In a pitch black space, he thought, *even the smallest flame can banish darkness. The opposite is never true. Let my soul be filled with light.*

He went through the steps, purifying his chakras and mentally tracing the multicolored pentagrams in the air. To his relief, the four archangels sprang to fiery life around him.

"Am I glad to see you," he spoke in Enochian.

The angels did not respond in kind, but Quintain sensed that the feeling was appreciated and returned. The spirits were eager and glad to be there, fulfilling their duty and purpose.

The hopes of his friends, his people, and his disincarnate allies propelled him, and his etheric body rose to its feet. The third-eye gem in his forehead shed a potent astral light. "Let's go," he vibrated.

TWENTY-SEVEN

The sky-tram arrived at the Temple of Understanding and Alouine scooped up a long shard of broken glass off of the floor. She looked at her friend. "It's likely that those who saw us at the Temple of Domination have already alerted the guards here."

"That's my guess." As the tram came to a stop and the broken door clanked and clattered open, Thaira gestured for the Last Men and Women inside to get out first, prodding them along with the muzzle of her pistol. Every eye tracked the weapon as Thaira precisely waved it at the hostages.

Alouine, pale and shining with a thin sheen of cold sweat, followed slowly, leaving the dead Lictors in the carriage.

"Are you going to be all right?" Thaira whispered to her.

"Yes," she said simply, though she felt somewhat breathless. Drawing up in front of the group of men and women, she straightened.

"My name is Alouine Morningstar," she announced. "For the moment, all of you are my prisoners. If you cooperate, you won't be harmed, and you can join the other members once we're inside."

One of the men spoke up. "I knew I recognized you. You're the old High Chairman's daughter. Why are you doing this?"

"That will become clear soon enough. Suffice it to say that I've been betrayed." She gestured to Thaira. "We both have. Our Mark accounts have been deactivated. All you need to do is take us inside, past the Triary and into the main chamber, and you'll be released."

"I take it we don't have a choice?" the same man asked.

Thaira responded by cocking the hammer of the pistol. "This is your other option," she hissed.

The hostages showed their palms. "A convincing argument," the man muttered.

Alouine nodded. She looked straight at the lone female hostage. "Come here." Her prisoner, shorter than her by six centimeters, did as she was told. Alouine spun her and placed an arm around her throat, gripping her tight. With her right hand, she pressed the sharp point of the glass just under and behind the woman's earlobe. Her prisoner flinched and a bead of blood welled out where the razor-like glass pierced her skin. Alouine issued a warning growl. "Walk slowly and stay calm. This will be over soon."

As the group made their way into the pyramid, Alouine activated her data link and reconnected to the Enclave's network, trusting Thaira to keep the prisoners in line.

She sent a chiming ping to Carver Delano's channel. She didn't really want to talk to him, and was near certain that he felt the same way. No doubt he already knew that she was in the Enclave.

She just wanted to personally let him know that she was there. She wanted him to be thinking about her while, she hoped, the two Outlanders prepared a fitting gift of karmic retribution.

Thaira kept her pistol trained on the backs of the Last Men in front of her, pressing the weapon to the man's back who had spoken to them. The man kept his teeth clenched and the others glanced about nervously. However, no one did anything to draw too much attention as Alouine followed them from the tram platform, which was fixed by steel supports halfway up the slope of the formidable structure.

Triary guards spotted them as they walked fifty meters of

winding, caged stairs to the entrance. They snapped up their weapons instantly, but Alouine hunched behind her hostage, using her as a shield and exposing only slivers of her body to the guards' aim. She added some slight pressure to her makeshift stiletto, which caused her human shield to whimper.

Thaira did likewise with her own hostage, hiding herself behind the man's back and clearly letting the guards see her pistol trained at the back of his neck. She slowly weaved behind the man to prevent one of the guards from being ambitious and taking a shot anyway.

"Drop your weapons or your masters will die," Alouine said.

Thaira twisted the gun in the nape of the man's neck. He coughed delicately. "They're serious. Do as they say."

The squad's leader, grimacing, nodded and said, "All right. Stay calm, sir; ma'am." He gestured to the other guards and as one they all placed their rifles on the floor.

Using her head to gesture, Thaira ordered, "Kick them over the side." There was a gap in the railing, and the soldiers did as they were told, sliding the weapons with their boots off of the platform. They fell twenty meters before clattering against the slope of the Temple and tumbling down another kilometer. "Pistols, too," Thaira commanded, before adding, "slowly."

When the guards had dumped their firearms, the two hostage-taking women advanced.

"Put your foreheads and palms on the wall and don't move," Alouine ordered. When the Triary men had done so, the two women and their prisoners slowly, warily walked past. The soldiers, who valued the lives of Last Men alone above all the things on earth, let them go.

Inside the temple, Thaira said to the man she threatened, "Use your Mark account and lock this door."

When the outer door's magnetic lock engaged with a solid clack, Alouine momentarily released the woman she held, who instantly reached for the spot where the glass had pricked her neck. She stared at the blood on her fingers.

Alouine took her by the arm. "You're doing fine. This is nearly over. Hurry," she said, gesturing down the corridor which led to the main gathering chamber.

Minutes and hundreds of meters later, the group arrived at the spacious auditorium, the thick glass doors actuating and parting for them with a smooth hiss, triggered by the active Mark accounts of the hostages.

Alouine nodded to Thaira. "Here we go," she whispered.

Thaira wore a fierce look in her eyes. "I'm ready."

Alouine gathered her female hostage again. "Don't do anything. You'll be safer that way."

As soon as they entered the chamber, Triary soldiers and Lictors, forewarned by the guards at the tram platform, moved to create a cordon around the women and their hostages.

Before Alouine could say a word, Thaira began to shout in her most commanding voice. "Back up, damn you! If any Lictor comes within ten meters of me, he'll have to clean this man's brains off the floor!" She pressed her pistol into her hostage's temple. "Triary, drop your weapons. Now!"

Everything in the grand hall came to a screeching halt as every white-clad guard un-slung his rifle and dropped it on the hard floor. Many of the Last Men and women, unaccustomed to stress of any kind, dropped plates and champagne flutes as well, and raised their arms in submission.

Alouine might have found this comical, except that standing directly in front of her and holding a holographic tablet was a gawking Heid Acheson.

He took a halting step forward. "Lady Morningstar," he muttered, which sent a chorus of scandalized murmurs and gasps through the crowd. "This is not—"

"No shortage of blood on your hands, Heid, but never on your clothes, I think," she mused. "Another step and I'll splash you with hers." She held the broken glass tight to her prisoner's throat, and Heid retreated.

He reached over and placed his tablet on the tray of a nearby slave who, wide-eyed, was frozen as a statue. Showing his palms, he said, "Madam, please. This is reprehensible behavior from someone as high-born as you."

Alouine cut him off yet again. "You would know about reprehensible behavior, you toad. You learned at the feet of the master. Tell me Heid, how are things going in your Circle?"

The wiry, bespectacled man opened his mouth and closed it again, reminding Alouine of the time her father had taken her to see where the Enclave's salmon were spawned. He stuttered for a moment, and then said, "I expect my appointment to the Highest Circle within a day." Reining in his emotions, he said, "It follows when the chairman of one's circle is also the High Chairman of the Enclave."

More stunned murmurs wafted through the crowd as Alouine shot Heid an incredulous look. "Really, Heid, you're not that stupid. Carver Delano doesn't care about you." With her eyes, she gestured upward, keeping her improvised weapon to the throat of the shivering woman before her. "Is he up there with them now?"

Heid cleared his throat. "I imagine that the High Circle members are all dead by now," he admitted in a small voice. "Otherwise Lord Delano probably would not have been elected." Gasps and even indignant shouts of outrage rippled through the gathered Order members. Those close to Heid threw him murderous glares. "I didn't kill them," he whined defensively. "The new High Chairman did."

Thaira's hostage chose this time to speak up. "So, is there a reason we've all gathered here?" Thaira pressed the weapon harder against his skull to silence him, and the man squirmed uncomfortably.

Another Last Man in the crowd shouted, "Is this some kind of misdirection to cover up for your coup, Acheson?"

More voices heaped scorn on the hard-pressed scientist.

"I knew this was nonsense."

"You're going to pay for this!"

"Be quiet," Thaira screeched. "I issued the emergency order." The grousing crowd simmered.

"On my behalf," Alouine added, loud enough for her voice to carry. "I've known that Carver Delano has been up to something for more than a month. He murdered my father, and has been working to usurp his position! And this fool has been helping him," she cried, pointing her glass spike at the fumbling Heid.

"I've only been doing my duty to my Circle," he protested. He cried out for his Lictor and scrambled behind the beast for protection as the other Last Men hurled jeers and insults at him. The towering monster swiveled to try to meet every threat, his one thick arm extending to shield his frail and frightened charge.

"Lady Morningstar," a voice hollered from the crowd. Last Men and Lictors parted and a young man of perhaps sixteen years stepped through, not nearly old enough to be an Established Last Man. "My name is Eric Savoy. My brother James was thrown out of Lord—of Delano's circle. He had to go to our family in the Second City." The young man of slight build and sandy hair glanced around. "I want to know why."

"I'm afraid I don't know the answer to that, Eric," was all Alouine could say.

The young man pressed on. "You say that Delano murdered your father." He looked at Heid, who cowered behind his Lictor. "And you say he's planning to or already has murdered the other High Circle members. Why are we only hearing of this now?" Several other voices acclaimed the young man's question and demanded answers.

"I have not been in the Enclave for several weeks," Alouine replied. "Carver's plots forced me to retreat to the Outlands."

More shocked gasps, particularly from the women in the crowd, echoed through the chamber.

Eric Savoy nodded slowly. "So perhaps you can squash the rumors that this emergency gathering is due to an Outlander uprising?"

"I'm afraid that rumor is partially true. There are Outlanders in the Enclave. It's very likely that as we speak, they're already in this Temple."

More frightened murmurs rippled, particularly from female throats. Alouine could tell that they were imagining a most horrendous savaging at the hands of enraged, bloodthirsty Outlanders.

"How do you know?"

"Because I helped them get in."

— — —

He imagined himself for a moment as a charioteer, like the picture from that ancient book in his library. The straining horses of his angelic familiars impelled his astral self forward, drawn toward the demonic sentries of the Last Men like magnets zooming to collide with their polar opposites.

Quintain felt this keenly, felt the spirit beings' urgency and eagerness for battle. Their multi-colored forms shone with it, each brandishing a long, cruciform war sword of glittering, diamond-like brilliance. The magus did not direct them so much as he unleashed them; flaming, vaguely humanoid shapes which emitted a high, keening vibration through the astral plane, a war cry to accompany their charge.

As soon as the sentries heard this, they formed a phalanx of impossible gravity. Their forms, like stylized renderings, horrid creatures with leaden bones and flesh of tar and pitch, trailing a billowing, acrid, black smoke, brandished foulness and disease and perversity for their fangs and claws.

The warrior angels, immortal knights of the four corners of the cosmos, crashed into the writhing, roiling mass of fester and rot. Their razor blades of hardened ectoplasm, extensions of their own being, whirled and hacked with impossible accuracy, hewing off great chunks of their foes which disintegrated into nothingness.

In angelic tongue, the agonists bantered, the demons belching cruel, vitriolic taunts and the angels countering with their own grave promises.

As Quintain predicted, the archangel Michael, blazing with annihilating fire, took the steepest toll of the enemy. The other knights crowded around their general, borrowing from his almighty strength as they parried lunging, ripping claws and, in quicksilver motions, brought about violent riposte.

The familiars of the Order came in droving waves to crash against the spiritual bulwark of Quintain's allies. Their astral bodies went up like paper soaked in petroleum at a sparking touch from a keen, shining angelic blade.

The two guards, deeply rooted to the material plane, did not initially react. Astral violence swirled all around them, and yet they remained spiritually blind, deaf, and dumb to the melee. Finally, two of the demons entered into their bodies.

Both men moved. They immediately set off to find and destroy Quintain's sleeping body.

They seemed to look directly at him, floating there in astral form. He knew what they were doing—seeking the silver cord that fettered spirit to body to follow it back to its anchor.

On the verge of panic, Quintain called for Auriel's attention and was given it immediately. "Please stay and continue the fight," he pleaded. "I must retreat momentarily." The spirit did not nod or move other than to continue hacking at its enemies, but Quintain felt its acknowledgement.

He zipped back to his body and opened his eyes to the heightened realization of impending danger. Peeking around the pillar, he was immediately forced to duck backwards as rifle rounds, accompanied by sharp, echoing cracks, chewed at the granite in front of his face.

Wheezing and desperately trying to flick the dust from his eyes, he took several more steps backward, racking his brain. Running would be foolish; they'd shoot him in the back.

He had to let them draw closer.

Climbing up into the statue itself, he squeezed his body into the alcove formed by the gap between the sculpted, massive foot and leg, and hoped that this concealed him completely from sight. Mentally repeating mantras of power, he charged and energized his body with a deep, spiritual vibration and drew the banishing pentagram in his thoughts. His forehead gem shone brightly with clear light, illuminating the hollow into which he pressed himself.

As the pair of men came into sight, their rifles before them, seeking him, he forced himself to remain a calm reservoir of astral energy. When they appeared before him, he directed this banishing, five-pointed shield through his arm and out from the tips of his index and middle fingers, thrust at the men like a dagger.

The astral energy, shaped to his intent, exploded outward in a giant, slowly rotating and multicolored pentagram, and as it traveled through the two men, it pushed the inhabiting spirits out, as a dragnet scoops fish from a sea. The disc of mental energy continued on its path, hurling the demons away with incredible force.

Confused and blinking, the two soldiers staggered for a moment like men awakening from a deep sleep and overcome by the pins and needles sensation of demonic possession.

Quintain lunged at them, taking full advantage of their

disorientation, and thrust his fingers at the solar plexus of each one in turn.

Their wills were weak to begin with and were near non-existent at the moment of contact, and Quintain attacked these with vibratory energy and an unconscious, undeniable impulse. The shocks to their subtle bodies resonated down to the physical plane.

He gave each man a mild heart attack, inducing a limited cardiac arrest. Both soldiers immediately seized up with a grunt, their entire bodies tightening, and collapsed to the floor.

Quickly, the young magus used sacred healing to correct the broken signal link between brain and heart and put the two men in a deep, comatose sleep.

Only then did he finally remember to breathe.

— — —

Eric Savoy's look of complete puzzlement was echoed on the faces of the Last Men and Women all around him. The crowd, their emotions toyed with too much in too short a span of time, began to grow spiteful. "You opened the Enclave to Outlanders?" the young man asked. "That's nearly as bad as murdering the Highest Circle."

The Triary were befuddled in the absence of clear instructions or meaningful situational doctrine for this, so they continued to do nothing, but the Lictors all around were in tune to the growing anxiety and impatience of the crowded Last Men. Their grotesque faces loomed, tall and threatening.

Alouine did feel the pulse of the woman she held and had a tiny pang of sympathy for her; the torment of being held hostage at knifepoint was something she hoped to never experience. Still, she could not release the other woman as yet.

"I cut a deal with them," she admitted. Before furious accusations could fly, she continued, "To save the lives of as many people here as I could. Yes! I helped a small number of Outlanders get inside the Enclave. It was my decision. I can tell you this: had I not made that decision, we would not be having this conversation." She paused for effect. "You would all be dead by now."

Sneering contempt for the Outlanders poured from the crowd. Even young Eric seemed dismissive of Alouine's claim and disdainful of the idea that an Outlander would be within a rifle shot of his person.

"You protest from ignorance," Thaira shouted. "Alouine just told you that she has been there, been in the Outlands. It's a fact; I helped her prepare for her journey. You're going to doubt what she's seen with her own eyes?"

The crowd settled a bit.

"Yes," Alouine spoke loudly. "There is one among the Outlanders who has been planning to invade our city for some time! I have seen what he is capable of and what his weapons can do. So I made a deal with him. I agreed that I would hand over Carver Delano and the High Circle members to him, and in exchange, we Last Men would free our slaves and accept the Outlanders as equals."

Scorn issued from the lips of the crowded Last Men in waves.

Alouine attempted to shout them down. "The time has come for us to face facts, and, yes, consequences for our actions and the actions of our ancestors. I am no exception! We here did not accumulate the burden of our sins by ourselves, but we alone must bear it. It cannot be excused from us. Nor can we pass it on to our children.

"The world is changing. We must adapt to survive. As a people, we know nothing of struggle or hardship, and that has made us weak. If we cannot reach an accord with these Outlanders, whom we have abused and enslaved for generations beyond counting, they will destroy us. Our race will face extinction. We need a transfusion of new blood, and new ideas."

She pushed her hostage, the crying, shivering woman in her arms, away from her to stumble into the crowd. Thaira glanced at her, worried. "I believe we have more to offer the world than our corpses," she said clearly and evenly.

She strode forward a few steps, taking deep breaths and energizing her chakras. The faces of her people, staring back at her, ran the gamut of expressions from pensiveness to pure, abject hatred. She sighed. "I've chosen my Great Work," she said. "I will live in an open city, and in a world where there is only one humanity. There are those of you who will oppose me."

Making fists of her hands, she murmured, "Fight me, if you dare, but if you do, fight me with courage and a bold disregard for death." She exhaled and her body unraveled, coiling like a spring. "That alone will convince me."

Last Men began to argue loudly amongst themselves, until one of them finally gave his Lictor a shove and shouted, "Kill her!"

The main chamber of the Temple of Understanding exploded into violence and panic and Alouine met this as the birth pangs of her Great Work. Lictors dove at her from every direction.

She kept the dark energy of the Kali'prana at her fingertips, not quite manifesting it. Her hand was on the hilt, but she kept the dagger sheathed. She knew every cut and stab she made with it would be revisited on her, and whatever the outcome, she wanted to live to see it.

The Lictors were slow, clumsy brutes, accustomed to fighting creatures their own size, not a darting, agile, psychically propelled goddess of battle. They tried to pile on top of her, to bear her down and crush her, but she rose above them all, kicking off of shoulders and faces and flipping from one beast to the next.

Crashing into one another, the simple-minded monstrosities responded to inconvenience with violence, jockeying and coming to blows in their mad scramble to lay hands on her. An unlucky Last Man caught in the fracas was plucked from his feet by a backhanded blow and sailed through the air to land near the wall with a sick, twisting crunch.

Screams and the madness of fear billowed through the chamber.

Gunshots rang and Alouine spared a split second glance, to see Thaira, her hostage cinched tight in a headlock, opening fire on the Lictors nearest her. Grim-faced, she snapped her weapon about professionally, even with one hand, and aimed carefully for eyes and ear canals. Her firing prodded the Triary into action, opening the floor for their rebuttal, which was spoken through the muzzles of their rifles.

Bullets cracked and Alouine retreated, snapping punches and kicks, and Last Men trampled one another to get away. Lictors fell with shuddering thuds and then rose again, bleeding but no less deadly.

Through it all, she dared to hope. Many of the Lictors merely continued to guard their masters on the far side of the chamber. Eric Savoy dragged a fallen woman to safety by the wrist.

Alouine refused to despair and fought on. *Be without fear*, she thought, *or overcome it.*

— — —

The door was suitably massive, Quintain supposed, for its purpose—to fill those at its threshold with awe and even a sense of dread. He could see the seams were six meters apart.

He stood before it for a moment, trying to imagine the mentality of fear one would need to possess to even imagine, much less create such a barrier. It was the plainest symbol of the mental illness of the Last Men that the young man had yet witnessed.

The thought gave him hope. *Whoever is behind this door is more afraid of me than I could ever be of him.* Breathing deeply, he zeroed himself in and performed his meditative rituals of banishment. He advanced and laid his palm on the polished, black surface. To his surprise, it smoothly began to slide upward and open.

A cloud of smoke coughed from under the meter-thick door, and the unprepared magus caught a face full of it. The horrific stench of burnt flesh caused him to immediately bury his nose in the crook of his elbow. Tears welled in his eyes, his nostrils and sinuses burned. He gagged and retched. It was the smell of a funeral pyre without the wooden fuel—meat charred to constituent carbon, human bodies rendered to the finest dust. He inhaled what had once been people. The thought was revolting.

Squinting, he tried to wave his way through the haze with his free hand. Eventually the influx of clean air thinned the smoke enough, and Quintain was able to make out the massive hollow circle of the stone High Circle's table. Ringing it were twelve seated corpses, all of them burned to cinders and recognizable only as blurry black shapes. Similarly thrashed and mangled bodies the size of the huge, dead man in the elevator were scattered about the room as well.

On the far side of the chamber, he made out the shape of the man he sought, and after swallowing his disgust, he advanced into the sanctum sanctorum of the Order of the Last Men.

Waves of despair and agony filled the space, intruding violently on Quintain's astral senses. An all-encompassing wrongness, a complete and utter antagonism to life and happiness, pressed in on the boy from all sides. His thought-images of the pentagrams of the corners flared to brilliance to protect him.

Immediately, those subtle, interlocked spirit fields began to gutter under the strain, and the boy knew he would have to hurry.

Carver Delano appeared to be deep in thought as the door opened, and glanced at Quintain distractedly. He had to double-take when the figure meeting his eyes did not match the Lictor he was expecting. The man sputtered once, but quickly closed his mouth tightly, reined himself in, and started again. "Who are you?" he demanded.

"My name is Quintain. You're Carver, is that correct?"

The Last Man scowled. "That's right. How in the hell did you get past my Lictor?" Backing away a few steps as the Outlander drew closer, Carver leveled his microwave pulse-emitter at the boy.

Quintain showed the man his palms. "You mean the giant man who was in the lift? Harrow killed him."

Carver was silent for several long moments. His face flushed and moistened and a single vein throbbed in his forehead.

Quintain imagined an angry child whose favorite toy was taken away by a familiar bully. *The chances are slim, but I have to try.* He spoke gently but firmly. "I only want to talk to you. Please, take this opportunity. It might be the last one you have."

Sneering, Carver spat, "I create my own opportunities, you sniveling shit. What could I possibly have to discuss with the likes of you?"

The boy recognized instantly that the virtues he tried his very best to live by, lucidity, compassion, truthfulness and forgiveness, were absent in the other man, or at least buried so deeply in his psyche that only decades of treatment could rehabilitate them.

Quintain did not have decades; this needed to end now. Voice quiet, he muttered, "You're so afraid. When you recoil in horror from everything you don't understand, how can anything new touch you?"

"Afraid? I'm not afraid of you," the Last Man snarled. The young man could see that Carver's pupils were dilated. His eyes bulged, crazed. Sweat beaded on his forehead and his thinning hair was mussed. "I have; you want," he continued, mocking, disdainful. "That is the way of this world, Outlander. I could buy and sell you a thousand times. I own the future! I could wipe you out in an instant." A low hum filled the air. "Allow me to demonstrate."

There was a popping sound and Quintain instinctively reeled backward, falling on his bottom as a cone of heat distortion from the boiling atmosphere washed through the space his head had so recently occupied.

Carver stepped in to finish him, to cook him alive, but Quintain's hand found Harrow's pistol. The safety clicked off with an echo.

Carver wore shock and utter disbelief on his frowning face.

Four shots rang out.

Quintain was scared stiff by the bucking, blinding, deafening device he held. He couldn't keep his eyes open after pulling the trigger once, and nearly dropped the pistol. But he did not want to die, so he pulled the trigger again, and again, firing blindly until the weapon ran empty and nothing else happened.

When he finally dared to peek, he saw Carver reeling backward, his hands clutched over his abdomen. Blood, in startling amounts and a shocking scarlet color, soaked his shirt and ran down the front of his slacks, coating his hands and running over his knuckles.

The Last Man staggered backward, hyperventilating. Each breath which left his lips was a high-pitched grunt. Panicking, his back hit the wall behind him and Quintain thought for sure that he'd fall.

Instead, he teetered, curled into a ball around his wound before, with a strained shout, he wildly flailed for the door controls behind him. He smeared blood all over the panel but managed to get the door to open, and then he slid along the edge of the portal, nearly falling into the room.

Gradually, the young magus stood up. He discarded the empty pistol as so much useless weight and carefully, warily, followed Carver.

When he saw the bright light of the next room and followed the bloody trail of Carver's seeping wound into it, Quintain nearly fainted.

The Last Man leaned heavily on a pedestal in the center of the chamber, surrounded by pyramidal structures on every side. Atop the pedestal's mirror-smooth surface, a glowing geometric design danced; three layered hexagrams, one stationary and the other two rotating in counter directions. A droning, whining hum filled the air, thrumming as though alive. Arcane geometry formed every surface, and all available space was consumed by occult runes.

No mundane intellect would ever recognize the purpose of the chamber, but Quintain understood it immediately as a geometric, power grid-structure designed to create a synthetic Merkaba— a star-tetrahedral vibratory energy field that could be used as an inter-dimensional vehicle.

All humans could create these, but only through a lifetime, or more likely multiple reincarnations, of careful study, a cultivated desire for enlightenment, and the knowledge that the cosmos is simply consciousness, creating and inhabiting itself within that creation. A stable, living Merkaba, one of the highest goals of man, would in theory allow a human being to shift dimensions and travel throughout the universe.

The Last Man intended to cheat the natural process by which a man ascends to higher levels of consciousness. Severed from unity consciousness as he and all Last Men were, Carver saw the Merkaba as nothing more than a tool. With this chamber, he intended to create a cheap facsimile of the real power.

"Stop," the boy said emphatically, raising his voice to carry over the din. "You can't do this!" He recognized the danger as immense. Improperly constructed or built for the wrong purpose, which Quintain was sure this was, a synthetic Merkaba could open a dimensional tear in the fabric of reality.

"It's already done," Carver blurted, and blood spat from his lips, giving his voice a sickening gurgle.

Quintain approached the dying man slowly, with his palms showing, pleading with him. "Please, this is wrong. Life is a school for the human soul, so that we can evolve spiritually. You can't cheat this or skip steps." He sighed, breath leaving his lungs in a shudder. "You're very confused. I want to help you."

"You shot me," the Last Man snarled, dribbling more blood which pattered onto the glowing floor.

"Only to defend myself. Listen, there is another way. This is too dangerous. You are so used to perceiving duality that you can't see the unity-of-all!"

Carver's eyes fluttered. He tottered. Ignoring Quintain, he keyed in the start code for the Incarnation Matrix and spooled up his quantum device with its attendant emanation of wrongness.

"This kind of thing always ends in failure! Don't cut yourself off; creating a new reality doesn't make you a god. It makes you a maladjusted child in need of help. Your struggle to remove your restraints has become your very shackles! I can help you!"

"You already have," the Last Man gasped. He pulled his hand away from where he had been clutching his soaking wound and stared at it vaguely. "Now I have nothing to lose."

Quintain dove at the man desperately, trying to tackle him away from the glowing pillar, but he was too late. The chamber filled with the brightest, most blinding light and reality imploded upon itself.

All the young magus could do was to hurl a prayer into the void as intense, fractal light exploded through every rod and cone of his mind's eye, and he passed through the prism of conscious existence.

TWENTY-EIGHT

When the blinding, white light faded, Quintain was afloat in a sea of being—an impossibly intricate, liquid crystal lattice which expanded infinitely in all directions, undulating to some foreign, incomprehensible pulse.

Scintillating, kaleidoscopic, fractal shapes danced in every corner of his awareness. He could feel a hum of vibratory power echo through his body in waves, which emanated from a cosmic center that was at once inside of him, and yet so far away as to be ungraspable.

He was in his etheric form, his glowing, ghostly spirit projection. Peering down at his hands, they were larger than he remembered, and his feet were farther away. He had a sense of expansion and felt taller than he remembered, not that it had much meaning here, where orientation was a highly subjective exercise.

Consciously, he reached for his forehead, the imaginary representation of his mother's gem, feeling for it with his fingers. Relieved to feel its smooth hardness, he cast about a glance for the silvery astral cord which kept his projected consciousness linked to his body so that he could at least orient himself to the physical plane.

The cord was not there, and anxiety assaulted his mind. With no cord, he could not return to material existence.

He reached out to touch the incredible grid of light and shape, but his astral hand made contact with a strange, geometric shape first. The tetrahedral formation of his Merkaba flared into perceivable existence around him, insulating him from his surroundings. He was trapped in a star-shaped, crystal bubble.

The discarnate human wanted desperately to sink in, to merge his consciousness with the pervading unity and bliss around him, and he could not. He understood that there was a process and that he was being artificially held from it. The spirits of renewal should have been cleansing him, pruning his memories and purifying him of his negative karma so that he could rejoin the cycle of reincarnation.

Instead, he merely floated. Had he eyes, he would have wept.

So this is it, he thought. *Am I going to float here forever, with the essence of God just outside my reach?*

Worry not, young Wayfarer.

Blinking, Quintain spun in a circle. Confronting him was a spectral being—massive, towering and terrible in its magnificence. Its astral body was cloaked in scintillating fire and its face, looming over Quintain to such extent that it seemed to touch the sky, blazed with the brightness of the sun. Still, streaks of grey were evident in its form. "Who's there?" he asked.

The being's voiceless voice was akin to the Whispers of the Archive, in that he did not hear its words so much as feel them. Unlike the guiding spirits of the Archive, this voice was singular, strong and clear. It rang at a frequency that rolled through his entire being.

What you perceive before you is the Guardian of the Threshold. Hitherto, powers invisible to you have watched over all of your incarnations, Wayfarer. These powers, assigned to you by the law of karma, saw to it that in the course of those lives, each cycle of death and rebirth, each of your good deeds brought its reward and each of your evil deeds attended its own evil results. These powers shall now partly release you from their influence, and henceforth must you accomplish for yourself a part of the work they performed for you.

"The guardian of the threshold?" the boy murmured. Quintain recognized that his voice had changed. Without his silver cord or a body to return to, he supposed that his self-image had aged, that his astral appearance had begun to idealize itself. "Am I dead?"

Death is illusory, a simple phase shift. The concept is a common misunderstanding. All Things are one. The being's voice softened slightly, sounding almost sympathetic. *Destiny has struck you many hard blows, Wayfarer, without your ever knowing why. Each of these was a consequence of a harmful deed in a bygone life. The gladness and gratefulness and joy you found were likewise fruits of former deeds.*

Your soul shows many a beautiful facet, and yet still many an ugly flaw; these were of your making, for they are the result of all previous experiences and thoughts. They determined who you were, and now all the good and evil you have done will be revealed to you. Hitherto, they were ingrained deeply in your own being, but now they have become released from you and detach themselves from your spirit.

I am the very being who wove my form from your good and evil achievements. My own body is shaped of your own life's record. Now that I have come forth from within you, the work is in your hands alone. I must become a perfect and glorious being, or fall prey to corruption; and should that occur, I shall drag you down into a dark and corrupt world with me.

Quintain nodded slightly. The Order's machine had worked. His body had been destroyed and his consciousness preserved, set adrift into the universe. His life's Great Work had built for him a magnificent sculpture and monument to his purpose and intent.

As a form visible to you, I will never for an instant leave your side once you have crossed my Threshold. In the future, whenever you think or act wrongly, you will perceive immediately your guilt as a demonic and hideous distortion of my form. Only when you have made good all past wrongs and purified yourself such as to make further evil a thing impossible will my form be fully transformed into radiant beauty. Then, too, shall I become united with you once again, for the welfare of the future. It is only by transforming me to complete perfection that you can escape the powers of death and pass over into immortality, united with me.

"So what should I do?" the disembodied boy asked. "How can I perform good works if the living world is so far away?"

Within the kingdom you now enter, you will meet supersensible beings, and I myself must provide your first acquaintance with that world, and I am your own creation. Formerly I drew my life from yours, but now you have awakened me to a separate existence so that I may stand before you as a visible gauge of your future deeds, and perhaps also as your constant reproach. You have formed me, but by doing so you have undertaken the duty to transform me.

The being paused for a moment and Quintain felt the full measure of the spirit's scrutiny. *You belong to a community, a family, nation and race. These communities are souls of their own. You must know your own tasks and must also collaborate knowingly in those of your folk and nation. Higher spirits have made great use of your personality for this already.* A sense of loving and grateful pride welled from the mirror-being. *Now these spirits have withdrawn their guiding hands from you. The Merkaba which surrounds you has also isolated you. You must now accomplish your Great Works both for and by yourself.*

From the spot where the spirit entity stood, a great whirlwind emanated, which extinguished all of the glowing illumination of the crystalline lattice of light and cast Quintain into darkness. Only the brightness of the Guardian continued burning in the infinite black.

Step across my Threshold only when you realize that you alone will illumine the dark path before you. The lamps of the guides whom you have hitherto followed are no longer available to you. Take not a single step until you are positive you possess sufficient fuel for your own lamp.

Quintain paused to merely be in the moment. He felt a new kind of freedom which outweighed all of his trepidation and anxiety, and felt joy and intense gratefulness for the new duties and responsibilities he gladly took upon himself. He spoke softly but with a strong vibration. "I know what to do," he said, "but not how to do it."

Life, as you conceptualize it, may be yours again when you discover how to free yourself from your artificial cocoon, this Merkaba you did not choose and did not create. This evil done to you is not a sin but a reflection of destiny; through this, you have broken the cycle and maintained your Will beyond the dissolution of the body. Few others have done this in the history of your race. You are welcomed among the spirits of the Hierarchy.

"Few others?" he wondered. *Carver's soul form could be here, too,* he reminded himself.

The one in your thoughts is one of those to whom I refer. That consciousness has been quarantined to ascertain if it is a threat to principle functionality.

"Oh, he's a threat, all right," Quintain said. "The only reason he did all of this was to become a god and wreak havoc on the earth."

Intentions and desires of consciousness are irrelevant. Harmonic resonance has been determined and does fall within established limits. A Demiurge has made claim on that soul and it has chosen.

"What does that mean?"

All Things and Ways are open to you, Wayfarer.

Quintain considered for a moment, and thought that accessing the Experiential Archive from there was worth a try. The instant his intent manifested, so did the information he sought. Unlike his previous attempts to glean knowledge from the Archive, it manifested clearly and he could access it at leisure. *Not that I can afford to wait around,* he mused.

The priesthood of the Order of the Last revolved around two spiritual entities or Demiurges, spiritual adversaries whose nature was to corrupt and tempt men from virtue. One was Lucifer, a spirit of light which also enflamed the Order's pride and offered them their megalomaniacal delusions of divinity.

The other Demiurge, EL, as it was known to the highest priests of the Order of the Last Men, was the ruling spirit of the earth, a voluminous cosmic being in the spiritual hierarchy known by countless names in past ages; Ahriman, Satan, Saturn, Baal, and so on. It was the manifestation of man's psychological trauma, a principle of gravitas, limit, stricture, death and empty materiality.

This was the spirit being which had claimed Carver's soul.

The god-form whose power I have struggled to curb all of my life has a name, the astonished magus thought. He instantly sensed that the nightmarish force was one of the true, shadowy, spiritual powers behind the Order—a complete mosaic picture of all of their demonic familiars and the subconscious urge that had driven them to make the earth into a living hell.

Of course, if either figure was evil, they were certainly necessary evils, for they stimulated man's intellect and desire, and enabled him to forge technology and improve his quality of life. The young, bodiless magus had no hope or prayer of destroying EL, nor did he want to. To an extent, the influences of the Demiurges were necessary for the unfolding of human freedom.

It was the misplaced, one-sided influence of these beings to the exclusion of all else that had led humanity to this sad pass and built the Order of the Last Men.

Still, that men actually worshipped such beings gave Quintain pause.

A vast and mighty cosmic manifestation of mankind's self-hate, avarice and perversity, which wanted nothing more than to stamp out even the possibility of individualized human consciousness, had claimed Carver's soul, and what's more, he had chosen to accept that claim? Even now, with direct experience of higher realms, the man wanted to remain a pseudo-human homunculus, a spiritless, materialistic shade? The revelation was so unnatural, so antithetical to life and happiness, that Quintain was stunned to silence for long moments.

"So, that's it? He can just do whatever he wants?"

That consciousness cannot be held and will act according to its own will. The Guardian almost seemed to shudder in revulsion.

Quintain paused again to cogitate. The most advanced technocratic black magician in generations plotted to achieve the Ahrimanic goal of the complete crystallization and rigidifying of the earth, turning it to a frozen cosmic slag heap and the binding of all humankind into soulless automata, and Quintain was imprisoned and unable to intervene.

I have to return! But breaking the Merkaba will only thrust me back into the cycle of reincarnation. I'll end up in a womb somewhere; I'll be an infant, and that's only if I can find parents. He racked his mind.

Solid matter is not solid, he remembered, *but rather vibrational energy condensed to resonant frequency.* A plan formed. It was crazy and perhaps reckless, but he had to do something.

— — —

Buried in a roar that was not a vibration but an ultra-low, crushing thrum, an oscillating shudder of incalculably long, deep pitch, Carver was tossed and wrenched violently by intense, roiling thoughts of unending spite.

It was as though the sonic contents of his own heart were echoed and amplified by astral context and reverberated back, into and through him.

A booming, all-deafening snarl filled his entire existence.

WE ARE THE UNENDING GRUDGE AND THE DISMAL WISH TO HARM. WE ARE RESENTMENT GIVEN FORM, CONTEMPT AND DISDAIN AND LOATHING AND CALLOWNESS GIVEN BIRTH BY MALIGNANT PRAYER.

"Why am I here?"

YE ARE AND HAVE ALWAYS BEEN OURS, GIVEN THE RIGHT TO GAIN FEES DUE TO US. WHAT SACRIFICE DOST THOU OFFER US?

"What? Sacrifice? I don't understand."

WE HAVE CLAIMED THY SOUL FOR OUR OWN, RATHER THAN CONSIGN THEE TO DISSOLUTION. IN RETURN, WE DEMAND OF THEE A MARKED SACRIFICE, A BURNT OFFERING, A HOLOCAUST OF BLOOD AND LIFE.

"I have no blood or life of my own to offer."

YE SHALL RETURN TO THE MATERIAL PLANE AND DEMARCATE AN ALTAR AND SLAUGHTER A SACRIFICE, OR WE SHALL CONSUME THY ESSENCE AND CONSIGN THEE TO THE DAMNATION OF OBLIVION EVERMORE.

"But my body was destroyed," the Last Man pleaded. "How am I to—" he blubbered, but was cut off by the horrific roaring of the deity of unforgiveness and cruelty.

WE ARE MASTER OF ALL MATERIAL THINGS AND THOU SHALT TAKE PHYSICAL FORM IN UNASSAILABLE BODY, MOLDED BY OUR INTENT. NOTHING SHALL STAND IN THE WAY OF THY OFFERING. THIS IS THE INTENT OF THINE OWN HEART. IF THY SACRIFICE BE PLEASING TO US, THOU SHALT BE INITIATED INTO THE HIGHEST MYSTERIES AND DEEPEST SECRETS.

"Yes," Carver whispered. "My altar will be the entire city I came from, and my offering all those within it."

SO BE IT.

TWENTY-NINE

Alouine side-stepped another Lictor's wild blow, which smashed into the floor with such force it cracked the marble. She could not stand still for a split moment or she risked being crushed. Eight, ten, fifteen Lictors chased her about, howling their rage and snorting frustration as she evaded them—the ghost of a matador of centuries past, whirling away from the mindless brutality of a dozen bulls.

Cold sweat poured from her. She could kill them easily but feared the consequences; already her joints ached with every stretch and motion, and she felt she had aged five years in the last hour. The option to use the Kali'prana would scrape away at her life's duration and quality. It made her sick to consider, but it was rapidly becoming her only option. Grunting, she dodged another vicious swipe, backpedalling once more.

A spinning heel-kick thudded into the Lictor's eye socket and the creature staggered back, only to roar and renew its assault. Her psychic senses rang and she twisted and contorted around the bayonet thrust of a Triary's rifle before planting the hard, sharp point of her elbow deep into the Adam's apple of the soldier's throat. Hooking her heel behind the man's, she gave him a shove and the choking slave pitched headlong into the path of the charging Lictor as Alouine skipped away yet again.

Thaira was nearly out of ammunition for her pistol. She kept careful track of each expended round to ensure that she left at least one for herself. She stopped shooting at the Lictors, since only a lucky hit would bring one down, and she had not managed that feat. Instead, she once again pressed the pistol to the head of her captive. With her own back to the wall and a ring of Triary soldiers all leveling rifles at her, she took a shuddering breath and worked her dry throat. The cruel steel of their bayonets flashed in the light.

The Last Man locked under her arm whimpered. "Please, let me go. It's over for you." Thaira wrenched him upright to better serve as a shield but feared that he might be right.

The ring closed in tighter, like a monster's maw full of spear-point teeth. Separated by ten meters now, both women were hemmed in.

Both prepared to die, by bullets or stabbing blades or crushing blows or a final, soul-destroying conflagration of annihilating psychic energy.

With a glad heart and the hope that her example might inspire others to change what she could not, Alouine began to draw up the horrid power of the life-denying void. She felt it course through her guts and clasp her heart with clawed fingers of ice.

She hoped that her father would be proud of her.

Instead, a familiar but no less rattling roar, a deep bellow of ancient rage, quaking in its extremity, shot and echoed through the grand hall and shook everything to stillness; the war cry of ten thousand throats, the heart-clenching feeling of ten thousand fists in the air and the blasts of ten thousand horns overlaying the mind-breaking wail of nuclear obliteration.

All souls, Lictor, Triary and Last Man alike, clenched their ears and sank to the ground. Thaira's panicked cry was drowned out in the violent, all-consuming din.

Alouine grimaced. A terrible situation was somehow becoming even worse. The monster could sense her; she felt it in her bones, felt her hair bristle on end. It was coming.

SHADOW OF THE LAST MEN

The steel wall behind her and to her right heated to red and a thin coil of smoke boiled from the burning paint. It bulged inward, before the point of Onuris' spear pierced its weapon through, and then tore completely with a terrific, rending crunch, pushing the hole in the metal wider with its arms. It shouldered its way out, and as its superheated bronze boots found the floor on the inside, the surface they touched hissed.

Lictors and Triary members, despite their inherent inhumanity and brutality, drew back from the sight, blinking and bewildered and struggling to decide whether the image they saw was real. The Last Men were undone with sheer, mind-blanking terror. Some, utterly unstrung, merely fainted, while others vomited or stared, catatonic.

Sensing Alouine with its astral gaze, the horror approached the hard-pressed woman. Frozen and bound in chains of fear which seized every nerve, her thoughts jumbled; *life, fleeting, gone.*

It held its weapon horizontally before it in a simultaneous salute and admonition, and barked a single phrase in its harsh, guttural spirit tongue.

Alouine did not need to understand the words to recognize their intent: the spirit was exhorting her to fight alongside it. Shakily, she nodded once and followed the creature into the fray.

— — —

Onuris easily drove the Lictors back, slashing and scything through them with its typical, furious vengeance. The heat of a sunbaked desert, oppressive and hostile to all comfort and ease, blazed from the metal warrior whose birth-womb was a foundry, a forge, the crucible of struggle and anguish, and the thirst of steel for blood.

Taking full advantage of the complete panic, emotional exhaustion, and total psychological breakdown caused by the monstrous bronze phantasm, Alouine freed Thaira from the encircling ring of Triary. She whirled into their ranks, swept their legs, drove her diamond-hard knuckles and fingertips into their eyes and nerve clusters, and stabbed them with their own bayonets.

Once more, by flipping the switch and letting his astral alter ego use his body, Harrow had turned the tables and victory seemed imminent.

That was until the air instantly and utterly froze. All motion ceased. In the span of a breath, Alouine caught a lungful of crystallized water vapor in her throat and felt the tiny slivers of ice scratch her airways.

The entire pyramid pulsed once with a low, throbbing thrum. Not as direct as Onuris' astral keening but no less appalling, simultaneously audible and tactile, the deep reverberation washed through the whole of the building, leaving nothing and no one untouched.

The air crackled with astral power at the edges of her vision; black veins of lightning shot through the corners of her eyes, and a form appeared.

It manifested from nothingness, flowing together from an unseen realm and drawing itself together and into the world by the instant, becoming a distinct horror of totally separate aspect from the other astral invocation.

A skeleton of pure aphotic blackness took shape in the air at the exact center point of the rhomboid chamber; pitted, textured bones forced into material form by some unknowable process and constructed of substance that had no earthly equivalent. Hideous spurs sprang from every surface, each length unnaturally straight, angled, stylized and cruelly sharp. A leaden metal formed its joints and ropes of tar and pitch slithered around the bones to form muscle and sinew.

The vagaries of the creature's face and head could not hide its receding forehead and the frivolous, cynical look it wore. A lipless mouth peeled back to expose rows of inorganic needles that served no obvious biological purpose but rather the infliction of pain. Narrow slits for eyes in the creature's smooth, shiny, sculpted face cast about with aplomb.

The terror which Onuris spread was a side-effect, mere by-product. This thing exulted in the horror and revulsion of the onlooker. It spread its bony arms, tipped with claws wide as it hovered, ten meters in the air, to welcome the loathing and disgust its visage demanded.

It was too much for many of the Last Men, like still-cowering Heid Acheson, who tore at their hair and eyes. Women beat their breasts and clawed at their own faces to force themselves to wake from the living nightmare that had descended on them: first, the fire of vengeance, and then, the chill of the grave from which there was no escape.

Bipedal and roughly man-sized and shaped, though bizarrely, obscenely stunted in some areas and elongated in others, the brazen avatar of all Ahrimanic principles completed its incorporation and cast about its dread gaze.

When those eyes met Alouine's, a stroke of whitening fear tore through her chest, and she recognized that which was once Carver Delano. The creature's appearance had nothing in common with her memory of the man, but, to her keen psychic senses, it was unmistakable. In death, he had become the emissary of all he had not-so-secretly worshipped in life—the power to smother all other wills and lives in his grasp.

She blinked and it was on top of her, seemingly teleporting itself across the distance with the speed of thought and a ripple of astral-quantum power.

One bony claw cocked back to shred her, to scatter her blood on the floor as the first of many sacrifices. That horrendous mouth could not possibly form meaningful words, but the creature projected its thoughts at audible frequency. "May this death solidify my immortal service to EL, Lord of the earth," it hissed. "And may the others harden the chains of the earthbound and serve as my fee due."

Onuris, propelled as if launched by rocket, barreled into the creature from the side, leading with the point of its lance.

And the emissary of the dark spirit stopped that lance dead with its palm, showing no indication of effort or strain. It merely reached out, almost lazily, and stopped the unstoppable as though it were nothing. An embodiment of constraint, limit, restriction, inertia; the fury of Anhur, the bloodlust of Slayer-of-Enemies, was rendered instantly helpless and impotent before it.

What-was-Carver projected, "See this body, this weapon, this sacrificial knife? The king of darkness gave me this. I bought it for the price of my soul, and nothing can stand against it." The black being reached out and seized the bronze by the throat, throttled it with its claws, taunted it. "The abyss yawns before us and I will grasp every life I can reach and hurl it in. I will build my throne on the throes and convulsions of those I destroy."

It pulled Onuris toward it, face to face. "The whole existence you fight to protect, I will render into nothing. What pitiful hearts you have poured hope into, I will empty upon the altar of this city."

The bronze spirit kicked and stabbed ineffectually at the black, driving the point of its spear at the exposed ribs of its grotesque adversary. The hard steel point failed to penetrate or even scratch at the body of what Carver had become. It reached down and seized the spear in its claws and with a simple twist, broke off the blade.

The body language of shock was evident even in Onuris' featureless, smooth-faced visage as it glanced from its shattered weapon to the face of its antagonist. The oil-black entity almost appeared to grin before it casually hurled its fiery bronze foe away, discarding the metallic form as though it was mere refuse.

At the end of the trajectory, Harrow crashed into a bloody, crunching heap where the hard floor met the unyielding wall. KA-BAR, in two pieces, clinked and skittered and slid along next to him.

The broken man did not move.

— — —

Quintain's vibratory rate had reached a fever pitch. He felt fully capable of expending vast amounts of astral-spiritual energy to the material plane for healing purposes. A sense of accomplishment accompanied this realization, but he cut it off there.

Temptation, as always, gnawed at him—the temptation to view himself as a divine being, a special and praiseworthy entity who had been favored by God and chosen to bask in glory and exult in his pride.

He banished these thoughts of self-aggrandizement as useless, petty—the work of dark forces whose reach was long and could touch him even here. Quintain did not care. His accomplishments were meaningless if he could not help those he left behind. The sobering thought struck him: he was certain he could not interfere with the destinies of material entities at all—unless he was invited and requested by name.

Tuning his awareness to the etheric world, the plane of thought closest to the material, he saw great forests of consciousness stretching into the void; each tree the subtle body of a man or woman, and each of the leaves that budded, grew, served its time in the warm light of the God-Sun, and then withered and fell; these were thought-feelings.

I can't search for a single thought in all of this, he murmured to himself. *I have to seek out the correct source.*

He found Harrow's etheric body first, but this was stripped near bare of all consciousness, charred, and almost totally consumed. Weak, curled, tiny emotions remained, but these would fall away and die any moment. Nowhere in the man's mind were prayers or pleading for his intercession. Urgently, Quintain sought on.

Alouine was likewise too preoccupied with seeking to overcome terror and revulsion. A constant anamnesis of her own mortality pervaded her subtle field.

Finally, the disembodied astral traveler found a sapling; an aura vibrant and strong and bursting with faith in her friends, teachers and guardians; overflowing with hope for the future.

He had found Nina, and he had found her at prayer. Transmuting his vibratory rate and bending his own perspective, he projected his astral image across dimensions and appeared to her.

She looked up at him from where she sat on the cold floor of the sub-way station. Joanna snoozed nearby. "Oh," she said quietly. "Hello. Are you checking on me, Quintain?"

His ghostly form sank into a crouch. "I think it was more the other way around," he projected to her. "And I'm very glad for that."

"You look different," she said. "Older. What's happening?"

"I need your help, Nina." He knew that the girl was sharp but still had to remind himself to put the situation to her in terms she would understand. "I've lost my body," he said softly. "But my Work isn't finished, and the others badly need my help."

"You lost your body?" the girl murmured, worried. "It's not like a bowl or a book, Quintain. How did you lose it?"

He arched an astral brow. "That wasn't accurate," he said. "I didn't really lose it. It was destroyed. I can't get it back."

"Oh, no," she gasped. "Are you dead?"

Quintain wavered for a moment in how to answer her. "I suppose I am," he finally muttered. Then he shook his head. "That's why I'm here: the dead can't change the destiny of the living unless they're asked. Harrow and Alouine are in big trouble, and I need to help them."

Nina blinked. "So, help them," she said, shooing him with her remaining hand. "Hurry!"

Quintain gave her a wistful smile and with an energetic hum, his projection disappeared in a flash.

He streamed as a wave-particle duality toward the Third City Enclave, transmuting his vibratory rate and transferring his consciousness to where he was needed. As he did so, he began summoning the colored lights of his angelic familiars to him. The ectoplasm of his quantum body, given intentionality by the girl's prayer, hardened and sank to the physical world.

It rises from my soul, clear as air and harder than the bones of the earth.

Cosmic wisdom in the mind of a man became pure power, and a human being permeated with that power instilled horror in the spiritual forces of darkness. Quintain gathered all Light to himself, consciously took up the will of the archangels, of Michael and his hosts, who respect and desire human freedom. He took up, personally, the responsibility for that freedom.

And he flew into the heart of the devil to win the earth for good.

The Enclave and its dome was a horrendous maw yawning from the earth, a splitting, gaping cavity filled with draconic teeth, salivating with hunger for a meal of blood and souls. The home of the Last Men, ever a conduit for the spiritual energy of the darkest gods, was ready to cannibalize itself.

With a crackling snap, he arrived inside the belly of the ravenous pit. In an astral sense, the dark entity he saw there was the karmic fulfillment of all the desires of the Order. Their physical gratifications and entrapments and the empty promises of their mechanistic materialism had given rise to that emissary of EL. The god reached out through his servant-avatar to materialize, crystallize, silence and darken all animated, living forces into a fixed and rigid and frozen form, to kill that which lives.

This was the projected intentionality of the spirit of gravity and jealousy, to exceed its proper bounds and reach into the living world; to promote the illusory lie that matter, cold and unfeeling, is the basic reality, or worse, the only reality. It was the wellspring of all fear, lust for power, hatred, envy, perversity, and all destructive impulses.

A single, black magician had tapped into the source of all awfulness, and became its link to the world. He had fallen in love with the deadliest forces—forces which already held the upper hand and forces which threatened to consume the entire city.

The black figure, skeletal, demonic, had torn Harrow's spirit familiar away, casting it back into its faraway abode, and had left the warrior in a disfigured heap to die. Alouine could do naught but cower in the creature's presence. The terror and despair of the gathered Last Men and what few Lictors and soldiers remained seemed to empower it. It fed on these energies as a black hole draws in all that comes near, with a gravity which even light finds inescapable.

It tore into the scattered Last Men, rending them with its claws and spattering their blood on the floor, which had become the sacrificial altar, desecrated to that purpose by unfettered malignance. The creature did not move with ferocity or even haste, but with the methodical determination of a slaughterhouse butcher at work, mechanistically appearing before its bound, marked stock, and swiftly opening their throats with one hooked claw.

Only the wayfaring Light-worker once known as Quintain stood in its way, and with supreme effort of will, he began to project his consciousness into that maelstrom of malicious intent. He banished all fear and cloaked himself in the resplendence of the angels.

Crackling with pure, white fire and lightning, the Wayfarer descended onto the physical plane in a flash which lit the Temple chamber as a noonday sun. Summoning all his spirit power, he poured it into an exclamation which thundered throughout the space, coruscating through all beings present.

"Enough of this!" he shouted. White-hot sparks of righteous outrage flashed from his apparition's eyes, and even the horrid creature Carver had become was stunned motionless. The spirit of the young man approached the blackened, demonic being menacingly. "This time of blood, and of the bonds of blood, is over!"

Screeching and dripping hot venom from its fangs, the black emissary of hate crouched down and spread its claws wide, ready to fall upon the approaching Quintain and rend him to bits, astral body or no.

But the semi-transparent body of the young man disdained a violent encounter. His voice was full of grave promise as he growled, "I have seen how you gave yourself over to become a monster, and I'll do what I must to rid the world of you."

Reaching out before him, he tapped the radiant, angelic body of Raphael, instantly passing his intention to the spirit. The archangel flew to Harrow's fallen body and enveloped him in glowing yellow light, slashed through with mauve. Likewise, Quintain dispatched Gabriel to Alouine, who stood transfixed. She blinked and her mouth gaped as she was washed in hues of blue, shot through with orange.

A bond existed between these two that transcended the antagonism of their blood. By the power of the angels and adherence to an impulse of the soul, Quintain forged this tiny, frail thread of respect into an unbreakable chain, a spiritual bond between human beings which destiny ordained to replace the old, physical bonds of blood.

He could feel the Guardian of the Threshold, his spirit-mirror-being, smiling.

"Foolish man," Quintain murmured. "No force in hell can stand against the progress of my Great Work. A spiritual communion is born here which nothing will sunder."

Chains of glowing gold took form, stretching from the heart of Outlander warrior to Order princess in molten, living color. To the archangel Michael, attentive and vigilant at Quintain's side, he said, "Take this misbegotten creature and bind him."

The spirit of fire, empowered by the Lord of all, obeyed gladly. It took up a great slack in the golden chain and in a rush of unstoppable impetus, it seized upon the black servant of EL, wrestling and pummeling it down and wrapping the chain tightly over its limbs.

What-was-Carver screamed and thrashed about with utmost violence, slavering and frothing bile and poison from its jaws, but could not break the hold of the general of God.

Quintain fused the chain so that the links that bound the king of hate's now pitiful avatar could be separated from those that kept Harrow and Alouine.

His voice sank low as he pronounced sentence. "Throw this unrepentant wretch into the abyss." He turned to Auriel. "We shall take this chain and sew up the mouth of the void that is this place, and remove it forever as an affront to the God of life."

The angel nodded.

In a flash of nuclear astral fire, Michael vanished with its prisoner in tow, and likewise the other Archangels departed to their own tasks.

Quintain lingered for as long as he could. He moved to Harrow and was met there by Alouine.

"Once again, our comrade is in dire need of aid," he said softly.

Alouine cradled the warrior's head. "I'll handle this one." For a moment, neither party spoke, until she looked up at the glowing figure. "Thank you."

Quintain smiled. He knew that the spiritual events here would take time to matriculate down into the earthly realm, but they made a good start.

He was still smiling when the laws of karma took hold and, Nina's prayer for his intercession answered, he faded from view of the living.

THIRTY

Harrow woke slowly, his vision blurry for several moments, and he shook his head to try to clear the mist and dullness. His body felt heavy, weighed down by some sort of soft, thick material, as though caught in a warm jelly or slime. It took him a moment to realize that his skin was not moist beyond the thin film of sweat that covered him. He was wrapped in luxurious and thickly quilted blankets which had a clean, feminine scent. Without thinking, he nuzzled his face into the softness and breathed deeply. The smell was familiar, but he could not place it.

Wondering at himself, he sighed out a deep breath, pushed the covers away, and immediately he began to feel better. The room's ambient temperature was too warm to be bundled up. He looked around.

The place was utterly alien: clean, richly furnished, elaborately decorated. In the dim light, he could make out brass and mahogany tones with burgundy highlights and deep red velvet. He was in a bedroom, he surmised.

Then, it came rushing back: the fire, the feeling of despair finally catching him as he was buried in a crashing tide of foes. As the dullness faded, pain set in. Wincing, the warrior slowly swung his legs, one at a time, over the side of the high bed. The punishment he had endured made him feel sluggish.

One side of the lavishly finished double doors gently opened, swinging smoothly and silently on brass hinges, and Alouine walked in, holding a china cup and saucer in one hand which trailed steam as she moved.

"You're awake," she said, stepping close to the bed and sitting on its edge beside him. Her hair was up, pulled into a high ponytail, and she wore a loose fitting, strappy tank top and tight bloomers. Harrow was very conscious of her lack of clothing, her long, bare legs, and his own nakedness. He was oddly grateful that the finely threaded bed sheet had stayed put across his lap. Normally, a thing like modesty had no chance against his pride, but he was feeling especially vulnerable—wounded and in a strange place.

"Yes," he murmured, still not altogether feeling sharp. SIMON began a self-diagnostic. "I feel I've slept for too long."

"It's been twelve hours," she replied. "And that doesn't include the four you spent in the surgery suite. Considering how hard you fought, I could not bear to wake you." She offered the cup and the saucer, holding it up under his nose. "Drink this," she said. "It will help to clear your head."

Harrow inhaled deeply, sampling the somewhat bitter-smelling, dark brew. "What is it?" he asked, as he took the saucer from her.

"It's called coffee," the woman said. "I think you'll enjoy it. Be careful, it's served very hot."

He sipped the beverage haltingly. "This is," he mumbled, before drinking again, "very good. It's invigorating." The Outlander wanted to say more, but he concentrated on the drink instead. An awkward moment passed as they sat together, closer than strictly necessary, with their shoulders touching.

"I take it that we're in your home," he murmured, hesitant to break the silence that had fallen over them. He glanced around again, taking in the surroundings and noting the portrait on the table next to the bed. He'd seen images captured in time before, but had no idea of how it was made. In it, Alouine stood beside and slightly behind a seated man; they both looked happy and at ease.

Alouine blinked. "Yes, right," she said with a smirk. "Apologies; this must be strange for you." She smiled. "You're not alone in that," she added softly.

"What do you mean?" he asked.

"You are the first man I've invited into my personal quarters. I hope you found my bed comfortable."

Heat rose in the man's face. He stuttered once. "I, ah, yes," he mumbled, before clearing his throat. "Thank you." After a moment, he asked, "Where is Quintain?"

Alouine took and held a breath for a beat before slowly exhaling. "There is much I should tell you, a long story that will demand as much from your hearing as it will from my telling. Suffice it to say that Quintain, as we know him, is dead."

Harrow gazed at the carpet for long moments, and struggled against short, shallow breaths. His lips clenched tightly, the corners of his eyes bunched, and his hand holding his drink trembled. A great sadness sought to escape him, and he fought, tooth and nail, to restrain it.

"He is dead to this world," Alouine continued softly, "but not gone. I saw him, in the temple. His spirit lives on." She smiled gently and reached over to give his shoulder a squeeze. "Enjoy your coffee. I'll draw a bath, if you're feeling up to it."

He merely nodded slowly, haunted by his failure to protect the boy.

She reached out and touched his cheek with her fingers. "I don't think he would have you mourn him. It's not the kind of man he was."

Harrow nodded again and blew out a breath. "Yes," he said. "You're probably right."

Smirking, Alouine arched an expectant brow. "I usually am." She hopped up again from the bed and walked to the door. He noted the way her hips swayed. She appeared happy to be there, but it was more than that. She seemed happy that he was there with her. The thought was simultaneously nerve-wracking and intensely satisfying.

Setting his feet on the thickly carpeted floor, he took several long minutes and tested to see if he could stand. His toes sank into the soft fibers; even that luxury was foreign to him. Pushing off the bed, he felt it—agony, his lifelong companion, creeping about in his knees and thighs and crawling up his spine. It was a welcome reminder that he yet lived.

The sound of running water and the sight of steam from the next room got him moving, and he peeked through the doorway to see Alouine sitting at the edge of a tub as it filled with hot water.

"Come in," she said, although she hadn't looked up at him. Doing his best to hide his limp, Harrow creaked and shuffled his way to stand closer. He glanced down his nose at the tub and his host nearly laughed. "It's just water," she said, smirking. "Nothing too savory, I promise."

He nodded gratefully and gingerly stepped in. The bath was hot enough to seep into his bones, but not scalding, and the magnificent, smooth black stone was quite comfortable. He was reminded of the artificial pond at Mason Dixon. *This tub is nearly as large*, he mused.

"I'll leave you to it," Alouine remarked.

On impulse as she rose, Harrow reached out to catch her wrist. Her large, dark eyes instantly flicked their intense gaze down to where he touched her, and followed her arm up his shoulder and to his face.

He was instantly brought back to the first time they met, feeling the pulse of her heartbeat and her lips under his. "Wait," he said softly. She lowered her bottom again to the edge of the bath.

A long moment passed before Harrow even thought to remove his hand from her arm.

When another moment passed and he said nothing, Alouine took a shot in the dark. "I think," she murmured, pausing to collect her words, "that what we want" —she shook her head—"at least, what I want," she amended, looking into his eyes, "should wait."

"That is exactly what I feel we should discuss," Harrow muttered, his voice nearly inaudible over the gentle slosh of the water.

Alouine gave him a gentle smile. "We have ample time, Harrow. If you try anything other than sitting or standing for the next few days, you're liable to come apart like tissue paper."

Harrow didn't know what tissue paper was, but he imagined it was as frail as he felt. Still, with no other alternative, he launched in, grave and solemn. "I could be something," he exhaled. "—to you," he added. "I could be happy here, with you." He gazed into the water. "There were times I used to imagine having a lover, or a wife."

"This is all new to me also," she reminded him, guessing at his apprehensions.

He swallowed and fearing the worst, he said, "My war isn't over. There are other Enclaves and other Outlanders across the world." He sighed. "If my choice is peace or war," he mumbled, his voice trailing off. "I must choose war," he finished in a whisper.

"Can you not have both?" she asked simply.

Harrow shook his head sadly. "I am afraid that if I taste a moment's peace, I'll never again find the strength within to take up the struggle." He locked eyes with her again. "I'd grow to hate myself. Do you understand?"

"Yes," Alouine breathed. "I understand." After a moment, she stood once more. "You are a warrior and a captain of men. You will be a great general in the coming war." Taking a breath to apparently steady her nerves and possibly will away the moisture collecting in her eyes, she said, "And you will be a great statesman for your people."

Then, sudden enough to make Harrow blink, she leaned down with her palms on the lip of the bath and thrust her face down to his, their noses mere centimeters apart. "But know this, Outlander," she said, her voice gaining strength to a low vibration. "I am a princess of the Royal Seed."

A smirk graced the corner of her lips, which in that instant appeared to Harrow the most delicious things on earth. Her voice took on a teasingly threatening ring. "I do not take no for an answer."

With that, she spun on her heel and walked out, putting plenty of sway into her steps.

Harrow gazed after her, blinking, mouth agape for several seconds. Then he blew out a breath and dunked his head into the water.

— — —

Nina was happy.

She and Joanna had answered Alouine's call, and Outlanders had come to the Enclave. The princess had even invited them to stay in her home—her palace. It was a wide world of things that the girl had never experienced before. There were soft beds and clean clothes and sweet things to eat, plenty of them. It was warm here. Her Harrow was alive and sleeping and had won his princess. Her Joanna was safe.

She was safe.

The brave boy she had looked up to had given up his body of flesh and blood but lived on as a kind of ghost, and he appeared to her. His softly glowing, yellow-orange form gave off waves of kindness—a gentle feeling of inclusiveness, like a loving embrace.

"I'm sorry you died," she whispered to him.

The semi-transparent apparition smiled, grateful for the girl's sincerity. "As am I, but I have no regrets. I will live again. The cycle repeats endlessly for us all. This is only the end of the beginning."

"Can we live like this now? Is it all over?"

Quintain considered his answer for a moment. "There is still a monumental task before those who desire justice, my friend. Our brothers and sisters are still enslaved around the world. Humanity is not yet whole. Even within the confines of this city, it will be some time before the wounds of the past are healed, and the mutual hatred of Last Man and Outlander alike can be finally put to rest."

Nina glanced away for a few breaths. "So, does that mean that Harrow and Alouine will leave, to free the other people?"

The quantized memory field Quintain had become enveloped Nina in a hug, which tingled against her skin and made her heart feel full. "The inaction of good people has been the Order's triumph for hundreds of years. Good people have done nothing for far too long. We can put down our weapons for a time, but never our courage to do what is right."

Nina swallowed and thought. Finally, she said, "I think I'm ready to do what I can. Will you teach me what you know?"

Quintain grinned. "Only if you acknowledge that your teacher is still only a student."

— — —

Harrow was up before dawn. Before he had gone to his rest on the floor of the room set aside for him—the bed was too soft for his preference—he had summoned Joanna to the top of the pyramid, with explosives.

Together, they had demolished the machine which had claimed his young friend's life and nearly given their enemy the power to destroy them.

He pulled on his armored forearm and shin guards, and then dressed himself. He laced up his boots and stuffed a Death's Head pistol in the holster at his side. His scatter-shot gauntlets came next.

Still, without KA-BAR he felt strangely nude and vulnerable. The feeling did not stop him from situating a weighted rucksack on his shoulders, and finally slinging a rifle next to it, across his back.

He ran at the fastest pace he could sustain around the base of the pyramid Temple, nearly nine kilometers, as he did every morning.

It struck him as an insane thing to do, but that did not matter.

The question isn't whether or not I'm insane, he thought, breathing deeply, sweat pouring from him as his boots provided a hammering beat on the smooth stone.

The question is, how insane do I need to be?

ABOUT THE AUTHOR

J. M. Salyards lives in Maryland with his wife and daughter. In his rare escapes from "girly world", he enjoys shooting sports, football and tabletop gaming.

Shadow of the Last Men is his first step in becoming a man of a million words.

ACKNOWLEDGMENTS

First thanks to Emily for her infinite patience, love, and support, and to Adria for reminding me to always strive to make the world a better place.

My most sincere gratitude to Penny and McKenna, the best teammates I could ask for.

ABOUT XCHYLER PUBLISHING:

Xchyler Publishing, an imprint of Hamilton Springs Press, proudly presents Shadow of the Last Men by J. M. Salyards, Book 1 of the futuristic dystopian thriller series, The Next Man Saga. Follow the author online at:

www.facebook.com/JmSalyards

www.twitter.com/JMSalyards

ALSO FROM XCHYLER PUBLISHING

A Dash of Madness: a Thriller Anthology by M. Irish Gardner, Elizabeth Gilliland, Sarah Hunter Hyatt, Breck LeSueur, F. M. Longo, Ben Ireland, David MacIver, and Tim Andrew, edited by McKenna Gardner, July, 2013.

Mechanized Masterpieces: A Steampunk Anthology by Aaron and Belinda Sikes, Alyson Grauer, Anika Arrington, A. F. Stewart, David W. Wilkin, M. K. Wiseman, Neve Talbot, and Scott William Taylor; edited by Penny Freeman, April, 2013

Vivatera by Candace J. Thomas, April, 2013

Vanguard Legacy: Foretold by Joanne Kershaw, April 2013

Grenshall Manor Chronicles: Oblivion Storm by R.A. Smith, December 2012

Forged in Flame: A Dragon Anthology, by Samuel Mayo, Brian Collier, Eric White, Jana Boskey, Caitlin McColl, and D. Robert Pease, edited by Penny Freeman, October 2012

Look for more exciting titles from Xchyler Publishing in 2013-2014, including:

Mr. Gunn and Dr. Bohemia, a Steampunk action/adventure by Pete Ford, October, 2013.

Our Extreme Makeovers anthology, October, 2013, by J. A. Guay, J. Branden Hart, Ginger C. Mann, R. M. Ridley, Rachael Romero, Neve Talbot, Scott E. Tarbet, Scott W. Taylor, and Eric White, edited by Terri Wagner and Jessica Shen.

Primal Storm, Book II of the urban fantasy series The Grenshall Manor Chronicles by R. A. Smith, November 2013; sequel to Oblivion Storm.

Diamond Jubal: A Midsummer's Night Steampunk, an action/adventure with a nod to The Bard, by Scott and Julie Tarbet, December, 2013.

The Accidental Apprentice, an imaginative fantasy by Anika Arrington, February, 2014.

The Rose and the Alchemist, a young adult fantasy by Li Frost, Spring, 2014.

Darkness Rising, the long awaited fantasy adventure from Elizabeth Lunyou, 2014.

We here at The X pride ourselves in discovery and promotion of talented authors. Our anthology project produces four books a year in our specific areas of focus: fantasy, Steampunk, suspense/thriller, and paranormal. Held quarterly, our short-story competitions result in published anthologies from which the authors receive royalties.

Additional themes include: Back to the Future (Fantasy, winter 2014), and Around the World in Eighty Days (Steampunk, spring 2014).

To learn more, visit www.xchylerpublishing.com.